PRAISE FOR CHANDRA BLUMBERG

Blumberg gives apt consideration to the themes of the importance of family, obligation, individuality, and freedom. Romance fans will adore the well-drawn love story between these funny and lovable dinosaur lovers.

—*Publishers Weekly*

A sweet romance with a ton of heart, *Digging Up Love* is a charming story about unearthing your deepest dreams and finding love along the way! I loved Alisha and Quentin's connection, and the baker/paleontologist pairing was so unique. A delightful debut!

—Farah Heron, author of *Accidentally Engaged*

D0096097

STIRRING UP LOVE

OTHER TITLES BY CHANDRA BLUMBERG

Digging Up Love

STIRRING UP LOVE

A NOVEL

Chandra Blumberg

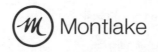 Montlake

Text copyright © 2022 by Chandra Blumberg
All rights reserved.

No part of this book may be reproduced, or stored in a retrieval system, or transmitted in any form or by any means, electronic, mechanical, photocopying, recording, or otherwise, without express written permission of the publisher.

Published by Montlake, Seattle

www.apub.com

Amazon, the Amazon logo, and Montlake are trademarks of Amazon.com, Inc., or its affiliates.

ISBN-13: 9781542038317
ISBN-10: 1542038316

Cover design and illustration by Liz Casal

Printed in the United States of America

To those who encouraged me to keep writing

CHAPTER 1

SIMONE

June

A sledgehammer would do the trick, or even a baseball bat. As much as she loved her restaurant, the dining room needed a serious design overhaul. Outdated and mismatched didn't fit her vision for the future.

But the rickety beadboard checkout counter would have to stay for now. Even the few run-down options she'd scoped out at the antique mart down the street were priced out of reach. With a renovation out of the budget, the only tool at her disposal was a flimsy paint swatch.

"Nautical blue? Nah." Her best friend, Chantal, used her fingertip to reveal the next set of colors. "Back in Chicago, with Lake Michigan nearby, maybe. But out here?" Her tone indicated just what she thought of the rural Illinois town. She tapped another hue on the swatch. "What you want here is *corn*flower blue."

Grinning, Simone shook her head. She'd missed joking around with Chantal. And nothing could dim her pride in the town's agriculture. Their corn fed the nation. Lake Michigan was picturesque but cold and forbidding half the time.

After seven years of self-exile among the hard lines of skyscrapers and concrete, being back among the rolling hills and groves of trees of Hawksburg was like tucking a handmade quilt around her feet on a chilly night.

Comfort. Serenity. Home.

She flipped through the swatches, then held up another to the countertop. "How about matte black? Classic but modern." If she couldn't demo the checkout stand, at least she could disguise the water stains and warped wood.

Chantal cocked her head to the side, her short afro—magenta this week, a change from last month's electric blue—was a splash of color in Honey and Hickory's dingy dining room. "I do like the black. But what about the tables?"

In unison, they turned their gaze toward the Formica-topped tables paired with red chairs, the glittered vinyl peeling off in some places to expose yellow foam underneath. Pops had purchased the seating years ago in an attempt to create a retro vibe.

Seated with her muck-covered boots up on one of the chairs in question was Meg Anderson, Simone's sister's best friend. She flicked her eyes up from the test she was grading. "Don't look at me—I'm the neutral party."

"We're not looking at you; it's the atrocity you're sitting on," Simone said.

Apart from the old diner chairs, Honey and Hickory's decor was an unironic blend of newish and not-quite vintage. A haphazard mix of local sports-team portraits, watercolors Gran had added over the years, and sepia photos from the restaurant's earlier life adorned the drab walls, lit by basic brass wall sconces. Not terrible, but nothing special either.

At least not on the surface. But this place was the heart of the town. The gathering space that fed farmers and lawyers, that hosted 4-H club meetings and Little League celebrations.

She'd grown up in this restaurant and cherished it with every fiber of her being.

But at twenty-five, after four years working at a downtown marketing firm, she now had enough experience to know a fresh, updated aesthetic would go a long way toward expanding the customer base and making Honey and Hickory the centerpiece of the new retail and entertainment hub she had in mind for the town's future.

At least the bones were good, with a high tin ceiling and wall of windows overlooking Main Street. If only she had the cash flow to implement her design ideas. But redecorating was just the beginning of her plans for an enterprise she hoped would expand beyond just a restaurant.

"Sure you can't swing for new tables?" Chantal tilted her head, finger pressed to her chin. "Because if you got some cheap ones, I could help you paint them out—"

Shaking her head, Simone set the black paint swatch on the *maybe* pile. "You didn't come all the way out here just to do my dirty work."

This was the first time Chantal had made the trek from Chicago since Simone had moved home last year, and they were supposed to be spending the weekend catching up. She'd wanted to get her friend's input, not con her into helping out.

"Sim, it's not a big deal. I know you must be overwhelmed with trying to overhaul this place."

"Overwhelmed" didn't touch Simone's baseline stress level over the past year. Owning Honey and Hickory was a dream come true but also had a steep learning curve. To go from working in the corporate world to running a small-town barbecue restaurant took a lot of pivoting.

And while the restaurant she'd inherited from her grandfather after his retirement had a loyal clientele and made a comfortable profit, between her student loans and operating costs, the large-scale renovation she dreamed of was out of reach. As was her dream to move beyond barbecue and make this town a destination. Put the spotlight on everything Hawksburg had to offer.

But today was all about achievable goals. Simone stepped through the swinging doors into the empty kitchen. The cook on shift, Brent, was tending to the smoker, cooking meat low and slow before they opened for lunch.

After passing by a long cooktop and walk-in fridge, she swung open the supply closet and pulled out the rusted dolly. She backed out, right into Chantal, who must've followed her in.

"What's that for?"

"To move the checkout stand." She steered the dolly around her friend, back out into the dining room. "Shifting it over by the soda machine will free up room for more tables eventually and make things look more spacious in the meantime."

She tried to shove the dolly under the counter, but there was no room between it and the floor.

"Plan to do that all by yourself?" Chantal asked. "You do know how physics works, right?"

Too out of breath to dignify her friend's snark with a reply, Simone pushed again.

"I can't watch this anymore." Her friend positioned herself at the opposite side.

"I don't want help." She set aside the useless dolly.

"But you need it." Meg hopped up from the table. She gripped the countertop, and they all pulled up. Nothing happened.

Another heave. Still nothing.

Arms straining, Simone blew a loose curl off her nose. "Whatever happened to your homesteading muscles, Meg?"

Meg panted out a laugh, immune to her snark. "You know full well your sister would be the best person for this job."

At that moment, the furniture came unstuck, and Simone nearly dropped the heavy counter on her feet. "You really think Alisha should be here in my place? How long have you been sleeping on that one?"

Brow bunched, Meg said, "Are you kidding?" The three of them baby-stepped toward the opposite wall. "Your sister lifts weights competitively. You don't think she'd make short work of moving this furniture around?"

Oh. Right. Simone wrestled a grin onto her face, aware of Chantal's assessing gaze. Her sister had been Pops's first choice. His only choice. After all, he'd given his blessing to her sister's decision not to run Honey and Hickory, but it was Alisha, not he, who'd handed down the keys.

"My sister may have the muscle power, but she's clumsy as all get-out," Simone said, kicking the dirt of deflection over the tracks of her insecurities. "Our toes would be toast if she helped us move this."

In reality, she'd never snub Alisha's help, but they'd agreed to quit mothering each other. And she needed to prove she could manage this restaurant on her own. Needed to validate her sister's faith in her and prove herself worthy of their grandfather's legacy. How could she expect to get the whole town on board with her vision for the future if she couldn't even pull this restaurant out of the past?

They reached the spot where she wanted the checkout counter, and she jerked her chin. "Here's great, thanks." Lowering it, they let out matching grunts as it hit the floor. One less thing on her to-do list for Monday morning, but that didn't make her feel better about taking advantage of her friend's offer to help.

Chantal walked over to grab a cup from the drink stand, and Simone took the opportunity to regain her composure. She dusted off her hands on the shorts of her romper and winced when the fresh blister on her thumb brushed against the woven fabric. She'd burned herself plenty in the past year as she'd become reacclimated to spending hours in the kitchen.

A hand fell on her shoulder. "You good?" Meg asked in an undertone.

She lifted Meg's hand off with a thumb and forefinger. "Of course." More than okay. Perfectly A-OK.

Willing Meg to drop it, she bent to retrieve the pile of paint swatches from where they'd fluttered off. She couldn't be mad at Pops for choosing her sister to inherit this place.

After all, she'd chosen to frame her self-imposed banishment from town as an escape. Kept up the ruse through Thanksgiving visits and spring planting with Gran and fishing trips with Pops. Sang the praises of city life while buying rounds at the Back Forty every time she visited Hawksburg.

How could she be upset that everyone in town had moved on without her when that was her goal all along? To exorcise herself from the only place she'd ever felt truly at home and never reveal how much she missed it.

Getting real with her family about how much she'd missed Hawksburg had been a long time coming. But sharing her authentic self with the rest of the town? Correcting the assumptions she'd fed into all these years? Much simpler to keep up the ruse.

But she was home now. Determined to stay and build a life in Hawksburg—the life she'd denied herself for years.

Simone shoved the swatches into the pocket of her romper, but when she looked up, Meg was still watching her, worry reflected in the depths of her green eyes.

"Am I upset I wasn't Pops's first choice? Not even remotely." She wasn't upset at Pops. Why would he choose her to take over Honey and Hickory when she'd moved hundreds of miles away? And in the end, it didn't matter, because Alisha had entrusted her with the job.

Upset? No. But maybe she was a teensy bit heartbroken that no one had known just how much she loved every inch of this place, every square mile of town, from the grassy town square to the two-lane dirt roads. And more than that, she loved the people. She just wasn't sure if they loved her back anymore.

Chantal added more ice to her cup and spoke above the rattle of the machine. "This place does look bigger now. Good call."

Bigger and emptier. Lately she only came out to the dining room when the restaurant was closed or service was winding down. Catching up with friends used to be her favorite part of this place—Pops had scolded her more than once about chatting while she was on the clock. Lately she couldn't bring herself to socialize, too worried she might hear that she didn't measure up in the role.

But dwelling on doubts wouldn't get her anywhere. She put her back to the door. "Ready for brunch?"

"My three favorite words," Meg said and shut her folder with a snap. She slid it into her tote, and the three of them stepped onto the sidewalk.

"I think we earned ourselves a mimosa with that furniture rearranging," Chantal said as Simone locked up. Honey and Hickory wouldn't open for a couple of hours. "Not that I minded, but next time you should ask one of the brawny dudes we played pool with at the bar last night to do the heavy lifting."

Simone laughed. "The last thing I need is a man's help in my restaurant."

Or anyone's for that matter. She needed to show the town she hadn't just inherited the deed to this place; she'd earned it.

Years of shadowing her grandpa at the smoker, cooking up batches of sauce, proofing dough, and working the temperamental fryer had laid the groundwork, and her experience in the city had given her the knowledge and vision needed to push this restaurant—this whole town—into the twenty-first century.

Most people still thought of Honey and Hickory as *Wayne's place*. But tomorrow everything would change. The first farmers' market of the season offered a chance to step outside Pops's shadow and stake her claim as the face of barbecue in western Illinois. Should be an easy coup since there was no other decent barbecue joint in the whole county.

Start with a fresh coat of paint, follow up with sales.

All part of the plan. *Her* plan.

CHAPTER 2

FINN

Finn fished the single key from his pocket and unlocked the door, shifting the bag of groceries higher on his hip. He sidestepped paint cans and a caulk gun, then dumped the paper bag on the counter. Glow from the streetlamps shone in through curtainless windows, and he fumbled around for a light switch. Retraced his steps and found one by the back door.

Then, after leaving the door ajar, he trotted down the back steps and reached in through the broken passenger window to hoist out his cast-iron skillet and giant stockpot from atop a tattered duffel bag. A basketful of clean laundry occupied the back seat, the chemical-laced freshness from dryer sheets fighting a losing battle against the stale smell of mildew from yesterday's rain showers.

Nose wrinkled, Finn looped the duffel bag over his shoulder, reached around and pulled a ziplock bag full of cooking utensils out of the sagging seat-back pocket, and hauled all the supplies inside. He kicked the door closed with his heel. The scuff mark wouldn't go unnoticed, but he'd clean it off before he left in the morning.

He set the pans on the sparkling new range and smothered a yawn with the back of his arm, worn out from a long shift at Bellaire, the fine-dining restaurant where he worked as a chef. But he popped open a Red Bull and did a quick circuit of the house to check rooms.

Wouldn't do to be caught unawares, not with his reflexes, or lack thereof. When he reached the spacious living room, he paused, adjusting the strap of the duffel where it dug into his neck.

A Darius Shield Realty sign had been hammered into the sod in the front yard—a warning his time in this house was running out. Warnings, the chance to reconcile himself with moving on; those were a luxury. Too often in his past he'd awoken in one home and fallen asleep in another, without a goodbye. Out front, a solid wood post anchored the *For Sale* sign, as sturdy as the insulated walls of the house around him, signaling to prospective buyers they'd get a solid foundation. A home.

Finn turned his back on the bay window. Home was a foreign concept to him, but the embrace of a warm kitchen was as close as he ever got. And these days, he conquered the loneliness through cooking. Healed the notion of insecurity by creating meals that made people stop, and stay, and savor.

Temporary, yes. But when he cooked for people, he created that sense of home he'd never had. And he hoped someday to use his culinary training to give others that same sense of hope. Of security, and a future, regardless of their past.

He scrubbed his hands at the apron sink and checked the clock on the gleaming stainless microwave. Five hours to cook and sleep would give him an hour's leeway to pack up and remove traces of his night here. Doable, if he got right to work.

Juggling a full-time job and a new venture selling homemade barbecue sauce would've been less stressful if he'd had a permanent address, but a small business loan required credit and assets, and since his net worth amounted to a leaky air mattress and a car on its last legs, his best friend, Darius Shield, had offered to let Finn bunk at his investment properties during construction.

Saying goodbye to the bedroom he'd sublet from a stranger off Craigslist hadn't been a hardship, and he'd used the money he saved on rent to fund his company, and in turn he hoped someday his barbecue sauce business would finance his bigger dreams.

Early stages now, though, and he had an idea for a new recipe that just might give his line of barbecue sauces an edge over other brands. He chopped the tops off a handful of garlic bulbs, then fired up a burner on the gas stove and glugged vegetable oil into his stockpot. Cranked on the oven—hot—and set the garlic in the cast-iron skillet and drizzled on olive oil.

To the pan on the stovetop, he added brown sugar and tomato sauce. Balsamic vinegar and molasses. Soon the scent of roasted garlic filled the kitchen, accompanied by the homey hiss and pop of bubbling sauce.

In the zone, he envisioned the components for his new blend as clearly as if they were scribbled on the subway-tile backsplash behind the cooktop like ingredients on a handwritten recipe card. Mustard, cayenne, salt, pepper. His hands moved with muscle memory—slicing, stirring, seasoning, blending the sauce to a fine puree. The earlier sense of intrusion was evaporating along with the extra liquid in the pot.

Lulled into security, he tasted the sauce—full of depth and layers of flavor—then turned around and flung the wooden spoon into the sink. Except he wasn't alone in the kitchen.

Behind him stood the tall and substantial form of his best friend in a three-piece suit. The sauce-covered spoon continued on its fateful trajectory and whacked into Darius's chest like it was a bull's-eye. It left a giant red splotch on his silk tie and clattered down, coming to rest not on the immaculate engineered-hardwood floor but atop Darius's gleaming loafers.

Finn made a belated dive to catch the spoon, but unfortunately so did his friend. They collided heads and wound up in a pile of limbs like football players grabbing for a loose ball. At least that's what he assumed caused football pileups. His experience was limited to what he caught from the kitchen during Super Bowl parties.

Hand to his aching skull, he surveyed the damage. Darius looked like he'd lost a battle with a ketchup-wielding toddler. Streaks of barbecue sauce covered his dove-gray suit and glistened on his no-longer-pristine shoes.

Finn's shoes, on the other hand, hadn't even been pristine when he first bought them from the neighborhood thrift store last year. His best friend was his opposite in almost every way—driven, successful, put together, with a stature that commanded attention.

Darius had to duck through the doorways in the old houses he renovated, and his gym-built muscles made quick work of demoing cabinetry and smashing through lath and plaster walls. Finn stood just shy of six feet, and the only muscles he could boast of came from spending hours at the cooktop at the restaurant and lugging boxes of inventory. And unlike Finn's unruly brown waves, Darius kept his black curls clipped close to his head, his face clean shaven.

Battling the feeling of inferiority that threatened every time his friend came around, he wiped a glob of sauce off his own scruff-covered chin. "You could've told me you were coming."

Darius fixed him with a death glare. "It's my house."

"But still, walking up on a chef without announcing yourself? You're lucky it wasn't a pot of boiling water."

Darius shook sauce off his hand, splattering the white cabinets in red drops. "Lucky, Finn? You're lucky I don't ban you from my properties for life."

"This won't even be your house for long."

"It will be if you ruin all my suits so I can't look my best for showings."

"Oh, there's an idea." Finn grinned. "Kidding, obviously. And don't worry, I'll pay for dry cleaning." Cutting off Darius's rebuttal, he said,

"You'd don't even let me pay rent. Least I can do is clean up my own mess."

"Okay, have it your way, Cinderella." Darius leaned onto his elbow and pulled a can of Lysol and a roll of paper towels from under the sink. He tore off a piece and dabbed at his loafers.

Finn spritzed the floor with disinfectant and resisted the temptation to spray Darius's shoes. To distract himself from the childish urge, he said, "So are you going to tell me why you're prowling around in a suit at midnight?" A thought hit him. "Wait, you're not meeting a girl here, are you?"

Darius made a face of supreme disgust. "Do you honestly think I use these flip houses as sex dens?"

He didn't, but he grinned anyway, just to get under his friend's skin.

"C'mon, man, no." Shaking his head, he went back to cleaning off his shoes. "You do realize I have my own place, right? I don't need to be bringing dates back to my flips."

Right. Darius was too classy to pull a douchebag stunt like that. Plus, no doubt the thread count on his sheets at home far outclassed whatever the room stagers had put on the beds in here. And he was officially done thinking about the state of Darius's bedsheets. "Which brings us back to what you're doing here. In a suit. At midnight."

Darius wiped his fingers on a paper towel, curling his lip at the damage left behind. "Why can't you get past the suit thing? I met up with some friends for drinks after work and didn't get a chance to change."

"And then you decided to come here and check up on me? Make sure I wasn't throwing a kegger?"

"Cut it out. You know I trust you. I came because I heard about an opportunity for you."

"And it couldn't wait until tomorrow?" Stupid to ask. With Darius, everything had a timetable.

"Tomorrow would be too late," Darius said, confirming his assumption. "There's a farmers' market about an hour away. Little town called Hawksburg, but apparently it draws a huge crowd, and this year it's expected to be even bigger."

"And you know this how?" Probably from hours of research on Finn's behalf. He claimed to believe in Finn's end goal to start a non-profit, but if he decided to go all in with the sauce venture, he knew his best friend would be ecstatic. A barbecue sauce business made sense on paper. His cooking-school dream? Not so much. Then again, he'd never been big on coloring inside the lines.

"Kendall—you know, from Hammerstein and Blythe?" Finn didn't, but he nodded anyway because he didn't need a who's-who rundown of Springfield real estate agents at going on one a.m., especially when he'd been on his feet for nearly twenty hours. "Well, she's got an uncle whose mother fell—"

"Dare, get to the point." His tiredness had crept up on him, and suddenly he wanted nothing more than to crash face first onto the air mattress waiting upstairs.

"The point is" –Darius loosened his sauce-covered tie—"there's an open slot at the Hawksburg farmers' market tomorrow."

"You keep saying the name Hawksburg like it should mean something to me."

"It should. It's the town where they found the dinosaur last year."

Finn stood up and looked around for a trash can. He ended up tossing the dirty towels into one of the empty grocery bags. "You do realize I am not a four-year-old child, right? Dinosaur news isn't exactly on my radar."

"Shut up. To be honest, I hadn't heard about it, either, but the way Kendall hyped it up, I thought maybe you might've. Anyway, I googled it and apparently it was a big thing last year, a dinosaur turning up in a swimming pool or something." Darius gingerly removed his jacket and laid it on the counter, which seemed like overkill since the damage was done. "They're planning to build a museum to capitalize on the interest. Smart, if you ask me."

Capitalizing on interest was basically Darius's motto. But since giving back was the other half of his personal mission statement, Finn couldn't fault him. Except when his friend's overzealous ambition morphed into meddling in his life.

"And all of this matters to me because . . ." His exhausted brain couldn't keep up, but he sensed meddling on the horizon.

"Because it's a great opportunity for your business."

Finn groaned, exhausted just thinking about trying to fit something else into his schedule. "Dare, no."

"Kendall already texted her uncle and got you the spot. It would be rude to not show up."

Trust Darius to use his people-pleasing personality fault against him. Luckily, charity trumped manners. "I have a shift at the meal-distribution center tomorrow."

Unmoved, Darius crossed his arms. "Call in sick. Or swap. C'mon, man, this is your future."

"I can't call in sick to the volunteer work. Pretty sure that's a cardinal sin." Or at the least, inviting bad luck.

"Then tell them you need to make money to pay for your landlord's dry cleaning."

"Funny." Finn sighed, rubbing his forehead. "What if I'm wasting my time with all this?" The likelihood of him ever making enough to launch a nonprofit cooking school on a chef's salary? Dismal. Hence the sauce business. The only problem was his heart wasn't in it. As much as he loved cooking, he didn't enjoy being on the other side: sales, marketing. Managing money? He shuddered, stomach tight. But he had promised himself he'd give it his all.

"You're not." Darius held his coat at arm's length and grabbed his keys. "Hawksburg. Nine a.m. Bring lots of inventory, and don't forget your credit card reader this time."

"Hang on." He dipped a clean spoon in the sauce. "If you're going to go around swinging deals for me, you should be the first to try this."

"A new sauce?" Darius took the spoon and slurped up a taste. Pounded the counter with his palm. "Get outta here, man."

"Right?" Exhilaration replaced exhaustion. He might have a real shot. "A trio is great, but four sauces offers something for everyone."

Eyes bright with an intensity that could only mean he was already running numbers, Darius nodded. "So you're actually considering a large-scale launch?"

"Considering it, yes. But Dare, I can't sink any more money into this if I don't start seeing profits." That was the whole point. Sell sauce, save money, finance his dreams.

"You want profits?" Needed them. "Then you can't be afraid to put yourself out there. This country market will be a low-stakes way to rack up some sales."

Low stakes. Perfect for his behind-the-scenes personality. Low stakes, low profile. He could do this. Start small and work toward making his big vision a reality.

CHAPTER 3

SIMONE

Downward dog in cutoff overalls and Birkenstocks was not how Simone had pictured this morning going. The first farmers' market of the season would set the bar for the summer, and her current inverted position didn't exactly exude powerhouse-restaurateur vibes.

Then again, she'd never shirked her share of grunt work, blisters or not. That's what mani-pedis were for. And setup would've been a breeze, except she'd loaned out her new folding table to Ruth. The backup one Simone had brought was rusted as all get-out, but a tablecloth would disguise the wear, if only she could unstick this bent frame.

"You're a lifesaver." Ruth's quiet voice came from above her. "Can't believe I forgot a table on the first market day of the season." Still soft spoken, she'd come a long way from the timid new kid Simone had befriended freshman year of high school.

Ruth had started her own business, which took strength and guts. Her friend had changed in the years she'd been away, and she'd missed the transformation. Catching up over drinks on holidays and long weekends relegated her to outsider status.

"Sure you don't need a hand setting that up?" Grass-stained Keds shuffled on the gravel next to her, and Simone pictured Ruth twisting a lock of red hair around her finger, like she'd done a lot as a new arrival to Hawksburg years ago.

Now Simone was the one on the outs, angling for an in, but even dripping with sweat and upside down, she'd never let her nerves show.

Simone managed another shake of her head. "Thanks, though. I'll be by later on to see your new stuff. I'm loving the lavender soap you sold me a few weeks ago."

"Oh good," Ruth said. "I've got a new scent I think you might like. Rosemary wheat. Except . . . shoot, did I bring the carton?"

Sun swept over Simone's shoulders as Ruth jogged off, taking the shade she'd cast with her, no doubt on a mission to make sure the rest of the day went smoothly, just like all the other vendors gathered.

The Hawksburg market was an eclectic mix of farmers, crafters, cooks, bakers, and artisans. Shoppers could score anything from a hand-stitched bag to cheese curds to a tall bouquet of gladiolus flowers. With so much local talent and flavor, Simone hoped to find a way to show-case it year round, but at this point, she'd settle for getting the table leg unstuck.

Teeth gritted, she lifted one foot and pressed her heel against the table leg behind her. Shifting her weight onto one hand, she tried to pry up the metal bar, but it wouldn't budge. Her shoulders trembled, and a trail of sweat snaked down her cheek.

"Are you playing some kind of solo Twister, or could you use a hand?"

Not Ruth this time. The voice was deep and came from somewhere close, not over her shoulder. Simone tucked her chin into her chest and peeked out from under her armpit. She sucked in a reflexive breath. Holy hottie, Batman.

A guy crouched next to her on the dusty grass, his elbows on his knees. He eyed her inverted position with a wry grin. Dark, tousled hair hung over liquid brown eyes so molten they were practically glowing.

His nose, slightly crooked, sat above full, sensual lips that looked like they'd just been kissed.

Her stomach dropped into her throat, not a difficult feat, because, gravity. But she sniffed and turned back to the stubborn piece of metal, giving it a tug.

"Nah. I've—" She yanked the bar upward, and it snapped into place. One final kick, and the rear table legs locked with a satisfying click. "Got it."

"I see that." The man's voice was as rich as honeyed coffee, smooth and deeply masculine, and a shiver pirouetted up her spine. She walked her fingertips back to her feet—one, two, three, four—letting the measured pace steady her pulse. Slow and sinuous, she rolled up from the waist, and telegraphed grudging thanks to Meg for dragging her to yoga all spring.

"Could *you* use a hand?" She extended her arm toward him, brows arched.

He chuckled and grabbed ahold, palm pressed to hers, and a frisson tingled at the base of her spine. A tattoo wound its way up his forearm to wrap his bicep in black designs. She rolled her tongue against her cheek, defense against the allure of the ink.

Tightening her grip, she leveraged him to his feet, and he gave her fingers a squeeze before letting go. "Thanks."

"No problem." Her voice came out scratchy and rough, and she surreptitiously forced a swallow.

"So, barbecue, huh?" He lifted his chin toward the carved wooden sign hanging at the back of the tent.

With his gaze averted, she took the chance to touch a palm to her temple. Catching a drip of sweat, she pressed her edges down, willing her hormones to follow suit. "Yep, best barbecue in the state."

"That so?" His voice held a hint of challenge, and his hotness meter fell a few notches.

"According to all my satisfied customers, sure is."

He gave her a brief smile and did a slow glance around at the stalls nearby. Other vendors were setting up their wares and sipping coffee from travel mugs. Tossing greetings into morning air already weighed down by soupy midwestern mugginess. "Anyone ever challenge that claim?"

Okay, time for this dude to move on. "Nope, I'm the only barbecue joint in town."

She stuck her hands in her back pockets and sized him up. Only a couple of inches taller than her—no big surprise, since she topped five nine in flats—and about her age, midtwenties she'd guess. Stubble dusted his jaw, glinting with burnt umber and cinnamon, and dipped down to cover a prominent Adam's apple. His scruffy beard and wind-blown hair brought to mind pirates and pillaging and all sorts of other yummy things.

Letting her gaze drift down from his faded T-shirt to his scuffed sneakers, she made a slow crawl back up, one eyebrow arched in an impersonation of the Rock she'd spent an entire summer perfecting in the bathroom mirror. "Not like I couldn't handle a little competition."

"You might get your chance. I hear there's a new vendor."

She hitched up her chin and looked him dead in the eyes, ignoring the hammering of her heart. "Oh yeah?"

"Yeah." He rubbed at his jaw, and she caught a glimpse of rounded bicep as he squinted down the row of tents. "Tim Brower gave up his booth. Had to go downstate, take care of his mom." His brown eyes swung back to hers. Slow, casual. "Something about a broken hip?"

"Tim *Brewster*, you mean?"

"He's the one."

Instinctively, Simone cocked her head to listen. Sure enough, she didn't hear any telltale bleating. Tim usually brought along a doe and kid to draw in customers for his goat-milk products. His cheese and yogurt were to die for, but she wasn't sold on the skin-care line.

Udder juice on your face? Blech.

"Anyway, I better get going, unless you need a hand flipping the table?" Mystery guy raised his thick brows.

"I'm good." She let her tone fall flat, and he stepped back, out of the tent.

Squinting against the rays, he sent one last crooked smile her way, looking less Robin Hood and more Sheriff of Nottingham by the minute. "All right. Guess I'll be seeing you around, Simon."

Simon? She glanced down and discovered her name tag had been knocked askew, maybe during her wrestling match with the table. The *e* sticker was missing. Must've peeled off in the humidity.

When she snapped up her head to tell him off, the tattooed stranger was halfway down the row of booths. He strode away on legs a smidge too long for his frame, headed straight toward Tim's spot.

Son of a—"Billy, you know about this?" She rounded on the father-son team next to her. Folks said their sweet corn couldn't be beat; come harvest time they'd sell out by noon.

Bill Lewis the younger pulled a sucker out of his mouth. *Better than a cigarette*, he always said when people teased him about the habit. "What?"

"That . . ." She cast about for a word sinister enough to describe the interloper intent on stealing her customer base. "That *stranger*—" she said, because in a small town, roots meant everything. "There's a new guy here to sell *barbecue* sauce, of all things. Did you know Tim gave up his booth?"

Billy slurped his sucker back into his mouth and spoke around the soggy stick. "Nope, first I'm hearing of it. Dad?"

Mr. Lewis shrugged, busy arranging heirloom tomatoes in a wooden crate. He wore a faded flannel button-down despite the heat, sleeves rolled neatly up to his elbows.

Billy used his tongue to push the lollipop into his cheek. "I know it's against protocol, but I wouldn't worry, Simone. No one can touch your grandpa's recipe."

Her mouth bunched into a knot of frustration. Her *grandpa's* recipe. She ducked under the thin rope anchoring the tent, then jogged down a few stalls to where Meg was unloading crates of eggs. "Margaret, did you hear about a new guy selling barbecue?"

Meg shook her head, sending her wavy brunette ponytail bouncing. She stacked the box with a grunt, then leaned out and shaded her eyes, but the guy had disappeared into the tent. "He cute?"

"His attractiveness is hardly the operative issue here," Simone said. "As always, your libido is off the charts."

"Which is a fancy way of saying yes, he's smoking hot." Meg gave as good as she got, and Simone couldn't help but grin. Trading jabs with Meg was one of her purest joys in life. But now was not the time for messing around.

"Why would Tim give up his spot to a barbecue guy? Everyone knew my plan to start selling Honey and Hickory's sauce this year."

"Maybe he didn't tell Tim what he was selling." Meg swiped at her glistening upper lip with her forearm, her fair skin flushed from the heat.

Simone squinted toward where the man had vanished. "He did look like a sneak. Wouldn't surprise me if he wormed his way in here under false pretenses." How could she ever make good on her plans to build up this town when she couldn't even manage to handle her small piece of it?

Becoming a regular at the market was supposed to show people how committed she was to this town. Prove she was still a local, despite her sojourn in Chicago. What if everyone flocked to the newcomer's booth and ignored hers?

A braver woman might have taken the chance to find out once and for all where she stood in the hearts of those she used to count as family. Too bad she'd used up all her courage on taking over the restaurant and starting fresh.

But bravado? That she had in spades.

She yanked her phone out of her pocket and scrolled through her contacts.

"What are you doing?" Meg's voice held an edge of worry. She'd taken over coddling Simone, since Alisha's cookie shop in Chicago didn't leave her extra time to keep tabs on her. Even though Simone missed her, she loved the new dynamic where they were just sisters, not each other's keepers.

"Calling in reinforcements." Asking for help never came easy, but she hadn't moved home just to sit on the sidelines. Time to rally the troops.

A show of solidarity just might be the thing to make the new guy rethink his choice of venues next week. She backed out of the tent before Meg could respond and jogged down the aisle, toward her pickup. If they agreed to come, her backup would need help hauling their wares.

One hour until the market opened. Plenty of time to launch an offensive.

CHAPTER 4

FINN

8:56 a.m.

Cutting it close, as usual. Finn switched his phone to speaker and set it on the dashboard, only half listening as he dug under the front seat in search of his credit card reader. A stray sock, a toothbrush—that's where it went—a spoon covered in dried yogurt. He really ought to clean out his car more often.

"Finn, are you still there?" Bella—his boss, mentor, and close friend—sounded exasperated, a notch above her default setting of mildly perturbed.

"Yeah." With a shudder, he shoved the crusty spoon back under the seat, and it clanked against something solid. His card reader? Leaning farther into the car, he said, "I think you should go with avocado puree for the tasting menu."

"I was asking if you'd heard from Victor."

Oh. He bent his shoulder to the floorboard, reaching with his fingertips.

"Another no call, no show. His third in the last week. I'm gonna have to cut him loose."

That made him halt his search. He'd vouched for the teen, whom he'd met while Victor was doing community service at the meal-distribution center for a vandalism charge. From what he'd pieced together, Victor had basically been on his own all year, bouncing between relatives after his mom's incarceration. The job was supposed to help him support his younger siblings without getting sucked into dealing or theft.

"Give me a day at least to see if I can get in touch with him, Bell."

The sound of pots clanging hit his ears. "Okay, but as much as I love your bleeding heart, I've got a business to run. Kid wants to work, he's got a job. If not, I'll give it to someone who does."

Victor did want to work; Finn believed that without a doubt. But sometimes it wasn't that simple. Still, Bella couldn't run the restaurant short staffed forever. "Heard," he said, knowing kitchen slang needled her when he wasn't on the clock.

"Quit with that, mister. By the way, if you're not delivering meals, why are you awake right now? Jade said you didn't get out of here until after midnight."

And he hadn't gone to bed until nearly dawn, but if Bella knew that, she'd be all over him about how sleeplessness fed stress, which is not something he needed reminding of, considering his therapist had reiterated that last week. But he struggled to find rest in temporary dwellings. Working long hours ensured he'd stay out until he was exhausted enough to sleep.

Digging his toes into the gravel, he jammed his arm under the seat as far as it would go and finally hit pay dirt, then used his fingers to maneuver the card reader out from under the seat. "Darius found a farmers' market for me to sell at. Long story—I'll explain tonight. Right now I gotta go before I get a reputation for running behind schedule."

"Too late," Bella teased. "See ya."

"Bye." Finn wriggled out of the car and grabbed the credit card reader and his last box of sauce.

The market had just opened, and already he had to dodge his way through the packed parking lot. At least the half hour spent tearing his car apart from glove box to trunk in search of the missing piece of technology hadn't been in vain.

And everything else was set up—mason jars on ice to sample from, pretzels and breadsticks laid out on covered plastic trays, and bottles of Finn's Secret Sauce on display, with extra inventory tucked in boxes under the tables.

In his absence, a small crowd had gathered around his tent. His heart beat faster at the prospect of making real money. Until now, he'd sold through word of mouth. But he hadn't drained his meager savings just to sell sauce at cookouts and block parties. Hopefully these potential customers had helped themselves to samples and were ready to make a purchase.

He set down the box outside the tent. "Hi! Sorry, I had to grab something out of my car." Dusting off his hands, he put on a shaky smile.

Sell sauce. Save money. Finance your dreams.

"Have you had a chance to—"

What. The. Heck.

Finn spun in a slow and dizzy circle. His bottles of sauce were gone, replaced by overflowing baskets of yarn. Ribbony yarn, multicolored yarn, and fluffy neutrals that looked like they came straight off a yak. Yarn knitted into scarves and hats and slippers and beer cozies and—he stepped closer to peer at something propped on a table—a knitted large-mouth bass on a plaque.

And next to it . . . a deer head, complete with antlers.

Knitted taxidermy? He shrank back in horror.

"Cute little fellas, aren't they?" A woman in what could only be described as a cape—also knitted—stepped up next to him and joined him in scrutinizing the deer. "We do custom orders. Care to browse our brochure?"

He shook his head and stepped back, hands out. "Maybe another time, thanks." He flashed his teeth in a half grimace, half smile.

Wrong booth. Time was ticking. He stepped around the woman, intent on locating his own tent, and strode down the walkway. Stopped. *Was that* . . .

Backtracking, he surveyed the interior of the far side of the booth. Bags of pretzel sticks sat next to plastic domed containers with bottles of his original and spicy blend arranged next to them. And hanging from the back of the tent, the vinyl sign he'd picked up from the printer yesterday.

So this was the right stall after all. Except, unless he was losing it—plausible, running on only a few hours of sleep—when he'd ventured out to his car, there hadn't been a single homespun yarn creation in sight.

As he stood there, hands on his hips, questioning his sanity, a woman in a knitted teal bowler hat bounced over to him with a smile. "You must be Finn. Of secret sauce fame." She nodded toward the sign. At least she saw it too. One tally in the *Hasn't completely lost it* column. "Becky Doyle," she said, and he realized that was an introduction.

Clasping her hand, he grimaced at her grip, wresting his expression into a smile.

"When we got word this stall was available, we couldn't believe our luck."

"But it's not," he said, to underscore the obvious. "I'm here." And all of his stuff. Right next to their wares, assuming she was also a yarn seller. At this point, he didn't have the headspace to figure out her presence. Had there been a mix-up with Darius's intel?

She grinned. "And we're glad to have you. Always nice to see a new face around here. Although"—she leaned toward him and dropped her voice to a whisper—"you do know you're bending the rules a bit." He was? How so? "But we'll look the other way, since you're being so good about sharing the booth."

26

"Sharing?"

"All the booths are double occupancy. Tim is one of the few vendors who rents both halves. He needs the extra space for his goats."

Goats? When had goats come into the mix? Finn's head was spinning, and not from the sun beating down, though that didn't help. He stepped into the shade, marveling at the other woman's composure in her thick hat.

"We went ahead and shifted over your inventory so you wouldn't have to."

An elderly woman on a scooter motored up to the tent. "If you need anything else set up, Aimee would be more'n happy to lend a hand. She's got young legs."

Next to her, a young woman in a flowy skirt with a knitted purse slung over her shoulder rolled her eyes. "Aunt Janet, quit trying to set me up with every man you come across." She scowled at the woman, then flashed a smile his way. "Not that I mind helping out."

Finn frowned. "No, it's okay. I . . ."

"Yoo-hoo, Patty!" Another member of the yarn gang leaned out of the stall. "I've seen you down at the shop buying skeins. When are you going to join up?" The woman kept her face forward, speed-walking. "Patricia Ann, don't make me chase you!" The knitter cackled, like she might make good on her promise, but turned toward Finn instead. She wore a fanny pack front and center on her pregnant belly with an indecipherable bedazzled logo.

He squinted, trying to make out the words formed with tiny crystals.

She pointed to it with finger guns. "The Yarn Spinners. Heard of us?"

Nope, but he doubted he'd ever forget the name. It would haunt his nightmares.

With a chuckle, she maneuvered herself around him, into the shade, and pulled out some bills from her bag. "When Simone told us this spot was open, we couldn't believe our luck."

Simone. Why did that name sound familiar?

She licked her thumb and started counting the cash. "And just in time for our annual membership drive too. Great timing, isn't it, Doug?"

The lone man in attendance, seated on a director's chair inside the tent, kept clacking away with his knitting needles. "Best news we've had in a while. The market organizers have had it out for us ever since—"

"Ancient history." The pregnant woman cut him off with a lopsided smile toward Finn. "But yeah, we haven't gotten a booth in years. So we really do appreciate you sharing."

The young woman in the flowy dress—Aimee—leaned out and shoved a brochure into someone's shopping trolley. Slipped another into the tote bag of a shopper who'd just stepped up to his table. The woman looked down at the brochure sticking out of her bag. Backed slowly away from the tent.

Great. Just stupendous. He'd been dealt the short stick. All his potential customers were now giving the tent a wide berth for fear of being roped in to the group of knitters. Someone named Simone had orchestrated this last-minute arrangement. Didn't narrow it down much, in a town full of strangers. But the name rang a bell . . . Simone, Simone, Sim—*Simon*. The gorgeous barbecue vendor he'd met this morning. She did this?

Leaving the knitters behind, he strode down the aisle, dodging dogs—he would not be distracted by those adorable smiling pup faces and wagging tails, and oh, those floppy ears . . . *not now, Finn!*—and kids in little red wagons, and gaggles of old ladies with wire shopping trolleys, all giving the Yarn Spinners' booth—*his* booth—a wide berth.

He found Simon/Simone right where he'd left her, except right-side up, her stunning long legs now hidden behind a table likewise returned to its upright and locked position. Twin glossy black braids hung over her shoulders, and she'd added a baseball hat with the words *Honey and Hickory* stitched in maroon letters to her crop-top-and-cutoff-overalls outfit.

Sexy country girl wasn't something he would've guessed he'd be into, but dang.

He mentally slapped his own cheek. Not sexy. The person responsible for making him share a stall with the equivalent of mall kiosk vendors with a sales quota to hit. The two braids and overalls made her look innocent, but her wide smile hid a devious soul; he was sure of it.

A line snaked away from her booth, packed with customers who should've been handing over cash in exchange for his no-doubt superior sauces. Infringing on profits he intended to use for the greater good. Pretty sure she couldn't say the same.

And sabotaging her only competition? Whatever'd happened to a free market? Her Mr. Monopoly play ended now. Bypassing the line, he marched straight up to the table. "I know what you pulled, and you're going to regret it."

"Is that a promise?" She had the nerve to grin at him, a bright and dazzling flash of white teeth and red lips.

Flipping one braid over her shoulder with a fine-boned hand, she swiped another customer's credit card. "I went ahead and threw in a smoked sausage for you, Tara. No charge. Don't worry about losing your loyalty card. We'll just start a new one, okay?"

Simone pulled out a hole punch from her back pocket and snipped the card, then dropped it in the bag. "See you next week."

"Definitely. And thanks!" The woman shuffled out of line, and Finn took her place.

The next customer pushed up behind him. "Maybe you didn't notice, but the line's back that way."

He didn't turn. Not because he couldn't seem to tear his eyes off the beautiful woman in front of him. Only because he couldn't afford to turn his back on someone so sneaky.

"This won't take long," he said out of the side of his mouth, willing his eyes back up from the path they kept trying to trace down to her lips. He planted both hands on the table and caught a hint of something crisp and herbaceous as he leaned toward her. Tempting as a cool drink on a hot day—and totally at odds with the fire in her amber-hued eyes.

"Got a minute, *Simone?*"

She pressed her perfect lips together and flicked her gaze down the line of customers, then narrowed her eyes. "One minute." She leaned sideways and shouted around him, "Meg, can you send Laney over to give me a hand for a sec?"

A woman with streaky blonde hair popped out of a tent a few stalls down, a baby strapped to her chest in a carrier.

"She'll take care of y'all," Simone said to the people in line, gracious but with no hint of apology in her tone. "I'll be back right, after I deal with this misguided out-of-towner."

Out-of-towner? How would she even know? And she said it like an insult. The opposite of the welcoming, if overwhelming, way the knitters had greeted him.

Simone crooked a finger at him and walked out the back of the tent without checking to see if he was following. His blood pressure cracked through his skull and vented out the other side.

He caught up to her at the back edge of the tent. "Be honest, you put the Yarn Spinners in my booth."

"Whoa, dude." She spun around, eyes flashing. "I don't owe you an explanation. But if I did, I'd guess Tim must've forgotten to mention all the booths are shared. He's getting up in years, you know."

Finn didn't know, considering he'd never met the man. But telling her so would've played right into her hands.

"Or maybe the market organizers made a mistake," she said, continuing to ramble on in spite of his silence. Suspicious. Or maybe she was just flustered by his accusation? "You could always give them a call. Though most of them go fishing on summer mornings. Hard to reach them out on the lake." She flicked her hand across her legs to shoo a fly, and his attention fell to her bare thighs beneath the frayed hem of her shorts. So. Hot.

Out here—so hot out here. *Jeez, Finn.*

He raked a hand through his hair, less certain now but in too deep. "I know you had a hand in this." In what, though? The vocal presence of the knitters would make selling his sauce a little more inconvenient. But even if she had been the one to tell them to take over half the booth, it wasn't like she'd engaged in some kind of nefarious foul play. If she wanted him gone, this was the perfect way to push him out without implicating herself.

"Are you one of them?" The intrepid leader, no doubt. No visible knitted attire on her, although maybe she was hiding it . . . a yarn bra?

His gaze drifted down again to the glossy hollow between her collarbones. Snapped back up. Was he seriously about to ogle her chest under the guise of checking for a *knitted bra*?

"One of the Yarn Spinners?" She chuckled, and he couldn't tell from the sound whether she was laughing at his accusation or his inner turmoil. "Please. They've been trying to indoctrinate me into their cult for years, but no thanks. They do make quality stuff, though. They could crochet you a tote to haul all your unsold merchandise back to your car." Her smirk was an ice pick to his soul.

"Do you realize this is my livelihood you're messing with? I reserved that spot, fair and square." Last minute, and through third parties, but still. Come to think of it, Simone might have been telling the truth about Tim Brewster's forgetfulness, but somehow he doubted it.

"If you're concerned about fairness, you should know we abide by an honor system here." Honor system. Ironic, coming from her. "Only one vendor selling each category of goods. In case you hadn't noticed, this is a small town."

"I didn't realize it was a town at all, because the only thing I've seen since I pulled off the interstate is cornfields."

Okay, maybe bad-mouthing the town was not the best approach. Her golden eyes narrowed under the brim of her hat, but her glare made him dig in deeper. "Besides, I didn't know about your little code, so you can hardly ban me from selling based on something I didn't agree to."

Her full lips pressed into a straight line, nostrils flaring. The motion pulled his attention to the freckles dusting her high cheekbones, scattered across her nose.

"You're right, I can't ban you. But good luck selling anything today with your new stall buddies driving away business."

Aha! "So you did have a hand in it."

Without a reply, she turned her back on him and crunched away over the gravel. Full of righteous indignation, he caught up to her in a jog, then angled to cut her off. She stopped short, just before their hips collided, and the hairs on his arms shot up.

Unnerved by his reaction to her nearness, he growled, "You big coward."

"Coward?" She didn't back down, uttering the question inches from his lips. He would not, *would not*, look at her mouth. Or her hips, a hairbreadth from his. How easy would it be to slip his fingers into the belt loops of her overalls and tug her closer? Breathing quick, he shoved aside the unwelcome thought.

"Yeah. Coward." Her calm, aloof expression shot fire through his veins. "You said you'd welcome competition, yet you went and pulled some strings to drive away the first person to challenge you."

"I told you already. There must've been a clerical error." She crossed her arms. "And scared? Please. My barbecue's the best—I could beat anyone's sauce, any day." Her voice squeaked on the last word, and he let one corner of his mouth lift.

"From what I heard around the market this morning, it's your *grandfather's* sauce, not yours." He'd heard precisely one person say that. But he knew how to fight dirty too. Hated doing it, but for once, he had something worthwhile on the line.

Her small, pointed chin lifted in defiance. "You heard wrong, then. Honey and Hickory is mine, and mine alone. And this is my town. You'd better find a new home base to sell your sauce." Turning her back on him again, she ducked under the tent flap, a haughty queen ending an audience with an enemy general on the battlefield.

Find a new home . . . little did she know that's what he'd been trying to do his whole life, without success. A family? He'd found people who cared about him, who had his back no matter what. But home remained elusive.

Simone had hit a nerve, but he was done being kicked out and pushed aside. Forgotten and replaced. He had a right to be here, same as her, and he intended to stick around and make her regret treating him like an outsider.

CHAPTER 5

SIMONE

Squeezing the reins, Simone brought her horse to a halt. Willow obeyed with a snort, and she rose in the stirrups, eyes shaded to peer across the field at a familiar silver truck kicking up dust on the main road. Meg, on her way home already.

Dang it. The only company she wanted right now was the four-legged kind. Horses didn't require chitchat and had zero interest in drama and gossip, which is why she'd come straight here after throwing down with Barbecue Boy at the farmers' market.

She'd drawn first blood with the knitting maneuver, but the new guy had hit back by refusing to let the Yarn Spinners' voracious membership drive deter his customers. He'd risen to the challenge and walked the aisle with samples to draw people in—a move that should've bothered other sellers, except he was so freaking gregarious that no one seemed to mind his foray into neutral territory—and hawked his second-rate sauce until closing time.

Word was he'd sold all his stock on the first day, with more than a few bottles going to other vendors. *Sellouts.*

They all agreed Finn—impossible not to remember the name on everyone's lips after their public showdown brought on by her ill-fated ploy to scare him off—had earned the right to stay. The consensus was that it would be rude to subvert Tim's wishes. Rude? Defiantly refusing to stay out of her market was the rude move. And breaking the unwritten code for a stranger, of all people? Doubly rude.

But whatever—she'd adjust. Today's setback had made it clear she needed to focus on the bigger picture and find a way to fast-track her plans to expand the scope of Honey and Hickory.

Leaning forward, Simone swung her leg off the mare and dismounted. She'd planned to ride for an hour, but the whole town had already witnessed her flounder; she couldn't handle any more scrutiny. Meg had known her since they were kids. She'd see right through her if she tried to play it off. Better to leave before she got suckered into a heart-to-heart.

Willow bumped her chest with her black muzzle. "You got off easy this time, girlie. But we'll get you back in shape soon enough."

Before moving away, she'd sold the mare to her riding instructor, who she knew would treat Willow like family. But the first thing she'd done after coming home was buy her back, all cash, so she'd never have to worry about being parted from her horse again. It took a hefty chunk out of her savings and meant renting a studio apartment above the restaurant with finicky plumbing, heated by a radiator, but she didn't regret it for a second.

Still, between the substantial cost of upkeep on a horse and student loans, things were tight. Profits from the market were meant to go straight into her expansion fund. Yet after all her hard work on the sauce venture, she'd gotten outsold by a smooth-talking newcomer.

Simone let her head fall back, gazing up into a wide dome of sky unmarred by power lines and looming skyscrapers. The open expanse usually invigorated her, but today the endless sea of blue left her feeling insignificant.

Sensing her stress, or maybe on the hunt for treats, Willow nudged her hand, her whiskers a ticklish brush against Simone's palm.

"Hey, Sim." Her head snapped up, for a moment thinking the words had come out of the horse's mouth. But a leggy figure walked toward the paddock. Meg, no doubt dying to hash out what had gone down today at the market. Simone wasn't in the mood to discuss today's shit show, not even with a surrogate sister.

No one needed to know how much today's defeat had affected her. Most people would've called solid sales a success; most people weren't perfectionists who'd been shoved off course last year and had been scrambling to pull themselves together ever since. Didn't help that she'd had a front-row seat watching Finn rack up sales. And her traitorous body hadn't gotten the memo that this guy was bad news.

Metal scraped against metal as Meg unclipped the fence chain. The clatter banished the image of Finn glaring at her from under the dark bangs that fell into his eyes, the errant strands of hair not doing a thing to lessen the heat of his gaze.

Maybe Meg's arrival wasn't the worst timing. For once, she could use a distraction. The same went for Willow, apparently, who set off toward the open gate at a trot.

Forget what she said about animals. The blatant disloyalty, jeez.

Stopping short, the mare nosed around Meg's pockets. She laughed and fished out a peppermint.

Arms crossed, Simone clucked her tongue. "I see you've been spoiling her. Guess I'll allow it, since you give our girl top-notch accommodations."

When she'd come home last fall, she'd moved Willow out to Meg's acreage. Her property was close enough to town that she was able to come out and visit the mare at least once a day, and she helped Meg out with chores around the farm in lieu of boarding fees.

"You know I love having her here. You're basically family, Simi."

True. But for some reason, the childhood nickname grated on her thin patience like a file on a hangnail. Part of her wondered if Meg only hung around to fill the gap her big sister had left. Only spent time with her out of obligation, for old times' sake.

Not like she should complain when the rest of the town seemed to have amnesia about old times. What she thought would be a joyous homecoming had turned out to be a town full of people who'd moved on without her. All except Meg, who just so happened to be her sister's best friend. Coincidence? Maybe, but her time in the city had left her second-guessing motives.

"Quite a day, huh?" Meg's question interrupted her thoughts. "I cannot believe you targeted the full force of the Spinners at that poor guy. The look on his face . . ."

Simone's mouth twitched in a smile. From the cover of her booth, she'd watched Finn's wide-eyed reaction when the knitting group had swarmed him. Part horror, part fascination. Fully adorable. His *expression*, that is. Not him. Never him.

Meg chuckled, and she couldn't help but join in. "Should I feel bad?"

"Do you?"

Did she? Her knee-jerk reaction could've cost him sales. But she'd been under so much pressure since last year—moving home, trying to prove herself worthy of her family's faith in her to run Honey and Hickory—that his arrival had been one complication too many.

Not used to this nagging feeling of being overwhelmed, she'd acted on impulse. If she was honest, rounding up the Yarn Spinners had been less motivated by a desire to see herself succeed than to push away the feelings he'd sparked in her.

Feelings of inadequacy, and nothing else. Not a kick of attraction in her chest so strong it took her breath away. Not guilt over the hurt in his eyes when he'd confronted her, like she'd betrayed him. Not the inexplicable urge to go out and call a truce at midday in hopes he'd turn his bright smile her way.

"I just needed a win." Her tone sounded close to whiny, and she hated that. She could forgive herself for a moment of pettiness. But self-pity? No way.

Meg's sympathetic nod confirmed her fears. Here came the pity pick-me-up. In three, two—"I get that. But you've got a good thing going. The market is just icing on the cake, right?"

"You've clearly been talking with Ali too much." Simone smirked to needle Meg for the baking reference. "And yeah, I knew the farmers' market wouldn't be a huge source of income, but I guess I saw it as a testing ground. A stepping-stone to becoming part of the community again. And then along comes . . ."

An unexpected rival who poked holes in the hull of her dreams. Left her floundering in a sea of uncertainty when she was used to navigating the shores of surety. Her past was interwoven in this place. Had everyone forgotten? Would her plans for Hawksburg's future be a laughingstock?

"Along comes a cute stranger?" Meg grinned.

"Along comes a competitor out to get me."

"Out to get you?"

"He insinuated I was just a proxy for Pops."

"Ouch."

But maybe he was right. If she couldn't launch her dream of making Hawksburg a destination, of showcasing the town's worth, then was she just a glorified manager of her grandfather's restaurant?

"This was a wake-up call. Now I know I need to go bigger."

Meg's brows arched.

The idea had come to her while she was circling the paddock on Willow's back. Riding always helped clear her head. "I've got an idea on how to raise capital for the expansion and get some exposure to boot."

"We're raising capital now?" Meg settled her hands on her hips, her T-shirt tucked into high-waisted jeans.

"*I'm* looking to raise capital, yes." Not that she didn't appreciate Meg's support, but it was bad enough being the girl who couldn't make it in Chicago. If she couldn't hack being solo back home, she'd never get the town on her side again.

"Just how big of a reno do you have planned? Because if you sit tight for a few years, keep on churning out great barbecue—"

"I want more than just a renovation." She licked her lips. Meg was a vault; that much she knew from trying to pry her sister's secrets out of her over the years, before she learned that was a dead end. And sooner or later, she was going to have to share her ideas with locals. Meg would be a safe sounding board.

"I've been looking at retail spaces to rent." Meg's brow pinched in question, and Simone went on: "I want to open up a boutique to serve as a showcase for local goods. And down the road, I'd like to create a town-square venue to host concerts and shows. I just feel like Hawksburg has so much to offer."

Meg was nodding along, lips pursed. "So you want to draw in more people to town? Open the borders, so to speak?"

"Exactly." Simone grinned, enthusiastic for the first time since Handsome—scratch that—Cocky Stranger had opened his mouth. Meg got it, no long-winded explanation necessary, which might mean her plan had merit.

But Meg's brow furrowed. "And so, in the spirit of that, you drove the first nonlocal vendor to ever grace the farmers' market out of town."

Simone's smile slipped, along with her jaw. She wrestled it back up. "I didn't drive him anywhere," she mumbled, and she pulled Willow's reins over her head, leading the mare out of the paddock.

"What's that?"

"I said, I may have *tried* to run him out of town, but he stuck like a friggin' leech." The crunch of boot heels in gravel let her know Meg was following her toward the barn. "And granted, I may have gone a little overboard in calling up the Spinners—"

"A little?"

She shot Meg a glare over her shoulder. "But they've been dying to be invited back! They deserved the chance to be there more than some random dude who, lest we forget, was selling barbecue. You know the code."

"The code is more of a guideline. You know we have, like, three cheese guys." They sold different kinds of cheese, made from different kinds of milk, but yeah, no arguing the cheese point.

They entered the barn, and the familiar scent of leather and hay engulfed her senses. Here, she didn't need to perform. To succeed.

Meg grabbed Willow's halter while Simone slid off her bridle, then she slipped it on and clipped two leads to it. "Plenty of loopholes. Which would've made it easy to welcome a newcomer."

Easy? To welcome that pompous jerk? But yeah, her conscience hadn't been the quietest all day. It was one thing to let him rattle her but another thing to mess with someone's livelihood. She didn't take that lightly, but something about Finn had stirred her to a desperate act when she should've taken a step back to assess.

That something had nothing to do with his sexy smirk and everything to do with his dig at her capabilities. Okay, so maybe it was ninety/ten. Sixty/forty.

But no matter which way she sliced it, she'd messed up. Meg was right. Her first chance to put her plans into action and welcome new people into town, and she'd failed the test.

She unbuckled the girth and hoisted the saddle off Willow's back. "I made a bad move today, but it was also a reality check." Honey and Hickory's sauce was just one among many. A drop of molasses in the bucket. "Selling at local markets is not going to generate enough income to fund my vision." Especially not with obstinate competitors in the mix.

She added, "You know that show *The Executives*?"

Meg nodded. "You used to torture me and Ali with reruns of that show on Thanksgiving break."

"Because it's amazing." She pulled off the sweaty saddle pad. "Where else can budding entrepreneurs get a chance to pitch their idea to big-time investors?"

"Someone's been brainwashed by late-night bingeing."

Simone laughed. "I may have bookmarked the contestant-application webpage years ago in case I ever came up with an idea good enough to land me a spot on the show. And now I have one. With their backing, Honey and Hickory could be on the map."

"But Honey and Hickory already exists," Meg said. "Isn't the show for new ventures?"

"Sometimes. But it's also for entrepreneurs who want to up their game. Broaden their reach." Show up smug competitors without resorting to subterfuge . . .

"Okay, so why not pitch your new idea?"

Because she hadn't even approached local vendors yet. She'd planned to build up camaraderie over the summer. Get back to being seen as a local, not someone who'd ditched town for the city.

"No need. If I get the investors to finance my Honey and Hickory overhaul, I can use the profits toward expansion." And make sure her new venture was all hers. As a woman of color, she'd spent her whole life having her achievements questioned. Put under review. Negated by her gender and race by those with a twisted view of the world.

She wanted to make sure that at the end of the day, no one could pin her success on someone else. Winning an investment would secure the funds to build her dreams while ensuring that the investors remained as partners of Honey and Hickory only, not her future businesses.

A compromise, but a worthy one.

If Finn was going to invade her territory, she'd have to spread a wider net. Where better to start than on a show that broadcast to the whole country, live?

CHAPTER 6

FINN

Energy drink at his elbow, Finn stood at the steel prep table, staring down a daunting stack of plastic clamshell containers. Ten meals prepped, 190 to go.

He'd swapped shifts with another volunteer to go to the Hawksburg market, and what a waste of time that had been. Instead of preparing meals to feed people in his own neighborhood, he'd spent the day battling an entitled jerk for the right to sell his barbecue sauce in a town he'd never even heard of a few days ago.

And the nightmare hadn't ended when he'd left Hawksburg city limits. Distracted at work, he had dishes sent back to the kitchen all evening—overdone pork chops, raw risotto—beginner mistakes. To make it worse, he'd spent what was left of the night tossing and turning.

If only he could blame his insomnia on a leaky air mattress. But nope, Simone-Not-Simon Blake—whom he'd learned more about from the Yarn Spinners than he'd ever cared to know, from her family tree to the points she'd scored in the regional championship basketball game eight years ago—had stolen more than his spot; she'd robbed him of his hard-won peace of mind. He complained about the long hours, but working until he was bone tired made sleep come easy. Kept him from spending nights staring at blank walls, conjuring up memories best left in the past.

But one run-in with that self-appointed barbecue queen had hit him like a jolt of unwanted late-night caffeine, and conflicting thoughts had left him restless and jumpy until dawn. Awake and staring at the popcorn ceiling in need of scraping, he'd been torn between wanting to go back to the farmers' market next week to stand up to that sauce tyrant and wishing he could start over, without the insults.

Not because he was haunted by how the light in her topaz eyes had faded when he'd rattled her. No, he only wanted her on his side because Simone was the kind of territorial maniac no one should have as an enemy. And okay, maybe he felt a little guilty for his part in stirring up trouble.

He sliced open a fresh bag of lettuce and grabbed a handful. Busywork left too much time to overthink. In a few hours he'd be at Bellaire, and the menu there was adventurous enough to demand his attention, as last night's slew of errors had proved. Until then, no one would fault him for indulging in a few more fantasies about Simone Blake.

Vindictive fantasies, that is.

A tap on his left shoulder made Finn flinch, like he'd been caught out. He glanced over his right shoulder, straight into the mischievous brown eyes of his best friend, not the wicked amber gaze he'd tried unsuccessfully to banish from his brain.

Scowling, he asked, "When have I ever fallen for that trick?"

"Always worth a shot." Darius snapped the edge of Finn's hairnet. "This is cute."

"You're a dick."

"What's up with you? Not enough additives in your system yet?"

Finn's frown deepened. "Exhausted, is all. Not all of us get by on excessive optimism and a desire for world domination." It was supremely unfair that Darius was both a morning person and anticaffeine. "I've been working doubles these past few weeks."

Only because he'd asked for the extra shifts. And normally the extra hours spent in the kitchen with his tight-knit group of coworkers left him energized, not exhausted.

Since he couldn't take out his frustration on the source of his lack of sleep, he took aim at his friend instead. "Come to think of it, my tiredness is all your fault, since you insist on forcing me to make a go of this barbecue sauce business." And insisting he sell his wares at places infested with antagonistic locals.

"*I* insist? Does this mean you found an investor for your project? Inherited some cash from a long-lost relative?" The second he said it, Darius's face fell. An easy slip, the kind of common phrase most people wouldn't even blink at. But his best friend knew better.

Finn's relatives weren't the kind who gave away fortunes. They were the kind who stalled adoptions by making a claim on him, then discarded him when faced with the daily reality of taking care of a child. Let him languish in foster care until he turned eighteen.

So no, he hadn't scored an investor, or a windfall inheritance. Which is the only reason he'd agreed to Darius's suggestion to market the barbecue sauces he'd come up with for a friend's cookout.

"Sorry, man. What I meant was this sauce business is your best shot at making good on your cooking-school dreams. Unless you've reconsidered my offer?" Darius had the funds to get Finn's plans off the ground, but while that made sense on paper, Finn wanted to make a go of it on his own.

He could fit everything he owned in the back of a car. No furniture, no sheet set. Nothing substantial to his name. But his dream of a culinary school for those hoping for a second chance? All his. Inviting an investor—even his closest friend—meant leaving himself open to having the rug pulled out from under his dreams.

And in his experience, if there was a rug to be pulled, it got yanked right out from under him. Better to keep the dream his own and never see it materialize than let someone else in and have it stolen.

At Finn's headshake, Darius shoved his hands in the pockets of his hoodie. "Didn't think so. And honestly, I get it." His lips tugged to the side, like he didn't, not quite. Understandable, from someone with a mom who laid the world at his feet. "But if you're burned out, have you considered quitting the restaurant to pursue the business full time?"

Quit the restaurant? He'd be walking out on his family. Bella was like a big sister, Peter Pan to their crew of lost boys and girls bound together by their passion for food. He'd sooner accept the mountain of debt from ditching the sauce business than quit Bellaire.

Finn added a handful of cherry tomatoes to the salad and popped on the plastic lid. "And go from being broke and unhoused to broke, unhoused, and unemployed?"

"Don't make your living situation sound like a negative. You're saving on rent by bunking at my flips. It's a sound financial strategy."

Sound financial strategy. Sometimes his friend sounded like a walking textbook. And his issue wasn't not having a house; it was his lack of a home.

"You're never going to reach your goals if you don't invest more time in your business. Great entrepreneurs don't get to the top by not giving it their all." Darius jabbed the prep table to emphasize his point, dislodging some tomatoes. He snatched them up before they rolled to the floor.

"I'm not an entrepreneur, I'm a chef." And he was also wondering why he'd ever thought taking a chance on this venture would be a good idea. He didn't have the killer instinct of a businessman. He belonged in the kitchen, transforming ingredients into something more than sustenance. Enriching the lives of others through the power of a hot meal, cooked with care.

"See, that's part of the problem." Darius popped a tomato in his mouth and chewed it. Swallowed. "You're thinking too small."

His friend had been instrumental in building him up, encouraging him to go to therapy, to see his worth. But sometimes Darius forgot that not everyone wanted to conquer the world; some people yearned to simply exist, happily, and help others do the same.

Finn finished another salad. He pressed the lid on, and it cracked. Great.

"Did you come by just to dump more unsolicited advice on me?" Not fair. Must be the rudeness of the girl from the market rubbing off on him. Another reason to stay away.

Still, he wondered why Darius had stopped by. As far as he knew, his friend's portfolio of charities didn't include the meals-assistance program, but then again, Darius was involved in almost every part of the neighborhood. Wouldn't surprise him to find out his charitable donations had paid for the lunch kits he was packing up.

Sounding less sure of himself than he had a moment ago, Darius said, "I actually came by to see if you want to grab breakfast. My first showing isn't until noon, and my personal trainer canceled at the last minute."

Personal trainer. Finn couldn't relate to Darius's lifestyle. At all. Didn't stop him from being happy for his friend. While at the same time being grateful he didn't have an overpaid PE teacher harassing him to do push-ups every morning.

"Can't." Finn tossed in a packet of italian dressing. "Headed into Bellaire for the lunch shift."

"Dinner, then?"

He shot a glance Darius's way. His friend's hands were stuffed in the pockets of his joggers, lips pressed tight, despite his casual tone.

Finn pushed the salad aside. "What's really going on? Did you find another farmers' market for me to embarrass myself at? Because I told you, it wasn't worth the trouble."

"How was I supposed to know that place would be patrolled by a militant barbecue despot?" Darius's face relaxed into a grin. "I'm sorry, man. But stuff like this only happens to you. You're a walking chaos magnet. And why did you have to take the bait?" The telltale line of disapproval was back, cutting between Darius's brows. "Could've been a big opportunity there," he added. "The least you could've done is play nice. Leave the door open for a mutually beneficial arrangement."

Mutually beneficial arrangement. Simone's fiery eyes and biting words snapped to mind.

"Yeah, somehow I don't think she was too keen on any sort of arrangement, beneficial or otherwise." Why did that sound equal parts filthy and appealing?

"That's because you thought like a man, not a businessman. But I know how to fix your problem."

"I have a problem?" Besides an off-base attraction to a terrible human being, of course. That was a big problem.

Darius swept a look down from Finn's hair, which hadn't seen scissors since Christmas, to the worn Adidas he'd scored at a thrift shop a few summers back. "Many. But let's start with your company. If there was a way for you to fund your vision debt-free, what would you say?"

"I would say I don't need your charity, Dare."

"It's not me." Darius's eyes were gleaming in a way that made Finn's stomach clench with nerves. "It's Constance Rivera and Keith Donovan."

"You just named one of the richest people in America." He didn't go around reading *Forbes*—another of his entrepreneurial failings, according to Darius—but everyone in America knew about Constance Rivera's astronomical wealth. "And who?"

"Keith Donovan. He's a quarterback from the nineties, went from professional partier to successful businessman."

"And they what, teamed up to bail out small businesses?"

"Yes!" Keyed up, Darius squeezed Finn's shoulder. He was about to be shoved headfirst into something; he could feel it. "Well, not bail them out, but to give would-be entrepreneurs a shot. Ever heard of the reality show called *The Executives*? Contestants get a chance to pitch their business idea, then the studio audience votes. If you score enough votes, Rivera and Donovan make an investment in exchange for a percentage of your company."

Darius stopped, squinting at him. "Have you really never seen it?"

"You know I pawned my TV last year." Not much use for it when he gave up the room he rented to put his housing budget toward start-up costs.

Darius winced. "Jeez, no, I'd forgotten. Sometimes your life sounds like a country song."

"It's not that bad."

"You're right, nothing is. Country." They shuddered in unison.

Leaning his hip against the prep table, Darius crossed one ankle over the other, the soles of his sneakers bright white against the cracked, dingy tiles of the kitchen. "C'mon, you said it yourself: your sauce company is a means to an end. Well, right now it's a dead end. Do you really wanna keep working your butt off for nothing? Sleep on the floor of my flips forever?"

Whatever happened to a *sound financial strategy*? Finn kept his eyes on the label stickers for the lunches. Peeling, sticking, avoiding. "I have an air mattress." One that he needed to reinflate after a few hours, sure, but not an issue since he only slept half the night.

"You know I couldn't care less about having you there." Dude wasn't kidding. Darius once offered to sell him a flip for two thousand bucks. But sleeping at his friend's properties was totally different from taking full advantage of his generosity. No way would he ever cross that line.

"But what's gonna happen when I find a buyer for this place? You can't sleep in the Eighth Street property. We're in the middle of asbestos remediation."

Not something he wanted to consider. The thought of packing his duffel bag and moving houses again walloped his heart like a meat mallet on a cutlet. Head down, Finn muttered, "Hasn't sold yet."

"Probably because you're up in there sending me bad vibes."

"If anyone's capable of that level of voodoo, it's Simone Blake." Shoot. He hadn't meant to bring up that she-devil again. That wolf-in-sexy-farmhand clothing. That—

Darius frowned at him. "It can't have been that bad."

"It was." Finn gave up on the salads, his concentration shot. "She basically summoned a tornado of destruction. I left to grab something from the car, and when I came back, a rowdy bunch of knitters had taken over half my booth."

"Hold up, did you say 'knitters'?" Darius asked. "*Rowdy* knitters?"

"Yes, dude." He hadn't given Darius the details for precisely this reason. The whole situation was laughable. And he was the butt of the joke. "Noisy, heckling, rowdy knitters."

He stopped short of calling them abrasive, because they hadn't been, not really. Once you got used to their unorthodox recruitment techniques, he'd found them charming. Like most people, once you saw past whatever front they put on for the world.

Somehow he didn't think that would be the case with Simone. He'd given her the chance to fess up, to start again, and she'd laughed in his face.

"They were holding some sort of membership drive. Scared off all my customers. And one of them told me that Simone had tipped them off to the booth being open, so I confronted her, and she denied it to my face."

"Maybe it was a misunderstanding."

The same thing Simone had said, but he wasn't buying it. "A coincidence that, after I told her I was there to sell barbecue sauce, a bunch of her cronies show up? I don't think so."

Darius took his phone out of his pocket and scrolled through it. "I gotta say, I kind of admire this woman." Of course he did. "To pull a stunt like that in only a few minutes? Impressive. You're saying she conjured those interfering knitters out of thin air?"

"I mean, they were very real."

Darius looked up at him like he was an imbecile. "Dude, obviously she is not a witch."

"Right. I just—"

Darius's eyes went wide, and he blew out a whistle. Finn tossed a tomato at him. Sometimes he still felt like a gullible teen loser around savvy, accomplished Darius, who'd been about to graduate college when his mother became Finn's guardian.

"Anyway, you're not going to let her scare you off, are you?"

"I'm not scared. I'm going to stay away because it's not worth my effort."

"So you're scared."

"I'm not scared."

"So you're going back next week."

"Darius . . ."

"C'mon, Finn. What's the worst that could happen? No way she's got another group of knitters on her payroll to muscle you out. Or are you worried she hexed your spot?" Darius waggled his fingers at him, and Finn flicked them away.

"I don't know what she's capable of." And he had no interest in discovering her capabilities. Professional or otherwise.

"So why not go back and carry on with your business? I'm sure this barbecue woman used up all her magic on the knitters."

"Okay, Dad," Finn said to end the argument. "But you can forget about that reality-show crap. I am not going to put on a suit and parade myself for entitled investors with a silver spoon up their butt." Guys like him did not fare well in the spotlight. And he wasn't a winner, plain and simple.

Darius sucked his teeth. "Man, you piss me off. When are you going to reach out and take a chance?"

"Are you forgetting I'm a grown man now? Stop trying to run my life."

"I would if you stopped holding yourself back."

Avoiding Darius's eyes, Finn crumpled the empty bag of croutons. "They're never going to pick me anyway."

Shoot, that sounded way more needy than he'd meant it to. He didn't *want* to go on some lame show. And besides, his track record in the getting-picked department was abysmal. Why get his hopes up?

With a self-satisfied grin, Darius held out his phone. "They already did."

"I'm sorry, what, now?"

Darius's grin broadened. "I said, they already chose you. Check it out."

Finn's eyes fell to the cell phone, and he scanned the screen. An email thanking him for his application, telling him he'd been selected to appear as a contestant on *The Executives*.

"I applied on your behalf. And they chose you to be on the show."

Finn felt the world tip, shoved off its axis by those three foreign words. *They chose you.* His mouth stumbled to catch up with his careening thoughts. "When? How?"

"A few months ago," Darius answered. "I knew you'd never apply." Damn straight he wouldn't. Waste of time. Except . . .

They actually wanted him? Out of all the businesses that had applied to go on the show, they'd picked Finn's Secret Sauce? Seen potential in *his* company?

The proof was in his hands, spelled out on the screen, and his heart began to pound.

"They want you on the show, man!" Darius nudged his shoulder, and Finn cracked a smile, excitement overtaking shock. "But I didn't accept for you. That decision is yours. Filming doesn't take place until later this year, but the deadline to respond is next week." He pointed to a date at the bottom of the screen.

December. Half a year away. Half a year until his life might change forever.

Half a year was no time at all to someone who'd grown up waiting for a miracle that never materialized. But would this show be a dream come true or another letdown?

His pulse slowed as reality settled in like an overcast sky. He had an invitation, yes. But the outcome was up for grabs. Uncertain. He might get sent packing, empty handed, hopes dashed. Why bother?

He had a good life. Friends who supported him. A fulfilling career, when he thought he'd been destined for dead-end jobs. Was it asking too much to go off in search of more? Was it greedy to want a place of his own in the world? Or was he mostly afraid to hear . . .

Maybe next time, Finn.

These things happen, Finn.

It's no reflection on you, Finn.

All the while wondering, What if it *is* me, after all?

CHAPTER 7

SIMONE

SUBMIT APPLICATION.

The cursor hovered over the submit button on the screen of Simone's laptop.

"Go on and click it." Tucked into the sofa next to her, Gran adjusted her glasses and squinted at the screen, then shifted her pale-green eyes to Simone. "What've you got to lose?"

"Her dignity, for one," her grandpa piped up from the other side of the couch.

"Dignity? It's barbecue, Pops, not a mayoral election." Though becoming the first Black mayor of Hawksburg sounded like a worthy aspiration.

Pops tossed a kernel of popcorn into his mouth. "I get you wanna make the place your own." He cleared his throat. Honey and Hickory had been his heart and soul for the past fifty years, and she couldn't imagine that letting go came easy. "But you sure this is the best way?"

"Very sure." Treading lightly, Simone grabbed a handful of popcorn. "My whole pitch for *The Executives* will be centered on the things we love most about Honey and Hickory: community, locally sourced ingredients, and straight-up delicious barbecue." The best barbecue in the state, no matter what Finn professed.

"The premise of the show is to fund up-and-coming entrepreneurs," she continued, "and I think they'll jump at the chance to invest in a community-focused business."

Pops let out a satisfied harumph and turned up the volume on the TV. "That's settled, then. Hit the dang button so we can get on with the evening. You know your gran'll fall asleep if we don't cue up this movie soon."

On the other side of Simone, Gran tossed a piece of popcorn at her husband. "You'll be the one snoring by the time the opening credits finish." Guaranteed.

Friday flicks was a tradition they'd started when she'd moved back to town. Her teenage years hadn't been smooth sailing, and with her move to the city, she'd lost some of the closeness they'd shared. But rebuilding the bond was a lot easier than she'd thought. All it took was opening up about her reasons for staying away.

Family was forgiving. But she couldn't count on her childhood friends to be as accepting. Especially since rumor had it she'd only come home because things hadn't worked out in the city. A half truth. They didn't know she'd never wanted to leave in the first place and had jumped at the opportunity to move back.

She'd have to show them she was right back where she wanted to be. Home, and determined to build the life she'd dreamed of, the one she'd denied herself for years. Once they saw her commitment to Honey and Hickory and to building up the town she'd stayed away from for so long, then she could seek to rebuild old friendships. All that hinged on getting this investment. Without it, she'd be treading water.

Decision made, she clicked submit. She waited for the confirmation page to appear, then shut her laptop. "It's done." The first step in her application to be a contestant on *The Executives.*

"Hmph." Her grandpa spoke volumes in a monosyllable, but she reached over and ruffled his thinning white hair.

"It'll be fine. Worst-case scenario, they send me home empty handed. But may as well try."

She could apply for a small business loan, but the idea of taking on more debt on top of her student loans didn't sit well with her. And the hours she'd spent bingeing *The Executives* in college had always left her wondering how it would feel to step out on that hallowed stage and present her brainchild for the investors to either gamble on or tear to shreds.

But in all her daydreams, her start-up had been nebulous, unable to take shape, because what she wanted most of all was to run Honey and Hickory. Pops could talk about dignity all he wanted; going on *The Executives* to pitch her plan for the restaurant would be a dream come true, no matter the outcome.

Putting her laptop into her tote bag, she said, "All right, you pair of old fogies"—she leaned over to plant a kiss on Gran's cheek and nabbed the remote from Pops in the process—"let's start up this movie before you're *both* snoozing."

"Are you sitting down?" Alisha never bothered to say hello anymore. Running an up-and-coming urban bakery left her in constant motion. Oh, how the tables had turned.

Simone was thrilled her sister had finally taken the leap and gotten her foot off the brakes of life, but Alisha had gone from zero to sixty in the past year, while Simone was puttering along in a car running on fumes.

Not that she wasn't happy for her sister, but sometimes it was hard to see her succeed when her own future was so murky. And judging by the bubbliness in Alisha's voice, she was about to be served up another helping of her sister's success. Maybe another food journalist had interviewed her, or she'd nabbed another high-profile wedding-dessert table.

Simone set aside a stack of paperwork and slid her feet out of her shoes, kicking her stockinged feet up on the desk. "Not only am I sitting down, but you have my full and undivided attention." None of the cooks would show up at the restaurant for at least another hour.

"Okay, check your messages; I just sent you a text."

Expecting a link to an article, Simone swiped to her and Alisha's thread. A selfie of her sister hugging her boyfriend, the sweeping Chicago skyline illuminating the night behind them, filled the screen, huge grins on both their faces.

"Uh, sis, I think you sent the wrong attachment. This is just you and Quentin . . ." Wait a minute. She zoomed in to confirm. "And a gorgeous diamond on your finger! He already asked you to marry him?"

"Yes!" Alisha answered with an uncharacteristically high-pitched squeal, probably the same way she'd accepted Quentin's proposal. "But hang on, what do you mean by 'already'? You knew?"

Loving her secret role in this, Simone grinned. "How do you think he knew your ring size? But he told me he wasn't going to do it until he got back from summer fieldwork."

"It was a huge surprise," Alisha said. "I said goodbye to him the night before. Thought his flight left in the morning. But then he surprised me after I closed and took me down to Lake Michigan. He said I was his forever, Sim." If anyone knew about forever, it would be a man who dug up fossils for a living. "And a whole bunch of other super-sweet stuff I forgot the second he asked, because I was in shock."

Simone laughed. "You picked a good one, sis."

A successful bakery, collaborations with big names in the industry, and now a fiancé. Her sister's life had swerved into the fast lane, while Simone's had downshifted onto the shoulder.

Knowing this proposal was in the works was one of the reasons she'd taken the leap and applied to be on *The Executives*. She'd turned down her sister's offer to use her huge social media following to boost Honey and Hickory's profile because she wanted to maintain her autonomy. But she needed capital to make the changes she envisioned, or else all she'd be was a cardboard cutout standing in for Pops at the helm.

Pushing aside the unfamiliar feeling of being the one left behind, she said, "You two are so in love it gives me a cavity just being around all that sweetness, but I am beyond thrilled for y'all. Truly."

"Thank you, Sim. I know bringing a new person into our family is a big deal—"

"A person who happens to be kind, considerate, and treats you like a treasure," Simone said. "I couldn't imagine a more perfect brother." Her heart warmed at the word, jealousy forgotten. "Now, gimme all the details."

Alisha chuckled, breathy, and Simone got the feeling her sister hadn't taken a full inhale since last night. What would it feel like to spend forever with someone who took your breath away?

CHAPTER 8

FINN

This was a bad idea.

Finn shifted back and forth on his feet outside Simone's booth. He'd come over to clear the air, but she wasn't around. Probably off planning mayhem. He jammed his hands in his back pockets and peered around at the nearby tents.

On the drive here, he'd decided to confront Simone. Tell her he had no intention of backing down but that he was willing to be civil for the rest of the summer. But she was nowhere to be found. Must not have expected retaliation. Not like he planned to stoop to her level.

More likely the local vendors were her eyes and ears, watching and ready to report any sabotage. Nobody seemed to notice him, but he couldn't shake the feeling of exposure, like the new kid in a middle school lunchroom.

His phone pinged from his pocket, and he fished it out.

Darius:
Quit stalking that woman and mind your business.

Finn glanced over his shoulder in reflex.

Finn:

I'm clearing the air, like we talked about.

Darius:

Like YOU talked about. I said it's a bad idea. If you can't play nice, you shouldn't have gone back.

Finn:

I plan to play nice. If she does.

Stalking, ha. He silenced his phone without waiting for a reply and took advantage of Simone's absence to get a closer look at her wares. Sizing up the competition. *A sound entrepreneurial strategy*, he thought, mentally parroting Darius's words and chuckling to himself. She'd arranged the bottles in neat triangles like billiard balls. The labels were matte black with swirly gold letters. Elegant and appealing on the outside, just like her.

Which probably meant the barbecue sauce inside was slimy and tasteless.

The tent flap lifted, jangling the brackets attaching it to the pole. He stumbled backward at the sound, but no one materialized. The white vinyl fabric fluttered again at the same time a hot breeze ruffled his hair. Just the wind, not his rival returning.

Well, he'd tried. Whistling, he shoved his hands in his pockets and backtracked. When he was a safe distance away, he spun on his heel and was halfway back to the safety of his own booth when a piece of paper blew across his feet.

After stomping on the litter, he bent down and picked it up. Legal jargon. None of his business. But on the bottom, below a scrawled signature, the name *Simone Blake* was printed in neat blue letters.

Interest piqued, he flipped the paper over to read the front.

THE EXECUTIVES LIABILITY RELEASE FORM.

The Executives? She planned to be a contestant on that dumb show hawking her barbecue sauce? But why? She already owned a restaurant. And judging by the long line outside her booth last week, she had no shortage of customers. What more could she want?

He rubbed his thumb along the edge of the paper, tempted to toss it in the nearest trash can. From the snippets of conversation he'd heard last week, the locals who thought she couldn't handle taking over her grandfather's restaurant were a tiny, grumpy minority. She had a whole town behind her, and yet she was out for more than her fair share. Figured.

Some people didn't know how good they had it. He'd gone to school surrounded by kids like her who took everything for granted. Family, community, unconditional love. Typical, and he shouldn't have been surprised. Not coming from a woman who hadn't wanted to relinquish even a smidgen of her profits to a newcomer.

Maybe if he tore up the form, she'd forget to send it in and lose her spot on the show. The perfect chance to get back at her. But he found himself retracing his steps. He scanned her booth and found a leather bag tucked underneath the table. Careless, to leave her purse out. Then again, she'd mentioned everyone here was like family. Everyone except him.

He refolded the paper along the seam and quickly slid it into the bag. Last thing he needed was someone to catch him and assume he was after her wallet. She'd probably press charges out of spite.

Good deed accomplished, he strode away, not looking back this time. The more he thought about it, finding out Simone wanted to go on *The Executives* aligned with his image of her. Cutthroat, soulless, and out for a big chunk of undeserved cash? Sounded like the ideal contestant for a reality show.

All the more reason to turn down the opportunity. If the producers were interested in someone like her, he'd be a giant letdown. She was a sparkler, and he was last year's birthday candle. Why volunteer for public humiliation?

He reached his booth and got to work setting out bottles of sauce. New strategy: pretend Simone Blake didn't exist.

Unfortunately, after unpacking all the boxes, he discovered that his credit card reader was nonexistent, again. But this time he had no intention of leaving his booth unattended to track it down. The Yarn Spinners were attending a needlework conference in St. Louis, which left half the booth unguarded, and he wouldn't put it past Simone to rustle up another tenant to pester him.

He actually missed the chatter and good-natured gossip of his stall buddies. He'd soon discovered the knitters were a bighearted group of people, inclusive and welcoming, if a bit over the top in their recruitment techniques. The next trick Simone had up her sleeve could be far worse than a bunch of noisy, nosy knitters. He didn't plan to leave the tent for so much as a bathroom break until closing time.

He was in the middle of writing a *Cash only* sign when a shadow fell across him.

"I see you resolved your little scheduling issue with the Spinners."

Ignoring the shivers of anticipation pricking the back of his neck, he straightened up. Simone's hair was slicked back into a ponytail, the puff of curls twirling defiantly toward the sky, a match for her arched brows and the upward twist of her lips. Rosy-pink today, not the ruby from last week.

A subtle change he only noticed because he had been trained to create visually pleasing aesthetics on the plate. People ate with their eyes first. Not that he was thinking of tasting Simone's mouth . . .

He gulped down a breath of air. "I never had an issue with the Yarn Spinners. As a matter of fact . . ." He bent and pulled a bright-red scarf out of one of the boxes and wrapped it around his neck. "They gave this to me last week as a welcome gift. Real alpaca hair." *Hair? Fur?* Whatever the case, he took their word for it, not being familiar with natural fibers. Or alpacas. "My problem is standing right in front of me."

The corners of her lips lifted a tad more. "I'd say your problem is that you're wearing a fluffy wool scarf in ninety-degree heat."

"Wool"—that was the word he'd been searching for.

"And I'd say you clearly have no appreciation for fine craftsmanship." He resisted scratching his neck where a trickle of sweat inched down. "If you came all the way over here just to pick on me, at least get out of the way so I can serve actual customers."

She stayed put. "Says the man who drove fifty miles to be a pain in my butt."

"Looked me up, huh?" That shouldn't give him a thrill. And it didn't. Not at all. Minor heat stroke from the scarf, manifesting itself in chills.

"It's on your sign, genius." She lifted her chin, and he glanced over his shoulder. Oh, right. *Springfield, IL.* Printed under his company name.

Another of Darius's suggestions. Studies showed customers felt more comfortable purchasing from someone with a backstory. Roots. Might explain his dismal sales. He could churn out big batches of home-cooked flavor, but at the end of the day it was all smoke and mirrors, inauthentic. A sleight of hand from someone who'd been transplanted so many times he'd given up even trying for the illusion of permanency.

But he hadn't driven all the way here to throw in the towel before the market even opened. He needed to get rid of Simone before her forked tongue scared off all his customers. "Is this chitchat a distraction so your minions can execute some evil plot?" he asked.

The soft curve of her lips blossomed into an outright smile, and he realized he'd been staring at her mouth. Again. He stepped back, and his heel collided with the cooler. Ice, that's what he needed. On his overheated neck, but also . . . everywhere. He flexed his fingers, jammed them into his pockets.

"I like that you think I have minions," Simone said.

"You would like that." Villains always twisted insults into compliments.

She sighed, like she was bored, but her fingers tapped a restless rhythm against her leg.

"Did you come over here to try to chase me away again?" He loosened the scarf but didn't take it off. That would be admitting defeat. "Or is there a higher purpose to your lurking?"

"Lurking? Please. I'm just here to see what you have to offer." She swept an appraising gaze over the table, like she was sizing him up and finding him wanting.

Two could play at that game. He spread his arms wide. "I'd gladly show you what I have to offer, if you feel like you could handle the experience."

She flicked a glance down his body with what might've been appreciation from someone else, but since it was Simone, he labeled the look as "disdain." She picked up the nearest bottle of barbecue sauce. "Naked Heat." She blew a raspberry. Definitely disdain.

"Hey, don't shoot the messenger. Sex sells."

She arched a single brow, and something in him coiled tight. "Guess it depends on who's selling it."

He hooked a hand on the tent pole above his head, gratified when her eyes traveled down his body. "Maybe you should give it a try and see for yourself. Samples are free." Was it his imagination, or did her tongue dart out, moisten her lips?

"No thanks. It's probably poisoned."

"Suit yourself," he said. "We both know you're scared."

"You don't know me well, so let me clue you in." She leaned closer, and so did he, because even in a baggy T-shirt knotted at her waist and loose linen pants, her body pulled him in like a riptide. "I'm not scared of anything."

He swallowed. Blinked. Tried to look anywhere besides her objectively perfect lips and ended up staring straight into the sun. He ducked his head, eyes stinging. "Everyone's scared of something."

"I'm not."

"Heights?"

"Nope."

"Sharks?"

"We live in the Midwest," she said. "Sharks aren't exactly a top predator."

"Goblins?"

"Goblins?" She laughed, the sound warm and husky, campfire coals and moonlight. His grip on the tent pole tightened like a vise. "What is this, Middle Earth?"

"So that's a yes, then." Why was sparring with this maniac so much fun?

"It's a big no." Simone rocked forward, fingertips on the table. "Heights, sharks, monsters, spiders . . ." Her eyes held his. "Bring it on."

"Failure." The word popped out, and he instantly wanted to wrangle it back in, because the spark in Simone's amber eyes vanished like a doused flame.

"What?" Her voice went flat, like hammered steel. A tone he recognized as the same phony apathy he used to disguise big feelings when they threatened to break free.

He'd hurt her, and he hated himself for it. But with the ease of someone with a knack for making bad situations worse, he said, "I bet you're terrified of failing. I bet your whole existence hinges on the image of success, of being on top, and without it, you're nothing." He searched her face, and his breath caught at the sight of the gold flecks in her eyes, the freckles scattered like constellations on her cheekbones. "Am I close?"

Simone set down the sauce with a thud. "What you are is an idiot, Finn Rimes."

Yup, that much he knew without her help.

The boulder teetered near the cliff's edge. Giving in to temptation, he put a shoulder to it and rolled it off. "Everyone fails sometimes, Simone. It's not that bad." The words stuck in his throat like peanut butter and jelly on white bread, cloying and pasty.

She backed away. How could she not? He was an expert at repelling people.

"And you've already failed once," he said, voice thick.

She stopped, wary, her defenses up. "How's that?"

"You tried to get rid of me. But here I am. And I'm not going anywhere." He wasn't going anywhere, but she would.

A voice piped up before he could silence it, telling him if he was anything special, anything worth holding on to, it wouldn't have been so easy for all the families to discard him. He didn't doubt that Simone, too, would tire of their squabbles and brush him aside like the cloud of gnats gathered overhead. He never held anyone's interest for long.

But for now, in this moment, he held all her attention. All of her focus, all of her fire.

She stepped closer again, and his pulse thrummed in anticipation. "You're wrong about one thing. I've failed plenty. But I'm not going to fail at this. And since you insist on staying, you'll get a front-row seat to my success. Enjoy the upgrade from the cheap seats."

She turned and sauntered away. Done with the confrontation. Done with him.

Cheap seats? Oh heck no. Insult his sauce? Whatever. Insult him? Fine. But she'd hit a nerve by smack-talking like a spoiled princess.

Dazzled by her beauty—and that was on him—he'd forgotten for a moment she was selling hand-me-down sauce from an inherited restaurant. Secure by birthright in comforts he'd spent his childhood chasing, only to fail, again and again.

Forget forfeiting. Not only did he plan to show up and outsell Simone Blake every week, but he'd accept the invitation to pitch his brand on *The Executives*. Win an investment and prove once and for all, in front of the whole country, that he mattered.

He might come from nothing, but he was going somewhere.

Cheap seats? She'd be watching his victory from the couch.

CHAPTER 9

SIMONE

December

The studio lights blazed down, cooking Simone like a slab of ribs, but she chastised her sweat right back into her pores. She refused to wilt, wouldn't think of flinching, and sure as heck wouldn't allow herself to be intimidated by the razor-sharp duo of investors seated at the other end of the mock boardroom table.

Six months ago she'd applied for a chance to appear as a contestant on the entrepreneurial reality show *The Executives*. Six long months of waiting to earn recognition in her own right. Six short months to prepare, to rebrand Honey and Hickory online, launch a marketing campaign for her sauce, and create a rock-solid expansion and renovation plan worthy of investment.

Six months of pushing aside the fear the investors might transform her beloved Honey and Hickory into something unrecognizable.

Those six months ended today in a Los Angeles television studio, encircled by an audience whose votes would be tallied in her favor, or not. No time left for second thoughts.

Win over the investors with her plan; win over the audience with her charisma. A two-pronged challenge. Not simple but achievable.

Get it done, Simone.

She stood at the end of the table in a black, puff-sleeved jumpsuit and her favorite pair of heels, chin up, arms folded in a rehearsed power pose as the host introduced her to the investors, audience, and millions of viewers tuned in live. Then the lights dimmed in a swooping rush until she stood alone under a bright spotlight.

Practiced. Poised. In control of herself, her restaurant, and her future.

Go time. She dropped her arms to her sides and opened her mouth.

"We've gotta stop meeting this way."

The voice came from over her shoulder. Smooth and deep as a sun-warmed lake, the voice masked an interior as slimy as seaweed lurking below the surface.

Finn freaking Rimes.

Simone kept her smile in place and prayed her expression didn't have the queasy quality of a beauty queen who'd had her crown snatched off by a runner-up. The cultivated calm inside her whipped up into reckless indignation at the sound of that voice. *His* voice.

Her archenemy, come to steal the show with characteristically terrible timing.

She wouldn't turn around and acknowledge him. Maybe this was a trick of her nerves, and the voice was all in her head. Maybe if she plowed on with her speech, the ghost of farmers' markets past would evaporate into the ether of her subconscious.

Nope. Finn strode out to join her in the spotlight. Backed up a step and hovered half in shadow, half in the glare. "Didn't expect to see you here, Simone," he said, squinting.

Liar. Like he hadn't expected to ambush her? At least he had the decency not to butcher her name this time. Hadn't mispronounced it since their first meeting, in fact, ever since she'd replaced the missing *e* on her name tag. Almost like it was an innocent mistake. Almost like he cared enough to get it right.

Maybe that would've counted in his favor if he hadn't kept showing up at her market. Every single week. All summer. Setting up shop like he owned the place and befriending all the people who were supposed to be on her side. Winning over the town one smile, one sale at a time.

Innocent mistake? More like insidious undermining, a calculated assault.

"You two know each other?" Constance Rivera, seated at the far end of the table, narrowed her eyes. Her black hair was styled into a razor-sharp bob, and she wore a maroon suit with satin lapels and a thin, black tie.

Two years after graduating from Yale, she'd sold her tech start-up for a whopping $70 million and created a nonprofit aimed at getting girls from underresourced communities involved in STEM. She'd branched out from her tech roots to invest in companies across a wide array of categories with an interest in socially conscious brands.

You two know each other?

"No," Simone said, free-falling, at the same time Finn blurted, "Yes."

Next to Ms. Rivera, Keith Donovan, a retired NFL quarterback as famous for his flowing locks as his pass-completion percentage, belted out a laugh. Half up in a ponytail, the rest of his signature dark-blond tresses fell to his shoulders in a glossy tumble.

A sucker for comeback stories similar to his own, Mr. Donovan was known for championing newbie entrepreneurs aiming to reinvent themselves as well as their businesses. "Well, which is it?"

Invisible behind the glare of the lights, the audience was surely on the edge of their seats in anticipation of Simone's answer, eager for drama. She wouldn't give them the satisfaction. The merits of her business proposal had earned her this chance, and she'd leave here with her dignity intact, deal or no deal.

"We've met. But we don't know each other well." Damage repair. A die-hard fan of *The Executives* ever since the pilot aired, she remembered countless times the investors eviscerating contestants caught embellishing the facts.

Uncrossing her arms, she wrestled a smile onto her face. "I mean, we're not friends. Barely acquaintances. We've just run into each other a few times." Too many times.

Often enough for her to notice he got his caffeine hit from energy drinks, not coffee. To see he wore the same pair of jeans every week, faded Levi's with a ripped hem on the left leg. Enough to know he had one small freckle under his eye, another on the side of his cheek, and a deep dimple in his chin, usually hidden under scruff that glinted russet brown in the sunlight, darkened to walnut on cloudy days.

Too many times. Enough for her to wish she hadn't tried to banish him on their first fateful meeting. But she couldn't let wishful thinking hold her back, not with her business on the line.

Brow furrowed, Donovan steepled his fingers, tapped them against his lips.

Finn stepped up next to her and claimed the spotlight, the closeness of his presence assaulting her senses with the scent of pine boughs and clean sheets. Appealing like breakfast in bed and late-morning sex and . . . holy crap, what was wrong with her? She bit down on the inside of her cheek.

"Simone didn't appreciate me infringing on her turf." He chuckled, like they were rival neighbors in an HOA battle when in reality he was hell-bent on poaching her customers and driving her to extinction.

"Only because you blindsided me." His specialty.

"You're from Illinois as well?" This from Constance. Her dark eyes shifted between them, drawing conclusions. Incorrect ones, no doubt.

"Yes, ma'am. Springfield." Finn smoothed a hand down his suit jacket, and Simone tried not to notice the cut of the fabric against his frame. From her completely disinterested observations over the summer, she knew he had the kind of unpretentious muscles born out of manual labor, not the gym, and the tailored suit accentuated his narrow hips and rounded biceps.

If she'd known Finn planned to be a contestant on *The Executives*, she would've pegged him for a guy who went with jeans, sneakers, and a branded T-shirt. That is, if she'd ever in a million years expected to go head to head with him here. But the allure of the show was that it allowed aspiring entrepreneurs a chance to pitch their ideas with the investors' undivided attention.

Never once in their ninety-six episodes had two entrepreneurs pitched to *The Executives* simultaneously, let alone two competing entrepreneurs with a business in the same category. She would know. She'd watched every single episode. Twice.

"Springfield, Illinois, that is. Not Missouri." Finn rocked back on his heels as if primed to dissolve into the shadows again. She wished he would.

"I'm aware which Springfield you meant, son," Keith said. At the word "son," Finn flinched. A deep-red flush spread across his cheeks. Sympathy flared in her chest like heartburn.

Sympathy and totally misguided lust. Because somehow, even flustered and blotchy, he was still gorgeous. Well, screw him with a rusty drill bit.

"All due respect," he said, and Simone snorted. Like he was so big on respect. "I was told it was my turn to pitch, but there must be some mistake . . ." He trailed off, fingers bunched into white-knuckled fists before he shoved both hands into his pockets. On someone else the gesture might have been intimidating, but on Finn, it read as vulnerable.

"No, no mistake, Mr. Rimes." Keith's genial smile morphed into a sneer, a condescending expression Simone would bet good money he got coached on prior to each episode. Reality? The whole show was a theatrical performance. "We have a very unique situation on our hands. You two come to us professing yourselves to be the god and goddess of barbecue."

Goddess of barbecue? Simone steeled her own smile to remain in place. She'd never once referred to herself as a goddess of anything.

She was an entrepreneur, not a teenager trying to launch a career as a pop star.

"If I may . . . ," she ground out, mouth dry.

"You may not, Ms. Blake." Constance cut her off before offering a smile, quick and fleeting. She played a tough game, a contrived persona Simone suspected she put on due to pressure from the producers, like Keith's pretentious smirks. But this artificial setting was the only way someone like her would ever get a chance in front of heavy hitters like Rivera and Donovan. "Let me explain the unique circumstances of our show today."

Unique circumstances? More like worst-case scenario.

Constance spread her hands wide. "Both you and Mr. Rimes applied to be on the show with a barbecue-centric business, so we can't very well offer both of you a deal. It would be a conflict of interest, for starters. And while your bid to expand the scope of your restaurant is viable, Ms. Blake, your sauce business seems like an afterthought. We don't need our entrepreneurs overextending themselves early in the game." Ms. Rivera turned her sharp gaze on Finn. "You only sell sauce, is that correct, Mr. Rimes?"

He nodded once, the thick hair that had flopped over his forehead all summer trimmed around his ears and held in place with just the right amount of gel. Gone was his perpetual scruff, revealing a strong, dimpled chin other women might drool over.

Then again, other women probably hadn't seen his snake oil salesman routine firsthand. The trespassing, no-good, stick-his-nose-where-he-doesn't-belong—

"Just sauce, and it's the best you'll ever taste." Finn's voice had lost any hesitancy and regained its rich timbre, and Simone's body turned traitor, her insides melting even as her heart remained a block of ice. "Right now, the bulk of my business is e-commerce, but I think Finn's Secret Sauce would do well on grocery store shelves."

"So you're not in any brick-and-mortar retailers?" Mr. Donovan frowned, and Simone wanted to break in and inform them that several local grocers stocked her sauce, but Finn steamrolled her.

"Not yet. My expertise lies in the kitchen, but I've been working around the clock to learn the business end." Other than the hours he spent torturing her with his presence. "I'm all in with this company. What I'd love is some expert guidance. Oh, and a little of your pocket change might help." He winked, and a chuckle rippled through the audience.

Once again, Finn Rimes slathering on the charm, rich and creamy as fresh-churned butter, laying it on thick to win everyone over but her. Simone bit back a gag at all the verbal dairy. She wasn't jealous he'd never turned his charisma on her. *Please.* His used car salesman schtick might work on the audience, but the investors wouldn't be fooled by a pretty face.

Would they?

Doubt crept in, and with it, urgency. Finn was here for himself; she was here for Hawksburg. To win an investment and then win over a town full of people who thought she'd left them behind. She needed to quit hesitating and get down in the muck with him before he stole the biggest chance of her career.

But before she could speak up, Donovan clicked his pen. "That's what we like to hear. A good product and a can-do attitude will take you far. Run us through your business plan, if you would, Mr. Rimes."

And he proceeded to. Articulate and measured, he laid out his vision for his company, concluding with what had led him to come on the show.

"My original plan was to sell online and make the circuit of local farmers' markets, but this summer, I realized to reach my goals, I had to think bigger. I have Ms. Blake to thank for the inspiration." He flashed Simone a tentative smile.

Blood boiling, she stayed mute, head inclined with what she hoped was a smile and not the rictus grimace of someone who'd been stabbed in the back. That . . . rat. Dirty, rotten, conniving rat. Somehow, he'd gotten wind of her plan to come on the show. Probably from one of his Yarn Spinner groupies.

She never should've told anyone in town. Would she never learn? Reveal your hand, and the next thing you know, someone else will take your seat at the table. Trusting the wrong person had cost her her job in Chicago. And now that same naivete was about to lose her a chance to bring revenue and jobs to the town she loved with her whole heart.

Simone licked her lips, dizzy. She unlocked her knees, and the heels of her stilettos slipped on the polished faux-wood floorboards. Off balance, she thrust out a hand to catch herself, flailing. Her hand whacked against the table behind her, and her fingers sank into something gooey. And wet. And sticky.

The audience gasped. Finn's jaw fell open like a nutcracker, and Simone would've laughed at his cartoonish expression if she weren't stricken with terror. Pulse racing, she ventured a glance. Yep, she was knuckles-deep in a bowl of her own barbecue sauce.

Abso-freakin'-lutely awesome.

If she were watching this episode at home, she could pause and rewind to before this catastrophe. But if she did, she wouldn't stop with the past ten seconds. She'd skip back two years and stay in Chicago, as much as she'd felt out of place. Better to be lonely and adrift in a huge city than in a tiny town.

How had she sunk this low? She was Simone Blake, go-getter. Name-taker. Winner. A success. Until she returned home with her tail between her legs, defeated. Taking over Pops's restaurant was supposed to have been her chance for a comeback. Grow her family business into a household name, all on her own.

Yet here she was, asking for handouts from strangers. Begging for scraps with sticky fingers, and about to be rejected, at that. The only thing that stung worse than hearing no? Asking for help in the first place.

Her eyes pinched closed. She pictured the gloppy sauce sinking its pungent undertones of garlic and vinegar into the ridges of her fingerprints, the molasses staining her cuticles, black pepper flecks marring her glossy manicure. Her will lost the battle against body, and sweat beaded her upper lip.

No help for it. She opened her eyes and pulled her hand out of the sauce with a squelch like quicksand. A giant glob fell off her fingers and splatted onto the toe of her suede stilettos. And the cameras were still rolling.

Finn's thick brows tugged inward, matching the puppy dog tilt of his eyes, twin furrows marking his brow. He closed the distance between them in a single stride and whipped out his paisley pocket square.

Paisley? Her spiraling mind snagged on that detail. She would've figured he'd go with something bold and brash, not delicate and refined. Full of surprises, this man.

If they'd met under different circumstances, she might've happily delved into uncovering his nuanced depths. Explored the reason for the zings of anticipation that sparked in her chest as he stepped closer.

Stopping inches in front of her, he clasped her wrist and gently wrapped the silky fabric of his pocket square around her fingers. The warmth in his palm shot straight to her core. She should have been insulted at his nerve. Galled by the fact he felt the need to come to her rescue like some sort of knight in shining armor when he was more Night King than Jon Snow.

Instead, she felt . . . seen. Cared for.

This wasn't an act. This was Finn, raw and real. The knowledge hit her like a slap to the cheek, stunning her out of her trance.

She didn't need Finn. Not his surprising kindness or his wide smile that made everything around her feel less heavy. There was no room in her life for a man, and she sure as heck didn't need a shoulder to lean on. Especially not when that shoulder belonged to a slippery snake like Finn Rimes.

"Thanks for the assist, *Mr.* Rimes." His fingers tensed around hers. "But this has me thinking . . . out of all the times we've bumped into each other, I don't think you've had a chance to sample my sauce yet."

His eyes narrowed, just enough to darken from honeyed chestnut to the warm brown of a woodland creek. Sun dappled and inviting, but she wouldn't dive in.

"You're right," he said. "Can't say I've had the pleasure."

"Here's your chance." Before she lost her nerve or questioned the ramifications, she crumpled the pocket square in her free hand, leaving her fingers in his. Then she raised their joined hands and extended her sauce-dipped pinky toward him. "Go ahead, have a taste."

A hush fell over the room, the air so still she could hear the sizzle of her chances at a deal evaporating in the heat of the spotlights. His eyes flicked down to her fingers, and the tip of his tongue slid into the corner of his mouth. Her breath picked up, pulse hammering so loud in her ears she felt light headed, like she'd passed out at base camp and woke up on the peak of Everest.

A whole life of striving. Of working. Of pushing. And it all came down to this. Lucifer in a three-piece suit, an audience of millions, and two investors who held her future in their hands.

In one fluid motion, Finn caught her wrist, long fingers looped, gentle but firm. Now he held her with both hands. Encircled her. Engulfed her with his touch.

The brush of his fingertips whispered across her skin, and when she raised her gaze, she found his eyes searching hers, a question in their depths. She granted permission with a nod.

Yes.

Now, before we lose our nerve.

The thoughts dancing across his pupils settled like silt in a streambed, and he looked down at their joined hands, charcoal lashes skimming his cheeks.

She trembled, anticipating. Finn dipped his head and slowly, deliberately, licked the tip of her finger. A quick flick of his tongue proved her wrong again. She didn't think he'd have the balls to take the bait. Didn't expect herself to not hate it. To *like* it. To enjoy the slide of his tongue on her skin, the quick brush of wet heat, gone at the moment she'd started to *crave* it.

Jelly jointed, she trembled and felt his hands grip her tighter in support.

Finn's chest heaved, shaky; then he raised his eyes. A grin spread across his cheeks, like spilled honey on a sunny windowsill. "Not bad, Simone."

She tugged her hand out of his grasp, and his smile grew wings, launched into a full-bodied laugh. A declaration of war.

Moisture broke out on her hairline, and nuh-uh, no way would she sweat out her edges for this fool. Finger by finger she wiped his slobber and the rest of the sauce off her hand. Biding her time. Reconfiguring for a frontal attack.

She folded the pocket square and handed it back. "Think you can do better?"

He accepted the sodden scrap of fabric without looking at it, brown eyes sparking like the strike of flint on stone. Dangerous. "You tell me."

And suddenly, like it was scripted—and for all she knew, it *was* scripted, and she'd been kept in the dark for authenticity—a guy with a headset, dressed all in black, rolled out a chrome cart laden with bottles of sauce and smothered meat.

Finn tucked the dirtied handkerchief in his pocket. He swept an arm toward the cart, careless yet controlled, like he licked sauce off women's bodies in front of live studio audiences every day.

"Care to sample Finn's Secret Sauce? I'll let you use a spoon, though." He angled a grin toward the executives. Mr. Donovan let out a guffaw, but Ms. Rivera pursed her lips.

He held out the handle of a spoon, a challenge in his eyes. "Go ahead, have a taste," he said, repeating her offer in that melodious coffee-and-cream voice that almost made her forget they were on live TV with an audience of millions and that this man was her *nemesis*.

He'd been an adversary before, but an upgrade—downgrade—seemed fitting. Especially because she was about to do the dang thing and try his sauce. She couldn't afford to appear petty. Even though right now she felt petty AF.

She dipped the spoon into a jar of sauce at random and shoved it in her mouth like cough syrup. Her treacherous taste buds lit up like firecrackers. Hoo boy, that did not taste anything like medicine. In fact, it tasted like failure. Not a single person in the audience would choose her sauce over that perfection.

Tangy and sweet, with a hint of fire. *Delicious.*

"Told you," he said, and she realized she'd admitted it aloud.

Beaming, he hoisted the tray off the cart and headed over toward the executives like a waiter in some ritzy restaurant. In the shadows, stagehands did the same and moved down the rows to hand out samples to the audience. But Simone was done hesitating, done being blinded by the force of his charm like a starry-eyed doe in the headlights.

It was up to her, and her alone, under the blazing lights and the influence of one of the best barbecue sauces she'd ever tasted, to make sure her concept, her restaurant, her hometown flavor came out on top.

"Mr. Rimes says he's new to the game. Fair enough. But the difference between a newbie and a veteran is dedication."

Finn had reached the table and was placing a sample in front of each investor. She spoke quicker, because if they tasted those sauces without hearing the rest of her pitch, then everything she'd worked for since high school, all her hopes and dreams, the empire she planned to build—all of it would crumble to dust.

Not to mention, she could never show her face in Hawksburg if she lost to a city boy.

"He hasn't approached stores, falls back on the excuse of inexperience. If he continues to justify his lack of initiative, he'll be out of this business within a year. I don't make excuses; I make goals. And then I meet them. I'm here to grow Honey and Hickory to a household name and make all of us a boatload of money in the process. Are you in?"

Keith opened his mouth, but not to reply. In went a sauce-dipped spoon, and out went Simone's chances.

Constance took one tentative taste, then another. She wiped her mouth with a cloth napkin. "Ms. Blake, you've tasted this. Can you honestly say what you serve up at Honey and Hickory is better?"

The sauce? Maybe not. Barbecue was the heart of Honey and Hickory, but to Simone, the sense of community, the love within the restaurant's walls, the feeling of homecoming every time she walked through the doors—those were the lifeblood.

She could open up about her ultimate vision. Share her plan to invest in Hawksburg. Appeal to the investors' penchant for community-focused businesses and earn herself a better shot at victory.

Or set herself up to be the laughingstock of Hawksburg. Open herself up to criticism and disdain as the city girl who tried to worm her way back into the town's good graces. If she couldn't convince the investors to take a chance on Honey and Hickory, how could she expect to get locals on board with her grander plans?

"Honey and Hickory has more to offer than our sauce; you said so yourself. That's the reason we're continuing to grow, fifty years after my grandpa opened up shop. I may not have started Honey and Hickory, but I'm pushing the restaurant to new heights, building on a legacy."

Uncertain of her standing back home, she made the split-second call to keep her biggest dreams tucked away inside herself. But the game wasn't over. She'd been playing defense. Time to sink the buzzer-beating three-pointer.

"Meanwhile, Finn's Secret Sauce is a floundering start-up with no roots, destined to fail."

CHAPTER 10

FINN

No roots. Destined to fail.

Finn's throat constricted like he'd been garroted with a wire.
Constance Rivera and Keith Donovan were still questioning Simone,
but their voices had turned into the static of a radio station gone out
of range. Simone had exposed his deepest fears and secret worries, laid
them bare in front of millions of viewers.

No family. No home. No roots. No future.

A failure.

Who was he, after all, to come here and expect validation? A chance
he didn't deserve? Still, tasting Simone's barbecue sauce had him thinking he might have a shot. Her product was great, bordering on amazing,
but no match for the variety of his full line of sauces.

Against all odds, he'd thought he might make it out of this room
with a deal. A chance to prove his worth. To matter.

And then in one smooth, haughty speech, she'd torn down his par-
ticleboard hopes and tossed a match on the pile. He'd been in plenty of
fights. Fights where his feet hadn't been fast enough to escape. Fights
where he'd been ambushed and outnumbered. Fights where he hadn't

seen the knockout punch coming until too late. But he'd walked into this arena with his eyes wide open.

Sure, he hadn't expected to go toe to toe with Simone, but he'd wanted her to see his victory. No time to be squeamish. Flight wasn't an option.

He was transported to the group home after lights-out, when Brian Warnke laid him out flat with a fist to the nose after discovering Finn had snatched a granola bar from his stash under the bunk. Hungry and seeing red, with trembling hands curled into fists at his chin, Finn had refused to back down. Now as then, the explosive pain of the unexpected blow flipped a switch in his brain from self-preservation to self-defense. He'd fight back; he had to, if he didn't want to watch his dream die.

"'My meal from Honey and Hickory came with a side of dysentery straight out of *Oregon Trail*.'" Finn now spat out the quote against the echo of Simone's accusation, reciting from memory a review he'd found on a late-night, liquor-fueled deep dive into all things Honey and Hickory. "That's a direct quote from a one-star review I found for Simone's *historic* family restaurant online."

Simone strode forward and claimed center stage. "Written by a disgruntled cook who was fired for never showing up to work. It hardly classifies as empirical evidence."

"Look, *Ms.* Blake," he said, leaning heavy on the honorific like she had, gratified when her eyes narrowed. "Beyond Honey and Hickory's subpar reviews, your generic flavors can't match the nuance of Finn's Secret Sauce. You're a mom-and-pop barbecue joint with no soul, stuck in the past." Directing his next words to the investors, he said, "Whereas I'm all heart, focused on the future of barbecue. Sustainable, organic, outside-the-box flavor blends."

Simone clicked her tongue. "Organic? Wow, super cutting edge. If this was 1999."

Hands on her hips, she angled away from him, toward the crowd. "Honey and Hickory was farm to table long before it was fashionable, and we cook with locally sourced meat and home-grown produce."

"Like you had anything to do with that? Your grandfather probably set up those contacts while you were in diapers." He turned his focus on the audience; two could play at that game.

"Don't let Ms. Blake fool you. She's been at the helm of the restaurant for less than a year, yet she's trying to convince you she played a role in Honey and Hickory's decades of success."

A low blow. He'd hit her where it hurt, and he couldn't bear to meet her eyes as he went for the choke hold. Planting his fingertips on the glossy table, he divided a steady, earnest gaze between both investors, heart jackhammering.

"Ms. Blake is asking you to invest in a company with a long track record, when the truth is, the Honey and Hickory she represents is an untested gamble. She can talk all she wants about longevity and dependability, but the fact is, she and I are both new at this. Traffic on my website and social media continues to climb, as do my sales."

He tossed what he hoped would land as a sympathetic smile toward Simone, but his grin faltered, attention caught by the quick sweep of her lashes against her cheek, the pouty fullness of her lower lip. Under other circumstances, there were much better ways to spend his time with Simone than arguing.

But she was a missile locked on this upward trajectory, ready to blow his future to smithereens, and he'd committed himself to staying the course, to seeing this through for the lives he could change with the money.

He dragged his focus away from the quick flash of devastation he'd seen painted on Simone's features, unable to look her in the eye while he threw down the gauntlet. "All I ask is you evaluate Finn's Secret Sauce and Ms. Blake's restaurant on a level playing field. And on that field, taste is king."

For a second, his words hung in the air. Instead of him savoring imminent victory, his mind swept back to the taste of her sauce on his tongue—woodsmoke and black pepper, sweet heat. Much better than he was giving her credit for.

But what knocked him flat was the smoothness of her finger—delicate, pliable, soft. So unlike her rigid poise, the angular cut of her high cheekbones. The slash of her pointed chin. Sharp edges that matched the cut of her words. Sharp edges at odds with the supple curve of her fingertip.

For a moment, when he'd slipped his mouth around her pinky, he'd felt a jolt. An awakening. An awareness that maybe the hardness on her outside didn't match the woman inside.

Best to ignore it. After this nightmare of a standoff, he'd never cross paths with Simone again. Knowing her vengeful side, she'd likely put out a restraining order against him if he tried. Win or lose, there'd be no more trips to the Hawksburg farmers' market. No more setting up shop across from her or offering a hand with teardown just for the pleasure of hearing the comeback she'd toss out.

Good riddance. He wouldn't miss this at all. Not the smack talk or her rare, elusive smiles, or the searing heat of her gaze.

A burning gaze she turned on him now like a vengeful goddess, lightning flashing in her golden eyes. "You know an awful lot about my company for someone who just happened to show up at my farmers' market this year." *Her* farmers' market. As if she owned the town, the rights to everything she touched. "Have you known all along we'd be pitted against each other today?"

She wasn't too far off, but the accusation ground glass shards into his pride. "You think I orchestrated this? You couldn't pay me to be in the same room as you voluntarily."

"So you didn't spend the summer showing up at the Hawksburg market just to rile me? Throw me off my game?"

Yes. And also yes. But he let his eyebrows inch up, fixing her with a straight stare. "If I wanted to rile you up, there are more fun ways to go about it than arguing about barbecue."

Her eyes drifted down to his mouth, and his pulse kicked against his rib cage. The electricity snapped between them in a sharp crack that had his hands flexing, his throat gone dry.

Then her eyes flicked up again, the heat in her gaze no longer a flame but a blowtorch. Hot as the July sun and every bit as punishing.

"Nice deflection, Rimes," she said, and he noticed she'd dropped the niceties. "I'll ask again: If you weren't part of this ambush, how do you know anything about my business or my role at Honey and Hickory in the past?"

Google and too much tequila is how. He couldn't exactly admit to low-key cyberstalking on live TV, but he could embellish one of the murmurs he'd heard around the market. A couple of old-timers liked to mutter about how Wayne ought to have chosen someone else as successor.

Every time they voiced their unpopular opinion, they got shot down. But the investors and audience didn't know that, and all he needed was the seed of doubt.

"Hawksburg might be your hometown, but not all the locals are in your pocket. From what I heard, people are worried you moved back home last year just in time to run your family's legacy into the ground. Not that the legacy was that shiny to begin with." He wouldn't know, since his pride had kept him from stopping in at the restaurant, too afraid to visit the lair of his sworn enemy. Too afraid he might never want to leave.

"Keep my family's name out of your mouth." Menace dripped from her words like venom.

He gulped and took an involuntary step back as she advanced on him, steady on her towering heels.

"And while it's true I haven't been running Honey and Hickory for very long, if you think I haven't put blood, sweat, and tears into that place over the years, you're dead wrong. I've been fighting for a seat at the table every step in my career, and self-righteous losers like you aren't going to stand in my way."

"Well, Princess," he said, "my money's on you being the one to walk out of here a loser. We're not in your precious hometown anymore. In the real world, you don't stand a chance."

A slow clap came from behind him, and Finn realized with a start where they were. Not the real world—not even close. He and Simone were fighting, gloves off, on the set of a reality show. Trading bare-knuckle blows in front of two of the wealthiest entrepreneurs in the United States. And their argument was being broadcast to a live audience of millions. *Millions.*

The blood drained out of his face and left his fingertips cold, and he watched what must have been a mirror of his horrified expression transform Simone's face, her light-brown skin turning ashen in a heart-beat, freckles standing out in stark relief.

"Bravo." Keith Donovan clapped again and kept his hands clasped together under his chin, green eyes gleaming. "That was quite a perfor-mance, but we'd best wrap now before you two tear each other apart. Can't have that, not when we want you both"—he paused—"intact."

Wanted them both? Roasted on a spit? Drawn and quartered? Out of the corner of his eye he caught Simone pressing her fingertips to the tabletop, as if to steady herself.

"What?" he managed at the same time she said, "Pardon?"

Mr. Donovan leaned his elbows on the table, face impassive under a well-groomed beard. "While you two kids were flirting, Constance and I had a little heart-to-heart." *Flirting?*

"We've decided we want both of you, or neither," Donovan clar-ified. "Our offer would be two hundred thousand dollars, contingent on a merger."

A merger? A partnership, with Simone Blake, of all people?

Keith went on, like he hadn't handed down a gift-wrapped prison sentence. "We want to franchise Honey and Hickory, get Finn's Secret Sauce into major retailers. We're investing in your personalities as much as your companies. There are many barbecue brands out there, but this spicy dynamic between the two of you? Now that's proprietary."

A murmur of agreement arose from the audience. Keith looked toward Constance, who inclined her head in a crisp nod.

"You two are dynamite together." She smoothly took the reins of the conversation. "Ms. Blake has the restaurant and far more experience in the business realm. Mr. Rimes's sauces offer a unique twist on traditional barbecue flavors. Combined, you're a match made in heaven." She smiled with a flash of canines. "Or maybe hell. And we all know that's way more fun."

Hell—that's exactly where he'd landed. Flat on his back, belly up, nostrils singed with the scent of sulfur and scorched dreams. On fire. Go into business with his rival, or walk away with nothing.

He could kiss his dreams goodbye or say farewell to his sanity. If he'd lost precious sleep over Simone when they'd crossed paths once a week, how much worse would it be to work with her?

The overhead lights spun toward center stage as the show's host strode out between him and Simone. "You heard the investors," she told the audience. "Using your tablets, you may cast a vote in favor of Simone Blake and Finn Rimes, or against them."

She spun in a slow circle to give the illusion of making eye contact with everyone watching. "Again, if you want our investors to take a chance on these entrepreneurs, vote yes. If you want to send them home empty handed, vote no. Is everyone ready?"

The audience pulled the voting devices out from under their seats, faces lit by the glow of the tablet screens. Finn bit his lip and shifted his eyes toward Simone. She stood frozen, taut as a sprinter on the starting blocks. Maybe she felt his gaze, because she flicked her eyes over, narrowing them, and his gumption crumbled to dust.

At this point, getting out of the studio alive would be a win. Thank God for an audience of witnesses. Otherwise, he was pretty sure Simone would've laid hands on him by now. Violent hands, not *those* kinds of hands . . .

And now he was arguing with his subconscious.

A high-pitched sound, like the beep of a scooter horn, interrupted his internal struggle. Finn coughed down a hysterical chuckle at the sound effect. But Simone wasn't laughing. In fact, she hadn't cracked a smile since he'd licked the sauce off her finger.

Since he'd licked the sauce off her finger. Licked. Simone's. Finger. On live TV. Shame engulfed him like a cocoon, but he couldn't hide from the memory. This insane proposed merger wasn't the only reason for her frown.

"All right, all votes are in." The host faced the investors with a dramatic sweep of her hands. "The results are now displayed on your touch screens. So tell us, will these two get a deal, or is their barbecue nothing but burnt ends?"

A hushed word went up from somewhere in the audience, quiet. *Deal.*

Then again. *Deal.* The chant gained steam, picking up among the members of the shadowed audience. *Deal. Deal. Deal. Deal.*

Despite his desire to flee the room in shame, Finn found himself caught up in the energy. Maybe they could make this work. Maybe the investors were right, and he and Simone were some kind of oddball dream team.

He checked her reaction. Eyes drilling into his soul, she very deliberately pressed the toe of one shoe to the floor and swiveled it back and forth, like she was grinding a bug into oblivion.

Or not.

Ms. Rivera held up her tablet. Raising her voice to be heard above the chants, she said, "The audience has spoken." The room went quiet, and Finn leaned forward, felt Simone do the same. Pulled by an invisible strand of spider's silk toward their destiny. Or their demise.

Constance grinned. "In our first unanimous vote in show history, you two have yourselves a deal."

CHAPTER 11

FINN

Finn jogged to catch up to Simone and dove for the exit, but she let go of the heavy door, which slammed back in his face. He jammed his foot into the opening and bit back a curse as it smashed his toes.

Shouldering his way out, he called after her, "Are we not going to talk this over like adults?" Pain gave his words an edge.

She spun on her murderously pointy stilettos, and he had to stop short to avoid running into her chest. A chest he'd never noticed, certainly not now, when it heaved with each breath. He swallowed hard but held his ground, not backing up.

"Don't you mean talk it out like *partners*?" The ironic emphasis she put on the last word hit him like a punch to the solar plexus. *Partners.* What torture had he signed up for?

Chest tight, he nodded. "Like partners. Sure. Yes."

"You'd love that, wouldn't you?" Her golden eyes held all the warmth of a sarcophagus lid. "Grab on to my skirts and ride your way to the top?"

"The last place I want to be is anywhere near your skirts." Not like he'd ever seen her in a skirt, and he'd certainly never imagined her in one—not the brush of fabric above her knees, or the way a dress might hug her shapely thighs. Obviously he'd never imagined anything like that. Never. "And as for riding . . ."

She rolled her eyes. "Classy as always."

"I wish I could say the same." The words scraped through his clenched teeth, but the next ones were even more difficult to grind out. "We. Need. To. Talk."

Simone drew herself up to her full height. In high heels, she bested him by a hair, but he didn't flinch. The studio-lot lights cast shadows down the rows of buildings, her face unreadable.

When she didn't speak, he shoved his hands in his pockets and settled in. Patience was a skill he'd mastered long ago. Patience, even when waiting for a lost cause. Patience, even with the outcome a foregone conclusion. Patience and hope in the face of impossibility.

But staring Simone down left him feeling impulsive and impatient. Anxious to end this argument and break the spell her presence cast over his senses. She was a contradiction of hard lines and soft curls, bold and elusive, and his mind sought distance even as his body swayed toward her.

"We're not partners." She broke the silence with a lashing snarl. Night had cooled the amber depths of her eyes, banked the fire consuming her dragoness soul, but it simmered beneath the surface like a lava flow. He could hear her anger. Feel it sizzle and pop between them.

"Not partners? That's not what you agreed to on set." They'd offered her more than she'd come in for. A franchise. Was she so entitled she would refuse to put aside their differences despite the chance to open locations across the country? Unreal.

"Are you really thinking of backing out? Because if so, great. Let's go in and make it official." To sell the bluff, he spun on the heel of the ridiculous loafers Darius had talked him into wearing, and she grabbed his hand.

"Not so fast." She let go as soon as he halted, but the heat of her fingertips lingered like the press of a tattoo needle, inscribing her touch into his skin.

"I'm not backing out. Yet. But we don't need to talk about anything tonight," she said. "And just to make it clear, once the deal is finalized— *if* the deal is finalized—you and I are *not* partners. We're two separate entities doing business with each other for mutual profit."

"So, partners." He poked the grizzly before he could help himself.

"We've got a few days before we sign our souls away. Can you at least not go tossing around that word until the ink dries?"

His chest loosened at the opening she'd left, the pressure easing just enough for a full breath. "But you will sign it, right? This deal will be the best thing for both of us."

Was it, though? Darius had pressed him to ask for an investment in his culinary-school dream. Told him the investors would jump at the chance to fund it. But all his life he'd been led on. What if they took his dream and tied it up in red tape? Delaying. Deferring.

Or worse, handing it to someone else. Someone they deemed more worthy.

After so many years of bitter disappointment, he couldn't bear to let the one thing that truly belonged to him slip through his fingers.

Anyway, his plan to pitch his sauce had paid off. If Simone kept her word and took the deal, he had a shot at making his vision a reality. He couldn't fathom walking away from $200,000 over a petty farmers' market feud. "Are you really considering backing out?"

She sighed, deep and long. "I'm not sure, Finn."

Nothing left to say, he nodded once. When he brushed past her, she was cool as marble. Somehow, he missed the scorching blaze.

CHAPTER 12

SIMONE

Alisha:

A franchise deal?? With farmers' market Finn?? Was this twist planned all along and you kept us in the dark???

Meg:

I knew that rivalry stuff this summer was a front. But if Finn is your business partner, does that mean you two can't date? Bc in that case you got a raw deal.

Simone:

1) Not planned. I was as blindsided as it looked like.

Simone:

2) $200,000 is absolutely worth Finn being off-limits, considering he was off-limits the second he showed up in town bashing my sauce.

Simone:

3) I'm not going into business with him. He sucks.

Alisha:

But you already agreed to the deal. On live TV. In front of millions of viewers.

Simone:

I want to bring jobs to Hawksburg, not open up a bunch of generic barbecue restaurants across the U.S.

Meg:

I get that, but you could make a boatload of money. Just think what you could do for our community if you're at the helm of a major corporation.

Alisha:

And they're not telling you to close the Hawksburg location.

Simone:

No, they're just asking me to give up half my company. If I take the deal, it will be without Finn.

Alisha:

How do you plan to screw Finn out of the deal??

Meg:

Sounds a lot less fun than keeping him around. Just saying.

Less fun? Granted, maybe she'd begun to look forward to their weekly back-and-forth at the farmers' market. But giving up half her restaurant? Turning her dreams over to a man who kept thwarting her plans? The opposite of fun and games.

Simone exited out of the thread without replying. With Alisha's wedding in less than a week, she'd be in for a slew of questions from friends and family once her plane landed. No need to start the torture early.

And Pops. Oh gosh, what had her grandpa thought when he watched her accept a franchise deal that would rip the heart out of Honey and Hickory? He wouldn't know she'd only said yes to buy time. A no would've been final, but this gave her a week to figure out a solution.

Heartsick, homesick, and needing distance from the situation, she tossed her phone facedown onto the freshly made hotel bed. But visions of black light inspections had her retrieving it a second later. A thorough swipe with a disinfecting wipe rendered the phone germ-free and innocuous, but she couldn't say the same thing for her thoughts, which suffered from worst-case-scenario-itis.

Not surprising, given the unimaginable outcome of the taping yesterday. In the space between commercial breaks, *The Executives* had turned the opportunity of a lifetime into her own personal hell.

Franchise her restaurant? The opposite of the Hawksburg-centered growth she envisioned. Work with Finn Rimes? Gag. Barf. Yuck.

She'd rather . . . well, Meg was spot on about what she'd rather do with Finn if she'd met him under other circumstances. But Simone didn't gloss over history or let go of grudges. That kind of forgiveness left people weak and vulnerable. Exposed.

All of which she'd been last night on the show. Lordy, she'd underestimated Finn. Between the messy hair and the boyish grins, she'd let herself think his arrival in Hawksburg was nothing more than a cosmic coincidence. Turned out he had sinister plans all along. He'd come to scope out the competition. Spent the summer gathering intel and planning his assault.

She shoved the phone in her purse. Six months to prepare, and now she only had seven days to concoct a plan to keep Finn's greedy paws off her company. The producers had set up a video call for a week from today to get footage of Finn and Simone signing the deal.

Which meant by the time Alisha walked down the aisle this weekend, Finn needed to be a tiny, insignificant dot in the rearview of Simone's life. A tight deadline to figure out a plan, especially since Alisha's bachelorette party would cut into her timeline. But she wouldn't rest until she found a way to cut him out of the deal, refused to let his impassioned plea in the studio lot sway her.

So what if she had heart palpitations whenever he stepped close? If the scent of pine and fresh rain that clung to him like fog on a mountainside left her swooning and delirious, all the more reason to stay away. Partnering with a man who triggered mysterious side effects would be downright dangerous.

But her visceral reaction to Finn might have had a logical explanation. For a homebody two thousand miles outside her comfort zone, any familiar face was bound to spark a response. Even after living in Chicago for the better part of a decade, she still felt disjointed away from the rolling hills and tilled fields of Hawksburg.

Falling into the familiar pattern of sparring with Finn on set had all the comfort of running into an old classmate at the airport. Except she'd never wanted to reach out and pull a classmate close like she had in the close embrace of darkness last night, when the yearning in his eyes outdistanced the question on his lips.

Are you really thinking of backing out? he'd asked, but the depths of his eyes cried out, *Don't walk away. Choose to stay.*

Choose me.

For a fraction of a second, suspended in time, she'd almost put her arms around him and held on. A perilous impulse, deadly even. Death to her career, death to her freedom and autonomy. Death to the self she'd been fashioning ever since she left home.

The avatar she'd designed to conquer the game of life wouldn't stop to hug her nemesis. Badass Simone would pulverize the competition.

Find his biggest weakness and exploit it in a tactical strike. Vengeance was the feeling she needed to hold on to, not the knee-shaking, pulse-racing vulnerability that sneaked up on her whenever they were alone together.

Honey and Hickory could be the heart of the community in more ways than one—she wanted to bring in goods from local farmers and artisans, sell products made by women entrepreneurs, like Chantal's jewelry designs.

With the opening of the dinosaur museum, tourists would be . . . if not flooding, then trickling into a town where for so long the only newcomers were of the four-legged variety. The first chance for progress in decades, and she wanted to seize on it. But a franchise deal would pull her focus away from Hawksburg.

And if she accepted the merger, would Honey and Hickory become nothing more than a shell for Finn to market his sauce and grow his side of the business? Their family's legacy, sold out to the tune of $200,000.

Her phone rang, and she collapsed backward on the bed and threw her arm over her eyes. *Argh.* She couldn't be social today.

But when the ringer cut off and started again, she grabbed her purse. What if it was one of the bachelorette party venues calling? Just because her world was crumbling didn't mean she could slack off in her maid of honor duties. Her sister deserved the best send-off, and she intended to give her one with a day of pampering and a night of partying in Chicago.

Holding her phone overhead, she discovered it wasn't a party-planning emergency, after all. She accepted the video chat, her face lifting in a real smile for the first time since last night. "Chantal!"

"Sim!" The voice squealed across the airwaves, and Simone's smile grew. "Can we talk about how you made history last night?"

Just as quickly, her heart fell. For a second, Simone had forgotten her best friend was the die-hard fan who got her hooked on *The Executives*, back when their undergrad study sessions were bookended by copious amounts of reality TV. No doubt Chantal had been watching the spectacle unfold from her couch with a frozen daiquiri in a bag and a heaping bowl of homemade Chex mix.

"I gotta say I'm a little hurt you didn't clue me in on the twist. Hurt, but also that was epic to watch in real time." Yep, Chantal had definitely been drinking last night if she thought that dumpster fire was epic. "Kind of glad you didn't spoil it by telling me."

Simone let her free arm flop over her forehead. Apparently this was a conversation she was going to be having a lot in the near future. "I didn't know. They blindsided me."

"Hello, Sim. It's me." Chantal sounded exasperated. "Did you sign a nondisclosure or something?"

Well, yeah, she had. Several of them. But not about Finn, because the conniving producers had wanted her shock to be authentic. "I wish I could say it was an act, but nope. I went in there thinking it was going to be a typical show. Just me, the investors, and the audience." She stood up and went over to the window, where she had a first-rate view of the parking garage. Fitting.

"And instead, you got to flirt your way to two hundred thousand dollars."

Put that way, the offer stung even more. "I didn't get an offer because of my flirting ability." Had she, though? Was she doomed to have all her achievements undercut by her proximity to a man?

"I didn't mean it that way." She turned away from the dismal view to find Chantal frowning at her on-screen. "I meant you got to have a little fun and still come out with a deal."

Fun? More like an unmitigated disaster. "Half of a deal, and a crappy one at that."

"A partnership with Constance Rivera and the funds to start a franchise is crappy?"

A fellow small-town girl chasing big-city dreams, Chantal couldn't seem to wrap her head around Simone's love of Hawksburg. To most people, the broader scope of the deal would've been the biggest selling point. No denying multiple locations would put a sheen on her résumé, add to the illustriousness of Pops's legacy.

But she didn't want her legacy to be a bunch of corporate barbecue clones spread across the country. She wanted Honey and Hickory to be community focused, to spark change and growth in her own hometown. And the scope of the deal wasn't her sole objection. "Constance is amazing, don't get me wrong. But add Finn to the mix—"

"Oh yes, please." Chantal disappeared in gloom as the camera compensated for her leaving the city sidewalk and entering her building foyer. "Let's talk about that snack of a man, and why you never mentioned he was scorchingly sexy when you complained about him all summer."

Simone's mind flashed to Finn's eyes on hers, dark and intense as his lips closed around her finger, his tongue sliding along her skin. The current of need pulsing between them before he pulled away and snapped it. Shattered her dreams without so much as a flicker of remorse.

"Can we not?"

"Are you kidding? If you're considering turning down two hundred thousand dollars and slighting my girl Constance, you'd best believe we're going to talk it out."

"It's simple. I'm not interested in a deal with a built-in liability," Simone said.

"By 'liability,' you're referring to the fast-talking guy you let have carnal knowledge of you on TV?"

Yeah, he'd screwed her all right, but unfortunately, not in the literal sense. "I did no such thing. It was only my finger." Whoops. Walked right into that one.

Chantal's grin hit her ears. "'Only my finger,' she says." She chuckled. "You're not wrong."

Simone's cheeks flamed hotter than the coastal sun filtering through the streaky windows, but her embarrassment had nothing to do with

Finn's mouth and everything to do with millions of viewers who'd watched him pull one over on her. "Glad my public shame is a source of entertainment for you."

Chantal's smile slipped. "Sim, it wasn't that bad. It was kind of cute, to be honest."

"Yeah, a random dude is about to become equal owner of my family business. Super cute." About as cute as a baby cobra and every bit as deadly.

The screen blurred to show greige carpet on a staircase, and Chantal's breathing turned labored. She and Simone had lived in the same fourth-floor walkup since college. A year into law school, Chantal took the leap and dropped out to chase her design dreams, creating an eclectic line of jewelry.

With her business taking off, Chantal had decided to turn Simone's old bedroom into a studio. She tried not to feel replaced—silly, when it was beads and thread, not even a new roommate occupying the space she used to inhabit—but an ache settled into her chest as she thought about the home that used to be hers. It wasn't only Hawksburg she was homesick for.

"I know you moaned about him selling sauce on your turf all summer"—Chantal panted—"but I don't see the big deal. Hawksburg is not exactly a destination." Not yet. But her vision was to make it one, impossible if she was trying to build a franchise. "How much money did his presence actually cost you?"

"That's my point! Why come back every week?" To scope out her weaknesses. Wear down her defenses. "He might not have cost me much all summer, but he just cost me half my business."

He'd played the perfect long game, and she'd admire his strategy if she hadn't fallen victim to treachery. Fool me twice . . .

"What if he didn't know you'd be on the show? Could he have been a pawn just like you?"

"He did know. And even if he didn't, a partnership would be a disaster. It would be a constant battle of wills, and that man has an ego bigger than—"

"Than yours?" Chantal's bubbly laugh filtered through the connection as she unlocked her door. "Doubtful. Besides, who cares about the size of his ego?"

"That's my line." One she reserved for rationalizing hookups with self-indulged men, not signing business deals with them.

"I know, I learned from the best." Her friend's grin was upshot by the phone, her tasseled earrings swaying as she took off her macramé tote. "I'm just saying, personal objections aside, aren't you curious what he might bring to the table?"

"I know what he brings to the table. He's got decent sauce, but he's been in business less than a year."

Chantal squinted at her. "Technically, so have you."

"Whose side are you on?"

"Yours, always yours," her friend said. "And I wish you weren't living so far away so we could talk this out in person." Something Simone wished for every day. To somehow be close to everyone she loved most in life. But she was thousands of miles away from everyone she cared about, facing down an uncertain future all on her own.

"I just don't want you to let He Who Shall Not Be Named ruin what might be an amazing opportunity for your company."

She refused to utter it after what he'd done, but the name Jason Whittaker was forever seared into her consciousness. He'd been her office bestie from day one, right up until he'd turned traitor. Jason had cost her her job, but if she let Finn into her company, she might lose everything. And this time, the blame would fall squarely on her own shoulders.

"A franchise might be a great opportunity, I'll give you that. But I'm not risking my future by going into business with a wild card. I've got to figure out a way to take Finn out of play."

"And you're going to accomplish this how? You do realize wedding stuff is going to monopolize your time. Trust me on this." Chantal had five sisters, all older, all but two married. Her closet was half bridesmaid's dresses at this point.

"I know it's going to be hectic, but the bachelorette party isn't until Thursday. That still leaves me a few days to strategize, plus a four-hour flight's worth of planning time." She'd need every minute to contrive a way to save face before she arrived back in town. She couldn't let everyone see her as the contestant not good enough to get an offer on her own. "Speaking of, I'd better get to the airport."

Her flight didn't leave for another few hours, but it never hurt to arrive early. And maybe a change of scenery—she cast a last disgusted look at the concrete monstrosity blocking the California sky—would help her brainstorm ways to get rid of Finn.

"Okay, I'll leave you to your ridiculous timetable." Chantal knew her too well. Downright annoying. "But when you're outlining your sinister plan, make sure you're not so fixated on getting rid of him that you wind up hurting yourself in the process."

Now was not the time to hold back. So what if her emotions went haywire around him? Her emotions were drunk and disorderly, downing Jell-O shots and singing karaoke. They'd led her astray before.

"I've got a few days to discover Finn's weakness and use it against him. Trust me: there's no downside to going it alone."

CHAPTER 13

FINN

"I need to get her to see this is the best way forward for both of us." Cell phone crooked into his neck, Finn dragged his duffel bag higher on his shoulder and hustled into the airport. The automatic doors whooshed shut behind him, silencing the chorus of honks and shouted farewells, sealing out night air thick with exhaust fumes and cigarette smoke.

On the other end of the line, Darius sighed. "Simone already screwed you over once. What's to stop her from doing it again? And this time, she could tank your company."

Brought up short by the vast size of the terminal, Finn hesitated. He didn't agree with Darius's reasoning. The only way Simone could screw him would be to *not* take the deal. Which, judging by their conversation last night, was a very real possibility.

Cell phone to his ear, he searched the bustling concourse for the check-in kiosks. "I did things your way and went on the show, and now you want me to throw away two hundred thousand dollars?"

"No, I just want you to be careful," Darius said. "Watching you two together . . ." His friend let out another sigh. "I just worry you're not thinking clearly. You've been at each other's throats all summer, and suddenly you think partnering with her is a good idea?"

Despite his hesitancy to go on the show, now that a deal was within his grasp—a chance for a future he'd been too scared to even dream of—he wouldn't throw it all away just because of personal differences with Simone.

Intense personal differences.

"Do I think a partnership with two billionaires willing to finance Finn's Secret Sauce to the tune of two hundred thousand dollars is a good idea? Yeah."

He finally spotted the check-in line and stepped up behind a couple with hiking boots and oversize backpacks. Only his second time in an airport, and the whole experience felt like he'd made the jump from tricycle to motorcycle, skipping the training wheels and ten-speed. He'd never expected to get the privilege to fly on a plane in his lifetime, and yet he was about to partner with two of the richest people in the world.

And one of the snarkiest.

The backpackers exited the line, and he stepped up. After reading through all the options on the screen, he selected one that made sense. The screen beeped aggressively. He tried a different option. The screen flashed alarmingly.

Darius was still muttering in his ear, and Finn refocused on the conversation: ". . . spent years working on your self-esteem. And I'm not convinced a merger with a woman who hates your guts is progress.'"

Trust his big brother stand-in to bring him back down to earth. But he'd come a long way, thanks to therapy and prioritizing his mental health.

"You do realize I'm not seventeen anymore, right?" He hit another button, and the screen froze. At this rate he'd be walking back to Illinois. "I can't believe I'm sitting here trying to convince you a partnership with some of the best business minds in America is a good idea."

The machine beeped an error message, and Finn swore. "An opportunity that you signed me up for, might I remind you. You know my credit is a wreck. Without an investment from *The Executives*, I'm back at square one."

"Then convince them to take just you! You don't need—"

"Except I do. That's the whole point." Fed up with the argument and the worthless machine, Finn shoved his credit card in the slot. It jammed. He crouched down and dug his fingers into the opening, which upon closer inspection was labeled *Boarding Pass*. Oops.

"It's a package deal. All or nothing." And he couldn't walk away with nothing. Not with hope in reach. "My track record with women might not be the greatest"—an understatement, given his penchant for always wanting to believe the best of people—"but even you can see this is different. It's not romantic. Partnering with Simone is a smart move."

"Smart, yes, but also risky. Just don't lose your head, Finn."

His card finally popped free, and he shoved it into his wallet. A crinkled boarding pass ground its way out of the slot and dropped to the floor.

Lose his head over Simone? "Never. But listen, I'm cutting it close. I'll text when I land."

Fumbling to end the call, he jogged over to the line at security and tapped the shoulder of the man in front of him. "Hey, sorry to do this, but my flight leaves in forty-five minutes. Is there any way you can let me by?"

The guy glared at him but stepped infinitesimally to the side, and Finn squeezed past, bumping into the retractable line divider. He righted the teetering stand, then repeated his entreaty to the backpacking couple, then a harried mother with three kids and a pregnant belly, who urged her children to get out of his way while shooting him a kind smile.

By the time he'd made it through security and found his gate, he was sweating through his jacket. A crowd of people were milling around, craning their necks and scrolling through their phones. Shoot, had he missed his flight? His stomach shot into his throat.

"Where ya headed?" Finn looked down to find a grandfatherly figure at his shoulder.

"Uh, St. Louis," he said.

"Not tonight you aren't." So he *was* too late. The man grinned, gleeful to be the bearer of bad news. "Snowstorms picked up, grounded all flights to the Midwest."

"Snowstorms?" Finn didn't see the connection. Not like a little snow would stop a jet airliner.

The man nodded and then pointed with his cane toward the rows of TVs mounted overhead, showing news anchors with their hoods up, shouting at the camera through whiteout conditions. "They're calling it the blizzard of the century. We might be stuck here for days."

Days? He didn't have days to spare. The way things had been left between him and Simone, he would be lucky to ever see her again, let alone convince her to sign off on the deal. If he didn't reach out soon, he might miss out on his chance at $200,000 and a future for his company. Lose out on a chance to affect so many lives.

But a quick scan of the displays confirmed the man's dire prediction. DELAYED flashed next to his flight number in red letters of finality. Like it or not, he was stuck, thousands of miles away from Simone and the chance to talk her into taking the deal.

All the seats were taken, so Finn sank down against the wall under the windows and rested his forehead on his knees. He never should've gone on the show. His pride and the chance to flick a big middle finger at the woman who'd underestimated him were what had gotten him into this mess. Now, instead of him showing her up, Simone was yet another person he'd need to convince to take a chance on him.

Exhausted and overwhelmed, he squeezed his eyes shut. Maybe when he woke up, this would all have been a nightmare.

Finn blinked his eyes open and met a stark color palette of porcelain-plate white and pâté gray, edged with burnt-bruschetta brown. The scent of coffee and hiss of a steamer brought him out of his sleep-fog. His brain registered suitcases and satchels lying on the floor by people's feet.

The airport.

He rubbed his eyes to clear the remnants of his dream away, which had had a lot to do with Simone's slender fingers and . . .

He sat bolt upright and shifted his duffel into his lap. Jeez, the last thing he needed to do was dream about his rival-turned-potential-business-partner. Clearly his hormones hadn't gotten the memo she was public enemy number one.

His cheeks flamed, embarrassment aggravating his fresh sunburn. Yesterday he'd planned to spend the morning before his flight with an all-out tourist binge on Venice Beach and Santa Monica Pier. No sense in wasting what might have been his only trip to the West Coast by staying in his hotel room.

But he'd made it to the ocean and then canceled the rest of his loose itinerary. The grit of the sand underneath his feet and hiss of the waves on the shore had made up for all the stress and nonsense of the filming. He'd gotten some much-needed clarity while walking the shoreline.

Yes, Simone hated him. Yes, she was an entitled jerk. But he couldn't do this without her. Or rather, not her, but the $200,000 that came along with a merger.

There had to be a way to get Simone to see she needed him as much as he needed her—in a purely professional way, of course. Was she already back in Illinois? If so, she was probably holed up in her lair, finding ways to worm her way out of the deal and demolish his shot at offering a better future for people who needed it most. People who didn't get second chances or do-overs.

Finn dipped his head between his knees and tugged at the roots of his hair. If only she would've listened to him after the taping. But she had to go and storm off like an immature, stuck-up—

"Venti, sugar-free mocha latte."

His head shot up.

"With oat milk, please, extra hot, extra foam." A fittingly high-maintenance coffee order from a voice belonging to the very woman who haunted his waking—and sleeping—thoughts.

Over at the Starbucks counter, Simone scanned her credit card and placed a folded bill in the tip jar. After years in the service industry, the action would've been a mark in her favor, if he hadn't known money was disposable to her. Someone who considered turning down $200,000 sure as heck better tip their barista.

A tan trench coat hugged Simone's slender curves, paired with short boots and sheer black polka-dot tights. He'd never had a thing for lingerie—it got in the way, with too many buckles and straps and frou-frou lace—and it's not like her tights were fishnet thigh-highs. And yet . . .

The barista called out her order, and she stepped to the counter. Retrieved her coffee and took a long sip. Her eyes rolled back in her head with pleasure, and he tightened his grip on the straps of the duffel bag. Her expression evoked pure bliss, like biting into a bittersweet raspberry truffle as the finale to a four-course meal.

Then her eyes snapped open and she frowned, as if regretting the public display of happiness. Her expression hardened, eyes sharp as she scanned the concourse, and he resisted the urge to duck like she was a prison searchlight.

Not delicious, after all. Devilish.

Her roving gaze neared his seat, and he looked down, wishing for invisibility. Shoot. He'd have to face her or live forever with the knowledge that being a big freaking chicken had kept him from $200,000.

When it felt safe, he ventured a glance and found her seated at a table in the café, tapping away at her phone. Should he walk up and offer to buy her breakfast? No, too close to a come-on. The last thing he needed was for Simone to think he was into her. Because he wasn't.

Heck no. Never. Not even if they were the last two people on earth, huddled in a concrete doomsday bunker to wait out a nuclear winter with nothing more than a kerosene lamp, and a twin mattress, and no blankets . . .

Finn, get it together!

Anyway, no buying of pastries. Maybe he could leave it to chance and hope they were assigned seats next to each other.

Yeah, no. With the universe's low opinion of him, now was not the time to leave things up to chance. She picked up her drink, brushing her tumble of curls over one shoulder, and Finn flicked his eyes away before she felt his gaze.

No need to walk over there yet, right? These storms would keep them stuck here for at least another few hours. Plenty of time to think of a plan for approaching the most beautiful woman in the terminal, a woman who wanted nothing more than to run him through like a hunk of meat on a skewer.

CHAPTER 14

SIMONE

An eternity at the airport, and Simone had spent most of that time pretending to be absorbed in her phone, her food, her laptop, the rows of runway lights, a conversation with the barista about the merits of Velveeta versus Cheez Whiz . . . anything to avoid eye contact with Finn Rimes.

She'd spotted him around midnight. He lay dozing on the floor by the window, his head pillowed on the bright-red scarf the Yarn Spinners had given him. At first, she'd been worried he'd notice her, but as the night wore on, it became clear he wasn't going to wake up. How anyone could get a full night's sleep in a crowded airport was beyond her.

As for her, she'd dozed fitfully from two to five a.m., an alarm set to wake her every thirty minutes so she wouldn't miss a boarding call and the chance of rescue from the terminal of doom. But the winter storm wreaking havoc back home kept them trapped, and with dawn came a new kind of torture. All morning she'd been trapped in a reverse staring contest with Finn.

Whenever she darted a glance his way—over the top of a *Forbes* magazine she'd picked up in a kiosk, or peeking around the side of the paper bag holding her grilled chicken wrap, or under pretense of scanning the smog-filled sky above his makeshift campsite under the windows—he'd been sprawled on his back, resting, or thumbing through a worn paperback, looking totally chill.

Couldn't he at least have the dignity to look exasperated? Annoyed? Impatient? To maybe pace the terminal or roll his eyes or clench his jaw like any other traveler who'd been trapped in an airport for going on a full day?

Not like she should've expected impatience from the man who'd showed up to every farmers' market all summer, implacable as a midstream boulder. Unmoved by her attempts to get rid of him, with his steady presence he forced her to adjust course like a kayaker navigating the rapids.

Through persistence and charm, Finn earned the goodwill of townspeople who tended to view outsiders as the enemy. By midsummer he was selling barbecue sauce caddies knitted by the Yarn Spinners, by autumn he went home each week loaded up with a free crate of parsnips or squash or rutabagas from the Bills, and at their last farmers' market of the year, she even caught Meg sneaking him a couple dozen eggs. Traitor.

As if stealing the hearts of her hometown wasn't enough, he had the utter audacity to butt his way into her appearance on *The Executives*. She should've seen this coming. She *would've*, if she hadn't been distracted by his crooked grins and his dancing brown eyes and his espresso-rich voice and his stupid scuffed sneakers.

Insufferable, that's what he was. And entirely too at ease with this long wait. Head pillowed on his duffel bag, his long legs stretched out and crossed at the ankles, one arm under his head like he was stargazing at Yosemite. She lifted her gaze to the ceiling tiles. What did he even see up there? Water-stain Rorschach tests?

She watched his chest rise, fall. A fresh pink flush spread across his angular nose and prominent cheekbones, like he'd spent the day at the beach. Like he hadn't gone from airport to hotel to television studio to hotel to airport like she had, never allowing herself a moment to look up, look around, lest she get distracted from her mission. Like he cared more about experiencing life than wrestling it into submission.

Another inhale and he shifted, turned his head, and their eyes met. Held. One heartbeat, two . . .

Simone stood up and marched away, wheeling her carry-on around a *Wet Floor* sign outside the restroom. Once in the shelter of a stall, she took stock. For one thing, she'd let Finn catch her staring. Bad.

For another, her tights were doing murder to her intestines. Worse. She'd planned to wear this outfit for a few hours, not a full day. A novice flyer, she'd learned her lesson the hard way. Next time she'd show up to the airport in sweats.

But a bathroom outfit change sounded impossibly yucky, so she settled on taking off the tights as a compromise. Holding on to the purse hook, she slipped off one boot and shimmied the tights down. Tugged off one leg, then switched. Ah, sweet relief.

Out by the sinks, she shook out the tights and folded them into her purse. After smoothing some hand cream into her knees and shins, she retied the belt of the trench coat she refused to take off—she wasn't taking the chance of someone walking away with the high-end coat she'd scored at a resale shop—and rubbed on some lip balm.

Feeling more human now that she'd freed her belly from the clutches of nylon, she strode out into the concourse, intent on continuing to avoid Finn until, well . . . forever. Getting to know him would make cutting him out of the deal messier. Like they'd been doing all night, her eyes went straight to his spot by the windows. For surveillance purposes, of course.

Except he was gone.

Her body went tight, tingles racing up her spine. Where was he?

"Looking for something?"

She jerked and dropped the handle of her suitcase. The bag tipped forward, knocking into the back of her knees and scraping its way down to her Achilles. She hobbled away, swearing, and slipped on the wet floor. Arms outstretched, she braced for the inevitable smack of tile, but Finn grabbed her around the waist and swung her up into his arms.

"Steady there, Tornado." Cradling her, Finn sent down a warm smile at her, and wow. *Yes, please.*

He'd just swept her off her feet like Lancelot, and used a nickname that might have been better reserved for a ranch horse, but for some reason she was all about it.

But he was setting her down already, his arms steady and solid around her. The second her feet hit the floor, it was a slap of cold, hard reality.

"I'm sorry, I didn't mean to . . ." He rubbed the back of his neck. "Um, startle you."

Lies. He always meant to startle her; his whole being was specially designed to knock her off balance. She bent and grabbed the handle of her carry-on, then headed back to her seat before someone else snatched it away.

"Are you really going to just walk away?"

Glaring over her shoulder, she said, "Did you want a thank-you for catching me after you made me fall?"

"I did not make you fall." He caught up to her, walked alongside. "You slipped. I caught you."

"I slipped because you snuck up on me."

"I did not sneak up on you! I just wanted to give you this." He held out her phone, and she scowled. She wouldn't put it past him to have pickpocketed it to get in her head. "You left it on the seat, and I figured it was worth losing our little avoidance game to return it to you."

So he'd been playing along? Didn't matter. Shouldn't make her heart squeeze. "It wasn't a game," she said to silence the pitter-patter of her heart.

"Oh, so we weren't playing staring-contest chicken?"

"You are so immature."

He grinned. "Says the woman who ran off to the bathroom when she lost the game."

"Did not." She totally had. "Besides, you already admitted you lost by coming over to talk to me."

"I lost the *avoidance* game, yes. But we looked at each other at the same time, so technically the antistaring contest was a draw." She hated that he was right as much as she loved that he'd given thought to the rules. "Anyway, if you don't want your phone, I can go put it back on your chair."

She snatched it out of his hand. Put it in her purse. Zipped it. He laughed, loud and full bodied, and several people turned their heads. The sound should've rankled her, but instead she had to force a scowl to keep from joining in. Finn Rimes was the flip side to her coin. She hated that.

Less comfortable in Finn's presence than when her internal organs were being crushed by elastic, Simone made a beeline for her miraculously empty seat. But as she got closer, she realized it wasn't a miracle at all—Finn's duffel bag was slung across the armrest, saving two seats. He picked it up and sat down, crossing his ankles.

She followed suit, folding herself into the uncomfortable seat. "If you noticed me all along, why didn't you come over sooner?"

He shrugged. "After the show, you made it pretty clear you weren't interested in chatting."

Funny, a man who listened. She'd thought they were myth. "I needed some space."

"Do you still need space?"

She needed him out of this concourse, out of the airport. Out of her life. But he'd been on the floor all night and half the day. Denying him a seat seemed egregiously cruel.

"If you like, we can go back to pretending to be strangers." Could they, though? Her body thrummed with awareness of him.

Finn stretched one leg out toward the center of the aisle, like he was at home on a sofa, not crammed onto a stiff pleather seat. Despite his laid-back posture, he kept himself to his side of the armrest, angled away from her. And yet his presence made the hairs on the back of her neck tingle in anticipation.

She pulled the *Forbes* magazine from her purse and flipped it open. Eyes on the page, she felt Finn tip toward her, still on the other side of the armrest. He ran a splayed hand down his thigh, smoothing the worn fabric under his fingers. The jeans looked soft with wear, and she wondered how they would feel under her fingers. Or how they'd look unbuttoned and hanging off his lean hips . . .

She snapped upright and crossed her legs. Undid the top button of her trench coat. Kept a firm grip on the magazine so she wouldn't slip up and fan herself.

"Hot?"

"Bothered," she said, and he laughed. Flexed his hand and palmed the back of his neck. Jeez, the man was a walking seduction. She should've taken him up on his offer for space. "Don't you have somewhere to be?"

He swept a hand around the crowded terminal, and she realized her slipup. "I think we all do. And yet . . ."

"And yet, purgatory." At best.

"I think this is the part where a twisted demon throws us together, yet again, for their own torturous amusement," he said.

Against her will, Simone's lips twitched. "My theology's rusty, but I don't think there are demons in purgatory."

"An angel, then?"

"Throwing *us* together?" She let sarcasm creep into her voice to stomp out the spark of hope in his eyes like a dangerous ember. "Hardly."

Finn sat on the edge of his seat, then slid back and put his elbows on his knees, fidgety, the opposite of the calm he'd displayed up until now. "I should apologize." Head down, he blew out a breath. "I came on pretty strong on *The Executives*. Said some things I didn't mean." He looked over his shoulder again, and this time his eyes collided with hers. His gaze was bare and honest. "Then again, so did you."

"I meant every word." But had she? Thinking back on it, she couldn't remember half of what she'd said. It had all come down to self-preservation. She'd dragged him under to save herself. Shame vied for anger in her chest. "Besides, I'm not the one who's been plotting to steal your company since day one." Even though he owed her nothing, was no one to her, the deceit still hurt in a way she hadn't known was possible. Not anymore.

"I told you I had nothing to do with that," he said. "I was as blind-sided as you." But his voice cracked. Like a liar. Like a cheat.

"Say that's true . . ." It wasn't. "You still responded by throwing me under the bus."

"What was I supposed to do, roll over and take it?" He straightened up and tucked his long legs under the seat, bouncing his knee, like talking to her left him restless. "Considering how hard you fought to keep me out of your precious farmers' market, I figured you'd respect someone with a fighting spirit."

He had a point. "Just because I respect your . . ." Underhanded tactics? Duplicity? She settled on a complimentary word (he had apologized, after all): ". . . ingenuity on an intellectual level doesn't mean I don't resent it on a personal one."

He stayed silent for so long that she went back to perusing the magazine. She flipped to a feature article on Keith Donovan. The ex-NFL star smiled up at her from the glossy page, as if he were trying to convince her to take the deal.

"Whether you like it or not, we're stuck together." The words could've come from Keith's mouth, but unfortunately for her, it was Finn she was trapped with.

She flipped the page. "For now. Any minute now, we'll be boarding and we'll never have to see each other again."

"Maybe."

"Maybe I'll change my mind and agree to partner with a man who's already tried to steal my business?"

"Not to be particular, but changing your mind would be changing your mind, since you already agreed to the deal."

It was official. She was going to kill him. It was going to happen. He slouched backward like his life wasn't in imminent danger and threw a hand over the top of the seats, fiddling with a rip in the fabric behind her shoulders.

Did the man always have to be so loose limbed and loungy? It was downright distracting. Disarming. Decadent, like hot fudge and lazy Saturday mornings. She resisted the urge to lean back and see what it felt like to have those fingers slide up into the curls at her nape.

"What I meant was," Finn said, apparently incapable of shutting up now that he'd started talking, "sure, there's a chance we'll be on the plane in an hour. But I've been checking the radar, and it looks like another storm front's coming through. We might be stuck here for a few days."

He was just trying to get a reaction out of her. "No way."

"See for yourself." He passed her his phone, and the openness of the gesture stunned her. It went against nature, like sharing underwear, or a toothbrush. But she thumbed through the weather headlines, avoiding the cracks in the screen. Page after page of the dire warnings meteorologists lived for. Shoot. He wasn't lying.

An ache in her jaw signaled she needed to unclench her teeth, but when she did, a headache popped up in its place. She passed over his phone and slumped back, right into his hand. His fingertips slid along the sensitive skin at her hairline as he pulled away, and she ducked her head into her hands.

"Sorry." He sounded genuinely upset by her reaction.

"No, it's not your stupid hand." Which wasn't stupid at all; it was soft, and comforting, in a way that made no sense. "It's that this can't be happening. I cannot be stranded in California for days."

"Oh." He paused, then spoke again, tentative. "There are worse places to be stranded."

"Not for me. My sister's getting married on Saturday, and I'm two thousand miles from home." The irony. Trapped with her worst enemy when her closest family member needed her most.

"Next Saturday, as in less than a week?"

"Yeah, but her bachelorette party is in just a few days." And Simone still needed to work on the decorations, buy the liquor and party favors, catch up on all the work she'd missed . . .

"Well, I mean, you could miss the party, right? She'd understand."

"No, Finn. I cannot 'miss the party.' This is my only sister we're talking about." Not to mention she'd already pulled focus away from Alisha by going on the show. Selfish Simone strikes again. She stood up. "I need to go talk to a ticketing agent."

"Wait." His hand caught at her wrist, gentle, but his touch seared her like a hot brand. "I have an idea."

"I hate it already."

He laughed, loud and clear, and the brick of ice in her chest thawed at the edges. "Drive back home with me."

"No way." She jerked her hand away and crossed her arms, her skin tingling at the loss of contact. *Drive back home with me*, as if he were her coworker clocking out to go home to the same apartment building, not her sworn enemy asking her to embark on a cross-country voyage.

Brown eyes alight, he said, "Look, *The Executives* played us—I think we can both agree on that." She refused to agree with anything Finn Rimes had to say. Now, or ever. "But that doesn't mean they're wrong."

"Shocking you'd take that stance, since you're the one who can't get into big-box retailers without their clout. You need the deal."

"And you don't? You didn't come on that show just for publicity. I may not know you that well, but you don't seem like the kind of person to waste their time."

Maybe she could forgo her pledge and agree with him. Once. "No, I'm not. I really wanted a deal." The deal she'd asked for, not the one they offered. But she'd be out of her mind not to partner with Keith and Constance, wouldn't she? Saying yes had bought her a week to think it over. No would've been final. "'Wanted,' past tense."

His lips tightened into a straight line. "So why back out? Just to spite me?"

"It's not to spite you. It's to protect my company. My dream."

He stood up, eyebrows dipping together. "What if you could trust me?"

"I can't."

"Two days, that's all I'm asking. Let me help you get back to Illinois in time for your sister's bachelorette party. What better way to get to know someone than on an epic road trip?"

"No way. You're not Harry, and I'm sure as heck not Sally."

"Obviously. Wrong road trip movie." Finn splayed a hand to his chest. "Clearly I'm the quick-talking, fast-thinking Louise." He lifted his palm toward her. "And you're Thelma."

"Please. If anything, you're the random drifter who Thelma—"

"Bangs?"

This time Simone couldn't contain a smile, and Finn's cheek bulged where he pressed his tongue into it, like he was pleased. She shouldn't care that she'd made him happy. His joy shouldn't pull the edges of her lips higher, but it did.

"Back to our predicament . . ."

"*My* predicament," she said, correcting him.

He shrugged, as if the distinction was inconsequential. It wasn't.

"Driving is the perfect solution. You get back to your sister's in time. And I get a chance to prove what an awesome, stand-up guy I am. Next thing you know you're ready to jump into b—" She shot her eyes toward him, and he grinned. "Business with me. Mind in the gutter much?"

She bounced the rolled-up magazine against her thigh to keep herself from smacking him with it. "And if I decide you're a despicable human being?" She already had, and no amount of groveling would change that.

"Then back out of the deal. Nothing changes. But Simone, give me a chance." He clasped his fingers together and held them under his chin. "Please. This is my future on the line."

There he went with the puppy dog eyes. Not fair. But even though she would probably be able to fly out soon, driving across the country might be the perfect way to find some dirt on him. By the time they got back to Illinois, she could have her ticket to freedom punched.

She stole a quick glance down from his folded hands to his strong, tattooed forearms. At least the scenery couldn't be beat. "Two days?"

"Two days."

"No detours?"

"No detours." One corner of his mouth hitched up, and she prodded his knee with the magazine.

"I mean it, Finn. It's not a joyride. We drive straight through, and if you don't convince me by the time we reach Chicago, I pull the plug."

"Like an overheated toaster."

Finn shrugged into his red-and-black buffalo plaid jacket and flipped down the collar. He pulled a beanie out of his pocket and slid it onto his head. Wavy hair poked out the front, and Simone willed herself not to swoon. He looked up at her from under the fringe of his hair. "Deal?"

Way too adorable for her own good, this man. "Deal. But I get to pick the ride."

CHAPTER 15

FINN

"Who rents a convertible in December?" Finn adjusted the mirrors and fiddled with the height of the steering wheel. With the low seats in this ground-hugging sports car, he'd have a crick in his neck before they even got out of the rental lot.

"It was only a little more than the sedan." Simone didn't deign to look up from her phone. She'd insisted he drive the first shift so she could take care of some emails. Assumed he didn't have any work to catch up on, or maybe she just didn't care. But since he'd been the one to suggest the road trip, he went along with her little power play.

Also, there was his whole convince-her-to-partner-with-him plan. Which meant he should be on his best behavior. Which would've been a whole lot easier around anyone besides Simone High and Mighty Blake.

"Because it's *December*." He shifted into drive and pulled out of the parking lot, stealing another glance her way under pretense of checking his blind spot. "No one wants to cruise with their top down in the winter."

Her eyebrows appeared over the top of the sunglasses. "We're in Southern California. I'm pretty sure that's standard practice."

"For now."

"Huh?" Her giant sunglasses swallowed up her face like she was some kind of Hollywood starlet.

It shouldn't have worked on him. But dang, just like the ridiculous trench coat that still hadn't revealed so much as a sliver of hem underneath—seriously, was she even wearing a dress?—the movie-star sunglasses were totally adding to Simone's allure.

"We're in Southern California—for now," he repeated. "What happens when we get closer to home? You planning on driving with the top down in a blizzard?"

"Good point." She pressed a button, and the roof made a buzzing sound.

The canopy opened a crack, and Finn slammed on the brakes, squealing the tires. "Hey! You can't do that when we're driving!"

"Why not?"

"I don't know, but it does not seem safe." Already this woman was a liability. He'd be lucky to arrive back in Illinois with his half of the deposit. He pressed the button again, and the canopy slid back into place with a clunk.

"Whatever." Simone turned on the radio. She scanned through a rock ballad, oldies, and a pop song but stopped the tuner on a country station.

Finn kept his mouth shut for all of thirty seconds. He considered it a win. "Maybe you had a point. Two hundred thousand dollars isn't worth this torture."

"Not a fan of country?"

"Um, no." He shot a look her way. She was mouthing the words, her shoulders bouncing along to the nonexistent rhythm. "You're serious with this. Wow. How did I get trapped in a car with the one human in existence who likes country music?"

"Hush your mouth." Simone turned up the dial and spoke over the excruciating twang of steel guitar. "You do know there's about a hundred million people in this country who disagree with you, right?"

"One hundred million country music fans? No freaking way." Finn turned the music back down to stem the bleeding in his eardrums. "Google it."

"Okay, I will. But if I'm right, I get to pick where we eat tonight. And I get dibs on volume control."

"You're on, Blake."

She shook her head, a hint of a smile playing on her lips, and his stupid stomach did a flip-flop. He'd complained about the music, but his real complaint was that the universe kept throwing him together with this sexy thunderstorm of a woman.

Simone thumbed through her phone, dark curls falling down along her cheek, and he clenched the steering wheel against an urge to brush her hair back, tuck it behind her ear. Touch her again, like he'd been dying to ever since he swept her into his arms in the airport.

Given their history, if she so much as guessed his thoughts, she'd probably drop-kick him out of this car, eighty miles an hour or not. He rubbed a clammy hand down his jeans, easing off the gas for good measure.

"What?" Simone hadn't looked up from her phone, but his cheeks still heated with a blush.

"Nothing."

"Hmm." The soft hum of her response had him biting the inside of his cheek. Dang. He needed to get a grip, and fast. He hated to admit it, but she'd been 110 percent right. This trip was a terrible idea.

Facing off against Simone in the gravel lot of the farmers' market, or going toe to toe on the set of a reality show, was one thing. But spending forty-eight hours with all of her sexiness and sharp wit an arm's length away, with no small-town busybodies or studio audience as a buffer?

"Ha!"

Finn gulped, hard. Was she a mind reader? But she lifted up her phone in triumph. He frowned. "You can't expect me to read that."

"I don't. You're driving, numb nuts, and I want to live. But it's my validation."

He smirked. "One hundred entire people in the US enjoy country music?"

She poked his ribs, and he flinched at the unexpected contact, liking it way too much.

"One hundred *million* people."

"No way."

"Hang on, I'll send you the link so you can fact-check. What's your number?" He rattled it off, and a second later his phone chimed.

"You read that stat recently."

"Nope." When he glanced over, she'd rolled her lips in on each other, squinting at her phone. Maybe she felt his gaze, because she looked his way and lifted a shoulder. "Numbers just come to me."

"Poof. Just like that?"

"Poof, yeah." She grinned, open and wide. "Something like that." Then she was back to her phone.

He should leave her alone. They'd reached a truce, and more interaction could topple it. But she awoke an urge to delve deeper, explore. "Looking for more proof?"

"Nope. I'm choosing dinner. Winner's prerogative. Anything you can't or won't eat?"

"It's your call," he said. "You won." Later, he'd check the link she'd sent him, make sure she wasn't feeding him a load of BS. But somehow, he trusted her.

"I won a bet, Finn. I'm not Satan." Debatable. She set her phone on the dash and undid the belt of her trench coat. Finn's hands slipped on the wheel. "If you have allergies or a strong aversion, now's the time to speak up."

An aversion? To hot women undressing in the passenger seat? He glanced over to find her fingers working at the buttons of her coat. Second button. Third button. He was no longer breathing.

"Vegan? Gluten-free?"

What? Oh, *dinner*. "Nope. I'm pretty much a goat."

Out of the corner of his eye, he caught Simone doing a full-body shudder. "Don't mention goats."

He chuckled, glad for an excuse to get his mind off her undone state. "Do I sense a story here?"

"Yup. You remember Tim, the guy who loaned you the booth?"

"I thought he loaned it to the Yarn Spinners," he said, messing with her.

Simone blew out a sarcastic breath. "C'mon, we both know I lied."

"Is that an apology?"

"It most definitely is not." She paused, and Finn glanced her way to find her working down one shoulder of her trench coat. He tightened his grip on the steering wheel and checked the mirrors. Turned on the windshield wiper fluid. Did not look over. Would not.

But Simone flapped an arm in his periphery, the sleeve hanging past her hand like she was wearing a giant's coat. "Do you mind, real quick?"

She wanted him to help get her jacket off? Forget purgatory. This was torture. Eyes on the road ahead, the stalled traffic, the speedometer, anywhere but the inviting lines of Simone's body, he reached across and pinched her sleeve between his thumb and forefinger. Tugged. The fabric slackened as her arm slipped free, and he let go on a harsh exhale.

Of course she wasn't naked in the seat next to him. *Of course* she wasn't. Right?

"Anyway, he's a goat farmer," she said, apropos of nothing.

"What? Who?" Confused, he looked over before he remembered she might be sitting there nude. But she was frowning at him in a tan sweater dress that hugged her body like a second skin, stopping midthigh. Not naked, but close enough.

"Tim Brewster," she said, and his frazzled brain finally latched onto the thread of conversation. "He raises goats."

"Just goats?" He was still trying to regain his composure.

"Is that essential to the story?"

Not at all, but he loved to needle her. "I'm your audience, and I want to know." Finn switched lanes to pass a trailer and fixed her with as flat a look as he could manage with a still-racing pulse. "So, yes."

She rolled her eyes. So cute.

Not cute. Irritating. He wanted to slap himself.

"Yes, to my knowledge, he exclusively farms goats," she said, crossing her arms with another exasperated huff. *Mission accomplished.* "Can we move on?"

"I wish you would." Riled Simone was his favorite Simone.

She huffed out a tiny snort of indignation, and he bit his lip. Definitely his favorite.

"Anyway, I was thinking about sourcing my goat cheese from him."

"You serve dishes with goat cheese at Honey and Hickory? I don't remember seeing any on the menu."

"So you *were* stalking me."

Oops. "Reading menus online isn't stalking. It's a hobby of mine. Professional research. I am a chef, after all," he said, and he realized she might not have known that about him. Realized how little they knew about each other at all, outside their mutual hatred and his one-sided attraction.

"Hmph." She made that sound again, deeper this time, and he squirmed in his seat. "Well, you're right, we don't have anything with goat cheese on the menu. Not yet, at least."

Would she accuse him of corporate espionage if he asked what she had planned for the menu? Not worth the risk when she was already on the fence about the deal. But his interest was piqued. Goat cheese at a barbecue joint . . . fritters, maybe? Spread on a toasted bun to complement a pulled-pork sandwich?

"Anyway," Simone said, her voice cutting into his culinary musings, "I drove out to his place to check out the cheese, and he offered me a tour of his farm."

Tour of his farm? Sounded highly suspect. "Is this Tim guy single?"

"Again, is this relevant?"

Finn smirked. This time he hadn't even meant to derail her. "Just wondering if 'tour his farm' is a euphemism."

"Jeez, Finneas." She shook her head, looking disgusted. "It was not. He's old enough to be my dad!"

Finn sucked through his teeth. "When has that stopped a man?"

"Ew. Just, no. Well, yes," she said. "Sickeningly, you're right. But in this case a nice gentleman just wanted to show me his goats, okay?"

Finn couldn't hold back his laugh. "Whatever you say. So is that why you don't like goats? A lech showed you around his"—he choked the words out between chuckles, making air quotes with his free hand—"'goat farm'?"

"Oh my gosh, no! Cut it out, Finley." Now she was laughing too. "Tim is so not a lech. He's a cool guy. Other than his error in judgment in letting you take over his booth. But *he* wasn't the problem. It was his goats."

That sounded ominous. "Now I feel like I don't want to hear the end to this story," Finn said between laughs.

"A GOAT HAD A BABY ON MY SHOES." Her words drowned out the speakers, and frankly, thank God. No more off-pitch yodeling. But also, her statement stilled his laughter.

"I have some questions." He shot a glance her way to find her eyes bright, cheeks flushed under her freckles. He held up a finger. "One, was it premeditated?"

She hiccupped, fingers pressed to her lips. "On the goat's behalf, or Tim's?"

He lifted a shoulder. "Either. Both."

"I don't *think* so?" This debate was ridiculous, but he was having more fun than he'd had in a long time. "I mean, the goats were all running around in the pen," she said. "We were out there among them. It's not like he singled out that particular goat."

Finn rubbed at his jaw. "Hmm. But they were his goats. He had to know on some level, right?"

"Maybe, but how long is a goat's gestation?" Simone tucked her leg up under herself, turning to face him, animated. He didn't look at her bare legs; he wouldn't. Would not. "I'm sure it's not an exact science. I mean for horses—"

"Oh no." He rubbed his brow, pressing his lips together against an errant smile. "Now we're bringing more livestock into this?"

"Horses are not livestock."

He switched lanes, then put on the cruise control, only for convenience's sake. It had nothing to do with leaving him more free to focus on Simone. "Pretty sure horses are the definition of livestock. What else would they be? Pets?" Hang on. He was beginning to sense a pattern. "Okay, wait. Country music. Horse lover. Am I in the presence of a bona fide cowgirl?"

"Boy, please." She flashed a wide grin. "The proper term is equestrian."

"I'll take your word for it, cowgirl."

She prodded his shoulder, but he felt it in his core. "Anyway, you can see why goats are a sore topic for me."

He tried not to picture it, but it was no use. "I mean, *on* your shoes? Direct hit? Were you standing under the goat's . . ." He flailed one arm helplessly.

"Vagina? No, Finn, I was not. But there was a lot of . . ." Now it was her turn to flail.

"Afterbirth?"

She nodded, the back of her hand to her mouth. "That."

"So I take it you're not one of those women who wants to birth a basketball team?"

"I can think of nothing worse. What about you?"

He could think of a lot of things worse than having a family of his own. But she was only asking out of politeness, not a desire for him to

125

dump his issues on her. "Nah, I've never been a fan of birth. The labor pains alone . . ." He faked a grimace. "Plus, I'm terrified of needles, so an epidural would be a no-go."

Simone laughed. "There's always adoption."

"True." Finn chewed his lip. *Don't ask, don't ask, don't*— "You've considered it?" *Shoot.*

"Adoption? No." There she went with the full-body shudder again, and this time it was less cute. "I meant it would be a great option for you. Skip the contractions and all."

He forced a tight smile. "Right." Because that's all adoption was. A lesser evil.

"Not sure I'd be up to the task," she said, apparently oblivious to the dip in his mood. "People who adopt are heroes."

Heroes. "For taking on damaged kids?" He didn't bother to soften the words.

"No, jeez." She gave him a sharp look. "I meant, for stepping up."

"Taking one for the team." God, this woman wouldn't let up.

"No. I just . . ." Simone put a hand on his arm. "Are you adopted, Finn? Because I—"

"No." Adoption was too good for him. "I just don't think adoption is quite the sacrifice you make it out to be." More like a paradise he'd been locked out of.

"I didn't mean it that way at all. You know what? Forget I said anything." She shifted to face forward, pulling out her phone.

For a moment there, he'd deluded himself into thinking Simone Blake had a heart.

Partners was the endgame. Anything less would be failure, and anything more? A highway to heartbreak.

CHAPTER 16

FINN

Finn dropped a party-size bag of Doritos on the counter and tossed a few jerky sticks and a bag of smoked almonds next to it for good measure. Never hurt to stock up. And what was a good road trip without excess sodium?

Although, *good* wasn't how he'd categorize this trip so far. More like the climax of a disaster movie. His earthquake of emotional baggage had triggered a tsunami, headed for landfall the moment they got back into the car.

Country music would be a welcome escape at this point.

The herbal scent of lavender and mint announced Simone's presence at his shoulder. She placed a granola bar and water bottle on the counter next to his stuff.

"That's it?" The question came out harsher than he intended. Feeding people had become second nature. His friends understood his urge to make sure no one went hungry. Too many times he'd lain awake, stomach cramps keeping him from the relief of slumber.

But Simone wasn't a friend, and from the scowl on her face, she understood nothing about him. Fine, he'd prefer to keep it that way. "Forget I asked." He reached into his back pocket for his wallet, but Simone hip-bumped him.

"I got this."

Sick of arguing with her, he said, "Whatever."

"I don't like to be indebted," she added, and his molars connected with a clack.

"It's five dollars." He ground the words out through gritted teeth.

"It adds up."

"Yeah, well, not everyone has the luxury to be so high and mighty about debt."

"Oh my gosh, is this about my family business again?" She slammed some bills down on the counter. Finn bit down on his reply, snatching his items and backing out the dirty glass door.

Twilight was falling, bathing the gas pumps in gloom. Fitting. Too quickly, she got her change and stalked after him across the empty parking lot.

"Because I've told you, Finn, my life isn't some rose-colored whatever you think it is!"

"Okay." He yanked on the passenger door. Locked.

"Okay?" She faced him over the dusty canopy of the convertible, barren desert stretching out behind her.

"Whatever you say." He jostled the handle again for good measure.

"No." She tried her door, yanking on it. "You don't get to be like that. You're the one who begged me to come along on this trip."

"And I'm regretting it." He crossed his arms, and the Doritos bag crunched against his chest. Great. Now he'd be eating orange dust. Salty orange dust. And he'd forgotten a drink.

"Because I paid for your snacks?"

"No." *Yes. Maybe.*

Bickering about pocket change brought his focus back to the $200,000 deal hanging in the balance of this cross-country drive. With an inherited restaurant, she was set. This was all a game to her, but with his future on the line, everything carried weight, the tonnage so heavy his shoulders sagged.

She tried her door again. "Keys?"

"You have them." Too late, he realized, nope—he did. He dug them out of his pocket and sent them sliding across the fabric canopy toward her.

"Careful!" She grabbed them, then unlocked the doors and disappeared inside.

Rolling his eyes heavenward, he had no choice but to follow. She jammed the keys into the ignition, hard. "You can pay for dinner. We'll be even. Happy now?"

"Would you leave it? I told you, it's nothing." It wasn't nothing, but he couldn't put into words the big feelings she set off in him, like the fuse to a firecracker. A slow burn. An explosion.

"I really wanna hear what your problem with me is." She let go of the steering wheel and turned toward him, eyes blazing. "It seems like you've got it out for me because you think I'm somehow spoiled?"

"Ever think that might be because you're turning your nose up at two hundred thousand dollars?"

"Ever think I might have a good reason?" At his silence, she cranked the keys. "But go ahead, assume it's because I'm flush with cash or whatever the hell it is you think."

"Jeez, it's not the money." Not really. How could he put into words how much it hurt to see someone so oblivious to their good fortune? "It's about you having this . . ." He sucked in a breath. "Okay, yes, this rosy view of the world. Like there's no place in your life for messiness or imperfection or struggle."

He stopped himself before he said more. She'd been handed a restaurant gift wrapped, so she could leave $200,000 on the table with zero qualms. She had a family who loved her, so of course she'd never considered offering one to kids who didn't.

"Hold up. You think my life is perfect?" She huffed out a scoff. "Is this because of what I said about adoption? Because I tried to tell you . . ."

He fumbled for the door handle. Staying would expose wounds he'd worked hard to heal in front of a woman who'd always wanted him gone.

She growled, a small sound in the back of her throat, and he could feel her eyes on his profile, her frustration as palpable as the stuffy air in the car. "You have this whole view of me that I'm a heartless jerk. And whatever, maybe I am. But I only said people who adopt are heroes because I was raised by them."

His fingers slid off the door handle, numb. Her *grandpa's* restaurant . . .

He'd been so caught up in his own issues he'd never stopped to question why her family business had skipped a generation.

"My mom died when I was in kindergarten," she said, confirming his suspicion. The signs he'd completely missed, blinded by his own baggage. "A year later, my father abandoned me and my sister. Started a new family. Calling him a 'sperm donor' would be an insult to families everywhere. But my grandparents stepped up and took over for their worthless excuse for a son. They raised us like their own kids. Never made us feel like a burden or an inconvenience or anything less than cherished."

She licked her lips. "So forgive me for not being certain I'd be up for parenthood. If I decide to raise a child, I sure as heck want to make sure I'm ready for a lifelong commitment."

"I'm sorry." The words didn't touch his sorrow for her. On impulse, he clasped her hand, and she didn't pull away. He should've recognized the smoke screens she put up, the first line of defense of the wounded and scarred.

"Don't be," she said. "I only told you because I'm sick of your condemnation. But I don't want your pity either."

He swept his thumb along the side of her palm. "It's not pity."

"Then what is it?"

Understanding. A barrier between them slipping away. "A wake-up call," he said, really seeing her for the first time. She was a person trying to prove her worth in the face of loss and abandonment, just like him. A person he'd spent months pushing away, when all he'd ever wanted to do was pull her close, a decision that was looking more idiotic by the second.

"If it's not pity, then why are you making a face that says you want to tuck me under your chin and pat my back?"

Probably for the best that his real thoughts weren't reflected on his face, because that gesture sounded way more tame than the things he'd like to do to Simone. Desire amplified now that she'd broken the barrier and let him in. Nearly irresistible now that he'd touched her.

"Am I?"

"You are." That was interesting, because judging by her unfocused gaze and parted lips, she kind of didn't seem to hate it. "And you're holding my hand. Which is super weird."

"Is it?" It was, given their history. But she hadn't pulled away. In fact, her fingers tightened around his. It was weird, but also kind of nice, to be touching her.

Better than nice.

"I mean . . ." She slid the tips of her fingers along his palm. *Oh.* His eyes squeezed shut. "It's different."

"Should I stop, then?" He breathed out the question. Opened his eyes.

"Stop what?"

"Touching you. Your hand."

She shook her head. "Not unless you want to."

He absolutely did not want to let go of her. If anything . . .

He licked his lips, and her eyes darted down. Lingered.

"Finn?"

"Hmm?"

"Are you planning to kiss me?"

He wasn't planning on anything, right now. All coherent thoughts had fled, leaving him abuzz with desire. "Do you want me to kiss you?"

"Yes." Her voice set him aflame like a breath to coals. "Please."

That word. The first time he'd heard her use it, so courteous compared to her usual bluntness, and it was his undoing. He leaned across the gearshift and slanted his mouth against hers. Her lips were so soft. So indulgently plump. Pliant and yielding. Unexpected.

She let go of his hand, and he pulled back, broke the kiss. Had she changed her mind? But she grabbed his shoulder, tugging him close. Slipped her fingers into the hair at the back of his skull, slotted her mouth against his, and oh. Her tongue was so slick, so wet. He gripped the console to ground himself, but then her hand dropped to his thigh, squeezed, and he was lost.

He let himself fall headlong into her heat, sliding his hand along her rib cage. Molding against her, drawing her closer. She moaned, deep, and it pierced him, sharp. His hand slid down over the small swell of her hips to the hem of her dress, the silky smoothness of her thigh, and holy crap, they were at pump two at a desert gas station.

He pulled back, breathless. "This is a bad idea."

"Says who?" Simone asked, looking dazed and drunk and decadent.

"It's just . . . we can't . . ." At this exact moment, the reason escaped him, but . . . "I'm not supposed to kiss you."

Her eyes flew wide. "Excuse me, what? Do you have a girlfriend, Finn Rimes? Oh, gosh. Don't tell me you're married."

"No! Neither," he said, and she collapsed back against the seat, still looking thunderous.

"I just . . ." It was hard to speak around the foot wedged in his mouth. "That came out wrong. I just promised my friend I wouldn't . . ." Worse. "I mean, we're supposed to be keeping this platonic. For the, uh, the business. The deal." Nail, meet coffin.

"Let me guess, your friend says I'm a dangerous wild card, and you should watch your back around me."

"Not exactly." Darius had said Finn was gullible, and naive, and, okay, yes, that Simone might take advantage of him. Which she hadn't. "He knows I have a history of trusting the wrong people."

"Wow. Holy crap, wow." Simone cranked the keys, and the convertible rumbled to life. "You are absolutely unbelievable."

"Simone . . ."

She slammed the car into gear and accelerated out of the parking lot. "I opened up to you, shared really personal stuff, and somehow I'm still the enemy?"

"You've never been the enemy. But you gotta admit you haven't always been the kindest to me, and maybe jumping straight from arguing to making out is skipping a few steps."

"And you've been a saint?" she asked. "You quoted my restaurant's worst review in front of the entire country."

"You tried to run me out of town!"

"Forgive me for being a little distrustful of someone who showed up in my town and tried to steal my business," she said. "Or don't. I couldn't care less what you do."

"*Your* town? You see, that's it right there." Vindication tasted sour, but sometimes the truth was bitter. "You don't own Hawksburg, Simone. You think the world revolves around you."

"Nothing revolves around me, don't you get it?" She slammed on the brakes at a stop sign, and Finn put a hand to the dashboard to avoid having his brains smashed on it.

"The restaurant wasn't even meant for me. My grandpa gave Honey and Hickory to my sister. In front of the whole town. A big fancy ceremonious passing of the torch. There's even a video, if you'd care to see." She glared at him, daring him to speak. "But turns out she didn't want it. So she pawned it off on me. I'm a friggin' afterthought, and I could probably just hand over the whole business to you and no one would care."

The air punched out of his lungs. Twice now he'd hurt her. Twice now he'd jumped to conclusions. Wrong conclusions. *Hurtful* conclusions.

"When you showed up at the farmers' market, I panicked," she said, hands trembling on the wheel. "I was set on proving myself, and selling sauce was supposed to be the beginning of showing I was the right person to run Honey and Hickory. Instead, you came to town and implied I had nothing to do with the sauce we were selling. So yeah, I lashed out. But you went on *The Executives* to try to steal my chance at a future, so you can get the heck off your high horse."

"For the last time, I didn't know you'd be there." A half truth. He had known she'd be there, just not at the same time as him. He hadn't meant to face off with her, but he had gone on to prove his sauce was better. To prove *he* was better. He hung his head.

"Maybe not, but you can see why I might be hesitant to trust a man who says he wants to kiss me in one breath and in the next calls me an entitled brat." Put like that, he was an absolute heel. "We've both done some shady stuff, but I'm done being the bad guy in your story. I am not the asshole here."

He forced himself to meet her eyes. "You're right." He'd been wrong to justify his feelings of inadequacy by making her out to be a villain.

"Yeah? Because ten seconds ago you were calling me a bad idea."

"Not you." God, he'd hurt her. "The kiss."

"Well, you were right about that. The kiss was a freaking terrible idea. But not because I'm a jerk. Because *you're* a jerk." She pulled away from the stop sign, eyes ahead, shoulders stiff.

He sure was acting like one. And he couldn't take back his words, but he'd made her feel attacked after sharing a piece of herself. The least he could do would be to reciprocate, even if sharing left him hollow and vulnerable. Especially then. "I'm sorry, Simone. I really am. I've been all up in my head, blaming you for my own issues."

"You think?"

She wasn't going to make this easy on him. Not that he deserved easy. He raked a hand through his hair, blew out a ragged breath. "I've been through some stuff. I've worked on it. Am working on it, but it still comes up sometimes." More so lately, he realized. Making a go of the sauce business, fighting for his dream. All of it dredged up his insecurities. "I wasn't lying earlier when I said I wasn't adopted. But I . . ." It shouldn't be so hard to tell people this thing about him. Shouldn't make him feel nonhuman. But it did. "I grew up in and out of foster care. And in the end, I aged out of the system."

Aged out of the system. Made him sound like a felon, or an experiment. A test subject at the intersection of bureaucracy and family life.

He clenched his jaw against memories of the couch at his aunt's house and a scratchy wool blanket, a blaring TV. Of unfamiliar beds in silent rooms. Of bunks and the sound of crying. Of shouting at midnight and stillness at midday. Of lying awake staring at blank walls or, worse, dressers covered with snapshots of other children.

Children who were wanted, their rights to home implicit. While his case was always pending, always up for review. And the determination? Unwanted.

And away he would go.

"So you have no family?" Her question was direct, and he appreciated that. But the answer wasn't so simple. His biological family existed in name only, but Bella and his coworkers were family. Darius and his mom Tori were family. But that's not what Simone was asking.

"None like yours."

She nodded like she understood, and maybe she did. *My mother passed away. My father abandoned me . . .*

"I'm sorry, too, Finn." Her apology was quiet but clear. The on-ramp was coming up fast, and she clicked on her turn signal. "Really sorry for things I said to belittle you. Sorry you had to endure a terrible childhood." She met his eyes for a fleeting second of clarity. "But I am not about to be anyone's regret."

He'd gone and ruined his chances. Again.

CHAPTER 17

SIMONE

Taillights began to blur into the horizon under an endless darkness. Three hours of night driving had put them on the outskirts of Phoenix. Simone rubbed her eyes, then smothered a yawn, straightening her spine against the ache in her low back.

So far Operation: Discover Finn's Weakness had amounted to Tell Finn Your Deepest Secrets So He Can Use Them as Emotional Blackmail, with a side of Best Kiss of Your Life, and a chaser of Abject Humiliation.

Which is to say, hitchhiking with a serial killer would've made for a better evening.

And the cherry on top of the cocktail of misery was that Finn hadn't been all wrong in his judgment of her. She didn't dwell on her father's absence and focused on her good memories of Momma, but did she take Gran and Pops for granted? Yeah.

Even though she knew they could've made a different choice, could've searched for other relatives to take them in, she never stopped to think where that might have left her.

A ward of the state.

Raised by strangers.

With her mom and dad being only children and her maternal grandparents gone soon after her birth, her future had been tenuous at best. Having relatives didn't equate to having a family.

Even at her loneliest in the early days of college, she'd never once doubted she had a place to call home. A soft spot to land.

Worrying about her rank in the Hawksburg pecking order suddenly seemed a lot more petty. And not the kind of petty she took pride in. The low-down, cringey kind.

"Hey." Finn's words broke the hours-long silence, and she looked over to find him holding out his giant cup of Coke. They'd stopped for fast food because collecting on her winnings by choosing a quirky roadside restaurant no longer held appeal. They weren't buddies. This wasn't a joyride.

After a wordless second, she took the soda and slurped gratefully. His lips had already been on hers, so what could a little more saliva swapping hurt? That's what her brain said, but her body clenched at the memory of the kiss.

She took another giant gulp.

Finn sucked.

She blinked at the time on the clock. Thirty hours to go.

This trip sucked.

The deadline to sign the paperwork counted down like an action-movie scene where the hero was torn between snipping the blue or red wire to defuse a bomb.

The deal sucked.

Bleary eyes on the road, she tried to set the drink into the cup holder, but it tipped forward, close to spilling. Finn righted it. Silently.

Two hours and counting of no words between them, and the awkwardness hadn't abated. How could it? They'd kissed, then gotten into another giant fight.

Around Finn, her emotions were a constant maelstrom, and her head couldn't seem to get aligned with her heart. New territory for her.

She was always in the driver's seat when it came to her feelings. But here she was, starting to like the guy who had his eye on taking over half ownership of her restaurant. The guy whom she was supposed to be finding a way to boot out of a $200,000 deal.

A sour taste filled her mouth, and she reached for the cup again. Finn held it up, and she put the straw between her lips. Biting down on it, she spoke through clenched teeth. "Why'd you get such a giant cup of soda?"

"It was the best value."

"Because you have to have hands the size of an NBA player to drink it."

"Is that a dick joke?"

She coughed up a noseful of pop. "Jeez, no. Although one might say your giant drink is compensating for something."

"My tiny bladder?"

At that, she let loose a laugh. "You're super weird."

"So are you."

"I am." Something she didn't show many people. Most people got cool, self-assured Simone. Not quirky, sarcastic Simone. That Simone she saved for her closest family and friends.

This forced-proximity experiment was killing her vibe. If they went on like this, she might wind up kissing him again, and that was not happening. No more letting her guard down with Honey and Hickory on the line. Which meant she needed to put some physical distance between them, fast.

"What do you think about pulling over for the night?"

"Like, here?" He gestured to the roadside flying by outside his window. "Um, no thanks. I choose life."

"Shut up. I meant getting a room." She shot him a warning glance, lest he get the wrong impression. Then again, that ship had sailed. Right off a cliff. "Two rooms. And sleeping for a few hours."

He frowned. "I thought you had to get back for your sister's—"

"Alisha." The name popped out without her thinking. Why the heck was she volunteering more personal details? That settled it. She needed out of this car and away from Finn. "And yes, I do need to get back for Ali's—" Dang it. *My sister's* bachelorette party. But as long as we drive straight through for the rest of the trip . . ." Oh gosh, all that time in a confined space with Finn and his soft lips and his sense of humor and his strong hands . . .

And his self-righteous attitude. Her resolve strengthened. "As long as we drive straight through, we'll have plenty of time."

He watched her, his face illuminated by passing headlights. "If you're tired, I can take over. That's the plan, right?"

"Yeah, but those airport seats were murder on my back. I don't think I can take another night of cramped sleep."

"Okay, well, you're the one on the timetable," he said, voice even.

"I can't believe I'm having to talk you into this. What's your hurry?"

"I don't have one." This new agreeable Finn was freaking her out. "Your agenda is my agenda. I just want to make sure you're happy."

Happy? Sure, the two minutes of their kiss had been bliss. Right up until he'd called it a mistake. Called her unkind. "You have a funny way of showing it."

He groaned, slouching down in the seat. "Are you going to hold it over my head this entire time?"

Definitely. "You kissed me."

"I'm aware," he said, in a way that made her all too aware, everywhere.

"And then called me entitled."

He dragged his hand through his hair, mussing it. "Because I was going off crappy assumptions. And my overprotective best friend got in my head."

That, she could relate to. Alisha was more protective than a father in an old-school country song. But still. "I get it, but you don't just come back from that."

"Agreed. We can't pretend it never happened. I've made a lot of mistakes since we met . . ." He sucked in a breath. She heard it, and oh Lordy, she *felt* it. "But kissing you wasn't one of them."

The GPS dinged. "Recalculating."

"Shoot." Stupid hormones and Finn. "Missed the exit." She checked her blind spot and switched lanes. "Can you find a hotel and route us there before we end up in the middle of the desert?"

"Too late," he said, but he pulled out his phone, and she exhaled. Smooth talker, that's all he was. Not like she hadn't met plenty. Made out with plenty. The difference was the only agenda the other guys had was to get her in bed, not weasel their way into part ownership of her business.

Finn pointed up ahead. "Take the next exit—there's a hotel a few miles off the highway."

"Does it have a good rating?"

"Yes." He squinted at his phone. "Hang on. There's a note about bedbugs. But we're in the clear: says here they fumigated the place last week."

"Hilarious."

He grinned, hitching up his hips to put his phone in his pocket, and she tried not to squirm in her seat. Stupid close quarters doing a number on her hormones. "Can we play a game?"

"We are literally minutes from being out of this car." Dangerously close to getting sucked into Finn's vortex, she needed distance.

"Yeah, but it's been quiet for, like, hours."

"I could put on country."

He slapped a hand over the radio dial, honey-brown eyes pleading. "Please, no. I'll be quiet."

One excruciating minute of silence later, she said, "What game? And don't you dare say two truths and a lie."

"That hurts, Simone." She didn't need to look at him to know he was making a pitiful face. "What kind of a person do you think I am?"

"The judgy kind?"

"I deserved that," he said. "However, this game is not two truths and a lie."

"Thank God."

He laughed. "Okay, so it's like the alphabet game. But instead of looking for letters, you say three things about yourself, and one of them is a lie."

"Finn." She was fighting a smile.

"I'll go first," he went on, like she hadn't spoken. "But don't think for a second you're getting out of it. I don't want any more misunderstandings—"

"Not a misunderstanding. You judged me like a Judgy McJudgerson."

"I don't want to *misjudge* you, and so that means that I need to know you better. But in the spirit of fairness, I'll go first."

"And I'll go never," she said.

"Second."

"Literally never."

Out of the corner of her eye, she caught a flash of teeth. "This is fun already."

Why was he so adorable when he was being annoying? He rubbed his hands together—again, equal parts annoying and adorable—and bounced his eyebrows up. "Ready?"

"I was really hoping we could hold off on the cheesy road trip games until at least day two." A last-ditch effort to forestall the inevitable.

"You're out of luck."

"Don't I know it." She sighed, heeding the GPS's instructions to take the next exit, her grip on the steering wheel loosening once she pulled off onto the city street. "Fine. But if we miss our turn because of your lame game, I'm gonna be pissed."

"As opposed to your attitude now, which is . . ."

"Sunshine and light, Finnegan. Believe me, if you deprive this girl of a soft bed and a full night's rest, you'll regret it."

He grinned like a wolf. "Far be it from me to deprive the lady of a good night's sleep." Then he winked, the reprobate. "You're gonna want the left lane."

She flicked on her blinker, jaw clenched, as he took a sip of Coke like he was whetting his throat for a speech.

Putting the drink back, he said, "Okay, so here's me: I got my GED at twenty-one, I aspire to own a ridiculous number of cats someday, and I've never been out of Illinois until now."

Easy. "The cat one's true."

"How do you know?"

"Because you said you gravitate toward people who aren't emotionally available. Cats are snobbish, uptight, and evasive. Therefore, you love them."

A beat wherein Finn clearly tried to come up with a rebuttal but ended up saying, "Also because they're really cute."

"Dogs are cuter."

"I notice you said cut*er*." Astute, this one.

"Because kittens are kind of cute," she said. "And I don't hate cats; my eyes are just open to their devious nature."

He laughed. "So you're a dog person?"

"I'm an equal-opportunity animal person."

"Me too." Finn's smile warmed the whole car. Made it too hot, in fact, despite the blasting air-conditioning. "But a houseful of cats seems way more reasonable than a houseful of dogs."

"How many cats, though?" She checked her blind spot, switched lanes to pass a slow car.

"A least three but no more than eight."

"Eight and you're definitely veering into wearing-a-bathrobe-to-the-opera territory."

"I can tell you've given this a lot of thought," he said, earning himself a shove. A mistake, since touching the rounded ridge of his shoulder was enough to bring to mind how he'd gone still and taut underneath her touch earlier. "Two or three would be nice, though."

"And at least one dog." Why was she building an imaginary menagerie with this man? Physical separation couldn't come fast enough.

"Do you have any?" he asked.

"Cats?"

"Dogs."

She shook her head. "I barely have time to ride my horse. If I got a pet right now, it wouldn't be fair. You?"

"No." He hesitated, and she looked over to find him palming his neck. "I kind of need a more permanent housing situation."

"Your apartment doesn't allow pets?"

"Technically my apartment has four wheels and a license plate."

It took her a second to make the connection. "You're living out of your car?"

"It's not as bad as it sounds. I don't have a permanent address, but my best friend flips houses, and he lets me sleep in them during construction." He picked up his drink. "I told you, I'm all in with this business. When I said I'd do whatever it took to succeed, I wasn't lying."

She admired that. Which meant it was time to change the subject, because admiration and Finn didn't go together. *Shouldn't* go together.

The light turned green, and she accelerated. "I'm going to say the second truth is that you haven't left Illinois before, because you've been drooling over the scenery ever since we stepped out of the airport."

"That obvious, huh?"

"Yep. But not like I blame you. This is so different from back home." Instead of grass and trees in the parkway, there were palm trees and cacti poking out of a rocky landscape. Different, and beautiful.

"Especially now. I'm not loving the idea of going back to six feet of snowfall."

"Please, it'll be a foot and a half, if that. And fresh snow is so gorgeous." She let a sigh escape at the prospect of a trail ride with Willow in the powdery snow.

"Oh no." Finn was squinting at her. "Is my partner a snow-vangelist?"

"Not your partner." Not now, not ever. "And a who-in-the-what, now?"

"A snow-vangelist. You're gonna want the right lane, by the way." He leaned in, grinning, and she felt herself tipping toward him. Righted herself before she tumbled into the whirlpool of Finn's charm.

"Someone who tries to convert everyone to share their misguided love of snow," he went on. "You're one of the people who post photos on social media of snow angels on the first day of winter. You categorize shoveling as 'healthy exercise.' And even though you're, what, twenty-five?"

"Gross, way to fish for my age."

"Twenty-six, then." She shoved his arm, and he laughed. "Even though you're twenty-seven—"

She couldn't help but join in. "You were right the first time, jerk."

Triumphantly, he went on. "Even though you're twenty-five—like me, not that you asked—you will mow down schoolchildren on the sledding hill who get in the way of your snow-induced glee. Am I close?"

"I hate you so much."

His bouncing laughter echoed around the car. "We make a good pair. Crazy cat guy"—he put a palm to his chest, fingers splayed, then bowed to her—"mad snow queen."

Spotting the hotel chain up on the right, she swung in under the covered entrance. "So, when did you graduate high school? Fifteen years old or something ridiculous, like Doogie Howser?"

"What?"

"Your lie," she reminded him. "You said you got your GED at twenty-one."

"Oh, shoot." He grinned, sheepish. "I forgot I was supposed to come up with a lie."

"That's literally the name of the game! The game you wanted to play, might I remind you."

"Games aren't really my strong suit."

"Ya think?" she asked, laughing, but caught herself. She didn't want him to think she was laughing about his diploma. "Can I ask why? You don't have to say."

"Why I dropped out of school, or why it took me so long to finish?"

"Whatever you want to answer."

The engine idled loudly in the silence following her question.

Finn looked down. "There are a lot of reasons, but the main one is, I didn't think I was worth it."

Didn't think *I* was worth it. Not *it* was worth it. The distinction wasn't lost on her.

The lights in the overhang cast oblong shadows across Finn, cutting his face into geometric planes. She wanted to reach out for his hand, wishing in that moment for a way to show him just how worth it he was, but then he was opening the door and climbing out. "I'll grab the bags and wait for you inside."

When he disappeared through the sliding doors, she drove off to a parking spot at the side of the building. Finn Rimes made it way too hard to hate him. She'd have to settle for dislike and hope that was enough to keep her heart intact when she booted him out of the deal.

❦

Finn was leaning an elbow on the glossy white counter when she strode in, all disheveled hair and rumpled clothes and hot man mess. When he saw her, his whole face lit up like a Vegas billboard. Like he was happy to see her. Like he *liked* her.

"Bad news, Simone. They only had one room left. Just one twin bed. " He tapped the key cards on the desk and bounced his brows, the corners of his mouth upturned. "Cozy, though."

"If you want me to believe these ridiculous scenarios you keep throwing out, at least have the decency to keep a straight face." Smiling like a hypocrite, she held out her hand for a card.

The clerk's eyes shifted between them. "We're not together," Simone said. "If that's what you're wondering."

"But we did kiss, just now. In the car," Finn added, unhelpfully.

"Not just now. Hours ago."

He tapped his chin. "Has it been that long?"

"Wish it had been longer."

The clerk cleared her throat. "Continental breakfast is from six to ten."

"Great." Simone took her bag from Finn and strode off toward the bank of elevators. He caught up in a few strides and stood by her as they waited.

"Which rooms?"

"Oh." He rocked back on his heels. "307 and 308."

The doors opened, and in they went. Bumped shoulders. Tried again. This time she all but ran toward the back of the elevator. Finn followed and stood next to her.

"Should probably hit the button," she said.

"Oh, yeah." He hit three. Returned to her side, when there was a whole elevator to stand in. She looked up. He looked away. The elevator dinged.

He let her go first this time, walking a step behind till they got to their rooms. They stuck their key cards in the slots at the same time. The lights beeped red. Wordlessly, they switched.

This time the light turned green, and Simone turned the handle.

"I really am sorry," Finn said. She paused, listening. "About calling you entitled. You should know I have a major, giant, inferiority complex."

"You're just making it too easy at this point."

"Simone."

She smirked, unapologetic. But she couldn't let herself off the hook so easy. How must it have felt to get muscled out of a market when you'd spent your life on the outskirts? No wonder he'd assumed the worst of her.

She wasn't as bad as he made her out to be, but neither was he, not by a long shot.

"But Finn, you've gotta know you're awesome." She cleared her throat, feeling naked in the space after the admission. "An awesome cook. Your sauces are above and beyond"—she'd sneaked samples this summer—"and you don't get sales like that as a fluke. If you think you're not worthy of an investment, you really do have a bad case of imposter syndrome."

"Says the restaurateur with a business degree."

"That's why you can trust me." That and it wasn't in her best interests to feed his ego, not with such high stakes. "If you won't take my word for it, at least acknowledge the fact that Keith and Constance believe in you. You walked into that boardroom and owned it."

"I kinda did, didn't I?"

She shook her head with a grin. "Looks like your inferiority complex isn't the only thing that's oversize."

"Another dick joke? Simone, I'm blushing." He was, too. Flushed and bright eyed, and biting back a grin.

"What you are is ridiculous, Finn Rimes."

Ridiculously cute, ridiculously fun, ridiculously charming his way into her heart. She shut the door on all that ridiculousness, but try as she might, she couldn't quite shut him out of her heart.

CHAPTER 18

FINN

The waffle iron beeped three times, and Finn took out the waffle with his bare fingers.

"Ouch!" He danced back, dropping the steaming waffle onto his plate.

"Ever heard of tongs?" Simone materialized beside him, curls hidden under a scarf, pajama pants draped on her long legs, knotted with a silk ribbon under the rolled hem of her belly-baring sweatshirt. How would that ribbon feel between his fingers? Slippery and smooth as he pulled the knot loose . . .

He scrubbed a palm down his face. At this rate he'd need a second shower. A cold one.

She reached around him for a jelly packet, her arm brushing his chest, and he took a step back.

"You're up early, sunshine," he said, voice rough with more than sleep.

"If you call this early, you'll be dodging a bullet if I back out of the deal." She ripped the packet open with her canines, and Finn dodged his eyes away.

Upending a bottle of syrup over his waffle, he lifted his chin toward the windows. "Sun's not even up."

"Yup. Best part of the day."

He wanted to tell her that technically it wasn't even "day" yet, but that wouldn't have helped his case. She spooned some dried cranberries into her bowl of oatmeal and added a scoop of pecans. Swept her gaze down. "Would you like some waffle with your syrup?"

"Now who's judgy?" But he looked down, and shoot, he'd been so busy thinking of a comeback he'd all but emptied out the bottle. Defiant, he jabbed in his fork and brought the whole waffle to his mouth, biting off a giant chunk.

"Taking the high ground, as always." But she sucked her lower lip into her teeth to cover up a grin. He loved that she thought he was funny. Well, he didn't *love* it. Found their shared sense of humor cool, in a detached, platonic way.

He added a few slices of bacon to the calamity on his plate, then trailed her to a table, chewing. "So what's on the agenda for today, boss?"

Sinking into a chair, she tucked both legs up under her, settling in like a cat on a sunny windowsill, cup of coffee cradled in both hands. "Uh, driving?" She bent forward and blew across the surface, lips puckered. Gosh, her mouth was pretty. "Oh, and after that, more driving."

"Seriously? We're in this beautiful desert and you have zero interest in taking in the scenery?" He picked up a piece of bacon—candied bacon, at this point—and held it out, brows raised. She shook her head, so he chomped into it. Not bad, actually.

"What part of 'my sister's wedding is in five days' do you not understand?"

"Yeah, no, I get that. I mean, that's why we're driving," he lied. "But you're not even the least bit curious about checking out what Arizona has to offer?" Time to execute the high-concept, in-depth plan he'd come up with while waiting for his waffle to cook. "The Desert Botanical Garden, perhaps?"

He rose up and pulled a brochure out of his back pocket, the one he'd found in a stack by the coffee cups, and slid it across the table. As expected, she shoved it right back.

"Hard pass."

He put another brochure on top of it. "Butterfly Wonderland?"

"Do I look like the type of girl who likes butterflies?"

"There's a type of girl who *doesn't* like butterflies?"

In answer, she dug out a scoop of marmalade with her spoon, plopped it on the oatmeal. Swirled it in. Even her hands were beautiful. Thin fingers tapering into nails painted a soft peach. At odds with her fiery temperament, and the contrast left him a little breathless.

He really wished she'd take a bite already. Not because he was watching her mouth or anything. Her luscious, plump—

"What?"

He sat up straight. "What, what?"

"Finn."

"Simone."

She blinked at him. He stared back. Sighed. He'd really been a complete idiot to ruin his chances of ever kissing her again. But if he couldn't kiss her, he could at least keep his composure long enough to seal the deal. The *business* deal, he reminded his libido.

Tipping onto the back legs of his chair, Finn used his fingertips to slide another brochure out of the rack. When he leaned forward again, her gaze shot away. Like she'd been checking him out. *Interesting.*

But not interesting enough to lose sight of his master plan. "Grand Canyon."

She shook her head, chewing. Swallowed and said, "That's three and a half hours north. We're headed east."

"Did you study maps all night or something?" Not answering, she took a bite, and he laughed. "Oh my gosh, you did, didn't you?" Actually, that played right into his hand.

"In that case, you're aware that the picturesque town of Sedona"— he unfurled the final pamphlet and held it up in front of his face—"is an hour closer. With scenery rivaling the beauty of the Grand Canyon."

"Ha," she said. "Is that gem written in the brochure?"

He put it down, scanned the trifold page. "It is not, but it should be." She was looking at the pictures. "Beautiful, right? Majestic, even." He was laying it on as thick as the layer of syrup on his waffle, but it seemed to be working.

After another moment's consideration, Simone sat back and folded her arms. "You promised me we'd get back in time for my sister's bachelorette party. That's the only reason I agreed to this drive."

He licked his lips. "Right, and we will. But you're the one who wanted to stop overnight. What's one more detour?"

"First of all, this wasn't a detour. Phoenix was on the way. And secondly, I needed a break from you, okay?"

Oh. Okay.

"Oh gosh, now you're doing it again. The pouty face."

He bit his lip. "The one that made you kiss me?"

"See?" She sat forward and shoved a spoonful of oatmeal in her mouth, talking while she chewed. "This is why I needed a break."

Ohh. That was new information. He pressed a thumb to his lips, to test a theory. Simone dodged her eyes down, quick, then coughed, and he smiled. "So you liked the kiss?"

"I wasn't the one who said it was a mistake."

She had him there. Except despite what he'd said, his only mistake was pulling away. "Okay. But Sedona . . ."

She laughed. "What is it with you and this sightseeing kick?"

Besides the joy of seeing the country—he wasn't faking an interest in exploring—he desperately needed more time to prove he wasn't a total jerk. "You're not the least bit interested in seeing cactuses up close?"

"Cacti. And what's so cool about them? They're basically pine trees' big bad cousins."

"What?"

This time she chewed and swallowed before answering, her thin gold bracelet sliding down her arm as she gestured. "The spikes. They're basically more aggressive pine needles."

He tipped his head back and laughed. "Wow. Just . . . wow." He bent and shoved a forkful of waffle in. Winced, regretting it. So. Much. Sugar. "So you really wanna drive straight back home?"

Simone nodded. "That's literally what we agreed to."

"Do not pass go. Do not collect two hundred dollars." Or two hundred *thousand*, because if they got back home with her still unconvinced, there went his chances.

She pillowed her chin on her knuckles and blinked at him, angelic. That couldn't bode well. "How about we drive straight home, only stopping for gas and caffeine. How does that sound?"

Finn gave a thumbs-down. "You make me sad, Simone." He picked up her coffee and took a big gulp before she could stop him.

"You make my head hurt, Finn." She went to take a drink but wrinkled her nose and stood up. She grabbed a clean mug off the stack. Something about the gesture was so petulant that it warmed his heart and pissed him off at the same time.

"Maybe I'll save you the effort of weaseling out of the deal, because I don't want to be in business with a party pooper."

She put the mug back, stomped over, and took a big, hearty swig of their shared coffee. "I am so not a party pooper. I'm the fun one."

He snorted. "Keep telling yourself that."

"I know what you're doing, and I'm okay with it, because I wanted to see the cactuses anyway."

"Cacti. And no, you didn't."

"Then why are they in my search history?" She pulled out her phone and swiped at it. Held it up for him to see.

He squinted at the screen. "You've been googling cactuses, and you sat there letting me give you the whole spiel?"

She shrugged and put her phone down. "It's fun to watch you do your thing."

Calm down, libido.

"Plus, we do need to get back to Illinois sooner rather than later." She poked her spoon at him to emphasize her point. "No more detours after this. I wasn't messing around about that part."

"Why are you the way you are?"

"I dunno," she said. "But I think you like it."

He smiled. Dang it. He did.

CHAPTER 19

SIMONE

Alisha:
Are you seriously driving back?

Alisha:
Answer your phone!

Alisha:
Why did I have to hear from Chantal
that you decided to drive back??

Alisha:
Why did I have to hear from Chantal that you're
DRIVING ACROSS THE COUNTRY WITH A STRANGER???

Alisha:
If you get murdered trying to make it back for my
bachelorette party, I'll never forgive myself.

Alisha:

I will NOT be haunted by you, Simone.

Alisha:

Fine, you're dead. Meg is now de facto maid-of-honor.

Simone pushed the call button, and a few moments later Alisha's laugh rattled against her eardrums. "She lives!"

"Shut up. I thought you were worried." Simone leaned back against the car, taking in the panoramic view of red canyon walls and green foliage. They'd pulled off at a roadside park, and she had to admit, the scenery was drop-dead gorgeous.

Maybe a poor choice of words, considering she was in the desert with a man she didn't know all that well . . . a man currently snapping close-ups of a chipmunk perched on a boulder. She really wasn't too concerned.

"Oh, I was worried. Very much so." Her sister's chuckle belied her words. "But let's be real. You're pretty much a gremlin: hard to kill and feisty as heck. I had faith in your ability to stay alive."

"Thanks for that gruesome vote of confidence." She hunched her shoulders against the brisk air and watched Finn spin in a circle, taking in the view.

He'd promised her to be out of here in under ten minutes, but she could already tell she'd have to drag him back into the car. The fresh air was so clearly his natural element—something they had in common. If only that were the only thing.

She shut her eyes to block out the unwelcome—natural—beauty and small *feeling* stirring in her chest. *Bleurgh.* A moment later, something warm brushed up against her. A hand tightened on her waist, and she shrieked, eyes popping open. Finn.

He leaned into her, warmth radiating from under his plaid jacket, his hair a brush of shampoo fresh against her cheek. "Say cheese." He clicked the camera button.

"Is that him?" On the other end of the line, Alisha was probably hopping up and down like an eager bunny. "Can I talk to him?"

"Why, so you can decide if he's a serial killer by his voice?"

Finn bent his head to the phone and said, "Not a serial killer."

She covered up the mouthpiece. "A little privacy?"

"No problem." He dropped his arm from around her, leaving her cold, and gave a jaunty salute. "I'll just be up the trail, then."

Simone gave him a one-finger salute of her own and was rewarded by his laugh. She didn't like making him laugh. Not at all. It was just easier than dealing with the aftermath of his pouty face.

"So are you going to at least tell me where you are?" The voice from her phone dragged her mind away from the way her body seemed determined to succumb to Finn's charm.

Ugh, her worrywart sister. "If I don't, are you going to report me to Pops?"

"No, but I sure as heck will if you don't tell me where you are. Seriously, Simone, this is a crazy stunt, even for you."

Simone sighed. "I've known Finn since spring, Alisha. He's not exactly a stranger. Besides, what would his motive be to kill me?"

"The same motive you have to kill him? Two hundred thousand dollars spilt zero ways instead of two?"

"Okay, but there'd be a huge spotlight on him."

"The very fact we're even having a conversation about you being on the highway with a potential murderer is insane. You realize that, right?"

She squinted down the path. Finn was nowhere in sight. Dang it. He'd wandered off.

"I said—"

"Yes, sis. I heard you." She opened the car door and reached in to grab her purse, then locked it. "And you don't have to worry about me. I've got everything handled." As in, she was busy racking her brain for a way out of the deal, with no solution in sight.

"Does that mean you're taking the franchise deal? Is that really what you want?"

She didn't know what she wanted at this point, but telling Alisha so would make her look wishy washy. Indecisive. Not up for the task of running a business all on her own. "It's the smart choice." Simone picked her way down the trail Finn had followed. "A way to secure Honey and Hickory's legacy." Pops's legacy. *Her* legacy. Was it wrong to want to forge a new path, one that might end in failure?

"And it will make you happy? Trying to re-create copies of Honey and Hickory across America?"

Not at all. That much she knew for certain. Everything she loved about the restaurant was tied to Hawksburg—delivering meals and catching up with locals, cooking with food grown in her neighbors' backyards, feeding the crowd that gathered to celebrate after the basketball team won the state championship.

But happiness wasn't everything. What mattered more was esteem, and with a successful franchise, no one would be able to deny her competence.

When the silence went on too long, Alisha said, "I'm sorry, Sim. You know I trust you. If you think this is the best decision, then I'm all for it."

She could speak up, share her worries. But then Alisha would know she had doubts, might start to think maybe Simone wasn't the right Blake to take over Honey and Hickory after all.

"That means a lot, sis. But I've gotta let you go because if I don't find this man, we're never going to make it home in time for your party."

"About that—you really don't need to worry about making it back in time for the bachelorette party. Matter of fact, let's go ahead and call it off now." Alisha letting her off the hook. But she didn't need to be cut any slack. She could handle it all, all on her own.

"That kind of lame attitude is exactly why I need to be there," Simone teased, refusing to take the out. "This is your last hurrah of freedom."

"Sis, I've never felt more free than I do with Quentin. Someday you'll feel this way too."

Maybe. But the prospect of losing a chunk of her business to Finn soured her against the idea of tying up her future with anyone else's. "Save that sappiness for your vows. You know what I mean about the party. This is a big deal. In just a few days you're gonna be a wifey, and we all know that man's been dying to put a baby in you since day one—"

"Sim!"

"So we need to bid farewell to your single life in a proper way."

"So that's why you're driving two thousand miles. Just to give me a big send-off?"

She stumbled on a loose rock. "Yup."

"Not because you might be catching feelings for this guy?"

"Like a head cold?"

"Something like that," Alisha said, a grin audible in her words.

Simone sneezed. "I'm immune."

"Right, well, in that case, I'll leave you to it. Don't text and drive."

"Never do."

"Love you, lady."

"Love you, sis." She rang off, rubbing her arms against the chill seeping through her down coat. At least her detailed packing list was coming in handy. But where the heck was her wannabe partner?

Simone crunched along the trail, listening to the leaves rustle in the canyon breeze. Alisha liked to tease her that she was a country bumpkin, but the truth of it was that she loved her small town. Knowing everyone was where they should be, doing what they'd been doing since she could remember. The orderly lines of plowed fields, knowing every turn of the winding gravel roads.

"Finn?" she called. Around her, the canyon walls stretched behind the border of trees.

Wilderness was disordered, chaotic. Unpredictable. The leaves flipped upside down, revealing their silvery undersides. She hurried around a turn and ran smack dab into a plaid-clad chest. "Oof."

She found herself with a noseful of fabric softener and pine. A combination that shouldn't have worked, but dang, it totally did.

"Found me." His hands were on her elbows. To steady her? That would imply swooning or knees buckling or something mushy like sour old grapes. Besides, the effect his touch had on her was anything but stabilizing.

If she believed in metaphorical butterflies—which she didn't—she might think they were fluttering around her throat. Since she didn't, she chalked it up to pheromones. Really strong pheromones. Industrial-strength pheromones.

"Too bad." She wrenched her elbows back, and he let go. "I was hoping a cougar got you."

"They have those here?" His eyes were bright.

"Why do you look excited? Planning to feed me to one?"

"Simone, if I was gonna murder you, I would've done it back in California. We were closer to the border." With a rakish grin, he started walking.

She trotted to catch up. "You do know cougars aren't house cats, right? You can't pet them. I worry for your safety—" *Oh.*

She looked up from watching her step on the rocky path to find Finn naked.

Okay, not naked, but halfway there. His jacket and shoes lay in a heap on the rocks at his feet, and he was in the process of tugging off his shirt.

"What are you doing?" She stopped, giving him a wide berth. She knew all too well that getting up close would only lead to bad decisions.

"I'm assuming that's rhetorical." His words were muffled as he pulled his T-shirt over his head. He let it drop at his feet, then met her eyes, seemingly at ease in his half-dressed state.

At her arched brow, he swept a hand toward the river. The motion highlighted the smooth lines of his obliques, his lower abs taut above the waistband of his jeans. "Swimming."

"You can't swim in this weather!" Maybe she wouldn't have to murder him after all. The elements would do it for her.

"But there's a natural waterslide here."

"For summertime. As you so astutely pointed out yesterday, it's *December*."

"In Arizona." He unbuckled his belt.

"Northern Arizona. They're predicting snow tonight." She licked her lips, eyes zeroing in on the button of his jeans. "Are you planning to take those off?"

"I am." He grinned.

"What?" Heat crawled up under her collar to blaze across her cheeks.

"I am"—his canines flashed—"planning to take these off."

He'd moved on to the button of his jeans now, his belt hanging open. She swallowed.

"Eyes up here, Ms. Blake." He snapped his fingers, and she jerked her eyes up, ears attuned to the sound of his zipper sliding down.

"You can't just skinny-dip at a public park in December," she hissed.

"Oh, so it would be okay in July?"

Was he actually about to strip down to his underwear right now, right here? And, more pressing . . . Did she *want* him to?

Heck yeah, she did.

A clunking sound reached her ears. His belt. Hitting the ground. She shouldn't. She must. She looked down. "You had swim trunks on this whole time?"

He nodded. "I'm not about to go to jail for public indecency. Then how would I torture you?"

"I'm sure you could torment me from the grave, Finnegan." But she cocked her head. The swimsuit didn't leave all that much to the imagination. Topless Finn was still a whole lot . . .

She shook her head to clear it and squinted at him. "Did you put those on when you woke up this morning, weirdo?"

"No, I put them on after you agreed to the plan." He stepped out of his puddle of jeans like all of this was commonplace. "The brochure mentioned a natural waterslide."

"Okay, park ranger. Did the brochure also mention hypothermia? You're shivering already."

"Am not."

"Are too."

On impulse, Simone stepped forward and wrapped her arms around him. The man was ridiculous, standing here half-naked—mostly naked—in freezing temps. She couldn't stand idly by. It would be irresponsible.

"Simone?"

"Mm-hmm."

"Are you hugging me right now?"

"I'm saving your life."

"If you're trying to do the skin-to-skin thing, you forgot to unzip your coat."

She shoved him away. "You are too much for your own good."

"Too much what?"

"You know what."

A half smile lifted the edge of his lips. "She thinks I'm handsome." He put his hands on his hips, his fingertips pressing into the dips. He looked away toward the trees, then bit his lip. Shook the hair out of his eyes before fixing her with a look from under the dark fringe.

Gosh, did he learn that in some class somewhere, under the category Smolder 101?

"Of course I think you're handsome. I kissed you!" It was the rest that she couldn't handle.

"Ms. Blake has a thing for pesky, irritating—"

"You are quite possibly the worst person I've ever met." She stomped off toward the water's edge and plopped down on a rock. Folding her legs under herself, she selected a flat stone from the ground nearby. She cocked her elbow back and flung the stone, sending it skipping along the surface.

A shadow fell across her. She pushed pebbles aside, digging out another piece of loose shale.

Finn sat down next to her, drawing one knee up to his chin. "Is that why you're so tense? Because you want to kiss me again?"

She tossed the rock, counting the skips, and he prodded her knee with his chilly knuckles.

"I'm not tense." She hated how huffy she sounded. "And if I wanted to kiss you again, it would be a moot point, because I hate you."

He snorted. "Got it." He drew up the other knee and clasped his arms around them, the dark ink of his tattoos a contrast to his fair skin, and rested his cheek on his knees. His deep-brown eyes watched her for a moment. "Is there anything I can do?"

She selected another rock. Tossed it. "Start wearing a bag over your head? And maybe like a postapocalyptic handwoven robe."

He laughed, and she couldn't help but notice the way his stomach tightened. "I meant anything I can do to make amends."

"Back out of the deal?" She twisted her lips in a rueful smile. "Yeah, didn't think so. You don't really care if I like you. You care if I trust you enough to go into business with you."

"Can't it be both?" He spoke softly, and she hated the vulnerability in his eyes because it mirrored her own. He couldn't take down her walls. If he disarmed her, what would be left? A shell no one wanted.

"So you admit you've been trying to steal my business from day one."

He jabbed his hands back through his hair. "How many times do I have to tell you? No. I never would've gone on that show if I would've known you'd be there, because I would've known it would be a waste of time. Put us up against one another, and nine times out of ten you come out on top."

He sat up and stretched one leg out toward the water. Didn't dip his feet in, she noticed.

"The tenth time was a draw. Those weren't odds I would've taken. But a miracle happened. I got a chance. And so did you. I'm not trying to steal your business. All I wanna do is build it." At her frown, he said, "*Add* to it."

"Take half of it." No matter how sweet he was today, if she gave in, on Monday she'd be signing her future away. "You've got to understand something, Finn. It's bad enough that everyone thinks I've got no business running Pops's restaurant. If I give you half, it will prove to everyone I couldn't do this alone."

His thick brows pinched together. "No one does things alone."

"What about my grandpa? He started Honey and Hickory with a couple hundred dollars and a smoker parked on the roadside. My sister opened up a cookie shop in Chicago, all by herself. And you went on *The Executives* with a sauce you created from scratch."

"And I launched it with the help of my best friend, Darius. You think I know how to create a website? Manage e-commerce? Without help, I'd still be a busboy."

"Yeah, but you're not. You're the owner of a barbecue sauce company that two of the richest people in America want a part of." She stood up, because she couldn't be here anymore.

"That's where you're wrong." He followed suit and scrambled to his feet at the canyon's edge. "They don't want a part of Finn's Secret Sauce. They want a part of us. You and me. We're in this together, whether you like it or not. If you back out of the deal, you think the executives will take a chance on me alone? Heck no."

"They don't want to take a chance on me alone either. No one thinks I'm good enough on my own." Never far off, the memory rushed to the forefront and out of her mouth before she could hold it back. "Junior year of high school, my grandma got sick. Cancer, just like Momma. And I dropped all my extracurriculars, picked up extra shifts at the restaurant, all to take pressure off Pops so he could take care of Gran. But then over Christmas break, my sister came home and announced she'd dropped out of college."

"Why?"

"Why do you think? To take care of Gran and Pops, because she didn't think I was doing a good enough job." She'd failed her family when they needed her most.

"I'm sure that's not why."

"Really? Alisha was one semester away from graduation. Why else would she drop everything?" To pick up her baby sister's slack. Simone's efforts weren't enough then, and they hadn't been enough to win her an investment either. "And what's more, Pops didn't even question it. Made it clear everything I'd done wasn't good enough. Would never be good enough. So I left."

"But you came back." His brown eyes searched hers, but he didn't need to know her reason for leaving Chicago. Didn't need to know she'd come back home out of necessity.

"When my sister offered the restaurant, I thought it would be a chance to do what I couldn't do all those years ago—prove to my family I had what it takes. Instead, all I've done is embarrass myself on national TV."

"Simone—" He reached out for her hand, and she spun around, in no mood for any more of Finn's pity. But her elbow knocked into his chest and sent him tumbling off the ledge.

CHAPTER 20

Finn

Like a boulder careering off a mountainside, Finn tumbled off the canyon edge and plunged into the icy water. Ho-ly crap. That stung. His only experience with swimming was in the heated shallow end at the YMCA, and even that felt cold on the first plunge. This wasn't cold. This was like diving into a brain freeze. Penguins would need mittens to swim in this.

And then there was the little detail that he couldn't swim. He kicked his legs and brushed gravel. Vaguely remembering something about pushing off the bottom, he jammed his toes in, tried to jump. Didn't get purchase, so he tried again. Kicked hard and broke the surface. Gasped a half breath.

He willed his feet to paddle, his arms to churn, but he sank under again. Struggled to bring his head above water and heard a disembodied voice shout, "Finn!"

This time when his head dipped under, a hand clasped around his arm and tugged him up again. He broke the surface, not drawing any air because he was panicked. Water rushed into his mouth and he inhaled it, then sputtered, coughing. His vision blurred with wavy drips.

"Can you kick, Finn?" Simone's voice was raw, harsh. "I need you to help me out here. Can you do that?"

He kicked, or at least he must've. He couldn't feel his legs, but the canyon wall drew nearer as Simone pulled him to the edge, her grip iron on ice.

"Grab the wall, Finn. You've got this."

With great effort, he raised his arm out of the water and caught the canyon rim. Dragged himself up while Simone tugged until his chest scraped against the rock, then his stomach, and he was free. Coughing, he rolled over.

"Jeez, are you crazy?" Her face appeared above him, her eyes angry. No, not angry. Worried. "If you can't swim, why were you wearing a swimsuit?"

Good question. But he'd only planned to wade, not jump in. Probably a bad time to mention she'd knocked him off balance, given that she'd rescued him and all.

She unzipped her jacket and pulled it off, and for a disjointed second he thought she was going to do skin-to-skin, for real this time. Even through the layers of bulky coat, her hug earlier had felt amazing, as much as he hated to admit it. But then she helped him sit up and slung the coat across his shoulders. Less nice than her touch, but practical. "Can you make it back, or should I call for help?"

His teeth chattered too much to answer, but he managed to shake his head.

Hooking an arm around his elbow, she tugged him up as he scrambled to his feet. He slumped against her thin shoulders, legs trembling from adrenaline, maybe, or cold. He hated himself for leaning on her, even more so because he liked it. She wasn't doing this to be near him. Feelings didn't factor in. And that shouldn't matter. Didn't matter.

They reached the car, and she pulled the passenger door open. Practically shoved him in. If he needed confirmation this was basic kindness and nothing more, then he had it. She jogged around to the other door and hopped in, turning on the car in the same motion, and cranked up the heat.

"D-d-don't you w-want the top down?" He tried to smile, but his lips were numb.

"Half-drowned and he's still got jokes." Simone made a disapproving face, but worry still puckered her brow. "Now take off your swimsuit."

"Excuse me, what?" Maybe his ears were clogged from all that river water.

"Your trunks are sopping wet! You need to get them off so you can warm up."

He crossed his arms over his chest, trying to look intimidating—hard to do when his whole body was a giant shiver. "I am not getting naked in front of you."

"Really, Finn?" She was sounding less worried and more exasperated by the minute. "You're gonna let your pride make you sick?"

"The first time you see my goods is not going to be when they're shriveled and—" He gestured vaguely to his crotch with a shaking hand.

"First time? As in there'll be a second? You must be delusional from cold." Her gaze was withering. As if his body needed any more excuse to shrivel up. "And dude, I don't plan to look. What kind of perv do you take me for?"

"The cute kind."

"Definitely delusional. Listen, I'm going back to grab your clothes," she said. "You can strip while I'm gone."

"That actually s-sounds less f-fun, come to think of it." But she was already out, jogging up the trail in only her T-shirt, and he realized she'd left him with her coat. She'd be freezing. Shame curled through his chest, but he arched up to peel off his swim trunks. He hadn't been kidding about the state of things down there. Now was not his time to shine.

His trembling fingers caught at the waistband of his swim trunks but couldn't seem to latch on. He managed to grab hold on the second try and shimmied the wet fabric down his thighs and kicked his legs free. And then he was naked in a rental car, the dripping water from his hair pooling on the seat back between his shoulder blades. Goodbye, deposit.

Simone opened the door with her hand over her eyes. "Decent?"

He scrambled to pull her jacket—the only dry clothing within reach—into his lap. Shoot, that was probably super creepy. Too late now.

"Good to go," he answered, the words coming out as a rough scratch, and he bunched the coat in his fingers.

Keeping her eyes carefully averted, Simone climbed in and put the car in gear, turning out of the lot onto the winding canyon road. Ten minutes of throat clearing, awkward shifting on the seat, and foggy windows later, they pulled onto a dirt road and stopped in front of a rustic lodge.

She put the car in park. Turned to him, all business. "Okay, so I'm going to see about getting us a deal on a room for a few hours. Worst-case scenario, we pay the full rate, but you need a hot shower and some warming up. If you die of hypothermia, everyone will blame me, and goodbye my chances of a deal with *The Executives*."

"And also, I'd be dead," he pointed out.

"That, I could live with."

"Right. Of course. So are you going to check in, or should I?" Finn acted like he was going to lift up the jacket, and Simone shot sideways so fast her elbow collided with the glass.

"No. I've got it. You just . . . sit tight."

She was out the door and up the low wooden porch steps in a flash, disappearing inside the leaded glass door. He shouldn't mess with her, especially when messing with her did a number on him. But she brought out the worst in him, in the best possible way.

He was sinking his head back against the headrest with a groan when his phone chimed. Shoot, that might be Bella, asking for a status update. Where had Simone stashed his clothes? He craned his neck, checking the back seat. His jeans lay in the footwell, and he grabbed them, then pulled out his phone.

Bella:
Your plan to get this woman on your side is really screwing with my schedule. I never realized how much you do around here.

Finn:
Careful, that sounded strangely close to a compliment.

Bella:
I'll flatter you all day if it gets you back to work quicker. Any progress getting that woman to see reason?

Progress? More like the mother of all setbacks. First the kiss, now his impulsive nature coming to bite him in the butt.

He was typing out a response when a knock sounded on the window.

He looked up, expecting to find an indignant Simone. Nope. A mountain-size man with a long red beard covering his gray peacoat stood outside the car, frowning.

Finn cracked the window. "Hello."

"Hi. If you're looking for the nudist ranch, it's up the road another couple miles."

"What? I—no. No, this is just an accident."

"You're accidently . . . naked?" The man's British accent made the word sound extra indecent.

"No. I mean, dude. I'm not naked." He pulled the coat up higher on his lap. "Well, clearly I am. But not exposed. I mean, I'm not about to flash anyone. And I am not a nudist."

"Look, *dude*," the man said, making the word sound like an insult. "No judgment. But we're not that kind of establishment."

The front door opened and another guy came out, thin and slight, with dreadlocks pulled back in a ponytail.

The guy who was a ringer for Tormund Giantsbane straightened up and disappeared from view, like a mountain shifting. "Elliot, I told you not to run that ad."

"For the last time, Carter, the ad is not the issue," the other man said, his accent bringing to mind nature-documentary narrators. "You can't keep turning away people just because you're worried about the noise."

"But this is a retreat. We can't have couples knocking beds against the wall at all hours of the day. And now this!" A finger came down level with the window, and Finn shrank away. "This man here is naked. Fully nude—"

"Again, not fully nude." Finn flipped up the head of the hood and shook it back and forth.

Goliath ignored him. "I'm off to the store. But Elliot, *handle this.*" He stomped off to a jeep that shifted as he settled his bulk inside; then he sped off in a flurry of gravel.

"I'm sorry. Really." The man on the porch raised his voice to be heard over the roar of the engine. "Your girlfriend explained the situation!" he shouted.

"Not my girlfriend," Finn said, and the guy cupped a hand to his ear.

"What?"

"I said—"

"Still can't—" The man waved a hand in front of his face and trotted down the stairs. "Know what? I'll just pop in and drive you there, shall I?"

Without waiting for an answer, he opened the door and got in. "Given the situation," he said, gesturing to the coat precariously covering Finn's junk, "I think it's best if you don't walk." He chuckled as he shifted the car into reverse, like people showing up naked at the lodge was an everyday occurrence. Maybe it was, judging by Mountain Man's reaction.

"Your girlfriend went on ahead. Said she wanted to get the heat on for you."

Finn pursed his lips. "Of course she did." Probably just thought it would be hilarious if he had to maneuver into the driver's seat while nude.

Navigating up a winding dirt road through pine trees, Elliot said, "You know, you really shouldn't go swimming this time of the year. A polar plunge might sound fun, but hypothermia is a real threat." He added, "And don't listen to Carter. I put you in one of the cabins, not the main lodge, so you needn't fret about the noise. Not that it matters, anyway. I keep telling him, if he turns away honeymooners, we lose half our business!"

"We're not—"

"Not married? Yeah, I gathered, but that won't stop you, eh?" The man grinned at him again, then tapped his thumbs on the steering wheel, face forward. "Er, sorry. Overstepped my bounds. And here we are!"

He slammed the car into park outside a small log cabin, and Finn snapped forward against his seat belt. "Well, I'll leave you to it, since you're, er . . ." Leaving the thought unfinished, the man got out and offered a quick wave, then headed up the path.

The half-typed text nagged at his mind. What could he tell Bella that would set her mind at ease? He knew she was worried about him, for all her talk about messed-up shifts. But he honestly didn't know where he stood with Simone.

He'd wait to reply until they got back on the road. In the meantime, he needed to shift his focus away from Simone, the person he was quickly developing a thing for, and onto Simone, the potential partner.

Finn glanced around to make sure there was no one in sight, then grabbed the keys, wrapped Simone's coat around himself like a towel, and inched his way out of the car. No need to subject anyone to an accidental peep show, least of all Simone. Talk about a bad start toward building a business relationship.

After tiptoeing up the wooden front steps, he twisted the brass doorknob with icy fingers and stepped inside.

CHAPTER 21

SIMONE

Simone knelt in front of a wood-burning stove, clueless and frustrated, clutching the fire-starter bundle that Elliot from the front desk had handed her, along with the room key, attached to—big surprise—another piece of weathered wood. This place really shoved rustic down your throat.

Which wasn't the worst thing. Under other circumstances, being stuck in a quaint log cabin with no Wi-Fi and someone as sexy as Finn would've definitely had its advantages. But now the perplexing heater was just another obstacle in her path.

The rest of the cabin had been rehabbed, from the inset lighting spaced between knotty pine rafters in the whitewashed ceiling to the gleaming white pine floors. Would it have killed the owners to put in a heater from the twenty-first century? Casting a glance over her shoulder, she listened for the rumble of an engine.

Finn would be here any second, and she needed to get the fire started. Needed to get him warm so they could get back on the road. Needed to find her mojo again, get back in control.

Turning back to the stove, she caught sight of a laminated paper shoved halfway under the stove. Aha! She slid it out with a fingertip, then rubbed the resulting soot onto her jeans. Step-by-step instructions. Her shoulders relaxed, the peace of diagramed order washing away the anxiety that threatened like storm clouds on the horizon. She arranged the logs and kindling according to the diagram, then flicked the lighter on, but it wouldn't catch. Tried again, and the door opened in a whoosh of cold air just as the lighter caught, extinguishing it.

"Hey!" Pivoting in her crouch, she nearly fell over at the sight that greeted her. Finn stood in the door with her coat draped around his hips like an ancient warrior returning from battle. Tattoos snaked their way around his right arm, up and around to wrap his shoulder in designs. His chest tapered down to a narrow waist, a delicious V framing the trail of dark-brown hair below his belly button—and that's when Simone realized she was ogling the line of Finn's happy trail.

"Like what you see, Blake?"

She took her time lifting her eyes to his face—no sense letting him know she minded being caught out—and twisted her lips. "What I see is a shivering mess who needs to get his butt in the shower before he succumbs to hypothermia."

He jerked his chin toward the stove. "A fire would help."

"I'm working on it."

"Need a hand?" Finn stepped forward, revealing a peek of hip bones and one long, hard thigh.

"No!" Simone shot out a hand reflexively—if he came closer she might combust, unlike the logs in the stove—and Finn stumbled back, knocking up against the door. His eyes darted around the room, and she followed his gaze.

With him inside, she realized how small the cabin was. The wood-burning stove she was fussing over claimed the corner of the "living room," with a tan leather couch next to it. Across the room lay a queen-size bed, topped with a wool blanket and bracketed by end tables. And that was it. A couch, a bed, and a door propped open with a rock—pray it led to a bathroom with indoor plumbing.

"Just one bed?" Their eyes met across the few feet that separated them, the deep surety of his voice gone strangled and hoarse. "Which is fine, because we won't be sleeping here. But if we were, I'd take the couch."

She rolled her eyes. "Everyone's chivalrous when it's hypothetical. Why don't you hurry and shower so we can get back on the road. If it comes to that, we'll duke it out over the bed later."

He grinned. "And when you say 'duke it out,' you mean of course—"

"Get in the freaking shower, Finn."

He laughed, scurrying toward the bathroom like a streaker. The lighter finally ignited again as he turned sideways to enter the door, his wide shoulders dipping down to a smooth back that ended in twin dimples above the curve of his butt . . .

Her thumb blistered in a burn, and she dropped the lighter onto the tiles. Distracting, infuriating . . . she shoved her thumb into her mouth, sucking on it and recounting all the reasons she could not pursue Finn's ambiguous take on the one-bedroom situation.

One: he was a customer-stealing rat. Two: he was an investor-stealing rat. Three: he'd called her entitled. Reason Four was on the tip of her tongue when Finn leaned out of the bathroom. "Good news! There's plumbing." Canines flashing in a bright grin, he disappeared again, and Simone fought against a treacherous grin and lost.

Reason Number Four why Finn Rimes was off limits: if it weren't for the business, she might actually be interested in him. Not just his flat abs and sexy smile, but *him*. The way he wore his heart on his sleeve and pushed all her buttons and managed to find a common ground with everyone. Even her. If she thought too hard about it, she might actually *like* the guy. And that was Not Okay.

"This is not okay," she repeated aloud, then latched the smoky glass door of the stove. That way lay madness. Pretty soon she'd be drowning in mushy nonsense like her besotted bride-to-be big sister.

Bad enough one Blake girl had bit the emotional dust. She needed to keep it together for both of them.

Behind the knotty pine door, Finn was singing a medley of show tunes, and the fact that it didn't curdle her blood meant something was very, very wrong.

On her feet in a flash, Simone went out to the car and fetched their bags. Set them up side by side on the luggage racks and unzipped them. Stepped back. Shook her head and carried her suitcase to the other side of the room, shoved it up against the wall. Pushed the couch up against the wall for good measure. Would've drawn a line down the center of the room if she'd had a can of spray paint handy.

By the time the shower shut off, she was waiting by the door, wiping her palms on her jeans, willing herself not to think of Finn in there naked and wet—*you've already seen him almost naked and wet*—and jeez, that wasn't working. She rapped with her knuckles in a quick one-two knock. He stopped humming.

"Uh, yeah?" He sounded wary.

"I have some clothes, since you went in there—" Don't say it, don't *think* it. "Naked."

The door creaked open a crack. His hair hung down over his brow, darkened with damp. "Thanks." He reached out a hand, but she held on to the bundle as he tried to tug it away.

"Didn't you bring anything comfier than jeans?"

"I guess the suit doesn't count?" he asked, and she rolled her eyes, allowing her annoyance to put some distance between them, because Lord knows she needed it.

"No, and I cannot believe you balled it up and shoved it in there. That's not how you treat a suit."

"All right, Fancy Pants. Anything else you'd like to critique?"

She opened her mouth to say yes. Planned to say that she couldn't stand the way he'd crammed everything into his duffel helter skelter. Couldn't stand the way he raked a hand through his hair when he was frustrated, or the way his eyes dimmed when one of her insults landed. Couldn't stand the perfect plumpness of his lower lip, which was currently pulled between his teeth, and oh for the love of . . . she was staring at his mouth again.

"Simone?" She blinked twice. Slow. Pulled the door closed as his laugh echoed on the other side. Why did he insist on torturing her? Why did she insist on letting him? Dazed and disoriented, she strode over to the couch and sank down.

Meg had texted her, and when she opened it, a picture of Willow frolicking in the snow filled the screen, and Simone smiled at the sight.

Simone:
Someone looks happy.

Meg:
Very. I would say she misses you, but I think it's safe to say she's living her best life.

Simone:
That makes one of us. Our trip hit another speed bump.

Meg:
What happened?

Simone:
Finn happened.

Meg:
??

Simone:

He fell into a creek. Getting warmed up now and hopefully back on the road soon.

Meg:

"Warmed up." Lol

Simone:

I hope your truck gets stuck in a snowdrift.

Meg:

Love you too.

Chuckling, she took a proof-of-life selfie and sent it to Alisha, along with: **Still alive, see you soon.** To her grandparents, who she was pretty certain had washed their hands of worrying about her after her first year of college in the city, she sent a text recapping the gorgeous scenery, but omitting any reference to Finn's ice bath and their current delay.

Half a day lost already, not even counting their overnight stay.

No missed calls, not even from Pops, who she knew must be wondering if she'd lost her dang mind in agreeing to the deal. But he'd vowed to let her run the place as she saw fit, and he trusted her. Much more than she trusted herself. She didn't want to talk to him until her plan was finalized. What would he think if he knew she was stranded and fighting for a do-over, rather than getting it right the first time?

The creak of hinges brought her eyes up, and she found Finn standing by the fire, toweling off his hair, in those same jeans from summer, feet bare on the hearth.

She needed to put some space between them. Like, now.

Her mind on the bathroom and a closed door and a cold shower, she leaped up and ran straight into Finn's chest. His rumpled—because seriously, someone needed to teach this man how to fold—shirt smelled like fresh laundry and home. Not Okay. His arms came up to steady her, and her heart flip-dipped.

"Whoa, Tornado. Where's the fire?"

She should've said, "In the stove," just to be annoying. But that would only be half-true. Because the fire was right here, between them. In the air, popping like static. In his eyes, gone dark and intense.

Her breath caught when she realized he was still holding her arms. "I was gonna shower. You're all fresh, and I probably smell like trail dirt and river water."

"You smell amazing." He spoke low, and she gave in to desire, her body arching toward him. "Like always." Finn's hands fisted in the hem of her hoodie, and he tugged her closer, bringing their hips together. She gasped. "Like a garden after a thunderstorm."

He breathed out a shuddery breath, and she found herself running her hands up his chest, gripping his shoulders, eyes on his cheeks, his lips, mind everywhere and nowhere.

She answered him mindlessly. "It's my hair cream. I make it myself."

Finn swept his hands up over her shoulders. "Of course you do."

"What's that supposed to mean?"

"It means, is there anything you can't do?"

Avoid him, apparently. "Well, I've never gotten the knack for soufflés."

Finn bit out a strangled laugh. "That's your biggest flaw? That you can't make soufflés? Simone Blake, you are so adorable I could kiss you."

She met his eyes. "Then do it."

"What?"

"Kiss me, Finn."

He searched her eyes for a heartbeat, brown eyes burrowing into her soul. She squirmed under his gaze but didn't look away. She let him take her in, hold her. Then his thumb swept over her lips, parting them, and the motion broke something in her. She slid her hands up into the hair at his nape, then tugged him down.

When their lips met, relief flooded her senses, so deep she lost her footing, knees weak. He stumbled, too, crashed into her, a wave of passion cresting between them, and she let herself be obliterated, found again in the wreckage, reimagined, renewed, reborn as a creature of fire and molten gold, searing and bright.

The back of her knees hit the couch, and she fell, pulling him on top of her, their kiss broken only for a moment before Finn's lips coaxed hers open, and she let herself melt. The fleece of her jacket, soft before, scratched at her collarbones, and she lifted her hips to free it.

A groan tore out of Finn, and he dipped his hand down, fingers fumbling against hers, and in a laughing tangle they tugged the sweatshirt over her head. She lay there in an old T-shirt hiked up over her waist, but his gaze roved over her like she wore silk lingerie. The look made her feel exposed, vulnerable, where she'd always felt certain, sure.

She tipped up her chin, daring him. "What?"

"You are the most gorgeous woman alive." Then he was back, a welcome weight, grinding her into the couch, and she slipped her hands over the taut muscles of his trembling biceps. Dipped one hand under the sleeve of his shirt, palmed the intricate patterns on his arm.

Seeking more contact, she drew her fingers down to his belly button and traced them back up, reveled as he shuddered at her touch.

"You're not bad to look at either." She grinned and yanked up on the hem of his shirt, happy when he pulled it over his head, then dipped his head to kiss her again, fierce and deep.

She breathed out a moan as his tongue swept over hers. Her hand strayed up to his chest, and his heartbeat thudded against her palm, tracing the same pattern that swirled along her eyelids. Finn's arms on either side of her caged her in, but she felt free. Wide open. Known.

No animosity in this kiss, nothing to prove, only the heat of pure need, echoed in the slant of Finn's mouth over hers, the press of his body, urgent and—

"Hello in there!" The door rattled on its hinges with a knock like the battering ram of an invading army, and Finn sprang off her in a flash.

"I've got the extra blankets you asked for." The man on the other side of the door may as well have been standing in the room for how clear his voice was. The walls must have zero insulation. Had he heard them going at it like a couple in a car at a drive-in?

Finn's eyes flicked toward hers, and she pulled the chevron blanket over her chest. He snorted. "Like you're the one with an issue."

She dodged her eyes down, then back up, cheeks hot. She grabbed her sweatshirt off the floor, ready to toss it to him, but he waved her off. "It's fine." Positioned behind the door, he cracked it open and peeked out, head and shoulders exposed. Simone caught a flash of red hair that cleared the lintel of the door.

"Not a nudist, eh?" The man shoved the blankets into Finn's bare chest and closed the door himself.

Laughing, Finn turned around and tossed the blankets on the foot of the bed.

"What was all that about?" Simone sat up on her elbows.

"There was a mix-up earlier. When you left me naked in the car." Finn hitched a creamy shoulder. "He caught me in a compromised position."

She arched one eyebrow, not passing up the chance to tease him. "Oh?"

"Yeah." Finn came over and framed her with his arms. "Come to think of it, that's twice now, thanks to you." He bent his head and pressed a soft kiss to her lips.

Every fiber of Simone's being wanted to arch up into him. To close her eyes and lose herself in the beautiful chaos of Finn. So she did the opposite.

She slid down and scooted out from under his chest, falling to her knees, and basically crawled forward until she was clear to stand, which she did, on shaky legs.

"Sim?"

Her heart cracked, hearing him say her name. She needed superglue, stat. "Just going to grab that shower. You'd better get under the blankets. You need to get warm."

"I'm plenty warm." But he sneezed. Sat down on the sofa, brow furrowed. "Look, Simone . . ."

"I can't, Finn. We can't." She took him in, brown eyes and mussed hair. Soft lips. Open heart. Wounded. She shut the door.

When she came out, Finn was curled up on the couch under a blanket. She tiptoed over, but his eyes were shut, his breath even. She bit the corner of her lip. Took another blanket off the bed and covered him up. Added another log to the fire. And crawled into bed in broad daylight, intent on getting some shut-eye for the overnight drive.

But she couldn't sleep.

CHAPTER 22

FINN

He was dead. Simone had murdered him in his sleep. Set the cabin on fire and left him to burn. That was the only explanation for the inferno in his skull. He squeezed his eyes shut tighter and prayed the end would come quick.

"I know you're awake. You can stop faking it."

He pried open his eyes, and a very blurry, very irate Simone came into view, hovering over him like the ghost of bad decisions past—starting with crossing her at the farmers' market and ending with dragging her on this cross-country exercise in futility. He blinked again, and she came into focus, curls framing her frowning face, her brow knotted in irritation.

He squinted, reassessing her expression. Not irritated. Worried. Maybe this was an apparition, after all. Human Simone would never be worried about him. "Am I dead?" His voice croaked out like a strangled frog, and he tried to swallow.

Not dead. Dead wouldn't hurt this much.

"If only I could be so lucky."

There she was. He smiled, and instantly regretted it, because even that small movement sent a bolt of pain through his throat. His skull pounded with the drums of a thousand marching bands.

"Drink," she said, holding out a bottle of water. "Can't have you dying on my watch."

He tipped up the bottle, shocked at how weak he felt, and took a sip. The water hit his tonsils like a cement truck, and he let out a gasp. Made himself go back for another swallow. Closed his eyes and collapsed back onto the pillow, spent like he'd just worked a double shift.

He felt a cool hand press against his forehead and sighed at the relief.

"Jeez, Finn, you're burning up." He might've been imagining it, but it seemed like her words held less judgment than the *You fell into a freezing river and I had to save you and you're now delaying my trip more than the snowstorm of the century* that he expected.

He opened one eye and found her unscrewing a medicine bottle. Light drifted in through the curtains—she must've shut them so the brightness wouldn't wake him. Shoot. He'd only meant to sleep an hour, not all morning. He pushed back the covers, ignoring the pounding in his head. "We need to get back on the road. Why didn't you wake me?"

"Because you've got a raging fever." She'd checked on him in his sleep? The thought was strangely comforting. "And you've been coughing in your sleep." That explained the tightness in his chest. "You're in no condition to drive right now."

She pressed a pill into his hand. Cyanide? With the delay he'd already caused, he wouldn't put poison past her.

"You must hate me." He eyed the bottle in her hands—the label read *Ibuprofen*, but he curled his palm around the pill anyway, taking no chances. Although if it was arsenic, she probably would've crushed it up in the water to be on the safe side.

"No more than yesterday," she said, and when he lifted his eyes, she was . . . well, she wasn't smiling, but she wasn't scowling either.

Whether or not she hated him didn't matter to him personally at all. Which is why he'd kissed her twice. To prove it didn't matter. He could get physical with her and suffer no ill effects because it was just an attraction—

"Finn, stop overthinking and take your pill."

Bossy, as always.

"Can't." He pushed the words past chapped lips.

"If your throat hurts, the medicine will help that too."

"No. It's not my throat." He lifted a hand to gesture at his neck and winced, letting it fall to the quilt. Jeez, his muscles ached with a constant shiver of pain. "Can't swallow pills."

She rolled her eyes heavenward, and if he didn't know better, he might've caught her lips moving in a silent prayer. But Simone Blake didn't rely on divine intervention. When she met his gaze again, she looked strained, with her sister's bachelorette party coming up and them stranded in the desert. Who could blame her? All because of his stupid scheme to get her to trust him.

But instead of tearing him a new one, she asked, "What do you do, then?"

"Take them with food."

"You want me to hide this in a banana like you're a zoo animal? You know what? Don't answer that."

Cool fingers fiddled in his palm; then the pill was gone. He closed his eyes again—avoidance was one of the few tools in his meager arsenal. A click signaled the door opening. He shivered at the gust of cold and pulled the covers up around himself.

He'd been trying to convince her she needed him. But at this point he was deadweight. His chances of winning her over had taken a nose-dive from improbable to downright impossible the second he tumbled off that ledge into the water. He shook his head at his own foolishness, and a cough racked through his body.

He was a screwup. A tagalong at best—and now, a liability.

At some point, she'd piled pillows under him like he was some sort of an invalid. *Hurry, Pa, Finn's got a fever, fetch the doc!* He laughed, which shifted his pulse to pound in his temples instead. But he had to admit, the angle was . . . nice. Comforting, even. And if he didn't move, or breathe, being upright eased the disaster stewing in his skull.

At least she hadn't rummaged in his bag again. But how would she know unzipping his bag was an invasion of the only private space he'd ever been able to count on? It was sweet of her to bring him clothes, especially when the alternative was marching out half-naked, which would've given her the wrong idea.

But if prancing around nude gave her the idea he was into her, kissing her confirmed it.

His fists bunched the blanket, and he fought down another cough, wincing at the pain in his chest and the memory of her shutting down after their kiss. Less than an hour after his vow to keep things purely business, he'd caved to his desires. Clearly this road trip had been a bad strategy. The sooner they got some space from each other, the better.

He pushed down the covers with pricking hands and willed his legs to swing off the couch, his feet finally hitting the floor with a thud that reverberated like an echo chamber in his skull. He had on one sneaker when the door swung open. Words were too much, so he lifted his foot into the other shoe, panting.

"Where are you planning to go, Superman?"

"You've gotta be back home soon." His voice lurched out like the sliding of gravel down a hillside. "Can't have you missing your sister's party."

"And if we head out tomorrow, we'll make it." Her breathing sounding strained, and he looked up to find her chin holding a lidded coffee cup in place atop what looked like an armful of snack bar. She squatted down in a slow plié like a ballet dancer, back straight, to deposit the load of fruit, granola bars, and crackers onto the coffee table. "But we can't go anywhere right now."

It was sad, and pitiful, and clearly a fever delusion, but his heart warmed at the word "we."

"You," she said, and his heart whimpered, "are going to stay in bed. Recuperating." She set down the cup and picked up the banana, peeling it. "As much as I might joke, you're no good to me dead, Finn."

Technically untrue. A dead Finn would solve a lot of her problems. "I'm no good to you alive either." He rubbed a palm over his face, remembering the pill. The room was spinning, but that could've been the slow effects of poison or the fever. Hard to tell . . . "Which means you're doing this out of the goodness of your heart. Or you like me."

"Don't flatter yourself." Her answer came quick, like she'd rehearsed. "I'm making sure you don't die on my watch because a murder investigation would be a huge time suck."

His laughter turned into a cough, demolishing his throat with stabs of pain, but his good mood remained. Something was really wrong with him if he thought her prickly sarcasm was cute, but he did. Really cute.

Simone set the half-peeled banana on the dresser and pulled something out of the bag, then tossed it into his lap. He picked it up and shook out the fabric, eyebrows tugging together when he saw what it was. "Cactus pants?"

"Pajama pants." Covered in tiny saguaro cactuses. "It's what normal humans wear for lounging."

"You bought me pants." He tried and failed to keep the awe out of his voice. "With cactuses." Like they had a history. A backstory. Inside jokes.

"Cacti." She fought to keep a smile off her face, and it only made him grin harder. "And stop making it sound like such a big deal. You packed the contents of a Levi's store and nothing else. Sleeping in jeans sucks."

As much as he wanted to disagree, the rough fabric on his overheated skin was murder. "Well, thanks. But I won't be needing them today. Because we're leaving."

"Are not."

"Are too."

"Finn, you're feverish and clearly delusional if you think I want to trust my life to you on the freeway in your current state." He narrowed his eyes, but she kicked his sneakers out of reach. "And if you say you'll just be a passenger, fine and good, but I can't drive twenty hours straight with no sleep. I know my limitations. So, we stay and you rest, because if I wind up missing Alisha's bachelorette party, you'll wish the cold killed you."

Glaring at her—for what, he wasn't certain anymore, but old habits die hard—he stood up, wobbled for a second, and puttered off to the bathroom, ridiculous pants in hand. Once inside the bathroom, he let out the cough he'd been holding in, doubling over.

"Heard that," Simone called from the other side of the door, and his coughs turned into a chuckle. Which hurt, a lot.

He shucked off the jeans—stiff and scratchy—and pulled on the pajama pants. Literal heaven. He could live in these pants forever. He could die in them.

Speaking of death . . . he met his reflection in the tiny square medicine cabinet mirror. Wished he hadn't. Scruff covered his jaw, and his eyes were rimmed with red, his nose a ringer for Rudolph's. His hair looked like his mother had mated with a werewolf, and he had the complexion of an anemic vampire.

Helpless to do anything about his appearance at this point, he pulled his toothpaste out of the travel case that he hadn't left on the sink. More evidence of Simone's well-meaning snooping. Sheesh, she had done a more thorough job on his luggage than TSA. He tightened his grip on the toothbrush against the irrational sense of violation.

He spit, his throat burning in a reminder that he was sick and royally screwed. He couldn't have sabotaged his chances with Simone more if he'd tried. He'd meant to drag out their trip a little longer to give himself more time to prove himself an asset.

Instead, he'd proved he was a liability. If they didn't make it back in time, he could kiss his chances for a partnership goodbye. She'd never speak to him again, let alone take the deal.

Except they'd kissed again. Could he blame that on delirium? No. He'd been fully lucid, every sense attuned to Simone. The peppermint from the gum she'd chewed to keep her eardrums from popping on the drive through the canyon; the warm, slick parting of her lips; the pressure of her hips as she rose to meet him . . .

He gripped the cold porcelain of the sink basin to keep himself from slipping away into the heat of the memory. A memory tainted by her breaking away, all but bolting out of the room. He'd only known her since summer, but the disappearing act she'd pulled was the first time he'd ever seen her flee.

All because of their kiss. Because of him.

Just when she'd started to let her walls down and trust him, he'd gone and ruined his chances by making things complicated. Messy. Personal.

Darius's words came back to him. Was he sabotaging himself? Or was he really falling for this pain-in-the-neck woman who also happened to be his shot at redemption?

A woman he couldn't hide from forever, at least not unless he retreated to perch on the toilet lid, because his legs had about another minute before they'd give way. He put his toothbrush away and zipped the bag. Tucking it under his arm, he opened the door.

"Do the pants fit?"

He jumped back in surprise and banged his hip on the vanity. Simone sat cross-legged, doing a puzzle on the coffee table. Her gaze slid down his legs, and his fingers tightened around the doorknob. "You look comfy."

Comfy was about the furthest from how he felt. In fact, if she kept looking at his . . . pants, then he'd have to retreat into the bathroom.

But she took a bite of muffin and went back to the puzzle. She *would* like puzzles.

"You got the fire going again." He eased out the door, holding his bruised hip, and took a defensive position against the wall, back pressed to the rough timbers. "Where did you learn how to do that? Girl Scouts?"

Simone pressed a knuckle to her lips while she chewed. Which only made him think of how they'd taste, dusted with cinnamon sugar, luscious as melted butter . . .

"I was too busy with 4-H for Girl Scouts."

He'd been distracted by her mouth, but still, *4-H*? "Half of those words make sense to me," he said, and she chuckled.

She pointed to a sooty piece of paper on the tiled hearth. "There's instructions." She stood and brushed off her hands on her pants—jeans, he noticed. Hypocrite. Then she leaned up and pulled the cord on the curtains, letting in slanting rays of afternoon sun.

He raised his arm to his eyes with a hiss.

A cackle reached his ears. "The vitamin D will do you good."

"Or turn me to ash," he scratched out.

"You're looking mighty gray, Finn." Disembodied, it was easier to hate her voice, though not by much. It was all raspy and warm. Jazz and scotch. "I thought vampires sparkled."

He wheezed out a chuckle. "Don't make me laugh."

A hand settled on his waist, and he almost collapsed at the shock of her touch. Dropped his arm and found Simone inches away.

Worry swam in her golden eyes. "Why don't you lie down before you fall over?"

No energy left to argue, he stepped toward the couch, but Simone boxed him out, their hips colliding. One way or another, this woman was going to be the death of him. He ventured a small move to the side and was stopped short by her outstretched arm.

"On the bed." She pointed, one hand on her hips. "I nearly drowned you—by accident, for the record," she said. "The least I can do is give you the comfy spot to recuperate. Ease my conscience."

He hesitated.

"Get in bed, Finn."

He hadn't realized he liked take-charge women, but dang. He almost didn't want to comply, just to see what she'd do next, but being stubborn wouldn't help his case for partnership. And whatever his growing feelings for Simone were, they had to take a back seat to his business. Darius would murder him if he found out he'd lost out on this chance because of an off-base infatuation.

He pulled back the covers and eased himself down onto the sheets, almost whimpering at the plushness of the mattress. "Are you sure you want to give it up?"

"Keep asking and I might change my mind."

Staking his claim, he pulled the covers up to his chin, and Simone snorted. She hefted a blanket off the sofa. "Warm enough?"

Despite his chattering teeth, he was burning up. "I'm good, thanks."

"Hungry?" She'd swapped the blanket for a peeled banana.

Finn narrowed his eyes. "Is that laced?"

She ducked her head, grinning.

"Jeez, Sim. That's not what I meant. I just need food *with* the pill."

She bit her lip, a foreign gesture on her for the vulnerability it revealed, and his heart squeezed. She poked her fingers into the banana and fished out a pill, making a face at the mess.

"Serves you right for trying to drug me," he said.

"Serves me right for trying to help you."

He chuckled, and her lips lifted in what looked like a reluctant smile. "Quit laughing, or I'll smear this all over you."

"You wouldn't dare."

She stalked around the bed, eyes never leaving his.

He put up both arms. "Stop, I'm sick! You wouldn't dare attack an ill man."

"Ill is right." She pulled down his arms, surprisingly strong for someone so slender, and squished a big dab of banana on his nose. "I never back down from a dare." Her eyes flicked down to where her fingers were still clasped around his arm, and he watched her chest rise, swelling against the thin fabric of her tee. His skin pricked with something other than fever, but then she let go and sat back.

She bit off the mangled part of the banana and handed it to him. Put the pill bottle on the bedside table. Brushed his hair off his forehead and ghosted a kiss across it, so quick he might've imagined the words brushing across his overheated skin. "Still burning up."

But he hadn't, because his heart was on fire too. Going down in flames.

CHAPTER 23

Finn

Crouched over a puzzle, Simone spent the afternoon in the cabin with Finn. She stayed quiet, gaze never straying from the pieces spread out in front of her, but whenever he dozed off, he awoke to the snap of a fresh log on the fire, a box of tissues on the bedside table, a fresh bottle of water with condensation slipping down the sides in crystal teardrops.

This time when he opened his eyes, the sun was setting. Simone sat folded up on the couch with a notebook, pen tapping a rhythm against her knee. The fire crackled behind the glass of the wood-burning stove, curtains half-drawn in a truce for his headache and Simone's insistence that natural light would improve his outlook and make him heal faster.

With her quiet company, this whole cabin felt robed in peace. Almost like home. Or at least the notion of home he sometimes traced at the outline of his dreams. Except she wasn't here in spirit. She was yearning for an out, and their time in this cabin was a fleeting reprieve from the pressure of her indecision.

The room offered a false sense of security, like so many others he'd stayed in. An illusion both too good to last and not quite good enough. A cozy fire. Sturdy timber walls. Fresh sheets and a thick blanket.

Rest. Peace. Shelter.

But press past the illusion, and the cracks begin to show. A misguided mission. Distrust. Two people drawn toward each other but ultimately at odds.

Different goals. Different dreams.

This truce was temporary. This cabin? No more permanent than a hotel stay.

If he hadn't gotten sick, they wouldn't even be here. When he healed, he'd be evicted from this sanctuary, his future once more uncertain, in the hands of someone else.

Wide awake now, he watched her from under his lashes, feigning sleep. The distrustful, jaded part of his brain wanted to think she was keeping tabs on him. Watching and waiting for him to reveal a weakness. She wouldn't have to look very far. Huddled under the covers, feverish and miserable, he couldn't have been more vulnerable.

With a quiet exclamation, she uncapped the pen and started writing, pen slicing across the paper in quick, decisive strokes.

His curiosity got the best of him. "Plotting my murder?"

"Nope," she said, not looking up. "Finished that during your nap. Now I'm deciding how to spend two hundred thousand dollars split zero ways."

"Kinda thought we were supposed to do that before appearing on the show." He figured she would've had a plan for that money spanning back years.

"I did." She stopped writing. "But that was before. Now there's the franchise and . . ."

And him.

"And now you've been offered more than what you asked for." He hadn't meant to bite out the words, but her contemplating turning down a better offer just because she didn't want to share it with him? That stung.

"I get it. You think I'm being spoiled. But you don't know . . ." She trailed off.

"Don't know what? Tell me, Simone." *Let me know you.*

She licked her lips, then took a deep breath. Closed her notebook, finger in the pages. "You know the Hawksburg market? The one you insisted on crashing?"

"Again, it's not crashing if you're invited to the party," he teased. Who knew six months later their fraught first meeting would no longer be a source of pain but of connection?

Her lips tightened to hold back a smile, but her eyes crinkled, and the urge to kiss her awoke so suddenly the blankets bunched in his fists.

"Well, I want to create a sort of permanent, year-round market in Hawksburg with places to eat and shop. Entertainment venues. Build off Honey and Hickory and create a marketplace for artisans, crafters, musicians, and performers. Diversify the job market, make the town somewhere everyone can feel at home, regardless of where they come from." Her eyes sparked with excitement, passion. "Honey and Hickory is the starting point but not my whole vision."

That sounded amazing. And the exact opposite of what Keith and Constance had offered. Her hesitancy began to make more sense. "So why go on *The Executives* at all?"

"Because I'll never get there on my own." Which explained why she hadn't turned them down flat out. Trapped like him, both chasing second best, they were more alike than he'd thought.

"What about you?" She got up and poured bottled water into a teakettle, set it on the wood-burning stove. "Is a barbecue empire your dream?"

Finn scoffed, which turned into a cough. "Heck no. I wouldn't have even created a line of sauces if I'd had a blank check."

"So you're just in this to make money?" Simone sounded disgusted, like he'd failed a test.

This might be his last shot to get her to take the deal, and he'd gotten off on the wrong foot. "Yes, and no. The profits are a means to an end."

"And I'm guessing that end isn't early retirement and a yacht anchored in the Caribbean?" She opened a tea tin, and he recognized the earthy notes of bergamot. Earl Grey.

He shook his head. "Can't swim, remember? A yacht would be a terrible choice," he said, earning a laugh. He could make a currency of those laughs. Dole them out on rainy afternoons and disappointing Monday mornings. Drink them down like hot chocolate on a winter night.

Steam was curling through the air, loosening his lungs. Unstacking the weight from his chest, and the words flowed out of him, swept along by a sudden urgency not to explain himself but to share his dream with her.

"I want to make money to fund a cooking school for people who need a fresh start. People who are experiencing homelessness or have a criminal record holding them back from employment. Sober addicts looking for a second chance. I'd love to make real-world fine-dining experience accessible for those who couldn't attend a traditional program. Give them a chance for a future that's a one-eighty from their past."

Simone put her hands on her hips, eyes narrowed. "Stop it with that nonsense."

"What?"

She ripped open a tea bag packet and gestured with the torn wrapper. "Now I've gotta scrap my whole murder plot. I can't kill a freaking philanthropist."

A philanthropist. More like someone in dire need of a reality check who should be more focused on making his business profitable enough to put a roof over his own head than building a pie-in-the-sky culinary institute.

"Never have I ever been called a philanthropist, but if it saves me from imminent death, I'll take it," he said.

"Now it's my turn to ask: Why the heck didn't you pitch your idea for a cooking school on *The Executives*? Keith would've eaten that up."

He bristled. "I don't need a pity win. And just because he'd admire the idea doesn't mean he'd want to invest, let alone Constance and the audience." The idea of subjecting his dream to their scrutiny left him feeling strangled with more than congestion.

"And I guess . . ." He blew out a breath and let his head fall back on the pillow. "Is it cowardly to say I didn't trust them with it?"

If *The Executives* shot down his chef-school idea, then it would feel like a personal condemnation. Better to put his sauce business on the chopping block than a piece of himself.

Her lips twisted into a rueful smile. "Maybe. But if that's the case, I'm a coward too."

She unwrapped two mugs from brown paper, and that's when he realized she'd bought the mugs. Bought the tea. For him.

Not showy, how she cared for other people. He'd missed it because he hadn't wanted to see the good in her. Hadn't wanted to admit his role in starting the feud, or in keeping it going all summer.

It suddenly occurred to him how very alike they were. Stubborn. Proud. Determined to make a change in the lives of others. A harder pill to swallow than the ones he'd forced down earlier.

His biggest rival might turn out to be his greatest ally if they could set aside their past. The offer from *The Executives* was starting to look less like a punishment and more like kismet. Could they accept a compromise for the sake of the bigger picture?

"It's a good dream, Finn Rimes." The laughter was gone from her eyes, replaced with an intensity that made his blood simmer through his veins like the water in the kettle. "No matter what happens, don't let it go."

Don't let it go. Easier said than done, when he couldn't see a way forward without this deal she was adamant to get out of.

She crouched down to put another log on the fire, jeans molded to her legs. Then she stood and poured boiling water into the mugs. If only he could walk over and wrap his arms around her again. Kiss her neck until she dropped the spoon. Run his hands up over the curve of her hips and . . .

He cleared his throat, which turned into an all-out coughing fit.

"Hydrate, Rimes."

Cheeks flaming hotter than the fever warranted, he leaned over to retrieve the bottle of water. "Did 4-H also teach you how to cook on a wood-burning stove?"

"Boiling water is hardly rocket science," she said. "But while you were sleeping, I went down a rabbit hole. Found a blog about how you can utilize wood-burning stoves for cooking. The trick is regulating the heat. Not much different than a smoker in that respect."

"I wouldn't know."

The look she shot him from under her brow could've melted iron. "You own a barbecue sauce company and you've never smoked meat?" She whistled low. "The indecency."

He laughed. "Maybe you can teach me, when we're partners."

"Nice try. You're not getting your grubby novice hands on my smoker. But I could point you in the direction of a few good YouTube tutorials."

"Sounds a lot less fun than a personal demonstration." He grinned.

"Don't be gross, Finn." But she was smiling too.

And whatever she said, using what he would've only considered a heater to make tea showed how resourceful she was. Everything he'd learned about Simone fed into one image: Capable. Strong. Independent.

All qualities he admired, none of which boded well for his chances of getting her to take the deal.

"Thank you," he said, a few minutes later, when she passed him the steaming mug. "No one's ever made me tea when I'm sick."

"Don't tell me these things." She settled in on the end of the bed, tucking one ankle under her knee. "My brittle heart can't take it."

"Because I'm pathetic?"

She frowned. "No, because the world is pathetic."

His heart warmed at her grouchy show of support. "Well, thank you, seriously."

She poked him with the round edge of her spoon. "Stop thanking me so much. It's creeping me out. All I did was boil water."

It was more than that, but he let it be. "Creepy is my specialty."

"No, it's not." Her cheeks shone soft in the fading light. "You're, like, the least creepy dude on earth."

"Why do you say that like it's a bad thing?"

"I didn't."

"You did."

"I like that you're not creepy." She blew on her tea, sending little waves across the surface. "That's why it's a bad thing."

Her words swept across the small space between them. A ripple of awareness.

They drank their tea in silence, but not the kind that crackled with unspoken animosity or weighed down the air with the pressure of indecision. This was a companionable silence that stretched and grew into an iridescent bubble of happiness. One word could pop these precious, fragile feelings expanding between them, so he didn't reply.

When she was done, she leaned over and put a wrist to his forehead. Cool and herbaceous. "Fever's gone." She let her arm fall, and he almost caught it. Almost smoothed his thumb over the fine green veins on the underside of her wrist. Raised her palm to his lips and kissed it.

Almost, but didn't.

Instead, he pushed down the covers and swung his legs off the bed. "Off we go, then."

She put out a quelling hand, fingertips brushing his thigh through the soft cotton of the pajamas, and his pulse skittered. "I already talked to Carter and Elliot about an early checkout tomorrow. One good night's rest. We can leave the key in the drop box and head out at dawn."

Her hand was still on his leg, and he exhaled slowly, tentatively, but a cough still caught the tail end. He raised his elbow to cover his mouth.

What a wreck . . . him. This trip. The deal.

"I'm sorry," he said, when he could manage words again.

"You're sorry your immune system sucks?"

He chuckled, chest burning. "Are you sure we can make it in time?"

"We'd better." She smoothed a hand down the comforter. "I'm already the town pariah. People would never let me live it down if word gets out I missed my own sister's bachelorette party."

This time he gave in to instinct. Reached for her hand and squeezed.

One thumping heartbeat, another, and then she was pulling her hand away, into her lap. Twisting the silver ring on her thumb. "I should go finalize some details for the party." She stood up and smoothed back his hair, her nails a soft scrape at his temple. "Try to sleep, so we can drive straight through."

But how could he sleep when her touch set him aflame?

CHAPTER 24

SIMONE

Darkness fell while Finn was still napping. Simone had washed out her delicates in the sink—she'd packed for two days, not a week—then gone to the business center in the lodge to place a rush order for premade gift bags for the bachelorette party, since she wouldn't have time to DIY.

To-do list handled, there was nothing left to do but stare at the ceiling and try not to implode from restlessness. She'd silenced a call from Meg—prompted by interference from Alisha, no doubt—and Pops—calling to ream her out for sacrificing her principles. Or so she assumed. She let both go to voice mail, too embarrassed to talk until she found a way out of this mess.

With Finn's deathbed confession about his passion project, he'd unknowingly derailed her plans to cut him out of the deal. But keeping the idea to himself on the show raised red flags. Had he concocted the whole idea just to get her on board? Then again, she hadn't felt comfortable pitching her plans for Hawksburg either.

She cast a glance his way. Still sleeping, like he had been most of the day, except when he was pestering her about her own hopes and dreams. Making her head spin with sappy, woozy feelings, like she was the one on cold meds. Experience told her his altruism was a ploy, but there'd been a vulnerability in his eyes as he shared his vision.

And the kisses they'd shared . . . earthshaking.

How was she supposed to make this huge decision when his body turned her brain to mush and his words turned her heart to gooey sap?

"Up for a game of checkers?" Finn asked, startling her.

She swung around and found him sitting up in bed, a bottle of water in his hands, watching her. "I take back what I said. You're creepy as all get-out. How long have you been awake?"

"About as long as you've been pacing like a cornered tiger."

She stopped, realizing that yes, she had been.

"Could've taken a walk, you know."

But then there'd be no one to keep an eye on him. "Bears," she said.

"Well, if you insist on staying in here to look after me—"

"Avoiding being eaten by a wild animal—"

"Then let's at least get you stationary for a few minutes. For my sanity," he added, forestalling her objection.

Maybe checkers wasn't a bad idea. Checkers required strategy. Planning moves might jump-start her to a problem-solving mindset to salvage the deal. And bonus, it wouldn't leave her any mental space to obsess over Finn and her feelings.

Feelings. Yuck. Feelings had big yellow eyes and sticky, slimy tentacles that wormed their way inside your heart and burrowed insidious seeds that spawned into more feelings until your entire body was overrun by a pestilence of touchy-feely emotions like tenderness. Attachment. Fondness. *Barf. Gag.*

Distraction from her feelings? Yes, please. "I'll get out the board. You stay put."

"I'm not the one who needs the reminder." But he was smiling, so she let it slide.

She poured out the pieces on the quilt, and he picked out the red ones, setting them up on the squares.

"Ladies first." Finn leaned his chin on his knuckles.

She moved a piece. He scooted one with a finger. She made another move. He countered.

She took three pieces in a triple jump. "You suck at this."

He grunted amicably and made another terrible move.

"Are you trying to lose?" Sure seemed like it.

He laughed out loud, and this time she noticed it wasn't followed by a cough. Progress. "Believe it or not, this is me trying." He paused. "To win."

She joined in because it was impossible not to, when his laugh was rambunctious and carefree and utterly guileless, like running full on into the surf at the beach. Like spinning, eyes closed, in a sprinkler on an August afternoon. His laugh was sunshine and summer.

"I didn't realize it was possible for an adult to be so terrible at a child's game," she said when the laughter had faded.

"Whoa, hold on. 'Child's game'?" Chin resting on his knuckles, he flicked up his eyes, dark pools of umber in the lamplight. "Checkers is the game of kings."

"Pretty sure that's chess."

"Maybe." He didn't sound convinced, brow knotted as he selected another piece and put it right in the line of fire.

She jumped it. "It's kind of ironic, isn't it?"

"Mmm?" His eyes were on the board, thumb in the middle of his lower lip.

"Your name—it rhymes with win."

"The universe is a cruel place," he acknowledged.

Lordy, he was cute. And quickly becoming her favorite, if she was in the business of playing favorites. Which she absolutely was. She jumped another piece and made her checker a king.

The game was about to be over, and then she'd have no distraction from the fact that she was no closer to finding a solution that didn't involve losing her autonomy or destroying Finn's dreams. He needed sleep for the twenty-plus hours of driving left, but a few more minutes couldn't hurt. "Jenga?"

His eyes lit up. "I'm great at Jenga."

They sat side by side on the love seat, Finn with a blanket draped over his head like an ailing grandmother. He nudged a block out of the center, and the tower wobbled.

"I thought you were better at this."

He shrugged, seemingly unperturbed. "It's relative."

Simone tucked her heels up under her and scooted a piece out. "Tell me more about your cooking-school idea. Has it always been your dream?" Not sly, as far as interrogation went. But a simple question might catch him out in a lie.

"No." Finn pushed the blanket off his head and tucked it around his shoulders. Bad. Now there was nothing to hide his absolute gorgeousness. "For most of my life the concept of having a dream never even crossed my mind."

Never? She couldn't imagine. Then again, one of her few memories of her mom, the ones she hoarded, was of Momma teaching her to tie her shoes. Telling her she could be anything. Do anything. That she was powerful and strong. She could guess how many people had told Finn that.

"I didn't set out to be a chef. Didn't plan on being anything, really." He shook his hair over his forehead, then pushed it back over his head. Buying time. But she waited.

"One day I was washing dishes at Bellaire—that's the restaurant where I work. Both chefs on shift called in sick, and the owner, Bella, was in a bind. Asked if I could help out. Turns out that despite growing up on a steady diet of chicken nuggets and boxed mac and cheese, I had a knack for cooking."

"So you stumbled into it?"

"More or less." Something in the way he said it made her wonder if he was holding back. "Doesn't fit your dynamic, I know."

She made a face, and he nudged her knee. Her heart sang like a treacherous canary at the unexpected contact.

"Oh, come on. Like you didn't have your future mapped out at seventeen?"

"Fifteen." She grinned, then her smile slipped. Over half a decade lost to saving face, a fish out of water in the city. "But my big plan was to take over Honey and Hickory, and we all know how that turned out."

"Yeah, perfectly." He leaned forward and nudged out another block. The tower leaned precariously. "Are you or are you not running the restaurant?"

"I am, but—"

"But nothing. Life isn't linear. Sometimes to get from *A* to *B* you've gotta take a detour right past *Z*."

Uncharted territory. Uncertainty. All the things she ran from. "What's past *Z*?"

"Heartache, usually." He rubbed at his wrist, smoothing his thumb along the curling tendrils of ink at his wrist. "But also hope."

Trusting the process sounded a whole lot like relinquishing control, trusting others with her plans. To get her mind off those uncomfortable scenarios, she asked, "Your tattoos, do they have meaning?"

He nodded and nudged aside the blanket draped over his shoulders. Made a fist and turned his arm over, exposing the underside.

"With all the moving I did, I didn't have many treasured possessions. The few I did got lost under beds or forgotten under pillows. I stopped carrying anything that couldn't fit in my duffel. Stopped bothering." He shrugged, like it wasn't a big deal.

"But my body is my own. Goes where I go." His smile didn't reach his eyes. "The perfect place to capture memories and keep them in plain sight, where they can't be lost or stolen. I got my first one at sixteen.

A really terrible bird. It was supposed to be a hawk, but it turned out more like a grumpy pigeon."

Simone bit her lip against a laugh. "Can I see it?"

He shook his head, grinning for real now. "Absolutely not. Got it covered a few years ago." He peeled up the sleeve of his tee, exposing more skin, and she swallowed. Bare branches of a tree wrapped his shoulder, clouds layered in whorls around the branches.

"So your pigeon has a roost," she said, unable to help herself.

Finn bumped his shoulder against hers. "Remind me again why I'm hanging out with you?" But he grinned. "You're right, though. The failed hawk is still underneath, even though you can't see it anymore. Just like a person's past. It's invisible, but it's always there. Which is why I shouldn't have judged you by your beautifully perfect exterior."

"A compliment and an apology?" Simone pressed her lips together. "Talk about a level-up." She shifted slightly. "I like these best, I think." She traced her fingers along the delicate sketches of herbs on his forearm. "Fennel and thyme. You might not have planned for it, but profession is a part of you now."

The corner of Finn's mouth lifted in a smile. "It is, yeah." He pulled the blanket around himself again, and when he spoke, his voice was scratchy, the effects of the tea having worn off. "I wouldn't be where I am today if Bella hadn't taken a chance on me. But she's not the only one. My last foster mom, Tori? She took a chance on me too. Never gave up, either, though I put her through it. She and her son, Darius, are the closest thing I've got to family, though I didn't meet them until I was seventeen."

He stopped, like that was the end of the story, but she knew it wasn't. So she slid out another Jenga block and set it carefully atop the tower, waiting.

"Halfway through junior year, I got placed with Tori, who's a doctor. I started going to a new school in a wealthier district. I was used to flying under the radar, but there I stood out. Kids started bullying me right off the bat. For my clothes, the fact I got picked up instead of driving my own car. Stupid crap."

He pulled his lips to the side, eyes downcast. "But it got so bad I started acting out just to get sent to the principal's office. With all the detentions, I earned a reputation for being a badass, which, to be clear, I totally was not." He shot her a grin, then sobered.

"Out of nowhere, a group of popular kids started inviting me to stuff. Parties, to play video games at their house. I thought things were looking up for me. With them around, the bullying let up. But after a few weeks, we were chilling at this one kid Owen's house, in his basement, and he asked if I could get them prescription drugs. I guess they figured I'd have access to stuff because of Tori's job."

Betrayal. A scenario she was well acquainted with, and her heart softened toward him even more, as if she weren't already a pool of melted butter when it came to Finn.

"Punks," she said, and the corner of his lip quirked up in a not-quite smile.

"I felt like an idiot. Here I was thinking I'd finally made some friends, when all they wanted was to use me." He swallowed, tense. "And I couldn't wrap my brain around why. They had everything I wanted. Families, stable homes. Never stopped to think that if I did what they asked, I could lose my place in Tori's home. Or maybe they just didn't care."

Entitled. Self-centered. She understood now why he'd jumped to conclusions and pushed her away.

He leaned forward and nudged out another block, and the blanket slipped off one shoulder to expose his tattoos once more. Memories painted on his skin. His heart laid bare, the opposite of the blank armor she wore, terrified of being seen as anything less than put together.

"Anyway, once they figured out they couldn't get anything from me, I went back to being nobody." Placing the brick carefully atop the tower, he said, "Nothing new, but I guess it was the tipping point. I quit trying. My grades tanked. I turned eighteen over Christmas break and moved out. Dropped out. But Tori never gave up on me. She and Darius stayed in contact. It took me years to believe I was worth the love they kept showing me. To get my GED, to go to therapy. But sometimes it creeps up, that worthless feeling."

A moment ago her heart had been a puddle. Now it was a thin sheet of ice, and it shattered at his words. "That worthless feeling can go shove it."

"Right?" Finn rubbed a hand across his lips, bashful. "But that's why I want to start the school. To show other people they're worth investing in. To give them a chance to prove their past isn't their future."

She wanted to hate him still. Wanted to think he was rude and conniving and judgmental. But how could she?

"You're a really decent dude, Finn Rimes." More than decent. Kind and caring and considerate. She flicked her eyes over the room, the checkers and Jenga blocks evidence of his selflessness. "Sick as a dog, and here you are playing games with me, getting me out of my own head."

He dodged his eyes away, like he was embarrassed at her praise. Not nearly as mortified as she was for saying those things aloud, but he mattered more than her pride. Mattered as a person, regardless of what might happen between them.

Regardless of what she so badly *wanted* to happen between them.

Finn coughed, but it was a looser sound, not as worrisome. "Speaking of . . . you could've warned me about the underwear situation in the bathroom. I may be sick, but I'm not dead. And jeez, Simone. Those black ones . . ."

She'd totally forgotten. "Consider it payback for the creek-side striptease."

He grinned, a bright flash of teeth against his stubble. "Fair enough." He leaned over, his finger poised in front of a block.

"Finn?"

"Hmm?" He paused.

"If you push that one out, the whole tower is going to fall."

"It might."

"It will."

"Are you helping me win?"

"I'm helping you not lose."

"Because you like me?" he asked, eyes on the tower.

"Because I don't hate you." Not at all. Not even a teensy little bit.

"Good. Because I've never hated you."

CHAPTER 25

SIMONE

"Ready to hit the road, sunshine?"

Her eyes shot open. Silhouetted by light spilling from the open bathroom door, Finn hovered over her, a cup of coffee in each hand. He took a seat by her feet and bounced. "This bed is a dream, right?"

Groggy, she leaned up on one elbow. Bed? She was supposed to be the one on the couch. Unless . . .

Memories of last night came flooding back. He'd pulled off a Jenga victory, then convinced her to play the board game Life for rights to the bed. She suspected he knew there was no other way her pride would allow a sick man to sleep on the couch. But he'd jokingly reminded her of how she'd warned him bad things would happen if she didn't get a good night's rest.

Looked like the couch had treated him well, because he stood there beaming like the poster child for vitamin C. Dressed and showered, from the looks of his damp hair, his brown eyes sparkling but no longer feverishly bright.

She called upon her dwindling reserves of animosity to fight back against the onslaught of charm. "How are you healthy all of a sudden?"

"I never stay sick long." Was he puffing out his chest? "Constitution of a horse."

"And yet one swim in an icy river was enough to do you in." She fumbled for the lamp pull and clicked it on, illuminating Finn's smile in all its predawn glory.

"But not for long." He winked. *Winked!* Ugh.

"Long enough," she said.

He laughed, like her barbs rolled right off him. Like she was more pine cone than cactus. And strangely, that didn't feel so terrible, to not be prickly.

He pressed a coffee into her hands. "You wanted an early start, right? Or I can let you sleep till sunrise. You could use the rest."

Stealing her lines, this man. Infuriating.

Irresistible.

She shook her head at his offer—no way would she allow him to one-up her—and then tilted the cup to her lips and took a sip. Sweetener, no cream. He must've remembered from breakfast in Phoenix. Another sign of his attentiveness.

Maybe she'd misjudged him too. One on one, he didn't seem to care about winning or losing, or choosing sides, and maybe he didn't want to steal her company and destroy her dreams either. Maybe he just wanted to carve out his slice of happiness and help others do the same, just like her.

Or maybe this was all a big scam.

She couldn't imagine Finn going to such lengths to trick her. Then again, she'd been wrong before. But Monday was still days away. Would it hurt to live in the moment, just this once? Shift her focus from the pressure to perform to existing, here, in this moment with Finn?

Fifteen hundred miles before the real world called, and they'd face a decision that might sever their connection and send Finn out of her life for good. But for once she wouldn't let tomorrow's worries mar today. But one question nagged at the back of her mind . . .

Would fifteen hundred miles with Finn be enough?

⊷

Sometimes it creeps up, that worthless feeling.

Finn's words from last night haunted her. She knew he'd healed. Developed strategies to refute self-doubt and fend it off. But she intended to give him another reminder that the worthless feeling was nothing but a lie.

The detour would take them two hours out of their way. A small price to pay for showing Finn he was the furthest thing from worthless. She might not be able to give him half her company, but she could give him this. A reminder that the things he cared about mattered.

He mattered.

Worried GPS would spoil the surprise, she'd memorized the route. But it turned out secrecy wasn't necessary because Finn dozed off on the shadowy switchbacks out of the canyon. His face was still pale under the stubble, and smudges lurked under his eyes like half-healed bruises from a fistfight, a jarring reminder of their battle royale on set.

The whole early-rising, healthy-as-a-horse thing must've been an act. A selfless ploy to get her on the road and not delay them any longer. Her heart squeezed. This man. This awful, thoughtful man.

Still, his weariness worked in her favor. With him asleep, she followed the Park Service signs that shone in the headlights. Swung into a spot in an empty lot and killed the engine.

"Finn." She kept her voice low, but he jerked to alertness and pawed at his eyes.

"Shoot, did I doze off? Why'd we stop? Gas?"

She shook her head at his flustered questions. "I've got a surprise. It's not the Desert Botanical Garden or a butterfly house, but . . ."

He blinked and looked out the windshield. "But you brought us to the freaking Grand Canyon!" He was out of the car in seconds, and she followed him out into the chill of early morning.

When she caught up, he said, "You do realize this wasn't on the itinerary, right? You could get us in big trouble with the tour director. She's a beast about staying on schedule."

"Yeah, but there's this pesky tourist who keeps bitching about stopping to smell the roses."

"He sounds like a tool."

"He has his moments," she said, and smiled.

They followed the path toward the canyon, the crunch of their feet on the ground the only noise, steps slowing as they came up to the rim. Rays of morning sunlight bathed the canyon in goldenrod and ocher, rose pink and mauve.

The sight took her breath away.

Tears sprung to her eyes. Actual tears. Of joy. The worst, most useless variety.

What kind of loser cried happy tears? She did, apparently.

She felt like a total and complete wreck. But it was the most extravagantly beautiful thing she'd ever seen. Finn's arm came up around her shoulders, and she let him pull her close. Sunk into his warmth, let him hold her up while she went to pieces at the sight of a hole in the ground, of all things. Layers of rust and sand, overhung by an endless sky. Eons and millennia stretched before her.

She ought to feel insignificant in the face of all this magnificence. But in Finn's embrace, all she felt was accepted. A crying, blubbering, accepted human.

A sob escaped her lungs. Finn shifted and wrapped her up in his arms for real, and she burrowed into his chest, her emotions overflowing in hiccups and snot and . . . oh, gosh, she was never gonna live this down. She'd come here to give him this moment, but he'd given of himself too. Like he had last night. Like he might keep doing, if she let him.

"I figured it would've been me to have an emotional breakdown on this trip." A suspicious layer of thickness coated Finn's words, and she looked up to see tears shining on his cheeks. He slid his thumb across her damp cheekbone.

"I don't cry."

"Yeah?" To his credit, he didn't call her on the blatant lie. "Well, I do." He laughed. "Quite a lot, actually. You would hate it."

She sniffed. Lifted the sleeve of her hoodie to dry her eyes. "Do you cry at movies where the dogs don't make it?"

"Oh God, yes." He tilted up his chin and blinked.

"Me too," she admitted. "Every time."

His chest moved in a silent laugh.

"Are you laughing at me?"

"No. I swear I'm not. How could I?" He cleared his throat. "I'm just really happy to be here. With you." A kiss settled on her forehead, and she felt it soak in. Take root. "Thank you."

"There you go again with the excessive gratitude." She tightened her arms around him and ventured another peek at the glorious tableau. With Finn's arms around her, she took in the sight, breath even and deep to match his. "Thank you for reminding me it's okay to let go."

Okay to let go, but he held on. His arms wrapped around her waist, and she leaned back into the shelter of his body, like it was the most natural thing in the world. Like they'd been intertwined for eons, millennia. And instead of feeling choked up, breathless at the grandeur, his embrace settled her like a calming breeze.

Here, with Finn, her impatience transformed into peace. Shallow breaths became full inhales. Oxygen and serenity. Like everything would work out. Like she didn't need to strive and push and finagle things to her definition of perfection.

A crunch of gravel sounded on the path behind them. A moment later a black Lab burst out of the sagebrush and covered them in doggy kisses.

"Sadie, where are your manners?" At the end of the leash, her owner whistled the dog to his side. He ruffled her ears. "Can't you see these lovebirds are trying to have a moment?"

Lovebirds? *Love?* The word caught at her like a snare, pulling her away from Finn. Breaking the spell.

This wasn't love. This was a simple crush. A vacation fling. Nothing deep or meaningful or lasting. She fled up the trail, past the man and his dog, both of whom shot her a confused look. Holding her breath against the tightness in her chest, she charged onward toward the parking lot.

Taking Finn here, turning the focus on his desires after months of writing him off—that was a kind gesture. A good deed.

But love? Love was an upside-down, topsy-turvy feeling. Love was sloppy and reckless and unpredictable. She couldn't surrender to love.

She reached the car. Nowhere left to run. Nowhere to hide from her feelings.

"Simone."

That voice. Finn's voice. The aural version of a *Welcome home* sign at the airport, scrawled in big, sloppy letters. A hug in auditory form.

She turned, and Finn was right there, his eyes darkened to pools of deepest midnight, his chest heaving. *One breath, two.*

When their lips collided, it was a gale meeting a hurricane. A whirlwind consumed her—Finn's kiss, custom made to sweep her off her feet. She yielded to the press of his lips, and his fingers cupped her jaw, slid down her neck in a caress. In an instant he had her backed up against the car. An inevitable force, this need between them.

Greedy and insistent, she rocked up against his body, deepening the kiss, breathing him in like oxygen, drinking him down like the sweetest water. He moaned, and all of a sudden his hands clasped under her thighs. He lifted her up and stepped impossibly closer.

Pressed against the car door, she wrapped her legs around him. Tucked her heels against his back and gripped tight as they chased this yearning into uncharted waters.

She brushed her lips against his, teasing them apart, and underneath her, his whole body shuddered. His tongue swept against hers, his touch flooding her senses like a river overflowing its banks. Her fingers found their way into his hair, tugged him down, and he rumbled out a groan that shot straight to her core.

This didn't feel like a bad idea, not at all. The connection between them felt powerfully, inescapably right.

CHAPTER 26

FINN

Finn didn't know where he ended and Simone began. Swept up in her windstorm, he kissed her like there was an eternity in this kiss. Time ceased to exist; there was only the two of them, clinging to one another in the eye of the storm. The taste of her left him winded and hungry and desperate.

Wrung out and wanting more. Wrecked.

She was a force of nature, and he let himself be swept away, lashed by the current of her body. She molded against him, and he answered her with a dig of his hips, a sweep of his tongue, searching for deeper and more. He wanted all of Simone Blake. He'd never been in love, but he imagined it would feel like this. Insatiable.

Passion snapped between them like a lightning bolt. Hunger and fulfillment. If their kiss in the car was an exploration, their kiss in the cabin a question, then this was the answer.

Yes. A thousand times, yes. For all his lifetime, yes.

She was his person. The truth hit him in the quiet space between heartbeats, before a bark pierced the air and doused the wisp of magic. Gasping, he pulled back, his breath coming hard and hot in vapors.

Simone pressed a shaky hand to his chest. "That's a heck of way to say thank you."

He tipped his forehead to hers. "You did tell me to stop saying it, so . . ."

"One of my better ideas."

He kissed her again, helpless not to. "I thought all of Simone Blake's ideas were good ones."

"Oh, you're slick, Finnegan." She kissed him again. Quick. Easy. Like she'd do it again in a heartbeat. "I think I'll keep you."

He let go of her legs and lowered her to the ground. And though he knew it had been a throwaway phrase, his heart beat a hopeful rhythm in his chest. *I'll keep you . . .*

They only had a day left. He should be used to temporary by now. Should be comfortable in impermanence. He scrubbed a palm down his face and opened the door. Got in.

Maybe, just maybe—went his heart—this time would be different. Maybe, just maybe, she might decide to keep him by her side. Maybe, just maybe, he would be enough.

They stopped for lunch in Albuquerque. He ordered a burrito smothered in green chile, and Simone got a bowl of posole and a Diet Coke. She said, "My sister fills the world with sugar; I'm doing my part to restore balance to the universe." So he went ahead and ordered horchata to go, just for the joy of seeing her roll her eyes.

They made a pit stop in Amarillo. Simone had drunk all of his horchata, and he'd finished off her sugar-free soda. When they met at the hood of the car to switch drivers, she brushed his hair off his forehead and told him maybe he should've packed mousse. He asked, "Mousse?" and she dropped her hand to his shoulder and kissed him.

They filled up the tank in Oklahoma City. Between the kiss and a bathroom-key fiasco—it was attached to a rabbit's foot, which they'd both refused to touch, and insisted the owner provide another or open the door himself—they'd forgotten to fill up in Amarillo. The sun had dipped below the horizon, and by the time morning dawned, they'd be home. Too soon, though not soon enough.

So while Simone was inside prepaying, he pushed the button and motored the top down. Opened the trunk and pulled out the parka she'd worn in Sedona.

Ankles crossed, trying to play it cool, he was leaning against the side of the car when she walked out.

"Finn," was all she said. But she pulled the coat out of his hands and slipped it on.

Midfifties and cloudy—not top-down weather, but Simone hadn't stopped smiling since she climbed behind the wheel, and Finn couldn't remember a time he'd been happier.

Happily en route to his own send-off. Speeding toward farewell in the passenger seat, but he'd lived through plenty of goodbyes, and this felt more like a see-you-later. There was still hope for him. For them.

Halfway to Tulsa, it started to rain.

Finn slapped the rain-slick trunk with frostbitten fingers. They'd pulled over on a side road to put up the roof, but the roof had other ideas.

Ten at night and they were stranded in middle-of-nowhere Oklahoma with a waterlogged rental car. His plan to win Simone over thwarted once again, this time by the double whammy of natural causes and shoddy technology.

"The tow truck will be here in half an hour." Hunched next to him in the icy rain, Simone fumbled to get her phone back in her pocket.

"Half an hour?" He dragged a hand through his soaking hair. "Hopefully the insurance covers water damage."

"Water damage," Simone deadpanned, and then they were both bent double on the side of the feeder road, cracking up.

When he managed to get his breath back, Simone peered at him through the rainy darkness. "Darn it, Finn, can't you manage to stay dry for once?" And then they were laughing all over again as she tugged him over to the car.

She climbed in and scooted over, and he vaulted over the side and landed next to her.

"Have you always wanted to do that?"

He nodded.

"Was it worth it?"

He nodded again.

"Good. Now get under here." She opened her coat over their heads, and he grasped one side to create a canopy. "Can't have you catching pneumonia."

"I'm not that fragile," he said through chattering teeth.

"Better safe than sorry."

They huddled in the darkness, rain pelting the coat, the seats, everything around them. "Why are you taking this so well?" he asked after a few minutes of shivering.

She grinned, a flash of teeth in the gloom. "Channeling Finn."

That caught him off guard. "Me?"

"Yeah, you seem really good at waiting. Among other things."

"Referring of course to my cooking skills."

"Those too." She kept her face forward, but a soft smile tugged at the edge of her mouth.

He couldn't get enough of her. The tiny freckles on her cheeks, the way her curls had expanded, grown into a dark cloud around her delicate face.

She angled a sideways look, bumped his shoulder with hers. "That was a hint."

"I'm taking my time," he said, and she gave one of those small, impatient huffs, and that's when he bent and captured her parted lips in a kiss. His heart pinched tight in his chest when her lashes fluttered closed. He kept his own eyes open; they were on stolen time, and he didn't want to miss a moment of Simone.

Their hands created an arbor with the coat while all around, rain pattered down. A curtain of sound, like they were kissing in a cave behind a waterfall.

He clasped her knee, and she hummed against his mouth and fisted her free hand in the front of his shirt. Gosh, did she know how crazy that made him? He lost his grip on the coat, and it fell on top of them, a tent blown over in the wind.

Laughing, they battled their way out from under the weighty fabric, and then she was on his lap, above him, and yeah, he'd stay under Simone's sway any day. Their tongues slid against one another, a relentless, rushing stream. The wind kicked up and sent icy rain pummeling into them.

"We should probably—" She pulled back, resting her forehead against his.

"Yeah, probably." But he tilted his chin up and sucked on her lower lip until she breathed out a moan and dodged her mouth down to his. The heady rush of heat from Simone's mouth, her hands, her body, swept away the last of his reservations.

Stranded in the elements with Simone, he'd found his place. On Monday she might take everything and leave him stranded, but for now she was in his arms. His shelter from the storm.

The tow truck driver flipped up the hood of her yellow raincoat and shoved her hands into the pockets, eyeing them askance. "Who puts the top down in winter?"

Finn raised his brows at Simone, but she grinned, mischievous. "Right? My question exactly." The little traitor. She'd pay for that later. If her good mood held, that is. She was taking this latest delay remarkably well. Her laid-back attitude was mildly terrifying.

"Anyway, I'll take the car to Rick's, and he'll get to work on it in the morning, but until then, is there somewhere I can take you?"

"Chicago?" Finn asked hopefully, and the driver laughed.

They didn't join in, and her laugh cut short. "Oh, you're not joking?"

Illuminated by the flashing orange panel of lights, Simone shook her head. "He's not. My sister's bachelorette party is tomorrow."

"Well, if it's just the roof, Rick should have you on the road bright and early."

"Bright and early gets us back tomorrow night. The spa day starts at ten, and then we have a whole afternoon of activities. Is there anywhere to rent a car?"

Rent a car in the middle of nowhere at going on midnight? The tow truck driver's answer confirmed what they already knew. "I'd call your sister and tell her to go ahead without you."

Simone opened her mouth, and he guessed she was about to tell the woman where she could stick her unsolicited advice, so he jumped in. "Could you drop us off at a motel?"

"Sure, or I can do you one better. My cousin Eunice owns a B and B down by the interstate. Doesn't get much business this time of year, and I bet she'd let you have it half price for the night. Only a few blocks down from Rick's too. Save you the trouble of calling for a ride in the morning."

She ushered them over to the passenger side. "I'll give you two a moment to talk it over."

Once they were settled in the warm cab of the tow truck, Simone hissed, "A B and B by the *interstate*? First of all, those words should never be uttered in the same sentence."

"Agreed." Finn looked over her shoulder into the night. Five hundred miles of darkness lay between them and their destination. "But the other choice is, what, Uber across three states?"

She paused like she was actually considering it, then looked away, but not before he'd caught sight of the defeat in her eyes. "You're right. There's no way we're making it back in time."

If he hadn't put the top down, hadn't pushed her to explore . . . scratch that—if he hadn't begged her to come along on this road trip in the first place, then she'd be home already with her sister. But no giving in to regrets. Not tonight. He wouldn't spoil what she'd sacrificed to take him to the Grand Canyon by wallowing.

They were stuck; that much was inescapable. But staying the night at a bed-and-breakfast, even one by the interstate, couldn't be that bad, right?

CHAPTER 27

SIMONE

A bucketful of rainwater sat in the floral-carpeted hall of the bed-and-breakfast, catching drips from a crumbling ceiling. A hard hat would've been appropriate, or at least an umbrella. Simone and Finn trailed the innkeeper-slash-tow-truck-driver's-cousin, Eunice, down a hallway, under the watchful gaze of the staring eyes in the sepia portraits.

They'd passed nine heavy, mahogany doors—she'd counted, in case this was an escape room in disguise—and now the woman stopped at the last door on the left and fished a key out of the pocket of her puffer coat.

"I'm sure my cousin told you, it's the off-season for ghost hunting, so you've got the place to yourselves."

Um, no. The tow truck driver had failed to mention that the B and B by the interstate was actually a *haunted* B and B by the interstate. "Excuse me, ghost hunters?" Hard pass.

Simone backed up and nearly passed out from fright when she collided with something solid and breathing and . . . *laughing*. Finn. The reason she was going to be spending the night in this death trap of a mansion, waking up to another full day of traveling instead of keeping her promise to her sister.

The enormity of the delay had sunk in as the tow truck chugged away with their only ride home, and now she'd gone from chill to pissed. And tired. And full of regrets for embracing Finn's nonsense c'est la vie attitude. Maintaining her calm had become a serious undertaking.

She crossed her arms and stepped forward, away from the enticing warmth of his chest. A quicksand of distraction is what he was.

The gray-haired woman smiled up at them, key in the lock. "Forgot for a second that you didn't book us through the website. But yep. We're the premier spot for poltergeist activity in the whole state. Legend has it my great-great-grandaunt and her bridegroom haunt the place. Lovers' quarrel gone bad." She returned her attention to the doorknob. "Poison. Sort of a reverse Romeo and Juliet. Anyway, there have been a lot of mysterious occurrences reported on the premises."

Nope.

Nope, nope, nope. Not cool.

Finn spoke up. "But, of course, none of that's real."

Eunice got the door unlocked and swung it open. "Wouldn't know, seeing as how I've never slept overnight in this place. Inherited it from my grandfather."

"Oh, something you two have in common." He bounced his eyebrows at Simone, and she elbowed him.

The woman frowned at them, clearly trying to get a read on their dynamics. "We usually have someone come in and cook weekend mornings, but since you showed up out of the blue, I'll pick up some doughnuts for you tomorrow."

"What about dinner? Any delivery places around here?"

How could he think of food when they were about to be sequestered in this nightmare?

"At this time of night?" Eunice chuckled. "You're welcome to what's in the fridge. I'd be sure and check the dates, though. Also, the stove's temperamental."

"Ghosts?" He sounded hopeful, the charlatan.

"Old wiring." Eunice shot him an exasperated look. "But like I say, make yourself comfortable, and I'll be by in the morning. Long as the ghosts haven't chased you away." She rasped out a hoarse laugh and shut the door behind her. A tiny shower of plaster rained down from the ceiling.

Simone immediately spun on Finn, hands slicing through the stale air. "No. Absolutely not. I will hitchhike. I will walk. But I am leaving. Now."

Clearly he had a death wish, because he went to put his hands on her shoulders. Saw her expression and must've thought better of it, because he shoved his hands in his pockets instead. "C'mon, Simone. You don't honestly believe in ghosts."

"I believe in the fact that this place is about to fall down around our heads. I am not dying in Oklahoma, of all places."

He tipped his head back and laughed.

"It's not funny!"

"What's funny is you think the ghosts are murderers. That's not a thing."

"Murder ghosts are totally a thing."

"I think you're confusing them with murder hornets."

She crossed her arms and stared him down. He blinked first and ducked his chin. "I'm sorry. About all of this. Sorry I made you miss Alisha's party."

Not as sorry as she was to let her sister down. Although when she'd put in the call, Alisha had assured her everything would be fine. She'd do the spa day with the girls, then skip the club and head back to Hawksburg early. They'd do a scaled-down celebration when Simone arrived back in town tomorrow evening. Nothing she could do about it, but that didn't mitigate the feeling of failure.

She turned on a lamp by the bed, not trusting the shadows. "To be honest, I think the party was more for me. She's got this thriving cookie shop in the city, and now she's getting married. Moving on in life when for so long she was stuck, and I was the one going places." She went to the bathroom—a claw-foot tub, horrors—and flicked on that light too.

She shut the bathroom door behind her. Mirrors and all. "I think I wanted to throw her this big party with all my connections in the city to show she still needed me." And to show she still had ties to Chicago, still had people there who cared about her. A safety net, if Hawksburg didn't work out.

"That stupid worthless feeling . . . it sneaks up on you." He walked over to the other bedside table and raised his eyebrows in question. She nodded, and he clicked on the Tiffany lamp. "Do you miss your old life, in Chicago?"

"It took me ages to get used to the city. It felt so sprawling and anonymous. But eventually I carved out a new community in Chicago. My friends and coworkers . . . that's who I miss. But my life?" She shook her head. "My life has always been Hawksburg. But most people don't know that. I did too good a job convincing them otherwise." She clasped the carved mahogany post of the canopy bed for support, stress and weariness catching up with her.

"I hate the idea of selling out our town, but maybe it's stupid to keep trying to re-create the past," she said. "If I take the deal, at least Honey and Hickory will be a success."

Finn was standing across the bed from her. "Success, that's most important? Because it sounds like community is for you."

Did he not realize he was arguing himself out of the deal? Maybe he was trying some kind of reverse psychology tactic. She rested her head against the bedpost, worn out from second-guessing his motives.

"Doesn't matter, because community is out of reach. To most people in town, I'm just the girl who was too good for Hawksburg and only moved back because she couldn't hack it in Chicago. I don't think they trust my commitment. Haven't given them a reason to."

"I know I can't claim the title of 'local,'" he said with a grin. "But I heard nothing but good things about you all summer."

"What about the people who said I wasn't living up to Pops's legacy?"

"I may have exaggerated." His cheeks reddened, as they should have, for all the shade he'd thrown her way for being sneaky. "It was one old guy, and I'm pretty sure he said it out of misplaced loyalty to your grandfather. From what I can tell, the whole town loves you. I bet they'd love your expansion plan too."

"The farmers' market on steroids?"

He laughed. "I thought you were the businesswoman. Don't you have a better pitch than that for your brainchild?"

"Okay, really?" She picked up one of the musty throw pillows and tossed it at him. He ducked and the pillow flew over his head, to land harmlessly against the wall.

"Violence is never the answer, Ms. Blake."

She tossed another pillow. "Except when it is."

"Last chance to get out of this," he said. "I won't hold back just because you're a girl."

She grabbed another pillow. "And I won't hold back because you're a boy."

"Oh, it's on." He snatched up a pillow and threw it, but she swung sideways around the bedpost.

"That all you've got, Rimes?" She clambered onto the bed, pillow poised overhead. Finn's eyes darted to the last pillow, and she bent her knees in anticipation, loving this. "Do it. I dare you."

The sound of a door creaking open broke the heated silence. Ghosts, for sure. She leaped off the bed, into Finn's arms. Or tried to. She wound up knocking him back and tackling him to the dusty carpet. A disembodied voice spoke from across the room.

"Forgot to leave the key."

She rolled off Finn and tipped her head sideways to see a frowning Eunice by the door. "Try not to break the furniture. It's antique." She shut the door with a parting glare.

Finn scrambled to his feet. "Hungry?"

The sudden shift in his mood threw her. With the deal hanging over their heads, she couldn't judge what was real and what was a play to get inside her head. But the rumble of her stomach cut into her thoughts.

"There's your answer."

She stayed close by him as they walked down the dimly lit hall and made sure not to make eye contact with any of the people in the photographs. Creeptastic. When they got to the bottom of the stairs, Finn flipped the light switch. Nothing. "That's weird."

"Weird" was one word for it.

He turned on his cell phone flashlight and led her into the kitchen, toggling all the switches. "Nothing in here either."

"This is not okay." Simone adhered herself to his arm with zero shame. Desperate beat dead any day.

"It's fine," he said. "I'm sure they have candles around here."

"For séances, probably." She shivered.

"Hang on." He tugged out the creaky wooden drawers, one at a time. "Aha, see?" He held up a plastic box of tapers.

"Okay, but what're you going to put them in?" Teasing him staved off the uneasiness.

"Any chance you'd hold them like Lumière in *Beauty and the Beast*?"

She gave him a look designed to shrivel extremities. Toned it down, just a bit. There was a perfectly good bed waiting upstairs, after all, even if it was an antique.

"No?" He nibbled his lip. "Wait, remember the candelabra in the hallway?"

"The one that looked like it was alive? How could I forget? But yes, let's use that."

Together—because no way would she stay in there alone—they found the candlestick and brought it back. Finn put the tapers in and lit them. He set the candelabra by the range, where it cast an eerie glow. "May as well cook as much as we can. No telling when the power will come back." He opened the fridge and examined its contents. Unscrewing the cap of a gallon of milk, he sniffed it.

"I'm good with a bowl of cold cereal."

Finn froze and looked over his shoulder, his affronted expression visible even by candlelight. "I know you did not just say that to a chef. Cold cereal." He shook his head, and Simone chuckled.

"Don't you ever want a break from cooking?" She hoisted herself up onto the small butcher block island, trying not to look over her shoulder into the empty dining room beyond. "Sometimes when I come home from a day at the restaurant, I never want to see another skillet again. I keep an emergency stock of Lean Cuisine and Hot Pockets."

"Okay, now you're just baiting me."

She wasn't, but his cute, affronted expression was a nice bonus. He opened cupboards and produced two mismatched pans. Set them on the stove and stood back, hands on his hips. "Now, how to light this."

She leaned back onto her palms, elbows locked. "There's probably a spell book somewhere."

"Or a match works." He lit the burner and shook the match. "Care to take over? You're the one with the MacGyver skills."

She shook her head. "I'm having fun watching tonight."

He looked at her over his shoulder with a wide grin. "Oh yeah?"

"Do you work hard to have such a dirty mind, or does it come naturally?" she asked, because teasing him was too much fun.

And it was also fun to watch him. He was unexpectedly precise in the kitchen. The opposite of his usual sprawling sloppiness. He rinsed and chopped the entire contents of the vegetable crisper, sautéing the veggies in a pan of butter along with an onion.

"What are you doing with that?" she asked when he did a totally bro-ish fist pump over a tub of cornmeal. She would check the pantry for canned corn, maybe make muffins or fry up some corn cakes and top them with a tomato jam. But he'd already used tomatoes in the ratatouille.

"Polenta." Finn shook some cornmeal into the boiling pot of water and milk.

Eh, not her favorite. The texture was hard to nail. "I'm not usually a fan."

"Noted." He smirked over his shoulder, and she got the feeling he relished proving her wrong. Another thing they had in common.

"This is like a private viewing of *Chopped*." Simone swung her heels, relaxed for the first time in what felt like forever.

"Does that mean I'm being judged?"

"Obviously." She grinned. "But the good news is, there won't be a bottleneck at the ice cream machine. It's all yours."

"Phew." Finn wiped his brow exaggeratedly before shaking some processed parmesan into the polenta.

"You're actually using that?" In her experience, chefs were finicky creatures who tended to think processed ingredients were below their pay grade. Her pastry-chef sister loved to rant about the scourge of cinnamon rolls that came in a tube.

"Why not? It's here. It's cheese." His mouth twisted. "Almost."

She pointed at him in triumph. "And there it is. You snobby, classically trained cooks can't help yourselves."

"I think the word you're looking for is 'chefs.'" He grinned, then opened the oven and pulled out the sheet tray with a towel, his easy capability sexier than a striptease.

On his next trip to the fridge, he took out a jar of olives and twisted off the top, bicep flexing. Hello, muscles.

He offered her the jar. "First course."

Fishing out an olive, she said, "Hard to believe you'd never cooked until Bella asked you to fill in. You make it look effortless."

Finn froze, then set the olives next to her. "It wasn't my first time in a kitchen. A professional one, yes. But when I was eleven, I got taken away from my aunt for the last time. She was . . ." He turned away and went back to the cutting board. "Well, anyway, I'd been there a year, but it didn't work out. For the first time, I got put in a home with no other kids. A couple hoping to adopt."

After taking slices of bread out of a bag, he cut them into triangles. "They were big on family dinners, which until then I thought were just a sitcom myth."

He dropped half a stick of butter into a pan and lit another burner. "At first I was scared my manners wouldn't live up to their expectations—my aunt was always on me for elbows on the table and crap like that. But they didn't seem to care. We just talked and ate. And the food was good. So good." There was a smile in his voice, though he kept his back to her.

Simone thought back to her dinners with Gran and Pops, the ones they still hosted Friday nights and Sunday afternoons. Of the imperfect perfection of sitting down with family and sharing a meal.

"The husband"—she noticed he didn't use the word "dad"—"he prided himself on cooking these elaborate meals. And he didn't kick me out of the kitchen or tell me I was in the way. I was too scared to ask to help, but I loved watching him. Afterward, we'd gather around the table and share the meal. Decompress. It was the closest thing to home I'd ever experienced."

He pulled open the oven and slid in the tray of buttered bread.

"So he taught you to cook?"

"More like let me shred cheese and open cans occasionally. But I learned a lot, just watching. I celebrated a birthday while I was with them, and they gave me a cast-iron skillet. A month later, the wife got pregnant. And that was that." He rolled his shoulders, like he was shaking off the hurt.

"Shit, Finn, do you have any good memories?"

He huffed out a chuckle, then looked at her over his shoulder. "Today is a pretty great one."

This time she didn't try to ignore the gush of warmth in her heart at his words. She was close to telling him she felt the same when steam hissed out of the polenta pan.

After taking the lid off, he gave it a stir. "And even with how things ended, those dinners are still good memories. I think those moments of unhurried togetherness are what I'm trying to recapture every time I work a shift at Bellaire or pack up meals. I might never start a culinary school, but hopefully the meals I cook offer people that same chance to gather and be renewed."

Family or not, Finn was creating a legacy through his food. Through his compassion.

"Do you still have the pan they gave you?"

"Nah. I left it. Too heavy to carry," he said. "But a few years ago, I bought my own."

"Not too heavy to carry?"

"Not anymore." He smiled over his shoulder. "I'm grown now."

Yes, he was. Not just physically, but in emotional maturity. Miles ahead of her, but he made her want to catch up. To do the work on unpacking her past like he so clearly had.

He sampled the veggies and rooted around in the spice cabinet. Seasoned the dish again. Then he plated the polenta and topped it with the ratatouille. Placed a garlicky toast point on the edge and passed it to her. "Dinner in a bowl, but at least it's not cereal."

"This smells divine." Simone drew the plate to her nose, inhaling, glad of the neutral ground. She scooped up a bite of polenta. Not gritty, or mealy, or soupy. Creamy and luscious. Just right. They exhaled in tune, and he raised his brows.

"Better than Cap'n Crunch?"

"So much better. You can cook polenta for me any day."

"At Honey and Hickory?"

The polenta turned gummy in her mouth in an instant, her stomach churning. Just when she'd started to think there might be something between them. Something that transcended the deal. Something more than the miles they'd traveled or the misunderstandings of their past.

Hands numb, she set down the bowl. "I'm not hungry anymore."

CHAPTER 28

FINN

"Simone, wait. I was kidding." Mostly.

He knew a franchise wasn't her first choice, but she'd promised to think it over. And with it clear they didn't have a problem with each other on a personal level, he thought she might be open to taking the deal, using the investment from *The Executives* as a starting point to their future. A future together, as allies. As partners. As *more*.

He grabbed the candelabra and followed her out of the room. She was already halfway up the darkened stairs. If she was willing to brave this house alone, he'd really gone and pissed her off.

"Whether you were or not, we can't keep pretending this deal isn't looming over our heads." She shouldered the door open and disappeared inside.

When he entered the room, she'd shut herself in the bathroom. He set the candelabra on the dresser. Stood outside the door for a moment, hand poised for a knock. Wound up retreating to a chair in the corner, not sure if she'd want him in the bed or not. At least Eunice wouldn't have to worry about them breaking any furniture tonight.

He'd spent nights in back seats that were more comfortable than this bed. Nothing wrong with the mattress; his discomfort had everything to do with his epic miscalculation in the kitchen.

He'd offered to sleep downstairs on one of the couches—*If you think I'm staying in this room for one second without another living, breathing human to keep me company, you're out of your mind*—and then offered to take the floor, to which she rolled her eyes and turned on her side.

Simone lay next to him under the covers, but with the gaping distance between them, she may as well have been back in Illinois. All the ground they'd covered in the past few days had gone up in a puff of smoke like an extinguished candle.

She was right: the deal wasn't going away. It had been stupid to pretend. Stupid to think this suspended reality could last forever. Soon they'd go their separate ways.

And Monday? At this point, he didn't know whether she'd even log in to the meeting with Constance and Keith.

Sedona had been a beautiful dream, and knowing it wouldn't last, he'd cut it short, preempted the inevitable by waking before dawn. But her surprise detour to the Grand Canyon had given him hope that maybe the haven they'd created could last beyond this trip.

"Remember when we first kissed?" Simone's quiet question punched a hole in the silence. "You said you had a history of trusting the wrong people. And I got angry because that wasn't me. Isn't me."

The pressure in his chest built. He knew that now. Wished he could go back in time and unsay it. Kiss her again and not retreat behind his walls. Soak up the fleeting moments of togetherness rather than worry them away.

She shifted, and the sheet slid along his shins, a phantom caress. "What I didn't tell you is you're not the only one with a history of trusting the wrong people. Last year, I worked on a proposal with a coworker who'd been my friend for years. He and I spent months perfecting our pitch, but then the week before we planned to present—"

"He stole your idea."

"It was our idea. But yeah, he took sole credit. And instead of the promotion I'd been hoping for, I got let go."

He wanted to reach out for her, but though they were inches apart, the distance felt too great. "They fired you? For what?"

"Because I pushed back when I found out what he'd done. Didn't go along with his version of the story, or take it lying down." She pulled the blanket higher, up to her chin, shrouding herself in the only armor available. "They had to do cuts. Jason had gotten wind of it, and that's why he passed the idea off as his own. Not only was I not an innovator, but I wasn't a team player."

The Simone he'd come to know—grudgingly—over the summer was the very definition of a team player. She preferred to be the captain, but leading meant she worked doubly hard to ensure everyone's success. He'd seen her come to the market early and stay late, helping out and pitching in. The people of Hawksburg were her team, just like the staff at Bellaire was his, and he could only imagine it had been the same at her job in Chicago.

"Anyway, getting fired brought me back home. I'm not mad about that part." She rolled onto her side, facing him now, for the first time since they'd come upstairs, searching his face. "But what drives me nuts is wondering, Were we ever really friends? Or was our closeness just a long game to get what he wanted?" The question split his heart in half.

He could barely force the words out past the boulder on his chest. "You think I only care about you because of the money? Because of a business deal?"

She hitched up a shoulder, and the sheet slid off. She tugged it up and rolled onto her back, but he rose up on an elbow, willing her to meet his eyes.

"Yeah, the mess with *The Executives* makes our situation complicated. But if you tell me right now there's no chance of you taking the deal, how I feel about you won't change a single bit."

"Won't it?"

Two words. A question, not an accusation, but it gutted him like a boning knife.

The outcome of the deal wouldn't change his feelings, but it would alter their reality. Would she still want him, a chef with no grandiose future? Did she even want him now?

At night, shadows always loomed larger, crowding out certainty. As the minutes ticked away in silence, drafts of doubt seeped under the covers and invaded the warmth he'd soaked up out west. Left him chilled and uncertain. Of himself, of his future.

And of Simone.

CHAPTER 29

SIMONE

Gagging on an exploratory bite of jelly doughnut—lemon filling, no thanks—Simone wordlessly passed the rest to Finn in the driver's seat. He bit off half in one bite, no sign of disgust, like she'd expected. The man hadn't been lying about eating whatever was put in front of him, and yet the food he'd made for her last night was as deeply nuanced as his barbecue sauce.

With him sharing Honey and Hickory, she wouldn't lose sleep over the quality of their menu. Was she being selfish to want to keep the restaurant as her own? The last thing she wanted was to hold back the scope of Honey and Hickory for a personal fantasy. But taking the deal would mean trading community for corporation. Abandoning her principles for profit.

But if she bowed out, Finn would lose everything. Both of them or neither, those were the terms.

As they crossed over the Missouri–Illinois border, she felt more lost than ever.

Simone could've driven the last few miles in her sleep, which was lucky because by the time they exited the freeway after seven hours in the car, she was fighting drowsiness and decision fatigue.

Exhausted from trying to separate her growing feelings for Finn from all the turmoil surrounding *The Executives*. Ready to put some physical distance between them to clear her head.

Ever since his offhand comment, things hadn't returned to normal between them. Gone was the flurry of insults, but missing, too, was the playful banter.

Gone was Finn's openness, his easy laugh. His patience, too, seemed frayed at the edges. He kept scrolling through his phone. Adjusting the vents. Fiddling with the radio. Maybe she only noticed because it had been a long few days cooped up on the road. Was he having doubts about the deal, or doubts about her?

She turned into Meg's dirt driveway, the headlights barely making a dent in the country dark, and pulled to a stop in front of the corrugated metal pole barn that housed Meg's farming equipment.

"I'll be in touch Sunday to go over our strategy for the video call, after all this fuss with Alisha's wedding is over." Inadequate. But what else could she say?

Not expecting a reply, she climbed out, but Finn met her by the trunk.

"You can turn it down," he said. "You can walk away, and I would understand."

She wanted to believe him. Wanted to go back to not caring if he understood or not, even as she desired him more than ever, there in the softly falling snow and country darkness.

"What about you?" She'd been scared to ask. Scared of what his answer might do to them. "Do you want it? Really want it?"

He looked away, jaw bunched tight in the red glow of the taillights. "I don't see another way to make my culinary school a reality. And I don't know if I believe in a higher purpose, but . . ." He trailed off. This time when he met her eyes, she saw need, raw and bare. "Yeah, I want it. But I want you more."

There he was, the Finn who'd been missing all day. Cards on the table when she kept hers close to her chest. And unlike him, she wanted it all.

CHAPTER 30

Finn

The whole entire purpose of renting a car and driving halfway across the country was to convince Simone to take the deal. And his parting words? His monumental closing argument?

Yeah, I want the deal. *But I want you more.*

The worst part? It was true.

Last night she'd asked him if her not taking the deal would change things, and he'd hesitated. Hesitated all day, for every mile of the drive. So could he blame her for merely nodding at his declaration? For taking her suitcase out of the trunk and saying, "I'll text you"?

What more could he ask when a week ago they'd been enemies? The twisted terms of the deal pitted them against each other, even in a merger. There was no winning. Not for both of them. Maybe not for either of them.

Shifting into reverse, he craned his neck back to navigate the long drive. He braked with a curse, car idling in the drifting snow flurries. Simone's purse lay on the back seat. For a cowardly second he considered pretending he hadn't seen it to avoid facing her after his embarrassingly one-sided declaration.

Should he hang it on the doorknob, knock, and run away like a prankster? Super weird. Then again, the vibe he'd been getting from Simone was very much *I've-spent-the-past-few-days-with-you-and-now-I'm-home-and-reality-is-setting-in-and-I-fully-regret-kissing-you.* Which meant she might appreciate the leave-the-bag-and-run maneuver.

Still, even though this house sat on the edge of nowhere, leaving a purse unattended outside at night seemed like a bad idea. So he braced himself for a quick, face-saving getaway and knocked.

Laughter, then the door swung open to reveal a woman with a short blonde afro wearing a matching tie-dye lounge set. She broke into a wide smile. "Simone, you little minx. You ordered a stripper?" She sized him up, and her perusal stopped at his open collar. "Tats too? Ooh, he couldn't have come cheap."

His cheeks flamed. What had he been thinking, crashing a bachelorette party?

"Chantal, quit torturing him." Simone entered the room, a jar of salsa in her hand and an unreadable expression on her face. "What are you still doing here?"

Talk about a gut punch. Was it too late to toss the purse into the room like an unpinned grenade and run?

Feeling like a caveman who'd clubbed a rat and brought it home, only to discover a pig roasting on the spit, he held out the purse. "You left this in the car."

"What's Barbecue Guy still doing here?" Meg entered the room, carrying a bottle of Fireball whiskey, and he instinctively smiled at the familiar face, but a second later his brain registered the fact that she knew his name from the farmers' market and hadn't used it.

He took a step back, a cold wind blowing at his nape. "I was just leaving."

"You can't go without some refreshment." This from a fourth woman he hadn't noticed because she was folded up on the couch under an enormous bowl of tortilla chips. Her eyes were darker than Simone's, but the sly smile was the same. Must be her sister, Alisha.

She bit off a corner of chip, talking around it. "I, for one, am super happy you're not a stripper, because I would've had to murder my sister. I expressly said no penises."

No penises. "Got it." He took an involuntary step back. Self-preservation. "Wouldn't want to violate any rules."

Alisha laughed. "The 'no penises' rule only applies to naked ones or fake ones."

"Oh, well, mine's real." His cheeks blazed. "And covered, as you can see."

The woman nearest him—Chantal?—snickered at his discomfiture. He got it; her allegiance was to Simone, and the last time any of these women had seen him, he was dissing her on set.

What had she told them in the time since? Nothing good, it seemed.

"Anyway, here." Feet planted on the far side of the welcome mat, he leaned in and thrust the purse into Chantal's hands.

"Wait!" Alisha fought herself out from under the vat of chips and waved him in. "As the bachelorette, I insist you stay and have some snacks before you get back on the road."

He looked toward Simone, who raised her shoulders in the barest of shrugs. Not exactly a resounding invitation. He'd grab one bite of food and make his escape. Give her time to process the past few days. To decide if she wanted a partnership, let alone a relationship.

Dragged over to the couch, he found himself planted between Alisha and Meg, who'd passed him a mug of what was billed as apple cider but what he discovered was roughly two-thirds cinnamon whiskey.

Cradling the mug, he took another tentative sip and winced, then set it on the coffee table. "I'm sorry we didn't get here on time. Simone so badly wanted to be here for your party."

Alisha took a hearty glug of her own drink, then wiped her mouth. "She is here."

"I meant in the city. You were supposed to go out, right?"

"To be honest, you did me a favor by keeping her away." Alisha's dark-brown eyes twinkled at him, a more mischievous version of Simone's golden ones. He opened his mouth to say this wasn't the plan, but she went on, "Clubs and bottle service are not really my scene."

"Yeah, I'm still not convinced she didn't hire you to delay me, just so she could weasel out of a night of drinking and debauchery." Across the room, Simone sat down on the hearth next to a crackling fire. After so much time on the road, even the few feet of distance left him yearning to pull her close, his body tuned to her frequency.

Pulling himself back to the conversation, he said, "Well, this is definitely more low key than VIP." Shoot, that rhymed. He slumped deeper into the couch, but on the other side of him, Meg snorted into her drink.

"He's trying to say you're basic, Ali."

Not at all, but she smiled.

"Uh, duh. I know I am." Her good-natured grin put him at ease. "But the last year has been exhausting. Wonderful but exhausting. Between launching my bakery and planning this wedding, what I wanted most was a break, not another all-nighter. So this is perfect."

"Yeah, she's such a celebrity now, champagne and parties are ho-hum for her." Chantal came back in with a tray of shot glasses and more liquor, grinning.

Alisha covered her face with her hands. "I got featured in *Foodie* magazine once. Once! And they won't let me live it down."

No wonder Simone fought so hard for her restaurant. Food ran in the Blakes' blood. And with her sister's success . . . no doubt she'd pressured herself to live up to more than just their grandfather's legacy.

"*Foodie* magazine, are you serious?" Primed to make his exit, Finn took a second to congratulate Alisha. "As a regular Joe who never even made it into my high school yearbook, I have to say I'm super impressed."

"Well, thank you." She rubbed the rim of her mug with her thumb, still looking embarrassed at the attention, then smiled. "Though to be in our yearbook, you just had to be enrolled. And with a graduating class of thirty-five, making varsity in any sport was as simple as showing up to practice."

"Wow." He chuckled. "I'm pretty sure there were thirty-five people in my homeroom."

Chantal leaned across to grab a handful of chips. "What were you voted senior year? Most likely to lick a condiment off a woman on national TV?"

He choked on a lungful of air. She didn't pull any punches. "Uh, no. Actually—"

"If I had to guess, I'd say most likely to charm his way into people's hearts." Everyone's heads swiveled toward Simone, and her eyes went round.

Charm his way into *people's* hearts, or *her* heart?

The room stayed silent a second too long, and she leaped to her feet and snatched up a bottle of tequila from the table. "Shots?"

If he could give her nothing else, he could give her an out. Revealing her feelings for him—if she had them, and oh, how he hoped she did—in front of her friends and sister right now would leave her exposed in a way he knew she hated.

Clearing his throat to claim everyone's attention, he stood. "Is there a bathroom I can use? Then I'll hit the road and leave you ladies to celebrate in peace."

"Not so fast." Meg stretched her legs out to the coffee table, blocking his escape. "Liquor's optional, but you've got a job to do."

A spool of ribbon in his lap, Finn tied off a neat bow to match the sample favor box set in the center of the table. Turned out the job Meg had in mind involved gratuitous crafting and not gratuitous nudity like he'd feared.

No striptease, and the only packages involved were 250 small boxes of macarons, destined to become wedding favors.

He still worried Simone didn't want him there and hated playing a part in making her uncomfortable. But she'd been the one to hand him the scissors and ribbon, which he took as a sign she'd rather he stay than make a scene with a hasty exit.

"That is the worst bow I've ever seen." Chantal's voice broke his concentration, and he looked up to find her taking a box of macarons from Alisha. "You're relieved of duty, bachelorette. Go take thy lack of crafting skills elsewhere. You're a disgrace to bakers everywhere."

"Excuse me, Chantal, but have you seen my bonbons?"

Chantal laughed. "Can't say I've had the pleasure."

"What my sister means to say is her sugar work is top notch." Simone eyed the bow critically. Probably because she was the only sober one. "Unfortunately, looks like that skill doesn't transfer to nonedible items."

"Hey now." Finn picked up the box of macarons and brought it close to his face. A little blurry, but the knot looked great to him. "I think this is excellent. You can't let them roast you, Alisha. You're the queen tonight."

"Oh, okay. I'll take that." Alisha giggled and poked her sister. "Hear that, Sim? Finnegan Begin Again thinks I'm a queen."

Finn sneaked a look at Simone, who snorted with a half shrug. "Cheesy nicknames are a family trait, I guess."

He picked up his own spool and measured out a length of velvet ribbon, but as soon as he cut it, Simone took away his scissors. Party pooper.

Tying a knot to create a long loop, he beckoned to Alisha. She elbowed herself up off the couch, and he slipped the ribbon over her head like a sash. "We're supposed to honor the bachelorette. Bow down to her, in fact." He stepped back and bowed at the waist, stumbling. Okay, so maybe that last shot of whiskey had been a mistake.

But Alisha laughed and smoothed the ribbon. "I accept your tribute, my liege."

"Oh my gosh, y'all. The cheesiness. I can't." Simone buried her face in her hands. So cute when she was mortified.

Finn collapsed on the rug next to her and put his head on her shoulder to steady himself. Whoops. He straightened up, but not fast enough, because Chantal narrowed her eyes.

"So you and Simi, this a thing now?" She bent her head and bit off a stray thread, light-brown eyes trained on his. "Or is it a case of keeping your friends close and your enemies closer?"

The spiked cider and tequila mingled in his stomach, turning sour. Simone's shoulders went stiff under her formfitting turtleneck.

"Ooh, guys, guys!" Alisha broke in, drumming her palms on the table, eyes bright. "Forget the favor boxes. You know what we should do next? Home movies."

"No, Ali. This isn't Christmas vacation," Simone said.

"Um, yeah, it kinda is." She pointed to the snow swirling outside. "And it's my bachelorette party. What I say goes."

"Your sister's right," Chantal said. "She's the boss. And also, I'm intrigued. Home movies?"

Simone groaned. "We had a tradition of watching home videos every Christmas break, which Alisha started because she's a big ham ball." Warmth infused her tone and belied her objections.

Alisha's chin hit her collarbones in a nod. "Guilty. I'm a big ball of cheesiness. And there's no point in debating it because I already called for a ride."

"Who? Laney's got a toddler, and—"

The door burst open in a flurry of snow to reveal a man in a tan work coat and beat-up baseball cap, his arm covering his eyes. "Everybody decent?"

Finn huffed out a laugh. "What does he think goes on at these?"

The man dropped his arm, and his blue eyes shot straight to Finn. "What's a dude doing here?"

"Finn's our stripper!" Chantal declared.

The guy squinted at him, not in an aggressive male-dominance display, but more like, *This puny fella?* And really? Ouch. Also, who was this guy? He still hadn't explained his presence, but everyone else seemed fine with the intrusion.

"Wait a sec." The man's stare turned into a glare, beefy arms pulling across his chest. "You're the guy from *The Executives*. The one stirring up trouble all summer at the market."

Great, he had a reputation. Finn narrowed his own eyes. "And you are?"

Simone stepped between them before the newcomer could reply. "Finn, meet Shawn. He's an old friend of ours. Graduated in my class. And our ride, I'm assuming?" The guy nodded, and she grabbed her coat off the hall tree. "Can't believe Ali roped you into this."

"It's her big day this weekend." Shawn's face relaxed into an indulgent grin. "And this gives me a chance to test out the new snow tires."

"Well, thanks for humoring her." Simone pulled open the front door. "If we're doing this, let's go before we get snowed in."

Grabbing his jacket quickly lest he get left alone with the bouncer look-alike, Finn shoved his feet into his shoes and made his way through a few inches of fresh snow to a giant pickup idling in the driveway.

He opened the back door and climbed in next to Simone, who was buckling her seat belt. Seizing the moment they had to themselves, he said, "I'm sorry. I swear I didn't plan to stay."

To his surprise, she grabbed his hand. Squeezed. "I know. But this—"

The door opened in a flurry of snow, and she let go. Pulled away.

Chantal climbed in next to him, bumping him over with her hips until he was squashed into the middle seat. Alisha climbed in up front, and Simone tipped forward to ask, "No Meg?"

"She'll meet up with us tomorrow. You know how early she gets up."

The driver's side door opened and Shawn slid in, bringing a gust of cold air with him. He met Finn's eyes in the rearview. "Ready to go, ladies?"

"Sure are." Finn pulled his lips tight in a fake smile, and Simone bumped him with her knee.

"Behave," she whispered. "He's just looking out for me. As far as everyone in town knows, we're still sworn enemies."

Easy to forget after the eventful past few days that to everyone in town he was still the guy who'd thrown down with her on live TV. Not exactly the image he wanted at the forefront of their minds. "But you do plan to, like, set the record straight at some point, right?" Whoops. He hadn't meant to ask so bluntly, but the drinks had affected his filter.

"So a franchise, huh?" Shawn spoke up, gruff.

Simone went stiff, and if they'd been alone, he would've slid his hand into hers. But he settled for pressing his shoulder against hers in a show of support. "That's the plan," she said. *Was it?*

Turning on the wipers, Shawn pulled onto the main road, a glorified dirt path covered by drifting snow. "Gotta admit . . ." He trailed off.

"What?"

His eyes shifted to the rearview again, and then he cleared his throat. "It's nothing, Sim. You gotta do what's best for you."

"You don't think the franchise is what's best?" Her tone was clipped, taut.

Shawn tugged at his collar, and Finn didn't blame him for the unease. "We just thought you were staying this time."

The car fell silent. Finn held his breath, waiting for her response. Dreading the reply that would take him out of the equation. But next to him, Simone stayed silent, facing the window.

After a moment, Shawn cleared his throat, awkward after the rock he'd tossed into the stream of conversation. "So does Finn have somewhere to stay?"

Ah, back to speaking about him like he wasn't there. Classic. "Finn will figure something out," he replied, tipsy enough to counter Shawn's passive aggression by referring to himself in the third person.

"He's staying at my place," Simone cut in.

Feeling chastised for letting Shawn get under his skin, Finn bent his head toward Simone. "I could sleep in the car," he said in an undertone. The last thing he wanted was to be a burden to her anymore.

"Are you serious?" she whispered back. "It's a freaking blizzard out there."

So it wasn't that she wanted him with her; she just wanted him not dead. He'd confessed that he had feelings for her, but all she'd offered in return was common decency. Pretty clear where he stood.

Shawn took a turn, and they bounced along a driveway bordered on both sides by lit-up candy canes jutting out of the ground like runway beacons. Outlined by flashing, multicolored strands of lights, a farmhouse was visible through the whiteout.

"This is your place?" He somehow pictured Simone living somewhere less Las Vegas meets North Pole landing strip.

Alisha laughed. "No, this is our grandparents' house. We're on a mission to retrieve the movies."

"Not 'we.' Me," Simone said, correcting her. She opened her door, and snow blasted in like it'd been shot from a confetti cannon. "Y'all are so drunk you'll wake up Pops and bring down the wrath of God on us."

"Will not, Bossy Pants." Alisha opened her door with a flourish. "I'm coming too."

Stomping her feet against the cold, Simone popped her head back in. "Finn, can you help? I can't babysit her and find the DVDs."

"What about me?" Chantal asked.

Simone flicked her eyes toward Shawn, then jerked her chin at Finn.

"Oh right. Leaving these two dudes alone might not be the best idea," Chantal said aloud, earning an eye roll from Simone. Discreet? Maybe not. But yeah, he didn't trust this dude not to dump him in a snowdrift somewhere as a show of Hawksburg solidarity.

Finn followed Simone into the supercharged snow globe. The ground nearly hit his face when he hopped down out of the outrageously jacked-up truck—seriously, was the guy trying to compensate for something?—and by the time he recovered, the women were halfway to the house.

A rut in the driveway sent him into giggles when he thwarted its attempt to trip him. Simone shot him a narrow look over her shoulder. "Not you too."

"Not me." He shook his head and realized he was still shaking it. To cover, he jogged up and took Alisha's elbow.

"Thank you, my kind sir," she said.

He bobbed into a curtsy midstride, and stumbled. "Milady."

Simone shook her head, fitting the key in the front lock. "You two."

"Us two," Alisha said, and tipped her head to his shoulder. "Us two." They giggled.

Leaning an arm against the doorframe to steady the porch, Finn said, "So your grandparents live here? Very quaint." *Quaint.* He chuckled. What a word. But it fit the house: porch lights flanking the glass-paned front door. A pair of potted evergreens. Homey, in the truest sense of the word.

"This is new." Alisha tapped a jingle bell hanging over the door knocker, and it jangled loudly.

Grabbing the bell to stop the ringing, Finn said, "Shh. You're going to wake the parentals."

"*Grand*parentals," Alisha corrected. They both dissolved into laughter in the vestibule.

"Why don't you hot messes go grab some water? I'm gonna get the DVDs, and then we can jet." Back in her hometown again, Simone had pulled away. Not even a backward glance as he stood in the entryway, lost.

"This way." Alisha pointed him down the hall. "C'mon." She tugged on the end of his scarf until his feet got the memo. But a wall full of photos brought him up short. This was the hardest part in family homes. The pictures. The history.

Hands in his pockets, he stared down a man about his age. Alisha came back to stand at his shoulder and shook her finger. "No. Don't look at that loser."

"Your dad?" His eyes were still on the photo. Dismantling it. Searching for the why. Knowing from experience he'd find nothing but a hollow frame beneath.

"Marginally."

That broke the spell, and he gave his head a shake, meeting her eyes, but she turned away and started walking. He spoke to her back. "I'm sorry."

"Don't be." Alisha waved a hand, still moving. "Best thing that ever happened to us."

"And that's your mom?"

She stopped.

"She's beautiful," he said. "I'm sure it's hard, to not have her here for this."

Alisha cut him a sharp look over her shoulder. "Simone told you?"

"Yes, she . . ." Had he already revealed too much of their bond? "I really am sorry."

"No. It's fine." Alisha leaned a shoulder against the wall, bumping one of the frames askew. "Well, it's not . . ." She rolled her lips together.

"Anyway, she keeps things close to her chest. We both do." She huffed a laugh. "So I'm surprised she told you, is all."

Then she was off down the hallway, and he followed, more slowly. Piecing together a clearer image of Simone. The woman he yearned to build more memories with.

When he got to the kitchen, Alisha was fumbling with the tap.

"Allow me, Your Highness." He reached over her and flipped on the faucet, but the spray nozzle was on, and it sent water shooting all over his shirt, the counter, the floor . . . Alisha doubled over with laughter, and Finn gripped the edge of the sink, fighting his own laughter. He raised a finger to his lips. "Shh!"

"Ali, what in the heck?" a man's voice demanded.

Alisha raised wide eyes to his. "Uh-oh."

"The grandparentals?" he asked under his breath, and Alisha dissolved into giggles again, clutching his arm and nodding.

"Grand who?"

Finn turned around, and an elderly white man who must've been Simone's grandfather crossed his arms. In that moment, he regretted every single word he'd ever uttered against Honey and Hickory.

"Hello, sir." He tried to do the dude-nod thing but realized with devastation he'd dipped into another curtsy. Stupid whiskey.

Wayne Blake was not amused, judging by the set of his jaw, which was a ringer for Simone's when she was pissed. That only made Finn more terrified—he was well acquainted with the wrath of a displeased Blake.

"Alisha Marianne, your groom is upstairs sleeping at this moment," her grandfather said. "What're you playing at, bringing home another man two days before your wedding?"

Finn opened his mouth, but Simone's pouf appeared over the man's shoulder. "He's mine." Her grandpa's eyes shot wide, and she amended, "I mean, he's with me."

She'd claimed him? Qualified it afterward, but still. His heart warmed, but it cooled just as quickly under their grandpa's gaze.

"I'm just here as the bride's escort." The words replayed in his mind, and his cheeks flamed. "Er, not *escort* escort. More like a bodyguard? Or—"

"What he means is"—Simone cut off his rambling as smoothly as a karate chop to the windpipe—"your beloved eldest granddaughter is drunk, and Finn came in to make sure she didn't get up to any trouble while I grabbed these." She held aloft a stack of DVDs with handwriting scrawled on the spines.

"But what's a man doing at Ali's bachelorette party?" The question of the evening, apparently. Simone's grandfather fixed him with a glare. "And is this the meddling barbecue man?"

"It is," he said, happy to have an answer. "That's me. The meddler." Alisha giggled. "Finn Meddler."

"Ignore these two." Simone stepped past her grandpa. "Meg was pouring."

"Ah." Understanding dawned in Wayne's dark-blue eyes.

A tiny woman who looked very much like a fairy godmother appeared at the entrance to the kitchen with a stack of bedding in her arms. "Would the young man like to stay here for the night?"

He shook his head. No, the young man would not like to stay the night. The young man would prefer not to wake up dead after being smothered in his sleep.

"It's okay, Gran," said Simone, who at the very least had proved her desire to keep him alive. "He's gonna crash at my house."

"No, he'll stay here." Her grandmother's flinty gaze hadn't left his face, and he had the distinct feeling if he made a run for it, she'd trip him flat out with zero qualms.

He took the stack of blankets from her. "The couch sounds great."

CHAPTER 31

FINN

Finn cracked his eyes open and instantly regretted it. Sunlight reflected off dazzling white snowbanks outside a bay window across from him, the curtains drawn wide. These Blakes had a thing for excessive light. He closed his eyes, biting back a groan.

"Tried to keep up with Meg, huh?"

He shot up, his pounding skull an admonishment for the quick movement. A tall Black man sat in the recliner in the corner, holding a steaming cup of coffee. In the corner next to him stood a three-foot-tall statue of an angel. Avenging or guardian, he couldn't be sure.

On the tail end of a nod, Finn let his head fall back into his hands. "Yes." His throat scratched like he'd gulped down another lungful of canyon river water.

The guy laughed. "I made that mistake last summer and haven't been the same man since. Fireball?"

"Ding-ding-ding," he said, his vocal chords protesting. Simone's grandpa had said something last night about Alisha's fiancé, Quentin, sleeping upstairs. "So I'm guessing you're the groom?"

"The fiancé." He gave a stiff smile. "Wouldn't want to jinx things."

Finn's brows pulled together, and he eyed the dude, who looked dead serious about the superstition. "Right." He peered around the room for evidence of the grandparents, then whispered, "Are you by chance also my watchdog?"

Quentin smiled. "More like a bouncer," he said. "For them, not you. I didn't want Wayne's to be the face you woke up to."

That was unexpectedly decent. And probably more than he deserved, considering he'd gone and *curtsied* to the man last night. "Thanks for that. So my first impression of him was correct?"

"Um, yeah. I'm sure you'll be getting twenty questions at breakfast, but I figured you should at least have some coffee in you first." He lifted his chin toward the end table, where a steaming mug of what looked like a fifty-fifty blend of cream and coffee sat. Salvation in a cup.

Finn raised it to his lips, slurping down the liquid antidote. "I'm beginning to see why you're marriage material." Quentin laughed as he swallowed down another burning gulp of coffee. "No partying for you?"

"Last night?" Quentin shook his head. "I spent the evening going over table numbers and ironing my nieces' flower girl dresses, because my brother is clueless. My bachelor party was last week in the city." Like Alisha's would've been, if Finn hadn't screwed things up.

"Chicago?"

"Yeah. Forgot it's not *the* city around here. You from St. Louis, then?"

He shook his head. "Springfield."

"But now you're here?" Quentin's brows rose in a clear older-brother move that Finn didn't need to have a sibling to recognize.

"Are you asking what my intentions with your future sister-in-law are?"

Quentin laughed again. "If Simone didn't leave you stranded in the desert, I figure she wants you here." Did she? In the cold light of day, he wasn't so sure. "But I saw you on the show. She and you were at each other's throats." The question went unasked, but he needed to answer. For himself as much as for Quentin.

"I went into survival mode, and I think she did too. I thought I was fighting for my life, but it didn't take long for me to realize we aren't on opposite sides."

"And Simone?"

His exhale rippled across the murky surface of his coffee. "She's been sort of a lifeline, actually."

Quentin's brows shot up. "She know that? 'Cause Sim doesn't need to be anyone's life preserver."

She had been, though, literally. Saving him from the canyon stream. Taking the time to listen, to do what mattered to him. What had he done, besides slow her down? Take away her chance at the investment she'd worked so hard for?

"That's the last thing I want. I—" His words caught on each other and ground to a halt. He winced out a smile. "I thought you were here to save me from the inquisition."

"Save you?" A deep voice came from over his shoulder, and he turned on the cushion to find a muscled guy with perfectly styled dark hair leaning against the cutaway doorframe. "Nah, man. Q is the inquisition."

"Hardly." Quentin stuck out a long leg toward the fireplace. "I'm just watching out for my family."

"Which you, my man . . ." The guy who looked like he lived in the gym sat down next to Finn on the couch. Close. He clapped him on the shoulder. "Are not."

"Cut the crap, Hector." Quentin shot his brother a glare. "Finn, meet my macho-wannabe older brother, Hector."

Ah, the brother of the groom. A whole welcoming committee.

Finn took another gulp of his coffee and eased away from Hector. "Did you sleep over too?" This place was basically a boardinghouse.

But Hector shook his head, finally leaning back and removing his arm from Finn's shoulder. "Nah. Most of the guests are staying at a hotel in the next town over, but my brother put me up at some crappy motel here in Hawksburg. Insisted I stay close to the venue."

Quentin grinned widely. "The Hawk's Nest."

Hector glared at him. "You suck. You promised me thousand-thread-count sheets."

"Did I? I must've misspoken. I meant flea-infested prison blankets." Quentin turned toward Finn. "I had to spend a summer in that hellhole when I was here working on the dig. The perfect payback for a meddling big brother."

"Oh yeah, I know all about meddling big brothers," Finn said, thinking of Darius and his push to get him to start the business, to go on *The Executives*.

"Is that Hector I hear?" Simone's grandmother appeared at the doorway, beaming at Hector. "Where are your girls?"

"Morning, Ellie." Quentin raised his mug of coffee in greeting.

She shot him a warm smile. "Good morning, Quentin. Hope you slept well?" He nodded, and her gaze shifted to Finn. "I see someone is a tad more sober. Finneas, is it?"

What was with this family and adding extra syllables? "Just Finn."

"Well, you can call me Ellie," she said, mistaking his meaning. "May as well drop the formalities. After all, you and my granddaughter have been gallivanting across the country unchaperoned." Unchaperoned? Was this 1955?

Not waiting for a reply, she moved on to Hector, a wide grin lighting up her green eyes, and shook a scolding finger at him. "And you, young man—What's the meaning of showing up without the twins?"

"They'll be coming down this afternoon with everyone else."

"Hmph. Better c'mon in and eat, 'fore you waste away."

"Yes, ma'am." Hector stood and shuffled out without a backward glance.

"So that's my future grandmother-in-law."

Finn covered his mouth, but a snort escaped. A matching snort came from Quentin's chair, and soon both men were laughing. Quentin helped him to his feet. "Guess you didn't make the best first impression."

"Yeah, but what's with her and your brother?"

"You know, I haven't quite figured it out. I'm guessing it has a lot to do with two reasons: my twin nieces, who could charm their way into anyone's heart." Quentin grinned. "It might take great-grandkids before I complete the transition from guy who tore up their backyard looking for dinosaurs to grandson status."

Did he say "dinosaurs"? Quentin kept talking as if that was a normal statement. "As for you? I know Simone's a grown woman, and I don't buy into that misogynistic nonsense about protecting her as her male relative."

"You don't?"

"I don't. But I feel like now might be a good time to give you a heads-up. You're the first man she's ever brought home. No pressure." Quentin clapped him on the back and strode into the kitchen, leaving Finn with a pit in his stomach that had a lot less to do with the lingering dregs of liquor than the worry he wouldn't measure up in this family.

Again.

***

"Dairy in the eggs—yes or no?" Carton of cream poised over a dozen beaten eggs, Simone's grandmother stared him down, green eyes narrowed. A test of his judgment, not his cooking skills.

"Your kitchen, your rules," he said.

Mrs. Blake let out a surprised chuckle. "Good answer, young man." She closed the carton and poured the eggs into a skillet on the stove, next to a cast-iron griddle lined with sausage links. "Never use cream myself. You mind?"

The spatula in her hand was a peace offering, and he took it, but she held on, her eyes sharp on his.

"Just so you know, it's gonna take more than diplomacy and fluffy eggs to dig yourself out of that hole you dug on *The Executives*."

Finn's hand went shaky on the handle, memories of how he'd thrown Simone under the bus all too fresh in his mind. "I didn't mean half of what I said on the show."

"Which half?" She fetched tongs off the counter. "The part where you said Honey and Hickory is a backwoods cesspool of food poisoning?" An exaggeration, but not by much. "Or the part where you denied Simone had any hand in making Honey and Hickory what it is today?" A contradiction that highlighted just how off base he'd been on the show. Silence stretched, long and hollow, in the crater left by her recitation of his words.

An answer was required. A reckoning.

How many times had he been in this position, close to a family, hedging for an opening, a way in, against all odds? Experience told him this was another long shot—nearly impossible. But he had to try. For Simone. For himself.

"I regret what I said about Honey and Hickory." He ran the spatula around the edge of the pan, then met her eyes. "But more so, I regret what it may have cost Simone, because if—" The thought hit him, sudden and real, that his words could've cost her everything. "Ruining this chance for her was never what I wanted. I let my emotions get the best of me."

Turning the sausage in the skillet, Mrs. Blake gave Finn a side-eye to rival Simone's. "You apologize awful quick."

Quick? He'd had days to think it over. A week full of regret . . . and wonder. "Only when I know I'm wrong."

Mrs. Blake shot him a sly grin. "Guess I see why my granddaughter saw fit not to leave you in the desert."

He'd dodged a bullet but walked right into a firing squad.

Wayne Blake sat at the head of the table, the platter of eggs Finn had cooked in his clutches. "What I'm trying to figure out"—Mr. Blake scooped all the rest of the eggs onto his plate—"is why you're at my kitchen table right now and not halfway home with your tail between your legs."

Because you held me hostage last night? Since that answer might not have gone over well, he opted for another truth. "I planned to be home by now. But Alisha invited me to stay for her party, and I figured it would be rude to refuse the bride."

"Hmph." Wayne shoved a forkful of eggs into his mouth, chewed. "Didn't seem worried about manners when you bad-mouthed me on national TV last week."

"Wasn't you he bad-mouthed," Ellie countered, and Finn flinched. She may have forgiven him, but her allegiance was clear. Still, she offered him the pitcher of orange juice, which he took before Wayne could snatch it.

"Sure he did." Wayne frowned. "Dragged my restaurant through the dirt."

Finn spoke before thinking. "Actually, sir, it's not technically your restaurant—" Technically not a point he needed to make right now, but five days with Simone had cemented the distinction into his head. "Not yours, uh—" He darted his eyes across the table. Quentin and Hector took a bite in unison, watching him like must-see TV. "Not yours anymore, I mean. Sir," he added, like a moron. Like it would help.

Wayne's bushy white eyebrows went up, and he wiped his mouth on a cloth napkin. "Sure as heck ain't yours neither. If you think my granddaughter's going to give up over half the restaurant to a vulture like you, you got another thing coming."

A vulture like you . . . the words pressed against an old bruise. An outcast. Ostracized.

She hadn't called or texted. Left him here to fend for himself. Without her to vouch for him, he was a stranger. An uninvited guest. A nobody who'd spoken out against their granddaughter in front of an audience of millions. How could he expect them to forgive him?

But Simone did. She was sarcastic, and blunt, and prickly as the cactuses—cacti—on the pajama pants she'd gifted him, but she'd let him in. Forgiven him. But stopped short of trusting him.

"No need for name-calling, Wayne," Quentin said, snapping him back to the present, "And as for the restaurant, Finn's right. That's Simone's decision to make."

Finn shot him a grateful smile. Already he could see why Alisha was marrying this dude. Heck, he'd marry him if he got him out of this conversation unscathed.

"What's my sister's decision?" Alisha appeared in the vestibule in a bright-red hoodie and leggings, dark circles under her eyes, looking like she could use an IV of electrolytes.

"Whether or not she plans to sign away half of Honey and Hickory," her grandfather said.

"Finn's right—it's her decision," Alisha told Wayne. At least he had the younger generation on his side. "And I know you trust her, because she would've told me if you'd been butting in, trying to run the place. So quit scaring the company." She kissed Quentin, then snagged his coffee and chugged half of it. Finn grinned despite his unease. The sisterly resemblance was uncanny. Coffee thieves, both of them.

"I'm on strict orders to drive Finn straight to Meg's so he can pick up the rental car," she said. "Simone's worried about how long she's kept you away from the real world." Or anxious to get rid of him.

Frowning at Finn's empty plate, Alisha nabbed one of Hector's three muffins and passed it across to him. "And also she doesn't want to waste another two hundred bucks on the rental. Her words, not mine."

But why hadn't she come herself? Probably busy with something wedding related. After all, she was supposed to have been home a week ago. He decided not to read too much into it.

Mouth full of bacon, Alisha asked, "Had enough to eat? Because I can wait."

He pushed the chair back so abruptly it tipped over and smacked the floor. Fumbling to pick it up, he said, "I'm good to go." His stomach rumbled, and he coughed. "Thanks for the . . ." He eyed the dregs of orange juice in his cup. "Wonderful to meet all of you." He looked at Quentin and Alisha when he said this, lest he get struck down by a bolt of lightning for a lie. "And again, sorry for staying over unannounced."

"That's not what you ought to be apologizing for—" Wayne said, but Alisha cut him off.

"Grandpa, I think Simone's got this." Another vote of confidence. She'd have a lot of people on her side if she decided to pursue her dream, he was sure of it. Alisha planted another kiss on her groom-to-be's cheek and grabbed Hector's neck in a half hug. "I'll see you boys later. Finn?"

He'd never been so grateful to leave a table hungry.

"Sorry, I'm sure you were probably expecting my sister." Next to him in the driver's seat, Alisha navigated one handed along the winding, hilly gravel road. Simone had said her sister loved city life, but she was clearly at home on these back roads too. "I think she was a little overwhelmed. She'd planned to do a lot of the prep for tonight ahead of time."

"Prep?"

"Yeah, for the rehearsal dinner. We're having it at Honey and Hickory, and the staff is great, but Simone wants to make sure everything is perfect."

Hosting the bachelorette party *and* catering the rehearsal dinner? Gosh, he'd really screwed her with all the delays. "Could she use a hand?"

"Are you kidding? Quentin's got more first cousins than my whole family tree, and they'll all be here in a few hours. She could definitely use a hand. But what about the car?"

"I'll pay for the extra day. I owe her one." Quentin's words echoed in his mind. *Sim doesn't need to be anyone's life preserver.* But she had been. The least he could do was repay her kindness.

"If you're sure . . ."

"One hundred percent."

∙⎯

After assuring Alisha he wouldn't hesitate to call her for a ride if Simone kicked him out of the kitchen—a very real possibility, given their history—he opened the back door of the restaurant and found himself inside Honey and Hickory for the first time.

Nineties hip-hop was pumping from a stereo on the countertop, and Simone stood at the prep table in olive-green leggings, an oversize light-gray hoodie pushed up to her elbows as she sliced shallots.

Her movements were fluid, precise. She palmed the pieces off the cutting board and dumped them into the pan. Smashed a bulb of garlic with the flat of her knife, and in went that too. The scent of browning butter and onions filled the kitchen.

His stomach rumbled, betraying his presence, but the music overtook it.

Into another pan went a stick of butter. Yolks into a blender. She turned it on high, then added the butter in a steady stream. Textbook hollandaise. She used a slotted spoon to fish one perfect poached egg out of the boiling water, then another.

A commercial came on, and she leaned across the counter to turn down the stereo.

"I thought you were serving dinner, not brunch."

She froze, hand on the volume knob. Met his eyes. "You're supposed to be back in Springfield."

"Yeah, well, your sister told me how much I'd thrown off your plans. I just came to see if I could help at all. Are you here by yourself?"

She nodded. "For now, but the others will be in later. I've got it handled."

He didn't doubt that for a second, but couldn't she see he wanted to help? "What's the menu? Eggs benedict, and what else?"

She rolled her lips together. "Actually, the eggs benedict are for Honey and Hickory, not tonight. I've been toying with the idea of offering brunch, and I came back so inspired and . . ." She trailed off, looking sheepish. "Anyway. I never do this. Go off script."

"Are you saying I broke you?" He tasted the sauce. Divine.

"Ruined me." But she was smiling. "Anyway, I know we've got a lot to talk about, but can it wait until Sunday? I'm sure you're ready to get home."

"I am, but I'm the reason you're in this mess. At least let me help you cook your way out of it. Consider me your sous chef for the day."

She wiped her fingers on her apron, brows raised. "You're not asking for head-chef status?"

"In your kitchen? Never." He wanted to press a kiss onto her lips, imagined how soft and pliant they'd be from the steam. But he wasn't sure where they stood, so instead he took off his coat and pushed up his sleeves. "Now put me to work like the tyrant I know you are."

"Finn Rimes, I've waited my whole life for someone to say those words." She handed him an apron. "Suit up, Minion."

CHAPTER 32

SIMONE

Nose cold, her arms laden with trays of meat from the smoker, Simone used her elbow to open the back door of Honey and Hickory a few hours later. Finn stood brushing a sheet pan full of cubed sweet potatoes with a smoky brown sugar glaze. When the door shut, he looked up at her, and his face broke into a smile so wide it pulled her in like gravity.

She'd never felt such an intense surge of emotion. Irresistible, bottomless. His eyes darkened and his smile slipped into something more intense. He felt it too. How could he not? And where did that leave them?

Trapped under the weight of a deal neither of them wanted but both of them needed. With a future tied up in one another, or on their own. And what lay in between? The unknown, and she hated uncertainty.

Forcing herself to break eye contact, she lifted her chin to the pan of potatoes. "Those will need to roast another thirty minutes; then we're set."

Nodding, Finn slid them back into the oven, the hair at the back of his neck curling with sweat above the collar of his henley. The man would walk in here after a night of drinking still looking like sex on a stick. How could she sift through all the decisions with him steaming up her kitchen in a henley and apron, of all things?

He closed the oven and shot her a speculative look, the same kind he'd been sending her way ever since the party. Hesitant. Vulnerable.

Her heart tugged her closer, and for once she obeyed, threading her arms around his neck. Giving him the reassurance she craved. "Thank you for staying. I would've been swamped on my own."

He pressed a kiss to her forehead, comforting as a fleece blanket by the fireside. "You would've done just fine on your own."

She would've. She always did. But having him here by her side . . . sharing her world with him—her home—felt more right than it ought to have. If she admitted to wanting him, would it amount to needing? To being bound and beholden?

"I can see why you love this place." One arm still looped around her waist, he rubbed a hand along the gleaming stainless counter. "This restaurant, and Hawksburg too. I've only been here a day, and already I feel like I know at least three people who I could put down as an emergency contact."

Simone laughed, because that summed up the locals perfectly. "You're either in, or you're out. And once you're in . . ." She stopped herself, because she'd almost said, *You're a part of the town forever, woven in like the stitches on the Yarn Spinners' designs.*

But that would mean she'd been the one keeping herself on the outs. But she hadn't imagined the cold shoulders, the canned pleasantries in place of meaningful conversations. Had she?

The back door opened with a gust of cold air, and Alisha and Quentin tumbled in, chased by snow flurries. She pulled away from Finn. The others must have suspected something, but she didn't need to confirm it.

But Alisha's brow bunched as she scanned the countertops, not seeming to register their closeness. "Where are you at with prep?"

Rude. "Um, since I'm doing this out of the goodness of my heart, I don't think I owe you updates."

"Everything's pretty much set to go except the salads," Finn supplied. She shot him a look, but she couldn't stay mad when she encountered his sheepish expression, shoulder half lifted in a shrug.

No guile. The complement to her surliness. The sweetness to balance her acidity. No denying they complemented one another. Did she want to test their compatibility with a merger when her future hung in the balance?

Across the kitchen, her sister and her fiancé shared a look. Quentin rocked up on his toes, hands jammed in the pockets of his black puffer coat. "So, say . . . and this is just hypothetically speaking—but say you had to feed a lot more people. Would that be feasible?"

"More people?" Meat took hours to smoke, although they could fire up the grill. Make grilled cheese for the kids . . .

"How many more?" Finn asked.

Quentin rubbed the back of his neck, face twisting in a wince. "Around two hundred."

"Two *hundred*?" Simone and Finn jinxed, and Quentin nodded with a grimace, then put up his hands in a quelling gesture.

"But not tonight. We're all good for the rehearsal dinner. Thanks, by the way," he said, and he flashed the smile that had no doubt won over her sister. "Our caterer lost power in the storm," he went on. "Their backup generator failed, and apparently no one knew because they hadn't been in all week. They lost all their perishable goods, and, well—"

"We've got no food," Alisha said. "For the reception dinner tomorrow."

No food, and the wedding a day away? The punches just kept on coming.

"So I was thinking, we could smoke some ribs . . ." Alisha pulled open the walk-in fridge, voice muffled. "I'm sure there's some coleslaw prepped—"

"No."

Simone turned, surprised at the surety in Finn's voice.

His Adam's apple dipped in a bob as he swallowed. "Not to shoot down your idea, but you don't want to be eating ribs in a wedding dress, right?" Alisha shut the refrigerator door, the look on her face answer enough. "What was the original menu?" he asked.

"Chicken and salmon," Alisha said. "We figured people would've had their fill of heavy meat tonight. But really, barbecue is fine. More than fine, when it's Honey and Hickory."

A barbecue buffet would be great at a lot of weddings. If her sister and Quentin were saying their vows in a rustic barn, or a fairy-tale reception in the woods, great. But their wedding aesthetic was classy contemporary. Lush, deep colors and an elevated tablescape. They'd planned the downtown wedding of their dreams despite the rural surroundings. Picnic fare wouldn't do.

A great cake and spectacular food topped Alisha's wedding must-have list. And as maid of honor, Simone had accompanied the couple to tastings. What their caterer had planned couldn't be replaced with potato salad and pulled pork. But while she could hold her own in the Honey and Hickory kitchen, she wasn't a professionally trained chef.

Already thumbing through her mental contact list of suppliers she could pull from to create a worthy meal, she swallowed her pride and turned to Finn.

She didn't need to say a thing. He'd already rolled up his sleeves.

CHAPTER 33

FINN

Plated dinners were out. Even with his extensive restaurant experience and Simone delegating, they couldn't pull that off for a wedding reception taking place a mere twenty-four hours from now. A whopping 250 guests, all needing to be fed at the same time? He'd thought Simone had taken on a lot with her plan to cater the rehearsal dinner tonight. But executing a last-minute reception dinner tomorrow? A panic chill swept up his arms at what they'd taken on.

Cocktail hour would be simple. A charcuterie spread, crudités. But dinner? For *250* guests?

His phone lay on the counter, screen dark after he'd read through the latest in a string of text messages.

Bella:

> You're on your own, kid. But if anyone can pull off this crazy scheme, it's you. Don't let doubt hold you down.

He'd put out an SOS to the crew at Bella's, but between the weekend rush and a death in Bella's family, there'd be no assistance coming their way from Springfield. But he was not on his own, not by a long shot.

Behind him, Simone paced the kitchen, phone to her ear, gesturing as she spoke with a local butcher. Boss mode, and it took all his effort to pull his attention away from the stunning confidence she exuded and back to the notes he'd scribbled on a piece of parchment paper.

Under the scratched-out plated dinners, he'd written *Buffet?* Simpler on short notice, but he worried how the food would stand up to sitting so long. A chicken breast could go from juicy to dried out in the blink of an eye. And the elegant element would be lost. Unless they found a way to put a playful spin on a traditional buffet . . .

"Sim," he whispered, and he prodded her arm with the pencil eraser as she passed by.

"Hang on just a sec, Mal." Scowling, she put her hand over the receiver. "What?"

He spoke fast, ideas keeping pace with his words. "What if we did DIY food stations? Macaroni and cheese, baked potatoes . . ." They could prep the garnishes and focus on nailing a few main dishes.

"But what about proteins?"

Good point. "A grill station? Kebabs, or fajitas? Those cook up quickly, and we could utilize tofu for the vegetarians."

She was nodding. "That just might work." She put up a finger, brought the phone back to her mouth. "Hey, Mallory, can I call you back in a few? We're still working out the details, but I'm guessing we'll be over in about an hour. Great, thanks." She hung up, then swiped at her phone, typing. "Lyndsey and Brent responded yes. My grandpa's right-hand man, Hank, offered, but he's like a second father to Alisha. I want him to enjoy the party." Frowning, she rolled her lips together. "That just leaves Rhonda, our most experienced cook, but she's not answering her phone. Regardless, with everyone else working the reception, we should be good."

"But what about the restaurant?"

"It's one day. Alisha's more important." No hesitation. Honey and Hickory meant the world to her, but she'd put everything on the line for those she cared about. Misjudged her? Oh yeah. He may as well have compared canned tuna to an ahi steak. She fought for what she wanted, yes. And fought just as hard for others.

She strode over to the door, took his jacket off the hook, and tossed it over. "The venue has a kitchen. Want to go over and scope it out? Then we can drive to the butcher and also see what we can rustle up in terms of seafood. Deal?" She froze, hands on the zipper of her coat.

Across the kitchen, their eyes locked. *Deal?*

"I'm in," he said, heart in his throat. But was she?

"All hands on deck" took on a whole new meaning in a small town. Simone had painted herself as the prodigal daughter, but all Finn saw was the town sweetheart. The venue had a bare-bones kitchen, but tableware was part of the catering package, now null and void.

Even with all the cutlery and plates from Honey and Hickory, they were woefully short. So yesterday Simone put out the small-town Bat-Signal, and people turned up offering chafing dishes, electric grill pans, cutlery, and place settings.

He'd finally made it back to Springfield late last night after the rehearsal dinner—which had gone well, thanks to all the prep they'd done before the catering mishap forced them to switch gears and focus on the reception—to get a few hours' sleep and return the rental car. Now he pulled his own car into a spot between two trucks in the reception hall lot.

Rubbing the sleep from his eyes, he tried the door. Locked. He pulled out his phone to text Simone and let her know he'd made it.

"Look up, silly." He did, and there she was, holding open the door. "Hope you brought a change of clothes," she said, giving his uniform and nonslip shoes a once-over.

"I came to work, did I not?"

"Yes, but after dinner's served, y'all get free range of the reception." *Y'all.* Like he was just another worker. "And of course I'll pay you what the Honey and Hickory cooks are getting."

Bristling at the insinuation, he said, "I'm here to help you and your family, Sim. I don't want money."

"This is tricky, and I'm trying to negotiate things as best I can."

"I get that, but I'm not here as your potential partner. I'm here as your . . ." He trailed off, because what exactly was he to her now? An enemy no longer, but more than a friend . . .

She reached up and rubbed a thumb down the center of his brow, her touch drawing him into the present. "I'm glad you're here, in whatever capacity." Almost shy, a smile tugged at the corner of her lips. "I'm getting kind of used to having you around."

He wouldn't push it, not this time. Last time he'd pressed for the answer, in the bed-and-breakfast, he'd scared her off. For now, he was grateful she'd let him stay. A one-eighty from summer, when she'd all but run him out of town.

He'd avoided touching her with everyone around, but with just them at the front door, he reached for her hand, heart squeezing when she threaded her fingers through his. "Thank you."

She tipped her head sideways. "For what?"

"For letting me help. This is your home. Your place. And I don't take that lightly."

A small smile lit up her face. "What did I tell you about thank-yous?"

Glancing over his shoulder, then peering over hers—there always seemed to be someone watching here—he stepped closer. Wound his hands around her waist and bent his lips to hers, murmuring, "That you prefer them like this." He kissed her, quick, light. But she swept her hands up to his shoulders and pulled him deeper.

Yes, this.

This is what he'd been missing ever since they'd arrived in town. Working with Simone was nice. But being with her? His true desire. His world. His home.

She pulled away, her hands still twined around his neck. "Let me introduce you to everyone real quick. I've only got a few minutes before I gotta head to hair and makeup."

"But it's, like, five hours until the wedding."

She patted his cheek. "You sweet, innocent man. How little you know of the realm of women." Chuckling, she pulled him down the hall to the kitchen. Rowdy voices and laughter spilled out the door, and he slowed to a halt just short of entering. All of a sudden, this task felt overwhelming.

Looking back over her shoulder, Simone asked, "Getting cold feet?"

"Nah." But he worried about what would happen after the party. Succeed or fail, he'd still want her. Would she feel the same?

CHAPTER 34

SIMONE

Simone dropped Finn's hand and led him into the reception hall's kitchen. In an alternate universe, she would've walked in hand in hand. Let everyone see just how much his presence meant to her. But she still didn't know if she should take the deal, and even though he'd promised he'd want her without it, in her experience, there was what someone said, and what they did. And only one of those two could be trusted.

Monday was only two days away. Defining their relationship could wait. If Finn still cared about her after the dust settled, then maybe she could trust their connection.

For now, all that was left to do was make a round of introductions and go over their game plan one last time before she got sucked into bridal party preparations. All three cooks from Honey and Hickory were hard at work on prep, working for double pay. And all but one had been enthusiastic about the challenge.

"Hey, Rhonda, thanks again for deciding to come in."

The reluctant cook looked up, her tidy dark-brown bun covered by a hairnet. "Always on shift Saturdays anyway. Figured my body wouldn't know what to do with the extra rest."

At a loss from the Eeyore-like response, Simone settled on a nod.

But Finn stepped closer. "What're your plans for the basil? Is that going in the pasta salad, or is it a garnish?"

Simone glanced at him sharply. He already knew the answer. But he gave a tiny shake of his head before fixing all his attention on the taciturn cook. Chin in his hand, he nodded along as she spoke.

Turned out introductions weren't necessary. She'd forgotten how great he was with people, the effortless way he made everyone feel important. Because to him, they were.

She went over and picked up their clipboard to do a final run-through, and Lyndsey stepped up to peer over her shoulder. "Would you look at that."

"What?" She turned and found Lyndsey's eyes not on the list, but on Finn and Rhonda.

"He's teaching Rhonda to chiffonade basil."

He was. Grinning at something she'd said, he rolled the basil leaves tightly, then chopped them with quick flicks of his wrist. Next to him, Rhonda mimicked his movements, and he slowed, the better for her to imitate.

"So?"

"So?" Lyndsey frowned at her. "Rhonda normally doesn't even take all the peel off the potatoes before boiling them."

"Because the mashed potatoes we serve are smashed."

"We serve them smashed because Rhonda doesn't like to peel them. C'mon. You don't think he's a little good to have around? The way I see it, the merger is a godsend for the restaurant. Not only do you get a chance to get out of Hawksburg again to start up the franchises, but Finn's heaven sent. He could kick-start our food to the next level. I know you're ready to stop treading water."

Treading water. Heaven sent. Finn had been in town less than two days, and already people thought he was more valuable to Honey and Hickory than she was.

Lyndsey leaned both elbows on the prep table and turned to Simone, eyes bright. "Do you think he can teach me how to flambé? I've always wanted to try."

Of course he could. He could teach them to fillet a halibut, or make a red wine reduction. But what did that matter at Honey and Hickory? "You planning to flambé a pork butt?"

Lyndsey shook her head.

"Then it's a moot point. Finn's here to help with the reception dinner—that's it."

Brows raised, Lyndsey said, "Heard."

●━━

"Is it hot in here, or is it just me?"

At the sound of her sister's voice, Simone spun from her haunt by the sanctuary entrance, where she'd been scrolling through Finn's updates about the meal, including a thumbs-up selfie of him and the cooks, all with huge smiles. Great news, and it shouldn't have made her feel left out. But it did.

Even though she still had doubts about leaving the reception food for her sister's wedding in the hands of someone who, up until last week, had been her sworn enemy, she knew Finn could handle it. She'd watched him in the kitchen this morning. He kept everyone on track without barking orders. Guided when they needed it and stepped back when they didn't.

And the man could cook. Could he ever. As long as Lyndsey didn't set the kitchen on fire with her sudden interest in flames, they should be fine until Simone could sneak away after family photos. More than fine.

She turned off her phone, allowing herself precisely one more second to worry that her feelings for Finn were clouding her good judgment—one second of *What will you do if he doesn't come through for you? And what will you do if he* does?—then she turned her focus to her big sister, the one whom she'd already let down this week by her fixation on the monster of a deal.

Today was about Alisha, and she wouldn't let any of her own issues—relationship, career, or some confusing mix of both—spoil that. She hurried around the corner into the hallway, where her sister stood with one hand pressed against her lace-covered stomach, the other resting on the wall like she might keel over. "I'm freaking out. I can't do this, Sim."

Okay, so this was bad.

"We need to send everyone home," Alisha said. "There's been a huge mistake. I'm not cut out for marriage." Above the plunging sweetheart neckline of her gown, her chest heaved. "I mean, I want to marry Quentin. I *really* want to. But what if I screw this up?" She flapped her hands at her face, flushed despite a layer of subtle airbrushed makeup. "Why is it so hot in here? I'm gonna puke."

"Sit." Simone punctuated the word by pressing her hands into Alisha's shoulders and backing her up toward a folding chair. Her sister sank into it and immediately dipped her head between her knees.

"Oh no, you don't!" Simone grabbed her bare shoulders just in time, stopping her.

No way was she going to let her sister get makeup on the ivory skirt of her wedding gown. Alisha worked harder for her sculpted muscles than most bros hogging the weight racks, and while she said she didn't do it for the looks, Simone had finally convinced her that if you've got it, flaunt it, at least on your wedding day. She'd steered her away from the ball gowns and into this mermaid-skirted confection of a dress.

With the dress out of imminent danger, she hooked a finger under Alisha's chin and squatted down until they were face to face. "Sis."

"Sis," Alisha parroted, a line between her brows.

Hesitating, she almost called for Meg. Her sister's best friend was the one with the amazing pep talks. Simone wasn't even sure she believed in marriage. But she believed in Alisha.

"Ali," she said, gathering her courage. "You are absolutely cut out for marriage. And not just marriage, but for marrying Quentin. The universe basically set you up. Put you on a collision course hundreds of millions of years ago." Alisha huffed out a teary laugh. "And besides, if you leave that man at the altar, he's going to need some next-level therapy."

Alisha laughed again, blinking up at the ceiling. "I would never."

"Okay. Well, then what are you worrying for?" She rubbed both hands down her sister's arms, prickled with goose bumps despite her heated skin. "Quentin is your forever. And you're his."

Her sister sniffed, her voice quavering. "Like you believe in forevers."

"I believe in *you*." Her mind shot back to the Grand Canyon. The eternity and immediacy all in one. To how her heart had kicked against her ribs the first time she and Finn met. To the confirmation in their kisses.

Did she believe in forever? A week ago, she would've said no. And now, the answer wavered, too murky to see. But she had absolute faith in her sister's capacity for love and commitment. She and Quentin wanted forever; that's what would make it theirs.

But first, she had to get her sister to the altar before her groom collapsed from sheer panic. Simone stuck out her hand behind her and snapped twice: "Margaret, water."

"Aye, aye, Sarge." Meg bolted forward from where she'd been whispering with Pops near a potted fern, both of them clearly concerned, and thrust out a water bottle.

Simone grabbed the bottle and brought it between them, lifting the straw to her sister's mouth. Hydrating people was becoming an alarming habit. "Drink."

When she pulled out the straw, a drop of water remained on Alisha's lower lip, and she dabbed it with her knuckle so the crimson lipstick would stay perfect. "Now, are you doing this?"

"I'm doing it." Alisha lunged forward and wrapped her in a hug as fierce as it was brief, then leaped up and accepted her bouquet from a relieved-looking Meg. An orange lily drooped low, and Simone jabbed it back in between a deep-blue gerbera daisy and a plum-hued rose.

The other members of the bridal party were milling around the foyer. At a nod from Simone, the first pair lined up. Ivy, one of Alisha's bakery staff who'd become her good friend, held out her arm to the groomsman she'd been assigned—one of Quentin's cousins, who'd arrived at the church with two minutes to spare and was still tucking the tail of his shirt into his pants. Ivy shot a grimace toward Simone, and she made a sympathetic face.

Meg and Quentin's best friend, Tre, were next, already in their positions, ready to go. Meg chuckled at something he said in an undertone; then they strode off down the aisle.

That left her and the best man. Hector's twin daughters peered into the crowded sanctuary, poppy-orange flowers tucked into their dark hair, chattering away. At a nod from Simone, he beckoned his daughters over, then knelt down in front of them. "I've gotta go in before you, so just listen to what Tía Alisha says. She'll tell you when it's time to start walking. And remember, it's okay to drop all the flowers in your basket, just not all at once, got it?"

At their nods, he stood with a smile and held out his elbow to Simone. Alisha moved up next to them, arm in arm with Pops. Gran stood by her other side, white-blonde hair teased to fullness. Her big sister shooed Simone and Hector with her free hand. "Hurry up and get on down the aisle so I can marry my man."

For once, she obeyed with no sass, taking Hector's arm and heading for the open sanctuary doors. Demons vanquished, Simone understood Alisha's urgency, even as she herself wished for time to slow down. To suspend them in this moment where Finn and Honey and Hickory and her dreams all coexisted in harmony.

But it was a precarious fantasy, and with each step down the carpeted aisle, she felt herself tipping the balance. One false move, and it would all come crashing down, just like a teetering stack of Jenga blocks.

"Brent, we're running low on shrimp, and Mr. Snyder's headed over." He'd cut out red meat since his stroke last year. Another reason she wanted to expand Honey and Hickory's menu, so they could serve every member of the community.

"On it." The cook hurried away, and Simone checked the rest of the stations to make sure they had enough to see them through. Everyone had come up at least once, and dinner seemed to be winding down. At the end of the buffet, Finn was stationed at the electric grill, chatting with all the guests who came through the line.

Tonight his easy smiles for everyone else were getting under her skin, like they had in the summer. Things had been strained ever since their stay in the bed-and-breakfast, but between orchestrating this dinner and their rendezvous in the hall earlier, she thought they might have been rounding the bend.

But now she wondered, yet again, if their connection was real, or a ploy to get her to take the investment. She couldn't afford a $200,000 mistake.

"You two pulled off the upset with this one, didn't ya?" Mr. Snyder made it to the table, his eyes on Finn at the grill. "Who would've thought, after seeing you just about kill each other on TV." He laughed, but she didn't.

He popped a cheese cube in his mouth. "I'm going to go give my regards to the chef for an excellent meal. What are you standing back here for, anyway? Your partner has this under control—you ought to be out there dancing with the other gals."

"As opposed to here, overseeing the meal I planned?"

"No need to get so prickly." He frowned and then snatched another piece of cheese, not bothering with the tongs. "Just wanted to make sure you enjoyed your sister's wedding." With a shake of his head, he moved down the line.

One day of this pseudopartnership, and already she'd hit a boiling point. Could she stand a whole career of people insinuating she was less than Finn?

She glanced down the row to see Mr. Snyder chatting with Finn, his belly bouncing with laughter. It should've warmed her heart to see people embracing someone she'd come to care about.

Instead, all she could think about were all the ways Finn's presence invalidated hers. She could share Hawksburg. Share her family and friends. But sharing Honey and Hickory meant handing over her part in it, one piece at a time. Admitting she'd never been the right choice.

Admitting she was replaceable.

With a last glance down the line to assure herself everything was set in case any more stragglers came along, she took off her plastic gloves. Finn had everything handled, and this was her sister's wedding. Time to quit wallowing and start partying.

●━━

Simone stepped off the dance floor as a love ballad came on, sweaty and smiling and feeling about a million times better than she had after Mr. Snyder's remarks. She glanced toward the banquet tables, ready to rope Finn into a slow dance, but he'd disappeared. Probably cleaning up.

Possibly avoiding her.

He'd been on edge ever since they'd arrived in town, and as much as she wanted to reassure him, she was in need of reassurance too. Tonight's celebration marked the last barrier between them and the deal. Tomorrow they'd have no more reason to delay talking through it, and she was no closer to coming up with a way to save both their dreams.

Hand in hand, Quentin and Alisha took the floor, and couples parted for them, pulling them in for hugs as they passed until there was only the bride and groom, spinning slowly on the parquet floor.

Quentin hadn't stopped smiling at his wife all day. First through a sheen of tears from the altar, and later around a million kisses they shared in response to glasses clinking and their own effusive love bubble.

And Alisha never stopped touching her groom. Holding his hand as they wound through the tables, resting her cheek against his shoulder when they sat at the head table. All the PDA would've been sickening if it hadn't been so supremely pure.

Teeth flashing in a grin, Quentin bent his head to whisper something in Alisha's ear, and she laughed, then ducked her forehead to his chest when he followed his words up with a kiss to her temple.

The unhurried kisses and besotted glances left Simone feeling bereft. She might not have been able to give a part of Honey and Hickory to Finn, but she'd already given him a piece of her heart, and no matter how the deal shook out, she didn't regret it.

She turned, bumped into one of the satin-covered chairs, and scooted around a tableful of guests finishing up their cake with cups of coffee or glasses of wine. With barely any time to prep, she and Finn had pulled off a wedding-reception dinner and saved Alisha and Quentin's big day. In the morning they could figure things out, but for now, time to find him and celebrate.

After reaching the bar, Simone leaned over to give her order. "Could I have two glasses of merlot, please?" Not traditional for a toast, but all the champagne had been used up in toasting the bride and groom.

Drinks in hand, she turned around and ran smack into Pops. Half the wine ended up on her, the other half on his white button-down, the tux jacket discarded. She looked down at her dress, saturated but unstained. Thank goodness for berry-toned velvet.

Pops grabbed a stack of cocktail napkins off the bar, but she waved them away. Didn't want white pulp marring her dress.

"I'm good. You're the one in need of a costume change."

"Pah. No one's lookin' at me today." His blue eyes twinkled in the candlelight and the glow from low uplights strategically placed along the walls. "Your sister makes a beautiful bride. Why aren't you out there with her?" He flipped a napkin toward the dance floor.

"Looking for Finn," she said, and she instantly wanted to bite back her words when a coy smile lit his face.

"Oho, are you, now?"

His smirk made her wish she'd downed the glass of wine now seeping through her dress. "We just catered a wedding for two hundred and fifty guests, so I figured another toast was in order."

He huffed his agreement, dabbing ineffectually at his stained shirtfront. "That all you're toasting to?" He kept his eyes down, but she knew what he was really asking. What everyone in her family was wondering: Was she going to take the deal?

"For now, yeah."

"I wasn't keen on the idea, to say the least." Pops tossed the useless napkins down on the table next to them. "And from what I hear from Ali"—he narrowed his eyes at this, letting her know just what he thought of her lack of communication over the past week—"neither are you. I promised I wouldn't butt in. Honey and Hickory's all yours now, to do as you see fit."

"But . . ."

"But as much as you might see 'franchise' as a four-letter word—"

"And you don't?"

"Never said I didn't. But all I've got to say is you've got a lot to consider. And I hope you won't let feelings get in the way."

Feelings? "I may have gone off on him on the show, and we had our share of arguments this summer, but I'm not going to let a grudge cloud my judgment."

"Wasn't talking about that kind of feelings, Sim."

Was she that transparent? She crossed her arms against the feeling of exposure, regretting it when dampness seeped into her skin. "If it helps, I'm not taking the deal. Not as it stands."

"That's what I'm worried about."

Confusion swept over her as the music quieted down.

"You have a history of pushing away things you love."

Love? "I don't love Finn." Her voice came out choked. Panicked.

She looked away, into the crowd, to avoid Pops's scrutiny. Her eyes landed on Quentin, standing across the room, the grin on his face bright with the full force of unfettered love. She followed his gaze to her sister, in the center of the dance floor, smiling back at him without an ounce of reservation. *That* was love.

No twist of doubt. No messy complications. Perfection.

The deal put everything in limbo, but it was more than that. Her feelings for Finn were too big to put into a tidy box, and that scared her.

"He's no one special to me." She couldn't let Pops see the depths of her messy, imperfect feelings for Finn. Not with so much on the line. Not with her heart on the line. "There's nothing between us. If anything, he's a liability."

Pop's gaze flickered up, over her shoulder, his expression solemn. "From the looks of it, that's news to him."

CHAPTER 35

FINN

There's nothing between us . . .

The music had cut out, bringing her words into sharp focus, captured like a photographer's high-speed lens.

Snap. *He's no one special to me.*

Snap. *There's nothing between us.*

Snap. *If anything, he's a liability.*

Snap. Her eyes met his. Wide. Startled. Unsure.

But before she could speak, Alisha's voice rang out, calling her sister to the dance floor for the bouquet toss. Simone half turned, and then the DJ repeated the call, coaxing her to the floor. A wall of women, young and old, eager and stoic, encircled the bride, waiting for Simone to join their ranks.

Decisive this time, she pivoted and wound her way through the tables, clapping her hands overhead as she swung her hips to the rhythm of Beyoncé's "Single Ladies." Brushed him off like she had at their first meeting. Turned him into a nobody. He'd entered some alternate universe where they'd never gone from jagged, biting words to tender touches. A world where *they* never existed at all.

He watched her jokingly jostle for position among the women, her lips turned up in a grin that didn't even have the decency to look forced. Alisha counted down from ten to the accompaniment of whistles and cheers. And then the bouquet was arcing overhead as a blinding series of flashes filled Finn's eyes with stars.

When he blinked, Simone was clutching the bouquet, petals scattered around the long skirt of her dress, jaw slack in surprise. She'd been tossed another future she didn't want. Just like the deal.

Just like him.

He backed away, driven by a need to hold fast to his composure before it flew away.

And it would fly away, desert him in a moment if he unclenched his jaw, let his chin fall. So he retreated—one step, two—until his back hit a door and he spun through it, out into the carpeted hallway. He had to get away. But he needed a minute to collect himself, to breathe.

Darting a glance behind him to check that no one had followed, he yanked open the nearest door and skidded to a halt on humid tiles. Everyone else had deserted the kitchen to go enjoy the open bar and packed dance floor. The remains of the cake lay on a prep table, only crumbs and frosting left. Too busy playing his role, he'd missed the celebration.

Alone, in these familiar surroundings—this refuge—all the mistakes of the past week crushed down on him, gravity amplified. Trusting too much, wanting too much, falling too soon.

His fault. He hadn't heeded his own heart's warning. Ignored years of experience that told him he wasn't someone people chose. Not for the long haul. Not for forever.

After surviving breakfast with her grandparents and pulling off this dinner, he'd deluded himself into thinking he might have a place with Simone.

But she'd never wanted him here. Never wanted *him*, at all.

The door swung open, and he darted over to the wall and flattened himself against it, next to an apron hanging on a hook. He held his breath, hoping it was just a cook looking to nab an extra piece of cake.

But Simone stepped into the room, bare feet soundless on the tile, the velvet skirt of her dress bunched in her hands to raise it off the floor. Her hair was braided close against her scalp and twined through with gold threads, the rest twisted into a knot at her nape. The maroon dress was cut down to just above the curve of her hips, accentuating the smooth sweep of her back.

His fingers tightened on the apron strings hanging next to him, and the hooks jangled.

She spun around. "Finn?"

No more holding his breath. No more hoping. "Surprised you came looking for me when I'm just a random nobody."

Her face fell. "I didn't mean for you to hear that."

"Didn't mean for me to hear it, or didn't mean it?"

"Both." She frowned. "If this was just nothing, do you think I would've let you come to Alisha's party? Let you meet my friends and family? I risked a lot having you here."

So had he. She'd risked her reputation. Her image. But he'd risked his heart. And he wouldn't be chancing it again. From here on out, it was all business. "And the deal? Did you mean what you said about that? I'm a liability?"

"Why do you keep asking about the deal?"

How could he not, when hundreds of thousands of dollars hung in the balance? When money and career and hopes and dreams were stewing in the stockpot of their relationship, ready to boil over?

"It's what you've been after all along." She challenged him with the statement, but he'd already answered; he didn't reply. "Is that why you stuck around?"

"I came for you. Like I told you." She would never believe him; he saw that now. Too convinced everyone was out to get her. "But you never wanted a part of this deal in the first place. And I'm done waiting on you to make up your mind. Are you going to sign the merger, or not?"

She hesitated, and he had his answer. "I still don't know if I can."

"Because I'm a liability." She shot her eyes to his. "You were considering the deal when it was just us. But here, with everyone around . . ." He gestured toward the door, where the pulsing thump of party music had started back up. "Were you just waiting for dinner to end to inform me my services are no longer required?"

Her eyes had gone cold. Golden resin hardened to amber. "I am not okay with your tone."

"My tone?" He pressed his lips together. "You deny knowing me, let alone all that's happened between us, and you're worried about my *tone*?" The nerve he'd always admired had now turned against him.

She balled her fists. "I was lying through my teeth, trying to save face!"

"Because it would be so terrible to admit you care about a loser like me."

"You've got it all backward. It's me people doubt. I'm the one who no one wants around." She gripped the steel table behind her, knuckles pale. "One day in Honey and Hickory, and already my cooks think you're the best thing to happen to the restaurant. Everyone out there keeps reminding me how I never could've pulled this off without you."

"They're wrong," he said. No matter what, he wasn't going to lie to her. "You've got nothing to prove." But he couldn't wait around until she figured that out.

He was done putting himself out there and holding his breath, waiting to be chosen, or not. "If you can't admit you might want me around because it might tarnish your image, then I'm out. I need someone who's sure about me. Not someone who doubts my worth."

"So you're walking away from the deal?" Her first concern. Because, of course.

Bowing out would leave her with no options. All or nothing—those were the terms.

"I'm walking away from *you*." While he still could, before the deal bound them together, for better or for worse. He couldn't spend a lifetime wondering if he was a means to an end. Couldn't make her a priority when he was her fallback.

As he pressed a shaky palm to the door, Simone said, "I wish what I'd told my grandpa was true. I wish you'd always been no one to me."

And honestly? Same.

CHAPTER 36

SIMONE

A very much not-heartbroken Simone cracked open the barn door the next day, her breath frosty, and stepped into the hay-scented warmth. Willow poked her head out of the stall and whinnied.

"Hey, girl." She found herself smiling at her horse's eager greeting. *See, you're not heartbroken after all.* Heartbroken people did not smile.

Heartbroken people might toss and turn all night, torn to pieces by losing someone they'd gotten slightly—or excessively, as it turned out—attached to. Heartbroken people might hug their pillow to their chest and cry because the man they sort of liked—very much liked— accused them of being a selfish, heartless jerk. And heartbroken people might feel like fools for falling in love with a man who could walk away without a second's hesitation.

But heartbroken people didn't get on with their lives the next day. They stayed in bed in holey pajamas and devoured copious amounts of ice cream, washed down with salty tears. They binge-watched sitcoms while sitting amid piles of unfolded laundry and take-out containers.

She, on the other hand, had risen early (a full ten minutes before noon), downed a homemade granola-and-goat's-milk parfait (managing to only reminisce a teensy bit about baby goats and Finn), and washed down her sensible breakfast with black coffee, not tears (those were all dried up), and now she was here.

Vertical, dressed, dry eyed, and fueled by a nutrient-dense breakfast. Take that, heartache.

Simone reached into her pocket and pulled out an apple she'd brought from home. Willow nudged her whiskery muzzle into her neck in a horsey thank-you, rocking her back onto her heels, and she chuckled. See? Not heartbroken.

After all, wasn't getting rid of Finn her deepest desire?

No, not anymore. She'd planned to screw him out of the deal. But in the end, he'd been the one who'd twisted the dagger. Ironic, in the cruelest way.

Somewhere between California and Illinois, her deepest desire had become her greatest fear. Losing Finn.

She swept a wrist under her dripping nose—she wasn't crying again; freezing temps always made her nose run, nothing new—and wrapped her arms around Willow's neck. Her watery eyes amounted to a reaction to all the pollen in the hay, was all. A reaction some people—misguided people—might blame on heartbreak.

Face pressed into her horse's coarse mane, she groaned. "This isn't what it looks like, okay?" Willow whickered but didn't pull away. More proof, not that she needed it, that animals were better companions than people. "Loving Finn would be ridiculous. *He's* ridiculous."

Willow snorted, like she didn't care either way, which made Simone feel like maybe she hadn't made her point well enough. She needed her horse on her side in this.

"Trust me, he's the worst. For one thing, he's got his head in the clouds, always searching for the beauty around him instead of being concerned with practical things."

She remembered how his eyes had crinkled with a grin above the fanned-out travel brochures, like the prospect of dragging her around to tourist attractions was the best fun ever. Like being stuck with her beat being anywhere else.

Except that wasn't true, because he'd walked away.

A swish of her tail showed Willow remained unconvinced. Fine. Simone had more ammunition. "I haven't even mentioned his smile, which is infuriating. Sexy and wholesome, all in one." She cleared the thickness in her throat. Allergies acting up again. *Ugh.*

If she felt like crap, may as well shovel some. She led her horse out into the aisle and clipped her lead to a post. Fetched a scoop and a wheelbarrow. She was halfway through mucking out the stall when Willow let out a loud neigh.

"Yeah, yeah. Almost done, Miss Impatient."

"Simone?"

Great. Meg, Care Bear in human form, harbinger of the touchy-feely apocalypse, she who must dissect every emotion, here to pester her about her feelings again. Nowhere to hide in a twelve-by-twelve stall, so she shoveled with renewed vigor in hopes Meg would take the hint and disappear in a puff of sparkly smoke to the fairyland from whence she'd come.

Unfortunately, she didn't, so Simone asked, "Aren't you supposed to be at work?"

Meg tugged loops of hose off the wall and walked in to fill up Willow's water bucket. "It's Sunday. Can't teach to an empty classroom." Pesky weekends. "Figured I'd come out and check on you."

"Gross."

Meg tipped her head back and laughed like the psychopath she was. "Do you want to talk about it?"

It being the fact that when she'd emerged from the kitchen, her sister's entire bridal party was lurking outside the door. They hadn't asked any questions, simply whisked her off to the ballroom and handed her a refill of the drink she'd spilled right before Finn showed up. She should've known Meg wouldn't be content to let it go at that.

"Why? So you can give me a patented Margaret Anderson pep talk? The one where you tell me all men are pigs and I'm better off without Finn? Because you can save your breath; I agree with you." She set the pitchfork aside and pushed a wheelbarrow full of poop toward the door. Meg scooted out of the way just in time.

"You can try to run me over all you want," Meg called after her, "but it's not going to take away your feelings."

Feelings. Bleurgh. But Meg was right. Nothing would make her feel better right now. Simone trundled the wheelbarrow over to the muck heap and dumped it. There. Out with the crap. If only it was so easy to get rid of pesky feelings.

Out of nowhere, someone wrapped their arms around her, hugging her from behind. Startled, she spun and jabbed, putting her kickboxing training to use. But she hadn't practiced since moving back home, so her elbow connected with empty air.

Meg gasped and jumped back. "What the heck, Simone?"

"You surprised me!" Simone dusted off her knees, torn between remorse and irritation, and irritation won. "You can't sneak up on people and hug them without warning."

"You're not *people*. You're my friend."

"Your friend's little sister."

"What?" Meg squinted at her like she was a student caught texting in class. "That's a super-weird thing to say. What is wrong with you today?"

Maybe the fact that Finn had walked out on her less than a day ago? "Ever stop to think I might be a little testy after losing out on two hundred thousand dollars? Without Finn, there's no deal."

Shoving her gloved hands into the pockets of her coveralls, Meg stepped aside. "So it's the money, then?"

She grunted an affirmative.

"Okay, if that's the way you wanna play it, fine. But for the record, you were wrong about my pep talk. I wasn't going to say you're better off without Finn."

That surprised her, but she covered up with sarcasm, per the usual. "Shocking. The woman who's on ten dating apps thinks I need a man. How very progressive of you."

"Two dating apps, and I didn't say you needed him. Will you just listen for ten seconds and let me explain?"

Simone ground her teeth together and started counting to ten in her head. *One Mississippi. Two Mississippi. Three Missi—*

"I can see your lips moving," Meg snapped. "I didn't mean ten literal seconds." She flung up both hands and disappeared into the barn.

The brush and tap of Meg's push broom greeted Simone when she came back into the barn after she'd decided talking about her feelings would be better than hanging out by the enormous pile of manure. Meg stopped sweeping and met Simone's eyes. "Why are you being so mean?"

Twitchy under her scrutiny, Simone said, "I'm always mean to you. We're mean to each other."

"We joke with each other, yeah. But this feels different. I was worried for you after what happened last night, but now I feel like something else is going on, and it's got nothing to do with money or a man."

Simone pressed her lips together. She would not cry again. Her throat ached, her head hurt, and all of this sucked. Like an unstable Jenga tower, her life was tumbling down around her, despite all her efforts to hold all the pieces in place.

The stress of a double-edged deal and losing yet another person who'd become important to her had set off an earthquake, and as terrible as it was to admit, this time she didn't think she was strong enough to withstand the fallout on her own.

"I'mjustreallyfreakinglonely."

Meg cocked her head. "I'm sorry, what?"

"IsaidI'mreallyfreakinglonely."

"What was that?"

"I said I'm lonely!" She paused, panting. "And it's really lame, and as much as I don't want to talk about it, Finn is gone and you're here, so I guess you win the prize of dealing with my emotional baggage. Lucky you."

Unable to look Meg in the eyes after her confession, Simone picked up a brush and got to work grooming Willow. "Everyone thinks I'm some hard-ass who doesn't need people. But the truth is, it's easier to push people away than rely on them. I moved back home, and everyone's moved on without me. I mean, I went on freaking national TV, got an offer from *The Executives*, and crickets. I love Chantal, but she's my best friend; she's pretty much obligated to care. Same for my sister. And no one else called to congratulate me, or check in, or anything."

This sounded petty and lame and selfish. After all, she had a best friend and a close sister. How many people could say that? But Chantal lived in Chicago, not Hawksburg. Ditto for Alisha. How was she supposed to carve out a life in Hawksburg without a support system here?

"Don't get mad, okay?" Meg leaned the broom against the wall and spoke slowly, like Simone might bolt any minute. And yeah, internally she'd laced up her shoes. "But what about me? *I'm* here. I texted after the show. I called when you were on the road. I've been here for you. Before. Now. Always."

Simone licked her lips, found them salty. "I know you have. And I appreciate it. It's just . . ." This was so freaking embarrassing to say out loud. Then again, a few minutes ago she'd argued a one-sided debate with a horse, so rock bottom was about ten mile markers back. "It's just the only reason you've stuck around is because I'm your best friend's little sister. And I hate being an obligation."

Hands on her hips, Meg said, "That is the craziest thing I've ever heard."

"You're telling me you hang out with me because you actually like me?"

Meg let out an astonished laugh. "Heck yes, I like you, woman!" She looked primed for a hug, so Simone stepped back, just in case. "I don't just like you, I love you. You and your little hedgehog self."

She stopped brushing Willow. "Hedgehog?"

"Yeah." Meg grinned, never a good sign. "You're spiny on the outside and soft and fuzzy on the inside."

"Hmph."

"But without the spines, you'd just be a squishy, boring hamster."

Simone shook her head. "You are an absolute freak, and I love you for it." She ran her fingers over the bristles of the brush with a sigh. "Am I being a needy, ungrateful loser?"

"Ungrateful, yes," Meg said, softening her words with a smile. "And needy? Maybe. But it's okay to be needy. If we aren't needy sometimes, then no one knows we're hurting. And Sim, I don't want you to hurt all alone."

Willow stamped her hoof, as if to punctuate the sentiment, and both women laughed.

"Permission to hug?" Meg held her arms outstretched like an over-eager camp counselor. Oh Lordy, this was worse than the sneak attack. She'd created a monster.

But for once, a hug didn't sound terrible. Simone spoke through teeth only half-gritted. "Permission granted."

Squeezing her, Meg said, "You know, I'm not the only one who loves you."

"Is this the boy advice you've held in this whole time?"

Meg's body shook with laughter. "Nope. I'm talking about all of us here in town. Did you know when you worked on the campaign for Crest, people bought so much the drugstore ran out of inventory?"

"They did not."

"They did," Meg said, releasing her. "And when you got fired, half the town said Chicago is dead to them. Everyone plans to boycott the whole city out of vengeance."

Chicago was already a four-letter word around town, with two strikes against it as a big city and the home of rival sports teams. "That's nothing new."

"Maybe not. But did you know Grace threw a watch party for your episode of *The Executives* at the Back Forty? Place was packed."

A watch party? Why had she never heard about it? Maybe because she hadn't stopped in at the Back Forty for a few months, too worried she'd wind up bellying up to the bar alone.

But Meg wasn't finished. "Ever since Matt heard you wanted to set up a retail shop, he's been dying to ask if you'll sell his jackets and bags—you know the studded leather ones?"

"Then why hasn't he?"

"Because he's worried you'll brush him off. You left and came back and didn't try to reach out."

"Because I was worried everyone would resent me. I wanted to prove how committed I was first."

"Resent you? Girl, most people adore you." An echo of Finn's words. *From what I can tell, the whole town loves you.*

"Don't you remember what happened when you asked the Yarn Spinners for help getting rid of Finn? They showed up on a moment's notice, no questions asked."

Simone rubbed a hand on Willow's forehead. "I know the town is full of kind people. That's one reason I love it here. It's just that everyone's created these rich lives of their own. They don't need me."

"Who said anything about needing?" Meg asked. "It's about wanting. You want to be in their lives. So reach out. Tell them."

"I tried that when I moved away. No one came to visit."

"Simone Eleanor Blake, are you really holding a seven-year grudge?" Meg clocked her face and said, "Don't answer that. But you do realize you were eighteen when you left. You've grown up. Maybe your friends have too. Open up, tell them you miss them, and see if they feel the same way."

"I guess it can't be worse than spending another year wondering if everyone hates me."

But she wasn't the only one who'd doubted their place here. Finn had been so uncertain of her feelings that he'd taken himself out of the equation altogether. All because she couldn't bring herself to admit she wanted him in her life.

Once she got started, talking about her feelings sucked a lot less than holding them in. "Since you're already imparting wisdom, may as well go ahead and tell me what you were going to say about Finn."

"Are you sure? You're not going to like it." Safe bet. "I was going to say you might not be better off without him. Not that you aren't whole without him. Your worth isn't dependent on anyone else, and I know you know that. But why is the possibility that Finn might make your life better so scary for you?" Meg asked the question without a hint of criticism. "Maybe if you sit with your feelings, it'll help you sort them out."

As opposed to her current strategy of avoiding her feelings like gopher holes in a pasture?

Could she maybe test out that advice sometime in the future? Like way, way in the future? "Tomorrow is my big meeting with *The Executives*," Simone said. "It's a long shot, but it's my last chance to salvage a deal. Now is not the time to have a heart-to-heart with myself."

"Maybe that's what makes it the perfect time." Meg said, back to impersonating a camp counselor. Maybe Simone had been better off not opening up.

Nah.

CHAPTER 37

FINN

Finn stood in front of the microwave and watched the frozen dinner spin in a gloomy pirouette. A full day gone since he'd walked out on Simone at the wedding. He'd fallen into bed last night, then worked a double at Bellaire.

But with his Sunday shift over and sleep elusive, there was no more avoiding his feelings in the stillness of the midnight hour. No more avoiding the fact that tomorrow he and Simone were supposed to videoconference with *The Executives*, and he wouldn't be on the call.

He'd walked away from the chance of a lifetime and screwed Simone over in the process.

The microwave dinged, and he flinched. Despite everything, she didn't trust him. Didn't trust his heart, his reason for sticking by her side. If she took the deal, she'd always wonder. And if she didn't, then he would.

So he'd made the choice for both of them. A choice that left him back in Springfield, standing in someone else's kitchen. But this time he didn't have the heart to bring ingredients to life and make it feel like home. Home was out of reach, and he was worn out from falling short.

He opened the microwave and pulled out the plastic container. Heat stung the pads of his fingers, and he dropped it on the marble countertop. He ripped off the plastic and stabbed a fork into the middle. Still frozen. He took a bite anyway, teeth crunching into icy shards of tomato sauce.

"This is brutal to watch." Darius had entered the kitchen in plaid pajama pants and a gray tee, laptop under his arm.

The latest flip house had sold while Finn was away, which left him nowhere to go except Darius's spare bedroom. Spacious accommodations that came with a heaping side of I-told-you-so. His best friend had been right. Impossible for him to separate heart and head.

Mouth full of freezer-burned pasta, he glanced around the kitchen. Top-of-the-line appliances—a six-burner range, double oven, Sub-Zero fridge stocked with organic produce and free-range eggs—and he was forcing down pasta somehow both cold and yet way past al dente. Bleak.

The thought of taking down a copper pan from the rack overhead made his heart seize with longing for what he'd given up. He wouldn't be able to fire up the burners without being reminded of Simone kneeling in front of the wood-burning stove in Sedona. The flicker of flame would remind him of how she'd healed more than his throat by taking care of him in the cabin, how she'd worked alongside him in the kitchen in Hawksburg.

But their connection hadn't been enough. *He* hadn't been enough. Turned out being the one to end things didn't hurt any less.

Pushing aside a chunk of icy marinara, he took another bite of mealy, frigid pasta. He grimaced as it stuck in his throat and pointed his fork at Darius, who was watching him over the top of the laptop he'd set up at the island.

"Don't say it." If he had to listen to a lecture about how much the past week had cost him—emotionally, financially—he might lose it.

Darius flicked his eyes down and tapped away at the keyboard.

Finn left the disgusting meal on the counter to reheat later and opened the fridge. The sight of full shelves and brimming crisper drawers didn't quell his anxiousness like it usually did. He bypassed bacon and a carton of eggs, brie and a jar of homemade apricot preserves, and fished out the milk instead, then rooted around in the cabinets until he found the boxes of cereal . . .

Rock bottom.

After another moment's hesitation, he caved and poured himself a bowl of bran cereal and shoveled a bite into his mouth. Depressing, as expected.

"Should I not have tried?" he asked his friend, unable to stomach the loaded silence. "You're always telling me to push past my comfort zone."

Darius kept his eyes on the computer. "In business."

"This was business!" Finn waved a hand, and milk dripped off his spoon. "Not my fault *The Executives* whipped up a sinister plot to boost their ratings."

"No, it's not. But things were already personal between you and Simone; then you decided to put them in a pressure cooker by inviting her on a road trip. It was never going to end well."

Never going to end well. He hated the emotions those words stirred up in him. For so long, he'd applied them to himself. Never going to amount to anything. Worthless. And hearing Simone tell her grandpa exactly that . . .

Emotion clogged his throat. "For a second there, I thought it might. We make a great team. And I think she saw it too."

"Then why'd you walk out before hearing her decision?" Darius closed his laptop, the better to shoot Finn a penetrating glare, no doubt. "You still had a shot at two hundred thousand dollars."

Maybe. Maybe not. And he was done being sure of someone when he was their option. He forced down another mouthful of cereal, trying to ignore the all-too-familiar slide of soggy mush going down his throat, the cold blandness of a meal he'd eaten countless times when he'd had to scrounge his own dinner.

The stool legs screeched along the tile as Darius pushed back from the island. "Enough of this." He took the cereal out of Finn's hands. "When's the last time you had a decent meal?"

He thought back to the breakfast he'd cooked with Simone's grandma. The Honey and Hickory barbecue he'd tasted. The rehearsal dinner he'd been too busy catering to make himself a plate.

"If you have to think that long, it's a problem." Darius pulled out his phone.

"What are you doing?"

"Getting you dinner. No one can think straight on an empty stomach. You taught me that."

"This is cheating." Finn balanced a compostable to-go container on his knee. After tossing out his depressing frozen dinner, Darius had called in reinforcements in the form of Bella, who'd brought takeout from an all-night diner. It wasn't that he was a food snob, but ordering takeout seemed lazy with a stocked fridge in the kitchen.

"Disagree." Bella sat on the other end of the couch, in sweatpants and a white menswear undershirt, her red-gold hair still pulled back in the braid she'd worn on shift a few hours ago. A night owl, she'd probably been on her PC, gaming to decompress after work, when Darius called. A pinch of guilt hit Finn for the fact that his friends felt the need to show up in the middle of the night for him, but a bigger part of him appreciated having their support. Bella raised a forkful of hash browns. "Takeout is self-care on days you just cannot bear to look at the inside of a pot again."

"Oh jeez, you sound like Simone."

Bella kicked her feet up onto the couch, then toed off her clogs when Darius shot a glare her way. "From what you've told me about her, she's driven, with perfectionist tendencies and a killer instinct." Accurate, but she'd left out caring, loyal, and flat-out hilarious. "Sounds more like Darius to me."

"Hey, now." Darius frowned, then brightened. "Actually, yeah. I am all those things."

Bella sat up, jabbing her plastic fork for emphasis. "Oh my gosh, you're dating the female version of your best friend. You totally have a type."

Darius grinned. "She's not wrong."

"What's wrong is how flattered you are by this," Finn told Darius. "Could you be any more full of yourself?" But he couldn't keep from laughing. That or cry. "What does that say about me, though?"

"That you choose to surround yourself with people who complement your personality." Bella tucked into her food again, then added, "People who help you be your best self."

Except Simone. She brought out the worst in him. Right up until they'd gotten to know each other.

The omelet on his lap was getting cold, and even though his appetite was gone, he wasn't about to waste any more food, so he dug in. Feta, mushrooms, spinach, and diced tomatoes. "This is fantastic."

"I know." Bella looked smug, but then again, she always did. "It's from the diner over on Elm. I've been keeping it to myself, but I figure walking away from your dream girl and two hundred thousand dollars deserves a good pick-me-up."

But he hadn't told her—

She cocked her head. "You think I don't know you well enough by now? That girl didn't break your heart. You walked away before she got the chance to show you the door."

He squinted at her. Bella was perceptive, but clairvoyant?

"And also, Darius might've filled me in when he called."

"You're lucky you fed me." Hangry Finn would not have been okay with this. He glared at Darius. "And you. Not cool. I would've told her in my own time."

"You don't have the luxury of time on this one. Isn't your videoconference scheduled for tomorrow?"

"Later today, actually. It's already past midnight," Finn said. He winced at the realization of how little time he had left to fix things, at how clueless he was about what he should do. What *could* he do after how he'd left things?

Darius must've noticed the uncertainty flicking across his face, because he said, "Talk to us. We want to help you, and you've got a few hours left to grovel."

"Me? I'm the one who should grovel?" Maybe he hadn't explained the situation well enough; it was as complicated as a beef wellington recipe.

But Darius nodded and took a bite of patty melt. When he swallowed, he said, "You're the one who walked away."

"I walked away because it was inevitable. I'm not someone who people pick—don't you get it?"

The room fell silent, apart from Bella's noisy chewing. After a moment she sighed and put down her fork. "*I* picked you. That night back when you were a dishwasher and we were in a bind, I chose you to step up."

"Because you were out of options."

"Because I made sure it looked like I was out of options." She set her food on the coffee table and sat back up, hands resting between her folded legs. "I told Jade and Zeke to take the day off. I wanted to give you that shot. And it's the best choice I've made since opening up the place." She leaned back. "Other than the pear risotto."

"That pear risotto was amazing," Darius agreed. "When are you going to bring it back?"

Finn tuned out of their conversation, his mind awash with the revelation Bella had just shared. She'd concocted a whole plot just to get him on the team?

No matter how much time he put in toward healing past wounds, he still thought of himself at the core as someone whom no one wanted but had worth anyway. If the world didn't want him, whatever—he wanted to do good for himself regardless.

But even if Bella hadn't chosen him off the bat, he'd never stopped to think how she'd chosen him ever since. She was here to cheer him up when she could've been at home relaxing after a long day. Darius had been choosing his friendship for eight years.

Had his misplaced insecurity pushed Simone away?

The fact remained . . . "Clearly you both think I'm in the wrong. Yeah, I walked away, but she didn't call me back." Hadn't called him since.

"Stubborn," Darius said, and Bella nodded.

Finally, they understood. "I know, right?"

"I meant you." Oh. "The deal was a big change for both of you. Do you blame her for being on the fence?"

Maybe a little. "I told her she could back out, that I wanted her more than I wanted the deal."

"Aw, look at you, Finn, with the grand declarations." Bella looked close to ruffling his hair like he was a puppy, and he scowled. "Too bad you followed it up with a tantrum."

"So glad you invited her," he mumbled at Darius. Then to her, he said, "And I get it. You think I'm impulsive, and emotional—"

"Nah, man," Darius broke in. "Can't speak for Bella, but as for me, I'm jealous of you."

"For walking away from two hundred thousand dollars?"

"For wearing your heart on your sleeve." Darius sat forward, hands locked between his knees. "Life has tossed so much shit your way, and most people would've closed off the world. But you've got this huge capacity for love. You don't hold back."

But he had. Closed off and shut down and walked away.

"You're not your past, Finn. Don't expect history to repeat itself."

"And if it does, we'll be here for you," Bella said. "We're not going anywhere."

Gratitude tried and failed to cancel out his sense of loss. "I know you think I should fight for her. But—" His food churned in his stomach. "I just can't right now. I'm exhausted from all of it. I have to leave it up to her."

And no matter what his friends said, her decision was a foregone conclusion.

CHAPTER 38

SIMONE

An hour before the scheduled videoconference with Constance Rivera and Keith Donovan, Simone sat at the corner table of Honey and Hickory, internally hyperventilating. WebMD would probably tell her that wasn't a thing, but it totally was.

Next to her laptop lay the paperwork sent over by *The Executives*, with both their names listed. She half hoped when she logged in to the meeting she'd see Finn's face on-screen, grinning, like it had been one big practical joke.

But she put the odds of him showing up as slim to none. She'd become another person who had made him doubt his worth, and that gutted her.

She'd asked for Meg's advice, so she may as well take it. Here she sat—not planning what to say in the meeting, not strategizing—just sitting and feeling the full brunt of rejection, which was freaking brutal.

A slow-motion video of Finn played out in her mind every time she sat still.

Finn, watching her under his lashes in the cabin, faking sleep. Finn, huddled up under a blanket, losing horribly at the game of Life and laughing about it. Finn, kissing her senseless at the Grand Canyon. Finn, lying beside her in a run-down mansion.

Finn, hearing her lie to Pops.

Finn, walking out the door.

Her phone rang, pulling her out of her spiraling emotions. *Alisha?* Why the heck was her sister calling from her honeymoon?

Expecting a dire emergency, and ashamed a threat to her sister's welfare offered a welcome break from all this emotional work, she accepted the video chat. "Please tell me you're not dead."

"I don't like how this is becoming our standard greeting," Alisha said, very much alive and apparently intact.

"Maybe we should work on it, but what the heck? Why are you calling me from your honeymoon?" She lowered her voice. "Do we need to have the Talk?" Not waiting for Alisha's answer, she said, "You see, when two consenting adults—"

"Cut it out, Sim." But instead of scowling at her for the taunting, Alisha giggled. Must've been the effects of marathon sex. "It's almost dinnertime here. We cannot have sex around the clock."

Maybe not, but they could at least make an attempt. What else were honeymoons for?

"I wanted to make sure you were okay, since I didn't get a chance to talk with you before our flight. Getting dumped at a wedding has got to be a top-ten worst-case scenario."

"I did not get dumped." Technically they hadn't been together. "And for future reference—"

"You're planning to get dumped at a wedding in the future?"

Simone kept talking over her. "For future reference, you phrasing it that way does not make things better." Boyfriend or not, Finn leaving her hurt far worse than losing a chance at an investment from Constance and Keith ever could.

But she didn't need to bring Alisha down on her honeymoon. "And getting dumped at a wedding reception barely ranks in the top-hundred worst-case scenarios. For instance, getting mauled by a rabid bear at a wedding? Way worse."

"What about getting mauled by a regular bear?"

"Also worse. See, you're proving my point."

"No, what I'm doing is letting you deflect. C'mon, Sim. What happened?"

Ugh, talking about her feelings was even worse than sitting here stewing in them, but her sister cared enough to call from Paris, and that mattered. A lot. "What happened is he thought I was keeping him on the line while I worked out a way to get the deal without him."

"Which, to be clear, you were."

"I was not!"

Her sister leaned closer to the screen, and the neck of her tee slipped off one shoulder. Was she wearing Quentin's shirt? Ew, TMI. "A week ago you told me you'd ruin him before you let him touch Honey and Hickory."

"Fair point. But things changed," she said.

"And he knew this?"

Simone blinked. "I mean, we kissed."

"So he knew you were attracted to him. That doesn't mean you liked him."

She hated having her own reasoning thrown in her face. "I told him he was a good person."

"Well, in that case . . ." Alisha rolled her eyes.

"What?"

"Sim, really? A good person is the bare minimum. You expect him to be reassured because you don't think he's the devil?"

"Considering I used to think he *was* the devil? Yeah." No. But she needed to hold on to her dwindling anger or she might break down in front of two billionaires in . . . she checked the clock. Shoot, less than half an hour.

"Anyway, I fail to see the problem. You didn't want the deal. Finn bowed out. Ergo, no deal, and you don't have the stigma of turning down a coveted offer from *The Executives*." A couple of days of being married to a professor, and Alisha thought she could claim the logical high ground. "The way I see it, he did you a favor."

"But he thinks I don't care about him." How did Alisha not understand the enormity of this?

"So?" Her sister leaned out of the camera and came back with a croissant. A predinner pastry snack? Simone wholeheartedly approved. Alisha took a bite, cupping her hand under the shower of flaky crumbs. "It sucks his feelings got hurt, but at the end of the day, you're better off."

This was infuriating. If she were there, she'd tear the croissant out of her sister's hands and throw it in the nearest trash. After she'd eaten half, of course. "I am not 'better off.'" She made air quotes and nearly dropped the phone.

"Why not?"

"Because I love him!"

Alisha grinned into the camera. Oh, crap.

"I hate you. I loathe you. I utterly despise you," Simone said, weighing the merits of crawling under the table. Who had closed last night? Brent, whose mopping skills left something to be desired. Slumping to the floor in humiliation was out, then.

Her sister was chuckling now. "I know I shouldn't laugh, because you're heartbroken—"

"Not heartbroken." Heartsick, maybe. Sounded less dire. Something that could be cured with an antacid, not surgery.

"Too late for that. But your face," Alisha said. "You should see your face. I'm surprised I haven't burst into flames from your laser-beam eyes."

She'd never wanted a superpower, but laser eyes? Sounded useful.

Alisha had stopped laughing, wore the serious big-sister face again. "I know this past week has been a roller coaster for you. But I honestly think this crappy deal is the best thing that could've happened to you. You two were content to keep living in this bubble of banter and bickering, but then you got tossed into the frying pan of six days of intensive couples therapy."

Alisha paused for breath, and Simone's frown turned into a glower. "And fell in love. So don't let a little miscommunication come between you."

Nothing "little" about him walking away from $200,000 just to get away from her. "He hurt me too. He imploded this whole deal without giving me a chance to explain myself."

A deep voice came from off screen, and Alisha waved a hand. "Be right there, my love." *Ick.* "I get that. But you didn't want the deal anyway, right?"

Simone shook her head.

"So, deal aside, what hurts is that he doesn't trust you."

Simone nodded.

"Well, have you given him a reason to?"

Had she? She'd stuck by his side during his sickness. Veered from her careful schedule for him. Told him things she hadn't shared with anyone else. But when asked point blank about their relationship, she'd denied having any feelings for him.

"Holy crap." Once they got into town, she'd distanced herself, wary of anyone finding out she had feelings for the man she'd been sparring with for months. And then belittled him—to her grandpa, no less. Anyone would've been doubtful. And given Finn's history . . . "Ali, what do I do?"

Alisha choked on her mouthful of pastry. "Wait, are you asking me for advice?" She looked over her shoulder. "You do realize this is Alisha. Your big sister—"

"This reaction makes me want to take it back."

"No, don't do that!" Alisha dove off the bed, and she cringed, waiting for the thump. But a second later she reappeared with a crumpled piece of paper, speckled with something dark. Probably vanilla extract, knowing her sister.

She was almost scared to ask. "What is that?"

"It's the speech I carry around in case this ever happened," Alisha said, like that was perfectly reasonable.

"*What* ever happened?"

"In case you fell in love, silly." The words should've made her angry, but all she felt was a weird sort of jumpy sensation in her belly. *In case you fell in love.*

Alisha unfolded the paper. "Simone, baby sister, little menace—"

"You're the menace," she interrupted.

"Hush and let me finish. You asked for this," Alisha said.

Eh, she'd asked for advice, not a full-blown speech, but she was in no position to be choosy.

"From the top: Simone, baby sister, little menace, I love you." She raised her eyes to Simone's, then went back to reading. "If you're hearing this, it's because you finally took down some of your walls and fell in love. I'm probably ninety and forgetful, which is why I decided to write it down."

"Accurate, since you've acted like a grandma all your life."

Her sister shot her a quick glare. "But now that you've let a man into your life, you might be regretting it. You probably think it makes you weak, which it doesn't, and vulnerable, which it most certainly does."

Well, that was the opposite of comforting.

"But being vulnerable is important, because only when we're vulnerable can we see there are people worthy of our hearts, people who crave the chance to love us and be loved in return."

But she still had so much to prove. So far to go before she'd reach a point where she felt like a success. How could Finn love a work in progress? How could anyone?

Then again, she loved Honey and Hickory, even though the decor was a hodgepodge of decades and the coleslaw was subpar. Imperfect. Great in some areas, lacking in others. Yet she loved the restaurant just the same.

Finn wasn't perfect either. He'd misjudged her and stormed off and cost her a chance at working with two of her favorite entrepreneurs.

But she loved him. Completely.

Alisha put the paper down. "If you love Finn, then find a way to show him. And if he doesn't feel the same way, then I'll help you pick up the pieces, and I promise, you'll be okay."

She would. She loved Finn, but losing him for good wouldn't destroy her. Didn't mean she wanted to test that theory, though.

"I mean it, Sim. If you put yourself out there and it all goes south, I'm on the next plane home."

"I would literally punch you in the face if you cut short your honeymoon for me," Simone said, and Alisha laughed.

"So are you going for it?"

"I am."

Alisha whooped, and Quentin's face took over the frame. "Does this mean I can have my wife back?"

"Take her away. I've got this." Action was her wheelhouse. Tell Finn she loved him? Terrifying. But show him? Heck yes, that she could do.

"We're rooting for you," Quentin said. "No matter what." Warmth fizzed through her chest at his support. She could get used to having a brother.

Leaning into view, Alisha said, "Hey, do you think you can ask for Constance's autograph when you—"

"Bye, Simone." Quentin sounded a tad less patient than he had a second ago, and Simone laughed as the call ended.

No, she couldn't get Constance's autograph, because a plan was forming in her mind, and if she decided to go for it, then she'd have a much bigger favor to ask.

CHAPTER 39

FINN

"There's someone at the door for you." Darius flung open the guest room door without knocking, interrupting Finn's *Top Chef* marathon. "Put on a shirt, right now. And pants."

He looked past the Cheetos crumbs on his bare chest to the cactus-covered pajamas he had definitely not put on to feel closer to Simone.

"*Actual* pants, the kind with a zipper," Darius said, then glanced around at the mix of clean and dirty laundry on the floor. "You know what? Hang on." He disappeared and came back in thirty seconds, handing him two hangers holding a dress shirt and chinos. "Put these on. And brush your teeth. I'll stall. You've got five minutes."

Finn bunched the clothes in his hands, watching Darius's fists clench at the impending wrinkles. "I don't want to see her, Dare." Except he did. So much his chest hurt.

So much so that he'd spent the past week hiding out in Darius's spare room, marinating in his unhappiness, venturing out only for his shifts at Bellaire and the meal center. He hadn't made any new batches of sauce, had taken the website offline.

What was the point? Monday had come and gone with no word from Simone. He'd lost out on her and the deal. Running a cooking school? That kind of future was for people who'd had life figured out since second grade. And developing feelings for a powerhouse like Simone? A recipe for heartache.

Darius was glowering at him from the foot of the bed. "You sure as heck better want to see her. This is your last chance."

His last chance had been at the reception, and he'd squandered it. He tossed the button-down and slacks on the unmade bed. He had half a mind to go out there shirtless—he knew what his body did to her. His skin prickled at the memory of how she'd traced his tattoos, circled his arms and gripped . . .

He snatched up a hoodie at random from the pile spilling out of his duffel, tugged it over his bare chest, and walked down the hall, dread and anticipation warring in his gut. Was she here to take him back or tell him off?

But when his eyes lit on the woman waiting for him, he backpedaled and collided with the corner of the wall. "Ouch!"

"Mr. Rimes?" Next to Darius sat a very poised Constance Rivera.

Clutching his elbow, he waved. "Ms. Rivera. Hi. Hello."

His friend's eyes went wide, and he mouthed, "What. The. Heck?"

Finn grimaced, helpless. He was an idiot. Also, Darius could've been more specific. He would murder him later, though. For now he had to figure out what kind of ambush he'd walked into. "I, uh . . . I wasn't expecting you." As if that wasn't obvious.

She let her gaze drift down to rest on his cactus pants for a brief moment. "I gather. Though I don't blame you. After you blew off the meeting, I'm sure I'm the last person you expected to see."

Wow, she held nothing back. Feeling more nervous than he had on the show, he bit his lip. "This is unexpected, yeah." Unexpected in the way a planet-killing asteroid would be. "Can I get you something to drink? Coffee? Water?" *Vodka, straight up?*

"No, thank you. I have something I'd like to discuss with you. Over dinner, if you're free?"

He was wearing pajamas at four p.m. Clearly he had nowhere to be. Refusing a dinner invitation from Constance Rivera would be even more brazen than turning down an investment from her.

Equal parts nervous and mortified, he said, "Um, sure?"

"What he means is he'd love that." Darius was across the room, or else he probably would've elbowed Finn in the ribs.

"Yes, I would," Finn lied. He had no good reason for turning down the offer, at least not one Ms. Rivera would understand. Was she here to demand an explanation? Serve some sort of legal notice for backing out of the deal? He gulped. "Let me just get changed."

"There's no hurry; you can take your time. Shower, maybe." Constance somehow managed to make this request sound gracious, not like a desperate plea not to force her to be trapped in a confined space with him in his current state.

He glanced down at the splotch of marinara on his hoodie. A fresh wave of heat crept into his cheeks. "A shower. Yeah." Avoiding Darius's eyes, he slunk to the bathroom.

Ten minutes later, droplets from his wet hair dampening the starched collar of the button-down shirt he'd changed his mind about, Finn sat in the back of a sedan next to Ms. Rivera, having flashbacks to his dripping car ride with Simone in Sedona.

At least he had pants on this time—wrinkle-free khakis, thanks to Darius's speed ironing, a skill that Finn had always teased him for. He made a mental note to cut that out.

"You know," said Constance, "I was taken aback when both of you declined our offer."

Both of them? Did that mean Simone had pulled a no-show too? He imagined the team from *The Executives* waiting. And waiting . . . but if so, why hadn't they reached out?

"But when Simone filled us in on the reason for your absence . . ."

That he was in love with her, and terrified she didn't feel the same?

"Let's just say I take some part of the responsibility. We created a volatile situation, and it's not surprising how things turned out. It's something I've spoken to our producers about, prioritizing drama over dignity."

She offered a tight smile. "I know it's poor consolation, but it's something I hope won't happen again in the future. As for you"—here came the reckoning—"what disappoints me more than your no-show is that you kept your dream to yourself."

How did she know about his dream?

"Sharing big goals can be scary. I get that. But in my experience, the hardest dreams to share are the very ones that need our voice behind them."

The car pulled to a halt, and he looked out the window, cognizant of their surroundings for the first time. They'd arrived at the street entrance of Bellaire. Constance climbed out, and he followed, at a loss.

The dining room was dim and empty, when it should've been ramping up toward the dinner rush. The door to the kitchen swung open, and Bella emerged in a navy dress, her auburn hair loose and tumbling over her shoulders, and he did a double take. He never saw her without it knotted atop her head or pulled back in a braid. And the dress? Even when they met up for drinks after work, she wore jeans and a T-shirt.

But shock eclipsed surprise when Keith Donovan followed her out of the kitchen. Had he dozed off during *Top Chef* and fallen into some kind of bizarre stress dream? The former NFL pro, current high-profile entrepreneur, stood in the Bellaire dining room wearing chef's whites.

"Finn, glad you could make it." Keith thrust out his hand, and Finn shook it, the contact proving this wasn't a figment of his imagination. "I'm sure you're wondering what's going on, but we asked Ms. Blake to keep you in the dark. After all, you blindsided us by changing your mind about our generous offer."

Jeez, they weren't going to let him off easy.

"And with stakes this high, we prefer to see how you perform without preparation."

They'd succeeded in catching him on an off day. An off week. He'd spent more time in bed than in the kitchen lately, and his mental state? Unfocused at best. And now he was about to be thrown into some trial by fire? He swallowed, grateful for the shower and fresh deodorant.

Mr. Donovan smiled at Bella. "Your boss was graciously giving me a tour of the kitchen when you arrived." Constance and Keith must've rented out the whole place, and knowing her, it hadn't come cheap. She valued her skills and the reputation of her establishment, as she should. "Excellent establishment you have here, and the dishes you made for me to taste? Phenomenal."

"Thank you." Used to Bella barking out orders or bestowing no-nonsense compliments, seeing her subdued kicked his nerves up a notch. They were, after all, in the presence of two seriously heavy hitters. And he was still clueless as to why.

Voice softer than usual, Bella said, "Ms. Rivera, it's a pleasure. Welcome to Bellaire."

"Constance, please." She shook Bella's hand. "Thanks so much for agreeing to this."

"How could I say no?" Bella smiled. "Finn is one of my best chefs, and I'll be sad to lose him." Her words reminded him of what she'd told him last week. How she'd fought to have him here. "But if you're going to help launch his vision, I'd be a miser to stand in his way." She raised a brow at him in a clear *Don't screw this up* pose that matched the shade Darius had been throwing his way all week.

Gladly, if only he knew what exactly "this" was.

Keith smoothed a hand down the front of his stiff white jacket and grinned. "We're not here for Finn's Secret Sauce. We're much more interested in your idea of a culinary institute that offers a second chance to people who need it most. In the spirit of that, we'd like to offer *you* a second chance."

A second chance. And he had Simone to thank.

"But there's a catch," Keith continued. "If you plan to head up a program like this, we want to know you've got the cooking chops."

Out of the corner of his eye, he caught Bella's smirk. She knew he had the chops; she'd trained him herself.

"My wife always jokes I couldn't fry an egg if my life depended on it." Mr. Donovan chuckled, but Finn was too on edge to join in. "Teach me to cook a meal from the menu here at Bellaire, and if I master the dish, then we'll sit down and talk. Those are our terms. Do you accept?"

Finn stood next to Keith at the cooktop, shocked into autopilot. He couldn't remember agreeing to their outlandish offer, could barely remember his own name, but he could train someone to season and sear a steak in his sleep. A handy skill, because his mind was toast.

The same woman who he thought wanted him out of her life had petitioned *The Executives* on his behalf. Constance's presence in the dining room was evidence of how much Simone cared. Keith standing here next to him, scraping a pat of butter into the pan under his direction, was proof of her confidence in him.

Somehow she'd forgiven him, or at least given him an opening, and he didn't dare squander her gift. He'd misjudged her, yet again. Didn't feel worthy of this huge opportunity. But that was the stupid worthless feeling talking.

Simone had granted him a chance beyond his wildest dreams, and he chose to believe himself worthy of investment. He would impart his knowledge to Keith to the best of his abilities, then go out and nail the pitch he should've given in California. The pitch that matched his heart's desire.

One of his heart's desires.

And then? Then, he'd find a way to win back his other heart's desire. Simone.

CHAPTER 40

SIMONE

It had been three weeks since she'd videoconferenced with *The Executives* and lost out on $200,000.

Three weeks since she'd asked them to give Finn a second chance.

Three weeks of wondering if the billionaires had decided to help fund his dream of giving others a future.

Three weeks, and she'd missed Finn every moment. But she hadn't wasted a single minute wallowing in self-doubt. She was done second-guessing her relationships and keeping herself on the outs. And she was ready to get to work on her own dream.

The first item on her list? Swapping out the beadboard counter for an upcycled glass display case. Then she'd called up Ruth, who'd been thrilled about the idea of selling her beeswax candles and handmade soap year round. She'd even offered to develop an exclusive line of scents for Honey and Hickory.

Next, Simone bought a refrigerated case secondhand to stock Alisha's cookies and local goods. Tim's goat-milk products were a shoo-in, now that she'd forgiven him for letting Finn take over his booth.

On a clothing rack behind the register went the screen-printed logo shirts she'd ordered back in summer and left in boxes in the office. Why wait for a storefront? She'd let her perfectionism hold her captive too long. It might take years to get the restaurant to her high standards, but if she held her breath for a celebrity investor, she'd be Pops's age and nothing would've changed.

Same with herself. A harder pill to swallow, but she was fed up with lonely days and nights spent on the couch. Done waiting to have her life in picture-perfect shape before seeking out friendship. People could either love her as a work in progress, or not.

Turned out her old friends were enthusiastic about making up for lost time and eager for the chance to have a part in her plan for the town as well. Derek, who'd married young and gone from spray-painting graffiti on road signs to teaching art class at the local high school, offered to paint a mural in the dining room and another on the alley wall outside.

Word of mouth had spread, and within a week, her front-of-house refrigerator was stocked with local foods, plus she'd added a dry goods section. The shirts sold out, and she put in another order for tees, adding sweatshirts and hoodies by popular demand.

Operation Farmers' Market on Steroids was a go.

But one person had stayed quiet ever since Alisha's wedding, the person whose blessing she wanted most, and he was sitting across from her, leaning back in his chair like he wanted to put some distance between himself and the platter of tempeh barbecue sliders.

"Vegetarian barbecue?" Pops made it sound like blasphemy.

She grinned. Silence was damning, but pushback she could handle. "Yep. I want to make sure there's something for everyone here. And expanding our options makes sense from a business standpoint. If we're getting more out-of-town customers, we need to offer dishes to suit a variety of dietary needs and preferences." She nudged the plate toward him. "C'mon, I bet you'll love it."

He picked up a slider and took a bite, then went back for another with a murmur of appreciation. "That's actually tasty," he admitted. "But why'd you go and make new buns? We've already got rolls on the menu."

"Yeah, but these are gluten-free."

"Quit lying." He twisted the roll around, scrutinizing it like he was trying to ascertain its chemical makeup, then took another bite and chewed, brow creased in thought. "Vegetarian options I guess I can get used to, even though we used to have a pig on the sign," he said, and chuckled. "But who comes to a barbecue joint looking for breakfast?"

"The same people who come to stay overnight and want more options than a muffin from the tea shop, or a greasy drive-through breakfast." She had numbers to back this up, but Pops cared about flavor. She valued both.

"Don't worry, I'm going to stay true to our roots and put a barbecue spin on everything. Like these home fries." Shifting the platter, she pushed another plate toward them. "I seasoned them with smoked paprika. Try them with some egg."

Pops swiped a cubed potato through runny yolk and held it up to the light on the tines of his fork. She stifled a smile. He looked just like one of the reality-chef judges he always roasted.

"This sounds like a whole lot more work than our old recipes. Sure the cooks are up for that?"

"With training, yeah." The word elicited thoughts of Finn and his cooking school. Had he met with Keith and Constance?

"If business picks up like you think it will, you're gonna need more staff."

"I hope we do. The more the merrier."

His eyes shot wide.

Her turn to lean back, arms crossed. "What?"

He wiped his mouth with a hankie, then grinned. "Just never thought I'd hear the day you were keen on inviting more people into the kitchen. Ever since your sister handed over the keys, you've held them in your hands so tight . . ." He made fists. "Heck, Hank's been scared to show his face in here ever since you ran him out in spring."

Her grandpa's right-hand cook was getting up in years. She figured he'd want a break. Never meant to make him feel unwelcome.

Blue eyes mischievous, Pops asked, "This mean you plan to let that Rimes boy have a go at the smoker?"

She shook her head. "Not even if he begs." Mistake. The image that conjured up . . . well, not something she wanted to imagine with her grandpa around. "And besides, he's got his own thing. Maybe." She told him about Finn's dream, and her part in giving him a second chance.

Even told her grandpa how she felt about her former rival, despite everything that had happened, not shying from the truth. Not covering up her feelings anymore.

By the time she'd finished, Pops had plowed through two more sliders. He swallowed a burp and said, "I like him, too, just so you know."

"You do?" Finn had told her about the starvation tactics.

"Don't look at me like that. Only boy my baby girl has ever brought home, and you think I wouldn't put him through it? Been waiting years to make a date of yours squirm. Can't expect me to pass up the chance." He grinned, face crinkling under white stubble. "But from what I can tell, he's a decent man. This culinary school sounds like a worthy idea. And his scrambled eggs put your grandmother's to shame."

"He won you over through your stomach? Typical man." He'd have to try harder than that with her. If he even still wanted her. She was beginning to wonder if she'd been wrong about their connection. Could she be the only one walking around under the gloom of a rain cloud, missing her sun?

Pops leaned his elbows on the table, serious now. "If he makes it up to you, don't let pride hold you back. You got a good head on your shoulders, but ain't nothing wrong with listening to your heart now and again neither."

CHAPTER 41

SIMONE AND FINN

The first cactus arrived on Tuesday. Simone was chatting with an old friend who'd stopped in to Honey and Hickory for lunch when the front door swung open and a man wheeled in a tall box on a dolly. "Which one of you is Simone Blake?"

She went to raise a hand, then stopped herself. "What is it?"

He peered at the mailing label. "Says here it's from Desert Sunrise Nursery. Out of Phoenix, Arizona."

She signed for it, then opened the box. A three-foot-tall cactus sat in a pot.

The next cactus arrived an hour later. Hand delivered from Loretta, the florist in town. A tiny, round, spiny thing in a pot. No note.

Simone discovered the third cactus when she sifted through the mail. It tumbled out from under a utility bill and fluttered to her feet. A pink-bloomed prickly pear on a postcard. She flipped it over and found only a return address: *Sedona, AZ.*

A sliver of happiness burrowed into her heart and took root.

The next morning a cardboard box was waiting on the back steps of the restaurant. She pulled off her gloves and used her keys to open the package, too impatient to go inside for scissors. A trio of succulents sat nestled in jars. An unsigned note said: *Not quite cacti, but too cute to resist.*

By noon she had cactus sunglasses, cactus oven mitts, and a cactus in a tiny glass terrarium.

At two, the door opened in a burst of cold air, and every single member of the Yarn Spinners came in. "We had so much fun with these," Mrs. Snyder declared. Each one of them placed a knitted cactus on the cash register stand. Twelve in all. "A cactus garden."

She only smiled because the knitters had spent so long on these handmade gifts, not because of how thoughtful it was. "I hope he paid you."

"Oh, hush now," Mrs. Snyder said, giggling. Which meant yes, he'd paid them well.

She transplanted the mini cactus garden to her desk in the back office, where they kept her company while she worked on payroll until nearly closing time, when the door creaked open and a six-foot blow-up saguaro cactus battled its way through the opening, propelled by Rhonda.

Simone buried her face in her hands. When she looked up again, the cactus loomed in the corner of the office, and Rhonda was trying in vain to frown. "You're running out of room."

By Friday, a string of cactus fairy lights wound their way up and around the office door. It had taken her entire supply of pushpins to put them up, and a trip to her grandparents' house for an extension cord. She could've left them in the box. But she hadn't.

A Christmas cactus sat on the edge of her desk, the trailing red blooms making her smile every time she looked away from her spreadsheets. Her cactus-shaped mug sat on a succulent coaster, and she was beginning to wonder whether this was an apology or an attack when a postcard slid under the door.

"Rhonda?"

No answer. "Brent?"

Hands shaking, she walked around the desk. Picked up the post-card, gritty with dirt from the floorboards. Not a cactus. A canyon. Red and gold and burnt umber.

She turned it over.

Roses are so overdone. And when it comes to thorns, they're second best.

She opened the door and found Finn on the other side.

Simone wasn't smiling.

"This is a shit ton of cactuses, Rimes."

She was, however, wearing the cactus sweater.

"Cacti." He raked a hand through his hair. "Do you hate them?"

"They're corny and unnecessary and superfluous." She picked up the hem of the sweater, which reached to her knees. Smoothing her thumbs over the fabric, she peered down at the appliquéd cactus.

When she looked up again, a grin lit her face. "And I adore them, you big weirdo."

"Oh, good," he said, and he realized his hand was fisted in his hair. He let go and ran his fingers over it, trying to tidy the strands. He'd had a whole week to plan out his apology, and he had, sort of. Broad strokes of *I messed up* and *Will you give me another chance* and *I want you, always have.*

But now that he was here and she was wearing the sweater—she'd actually worn it, even though it was tacky and hideous—all his thoughts were clashing cymbals of *She might still like you*, and all that came out was, "I'm sorry."

She crossed her arms, warping the cactus, and leaned against the doorframe. "I'm listening."

That was good. Really good. If he could dredge up something coherent to say . . .

"I didn't come over to heckle you, that first day," he said, surprising himself. It was true, though. "I came over because I thought maybe we could bond over barbecue. I came looking for a friend."

Simone licked her lips, head cocked.

"But then I saw you and—" His breath punched out of his lungs at the memory, at the reality of her here in front of him. "It was never going to be just friends with us."

She put a hand over her mouth, and her eyes turned suspiciously bright before she tilted up her chin, blinking at the ceiling.

"I know you probably think love at first sight is a myth, because you're practical and sensible and everything I'm not."

Hand still over her mouth, she breathed out in what might've been a laugh, or a snort, or even a sob.

"But I felt a spark that day," he said. "I tried to ignore it and write it off." Tried to *fight* it off. "I'm done trying, because how I feel about you is real, and it's grown into something deeper and more powerful than I've ever experienced. It's not rational and I can't explain how it happened, but I do know, beyond a shadow of a doubt, that I love you, Simone."

She dropped her hand to her neck, pressing like she was checking her pulse, and he stepped closer, put a hand on the doorframe so their thumbs were touching. "And it's okay if you don't feel the same way. Or maybe you only like me, just a little. Just enough to give me another chance to not screw things up by being up in my head and—"

"Stop."

He did.

Simone eased closer, her breathing quick. "You're not the only one who messed up. I lashed out because I was scared of how good we are together. I pulled away because I was so terrified of everyone finding out the truth."

She slipped her hand up along the doorway to cover his. "The truth is you're my favorite adversary. And the only person in the world I ever want to lose to, because I lost my heart to you. And I'd gladly lose it all over again, every day of my life, because I love you."

Finn's heart stopped beating. "What?"

"I said, I love you. How could I not? You're so perfectly lovable."

He pulled her close. "Can I kiss you now?"

"You can kiss me always."

Always sounded pretty darn perfect.

CHAPTER 42

SIMONE AND FINN

One year later

Simone and Finn carried the rough-hewn wood table across the room to create a long banquet-style table. Gone were the Formica-topped relics, replaced by these gorgeous tables Erika, a local woodworker, had fashioned from reclaimed barnwood. Another small step toward her big vision.

Today they'd invited friends and family for a celebration. Finn's first class of students had finished the program a week ago, and they'd planned the graduation party to coincide with the one-month anniversary of her boutique's opening.

The extra income from selling local goods in the restaurant and the wider customer base had paid for a lease on the retail space next door. She'd had to leave the wall of mirrors in place from its former life as a dance studio, but she now owned a store and a restaurant in the town she loved, her hometown. Spent each day in a life she'd always dreamed of—messier than she'd planned, but even more beautiful.

Especially when she looked up and met Finn's gorgeous brown eyes, the warm smile she'd stopped trying to resist.

Across the room, her grandpa popped a bottle of sparkling cider and poured it into plastic champagne flutes. Finn brought one to Simone, which she accepted with a quick kiss, then passed the cider back to him just as quickly. "One minute . . ."

She dashed out the front door and into the shop next door. Haleigh was arranging the latest shipment of necklaces from Chantal. The first few orders had sold out in weeks, and these newest ones featured tiny dinosaur charms in a nod to the museum. Simone flipped the sign to *Closed* as Haleigh glanced up, a puzzled look on her face.

"The party's getting started," Simone said. "C'mon over for dinner and cookies!"

Haleigh stayed put. "But you said never, under any circumstances, to leave the shop during business hours."

"I did, didn't I? Well, rules are meant to be broken. And if anyone stops by, I'll hang a sign to send them over to the restaurant." She stepped behind the counter and scribbled out a quick note, then taped it to the door.

Last year she would've been appalled it wasn't typed up. She'd come a long way, thanks in part to Finn's influence. "There."

But when she looked up, Haleigh was already halfway down the sidewalk. Hard to resist the lure of barbecue and her sister's cookies. She locked the door and made her way back to Honey and Hickory, accepting hugs of congratulation from latecomers outside the front door.

Finn was waiting by the counter, eyebrows raised. "Who's running the store?"

"I closed it down early. A wise-ish person once told me—"

"I heard the 'ish,'" he said.

"You were meant to." She grinned. "Like I was saying, a guy with a good handle on life told me it's okay to go with the flow sometimes. And this is a big day."

"Sure is!" Pops came over with his cup of bubbly. "This is the first meal cooked entirely by your graduates. Better be good." He winked and squeezed Finn's shoulder.

As she watched her boyfriend blush under the attention, Simone's heart became full.

"Just teasing you, son. If their cooking is anything like yours, I'm sure they'll nail my granddaughter's recipes."

She tensed, waiting for Finn to flinch at the word 'son,' but he beamed. "Thank you, Wayne. That means a lot."

Pops grunted, evidently full up on sappiness. She ducked her chin, thinking of her ongoing journey toward being comfortable with expressing her emotions. The apple didn't fall far from the tree, but she was putting down new roots in well-watered soil, thanks to Finn, Meg, Alisha, Chantal, and all the friends she'd reconnected with here.

Gran came out of the kitchen with a tray of Alisha's cookies. Simone and her sister were working on a plan to open a second Vanilla Honey shop here in town, hopefully by next year. But until then, the baked goods Alisha shipped from Chicago flew off the shelves.

Simone went over to help her grandmother with the tray. "Go ahead and find a seat, Gran. I think we're ready to eat."

Two of the graduates from Finn's cooking school hovered near the swinging door to the kitchen, looking nervous and stiff in their black Honey and Hickory aprons.

She walked over, smiling. "Hey, y'all. This is your celebration too! Kitchen's closed—get on out and enjoy the fruits of your labor."

They looked at each other, unsure, and she sought out Finn in the crowd. He was chatting with Bella, who'd taken a rare evening off so she could be a part of the celebration.

"Here, follow me." She led the graduates over to the table and ushered them to the empty seats. "Try not to scare them too much," she told Bella with a grin, and the other woman chuckled, her gray eyes sparkling.

"I'll save that for after they're fully initiated. Though there was this one dinner service where . . ." The cooks leaned in, rapt, as Bella recounted a kitchen horror story, while Simone stepped back to an open spot near the front of the room.

Public speaking never made her nervous, but tonight was different. Special. One deep breath, then she found Finn's face in the crowd. She was ready.

Raising her voice and her glass, Simone addressed the room. "Has everyone got a drink?"

There were nods and murmurs.

"Good, because I want to start off with a toast to the talented cooks who prepared this meal." The chitchat died down, and she went on: "We're so happy to have you both on our staff and can't wait to see what the future has in store for you."

She took a sip of her drink, gathering her courage. "Between the graduates and the grand opening of the boutique, there's a lot to celebrate." Cheers cut into her speech, and she waited for things to quiet down again. "I just hope I'm doing our part to give people more reasons to love our town, because there's so much goodness here."

"Got that right," Bill Lewis called out, and a chuckle swept through the crowd.

"Just one more thing, then I'll wrap it up, because I can see some of y'all giving me the stink eye, wanting to dig in to dinner." A smattering of laughter arose.

Her next words were meant for Finn, but she wanted everyone to hear. "Two summers ago, I met a man who turned my life upside down. It's no secret he and I clashed from the start. I thought I had life figured out, and then Finn Rimes showed up and blew my expectations to pieces. In the best possible way."

Leaning against the wall in the back of the room, Finn bit his lip, bashful, and her heart squeezed.

"I was worried he was out for my sauce, but it turns out he had his sights set on my heart." Their animosity seemed ages ago, long since transformed into ardor. "When I met Finn, I met my match, in every sense of the word. I can't think of anyone I'd rather spend my life with than the man I once tried my best to get rid of."

Heart thudding, she wound her way through the bentwood chairs and rows of tables toward him. "You are the perfect man for me. I couldn't not love you if I tried. And believe me, I tried."

He rolled his lips together, took her hand in his, and his warm touch filled her up with ooey-gooey mushy happiness.

Happiness that sent her down on one knee, where she knelt, looking up into his eyes, bright with unshed tears. "Don't you go crying on me."

"Too late," he said, and he breathed out a laugh.

She sniffed and squeezed his hand, drawing strength from it. "Finn Abraham Rimes, you are my most favorite person. You are brave and smart and strong and sensitive and stubborn as all get-out, and I love you. I adore you. I cherish you, and I want to spend forever showing you how much you mean to me."

She reached into her pocket and pulled out a small handcrafted wooden box. Flipped it open to reveal the key inside and held it up, hands shaky. "Will you do the honor of being mine forever?"

"Are you asking me to marry you?"

"You're really going to make me say it, aren't you?"

He nodded. "Just want to make sure I read the fine print of the deal."

Smiling, she shook her head. So sappy, this one. So perfect for her.

"Finn, will you marry me?"

He bent down and scooped her up under her knees, swooping her into his arms. "Yes, Simone. A thousand times, yes, I'll marry you."

She slid her hands around his neck, and he kissed her. Quick, soft, sure. Then he parted his lips and swept his tongue across hers. Bliss. Heaven.

Shouts and whoops pulled them apart, and he broke away, grinning. Looked down at the ring box cradled between them. "Is this the key to your heart?"

With a grin, she said, "No, silly. It's the key to our house."

"Our house?" His brow furrowed, and he set her down, running his hands up her sides, like he couldn't bear to let her go. And he would never have to.

Wordlessly, she took his hand and led him out the door and onto the sidewalk. Towed by a pickup with a vinyl DARIUS SHIELD REALTY decal, a tiny house sat parked in the middle of Main Street. The exterior mimicked the look of a log cabin, with a metal roof and paned windows.

"That's ours?" He swung toward her, capturing her other hand, his expression inscrutable, leaning toward utter shock. "You bought us a mini version of the cabin from Sedona?"

"Designed it, actually. And bought it. So . . . yeah." Nerves reduced her to rambling. Did he hate it? "Is it too cheesy? I know we only stayed there a day . . ."

Finn squeezed her fingers and broke out into a gigantic smile. "Cheesy? You bought us a house. It's not cheesy—it's the most thoughtful gift imaginable." He dropped her hands and pulled her into a hug, speaking against her shoulder. "It's perfect. I love it. And I love you, Simone. So much."

The truck door opened, and Darius hopped down, smiling wide. "I take it this means he said yes?"

She pulled away and nodded. "He did."

"Good, because I've been telling him all along: you're the best thing that ever happened to him."

"Ha, nice try." But she let herself be swept up into a bear hug by Finn's best friend. "I'm glad you were looking out for him. But if I ever hear you telling him to leave me . . ."

"Just be good to him, and I'll be on your side forever," Darius said, and she knew he meant it.

She slid her arm around Finn. Now that she had him, she didn't intend to ever let him go. "With our new ventures, a house was out of reach. But I figured it's time to get a head start on our menagerie, and we can't do it in an apartment. So I bought an acre off Meg. Figured we can start with this and, down the road, build a real house."

"A real house? What do you call this?" The sun broke out from behind the clouds, catching the glints of gold and chestnut in Finn's dark hair. His brown eyes sparkled down at her.

"Well, technically, it's a tiny house."

"Simone, you bought us a *house.*" He picked her up again and twirled her around. She inhaled a deep breath at the sight of the joy in his eyes and the warmth in his smile.

Finn didn't take her breath away; his presence bathed her in peace so deep she'd never need to hold her breath again.

"Not just a house. A home," she said as he lowered her to the ground, hands strong and sure at her waist.

"Our home," he corrected her, and this time, she let it slide. Because it was true.

Cars honked, people rolling down the windows despite the cold and waving as Simone led him around to the front door and pushed it open. "Welcome home, Finn."

Home. His heart burst with more joy than he'd ever thought possible, and he wrapped her in another hug as tears gathered in his eyes again.

"Back to having an address on wheels," Darius said from the small front porch.

"Yeah, but at least this one's got a kitchen." Simone tilted up her chin, meeting his eyes with an uncharacteristically uncertain gaze.

If she didn't already know, he planned to spend forever showing her exactly how perfect it was for him. How perfect *she* was for him.

Slipping his arm around her waist, he pulled her against his side and pressed a kiss onto her temple. "More importantly, this one's got you," he murmured. Then he let his eyes roam around the space, taking in the love on display around him. Four solid walls and cozy furnishings. And there went his tears again.

Darius was chewing on his lip, looking nervous as he leaned on the doorframe. A matching pucker of doubt crinkled Simone's forehead, and Finn pulled her in closer.

These two. How could they worry for a second?

"This is . . ." Finn tried to speak around the lump of joy in his throat. He cleared it and nudged his friend's boot with his toe. "You have a hand in this?"

"Maybe a little." Darius broke into a grin and stepped inside. Rubbed a hand along the countertop. "Your fiancée was pretty particular—"

"Me? You're the one who insisted on river rock in the shower." She wrapped her arm around Finn's waist and looked up at him, shaking her head with a smile. "Installed it himself. Said his crew was the best, but he was better."

Finn laughed. "Not surprised."

"And I made sure there's enough cabinet space," Bella said as she stepped inside. "Brought you this." She set his cast-iron skillet on the stove with care.

"That's . . . wow." With his free arm, Finn embraced Darius, who looped in Bella. The people he cared most about in the world, under one roof. His roof, thanks to the love of his life. "Thank you for this," he said, in the biggest understatement of his life.

Darius squeezed his shoulder, then pulled out of the hug, humor sparking his brown eyes. "What you should be thanking me for is introducing you two. If I hadn't sent you to that farmers' market . . ."

"Yeah, yeah, save it for your best man speech."

Darius's face lit up. "Okay. All right, then." He rubbed his hands together, peering out the window. "Any idea about the maid of honor yet?"

"My sister, Alisha," Simone said. "Happily married. But this town is full of single women, if you're ever in the mood to relocate."

"Never know. It's not that far from Springfield. How's the market for farmland? Got space for an office downtown?"

"Always room for more."

Bella stepped between them. "Enough of this business talk, you sharks." She tugged Darius's sleeve. "Let's give them a second to enjoy their new house in privacy."

With a wave, his friends clomped down the steps of the attached porch, and Finn shut the door behind them. "I thought they'd never leave."

Simone grinned. "You do realize we're in the middle of the street, with half the town waiting for us inside?"

He nodded. "Don't worry, I won't beg you to ravish me until this thing is parked. But then, all bets are off." He planned to say thank you in her favorite way, because in this case, words wouldn't even begin to do her gesture justice.

But for now, he kissed her, slow and deep, then dug a folded slip of paper out of his back pocket and pressed it into her hands. "I got you a present too. It's not a house, but—"

She unfolded it carefully, and it took all he had not to blurt out the news. "Oh my gosh. This is an adoption certificate." She looked up, eyes wide. "You got me a puppy?"

"I did."

"Where is she?"

Finn pointed out the window, to where Meg held a wriggling ball of brown, black, and white fluff. The Australian shepherd puppy who'd captured his heart at the pet shelter.

"That's her? She's adorable! Have you named her?"

He reached into his coat pocket and pulled out a collar with a heart-shaped nameplate. "I thought maybe we should name her together."

But Simone was staring at the collar in his hands, and he couldn't hold back his smile anymore, because there wasn't just an empty nameplate attached to the collar.

"Finn Rimes, is that a ring?"

He nodded, hands going clammy, even though she'd already asked the question. Even though he'd already said yes. Would say yes every day to life with this woman.

"Were you going to . . ." She put her hands to her mouth. "Holy crap, were you going to propose?"

"Great minds think alike, I guess," he said, biting his lip.

"I'm sorry. I didn't mean to steal the moment."

"Sorry? Are you kidding? It's *our* moment. And as competitive as you are, I'm glad you beat me to it. All I want is you."

"You've got me. I'm all yours. Forever." She pulled him down for a kiss, cupping his jaw. "And you're mine."

"I've been yours since the day you sicced those knitters on me."

"I had nothing to do with that."

He tipped his forehead to hers. "Did so."

"Are we fighting a few minutes into engagement?"

"It's never been fighting between us, Simone, and we both know it."

She kissed him again, long and deep. "For once, Finn, you're right."

ACKNOWLEDGMENTS

How surreal to be writing the acknowledgments for my second novel! The best way I can describe my heart right now is bursting with gratitude. What a journey this has been, and I'm thrilled and awestruck to be living my dream of writing books.

A giant thank-you to my all-star editor, Lauren Plude, for helping me push this story to its fullest potential. Our chats helped me dig deep, and this book is so much better for the questions you raised and the notes you gave me. Your insight is truly invaluable. Another huge thank-you goes out to my stellar agent, Rachel Brooks, who not only champions my books but also helps me navigate through this publishing journey. And thank you to the entire Montlake team for all the work you do to get my novels out into the world.

I truly couldn't have written Simone and Finn's love story without my husband's help on the home front. You took care of dinners and dishes and bedtimes and a million other things big and small for our family that gave me the time to finish this book. Having you in my corner means the world to me. From the bottom of my heart, thank you.

Thank you to my writer friends for your support, encouragement, and insight.

Last, but most certainly not least, thank you to my readers. I hope you enjoy reading this book as much as I loved writing Simone and Finn's story.

ABOUT THE AUTHOR

Chandra Blumberg writes funny, heartwarming love stories about characters that feel real and relatable. When it comes to her writing process, getting to that happily ever after is half the fun.

Born and raised in Michigan, Chandra moved to the Chicago area after majoring in English at Michigan State University. When she's not writing, she enjoys lifting heavy barbells at the gym, making a mess of the kitchen while baking alongside her four kids, and traveling with her family. *Stirring Up Love* is her second novel; she is also the author of *Digging Up Love*.